The Phone Call

Anna Belle Rose

Solstice Publishing - www.solsticepublishing.com

The Phone Call

By Anna Belle Rose

For Sam, who always believed it would really happen.

Prologue

Luke opened the door. "Alex! Come on in."

Alex handed him a bottle of wine and grinned, "Hey Luke. Peter has you serving as doorman?"

"I wasn't supposed to be, but" — he gestured down the hallway— "hear the music? They're dancing in the living room."

"Who?"

"Peter and his sister." Alex looked blank, so Luke continued, "Pete invited his baby sister to fill out the dinner table after you called and said that Diana couldn't make it."

"Oh, really?"

"Yeah. So a few minutes ago, she went in to put on some music, and a polka came on. The next thing I knew, they'd started polkaing around the room."

Alex tried to picture the drummer of his band dancing with a little girl. He pictured his tall friend bending down to lead a child half his size. Why on earth would Peter invite a *kid* to a dinner party?

Luke continued, clearly amused, "You have to see this."

Alex shook off the awkward image as he followed Luke down the hall. All he could see when he walked into the living room was Peter's back until the couple turned. Alex swallowed hard. This was no *baby* sister. This was a gorgeous woman wearing a simple dark green sweater with a scoop cowl neckline, and flowing black skirt that swirled around her ankles as she moved. Momentarily at a loss for words, Alex stared.

Noticing the stranger in the room, the woman stopped dancing, her face darkening with a heated blush.

She ducked quickly out of her brother's arms to shut off the music.

Looking around in surprise, Peter laughed out loud and casually draped an arm over his sister's shoulders. "Alex! Glad you made it. Do you want to polka? I'm sure Kat would be grateful for a less clumsy partner." Kissing the top of her head, Peter continued, "Alex, this is my baby sister Kat. Kat, this is Alex. I can't believe the two of you haven't met yet!"

Kat put out her hand, trying not to gawk at the stunningly attractive man standing in front of her. "Nice to meet you. Sorry for the polka…"

Alex held out his hand and felt the warmth of her small one sliding into his. "I'm Alex."

She grinned. "I gathered that."

"Huh?"

Her tone was teasing. "Peter just said so."

Alex pulled himself together and grinned back at her, "Nice to meet you too, Kat. Not to worry about the polka — I learned how as a kid."

Just then the doorbell rang again. Luke adjusted the stereo while the rest of the group moved toward the brightly lit kitchen and dining area. Moving ahead of Alex, Kat tried not to think about how much she'd liked feeling her hand in his.

Seated at the table, Alex was pleased to find himself across from Kat. As the boisterous group settled in, he realized that Kat knew the other two members of the band well, and even knew one of their dates. He passed a plate of antipasto across the table to her, "So how is it that you know Will and Dana, and even Maggie, but not me?"

She smiled, trying to fight the little surge of energy that came when she saw that he'd been paying such close attention to her. He was *so* classically handsome; his dark brown eyes met hers directly, and his chestnut hair waved almost to his shoulders. She abruptly realized that she hadn't responded to him. "Will and Pete have been friends for years. I met Dana last year when I was home for Christmas. And Maggie's mom is friends with ours."

"So how did we not meet?"

Her eyes creased as she calculated the timing. "I lived in Spain all last school year, and I only came home for a week at Christmas. Then I was back in the city for just a couple of days last May before going to Mexico for the summer, and then back to college. We must have just kept missing each other."

Not caring that he was ignoring the others at the table, Alex leaned closer. "From that explanation, I'd say that you are in college, and studying something to do with Spanish."

She nodded. "Yes and yes. I'm just about to begin my last semester of college, and I'm triple majoring in Spanish, Hispanic Cultures, and Literature."

"Literature?"

"Writing."

Just then, Peter gave a piercing whistle from the other end of the table. "Kat, Alex! Hello, join the rest of us."

Over the next few hours, the eight of them ate, laughed, and all but Kat drank numerous glasses of wine. Alex repeatedly found himself trying to draw Kat into more private conversations, wanting to get to know her better.

At the end of the evening, Alex joined the rest of the group that was leaving by the front door. He stopped in front of Kat. "It was great to meet you finally."

He noticed her cheeks turned pink, and hoped that it meant she'd enjoyed talking to him as much as he'd enjoyed talking to her. Her voice was husky. "Likewise."

"Maybe we'll see each other again."

"I'd like that."

***

As they walked down the street, Will said, "Shit, Alex, sorry that Diana bailed on you. As much as I love Kat, it must have been awkward to have to do all that happy-to-meet-you stuff, and then make conversation all night."

Alex responded instinctively. "No, I had a great time!" How could he explain how much he'd enjoyed himself without sounding like a babbling idiot?

***

The next morning, Peter handed his sister a cup of coffee. "You enjoy last night?"

"Yeah. It was fun." Kat gazed into her mug, feeling foolish as she thought about all the hours she'd spent thinking about Alex since they'd met, reliving every moment of the evening.

"Want to do it again?"

His question confused her. "When?" she asked, a little too eagerly.

"Remember how I told you that I wasn't going to be home tonight because I was going to the opera? *Don Giovanni,* remember? Well, we have an extra ticket because Alex's girlfriend bailed on him again. You want to go?"

The word "girlfriend" deflated some of the excitement she felt thinking about seeing Alex again. But, even if he had a girlfriend, she didn't seem to be around much, so what harm would going to the opera do? Her eyes sparkling, she responded, "I'd love to."

***

When Alex pushed the doorbell that evening, he was surprised that he felt a little nervous. Luke opened the door once again, and the two of them walked into the kitchen, laughing about déjà vu. Just a few minutes later, Kat entered the room, and Alex turned around. Even though she willed herself to not react, he was so handsome Kat could hardly breathe. Suddenly, she felt self-conscious in her new dress and wished she hadn't agreed to go. He had a girlfriend, for God's sake!

Alex swallowed hard. As he'd been standing and talking to Peter and Luke, he'd been telling himself that last night's reaction to her came out of a combination of good food and good friends, and a *lot* of really good red wine. He kept trying to remember that she was Peter's baby sister, but no matter how hard he tried to convince himself otherwise, what he saw was a gorgeous and interesting woman wearing a simple but sexy black dress, her strawberry blonde hair pulled up into a modest twist. He tried not to stare, but he followed the elegantly plunging neckline of her dress as it dove just deep enough to show an observant man that she wasn't wearing a bra. The shimmering fabric skimmed curves that would keep most men awake at night. High black heels accentuated her legs. At a loss for words, Alex tried to think of something intelligent to say.

Kat felt unexpectedly shy. "Hi Alex." Her cheeks heated.

"Hi, Kat."

Peter looked up from the sink where he was washing his hands. "Hey, isn't that the dress that Jess gave you for Christmas?"

She nodded, uncomfortably aware that she'd become the center of attention. "Yeah. Thanks. It certainly isn't an outfit I would have picked out."

Luke grinned. "Well, it should be. You look fabulous."

Kat walked around the center island to hug him. "Luke, I'm so glad to see you tonight. I didn't think I would see you again before I left! But thanks for the compliment," she said with a wink.

"It wasn't a compliment; I was just stating the obvious. Besides, I had to come over—you know how much I love the opera."

Kat wrinkled her nose. "And Peter."

He kissed her cheek. "And *you*."

***

At Lincoln Center, Alex hardly had to maneuver at all to wind up sitting next to Kat. He watched in fascination as she gave the performance her entire concentration. With sparkling eyes, she turned toward him at the intermission. "Thank you *so* much for the ticket, Alex. I had forgotten how much I love the opera."

"It shows." Alex looked at the glow of color on her cheekbones. "How long since you've been?"

Her eyes narrowed; Kat thought back. "Probably four years. My dad and I used to go pretty regularly, but with my schedule now, it's hard." Then she sighed happily, "But the last time, it was *La Boheme*, which is my all-time favorite."

After the last bow, Alex held Kat's coat for her and tried to hide his pleasure as he realized she was blushing just a bit when she thanked him.

Pete took her arm. "Okay, brat, how about some dinner now?"

***

At the restaurant, Kat hesitated for a moment, trying to figure out where to sit. Rationally, she knew she shouldn't be trying to pursue Alex. He was too old for her. Never mind that he was supposed to be with a date. On the other hand …

Before she could make up her mind, Peter and Luke sat together on one side of the table, leaving an empty chair next to Alex. After a slight nervous hesitation, Kat sat down.

The waiter quickly appeared, ready to take drink orders. The men ordered beers, while Kat asked for a seltzer. Alex looked at her quizzically. "You don't want anything stronger?"

She blushed. "Want has nothing to do with it. I can't."

Alex didn't understand. "What do you mean?"

"I won't be twenty-one until next fall."

Alex tried to hide his surprise, not wanting to embarrass her more. Holy shit! Last night when he'd heard Peter's little sister would be joining them, he'd thought she was a baby. Then, meeting her and spending time with her, he'd been thinking how attractive she was, and how much he'd like to spend more time with her, and yet now he realized that she was truly just a kid.

Just then, the waiter reappeared with their drinks, and they all ordered dinner. Over the meal, the four of them laughed and joked, and Alex began to forget about the six-year age difference as he enjoyed himself more than he had in months.

Coffee had just been delivered to the table when two well-dressed men walked by the table holding hands. One of them did a double-take. "Peter! Luke!"

Within moments, introductions had been made, and the two men had pulled up chairs. After finishing their coffees, the newcomers broached the idea of going dancing. Peter and Luke were both obviously tempted but hesitated as they looked at Kat.

She rolled her eyes. "Guys, just go. I'm tired anyway, so I'm happy to head back to the apartment and get a few hours of sleep."

Peter patted her hand. "No, we'll go home too."

She shook her head. "No, you won't. Go have fun. I'll be fine!"

As the two started to argue Alex held up his hand in a gesture of peace. "I'll walk Kat home. You guys just go have a good time."

Kat bristled at his tone, though conscious of a small thrill at the idea of being alone with him. "I don't need anyone to walk me home. You can go, too."

He tried to hide the excitement he felt at the idea of spending some time alone with her, even if it would be brief. Age difference be damned, he wanted a chance to get to know her better *without* an audience. "Kat, I'll walk you home, and then head home myself."

When they left the restaurant some time later, Kat still hadn't settled whether she should feel annoyed or pleased. When she didn't say anything for almost a block, Alex spoke. "Did I do something wrong?"

Her response was sharper than she intended. "No, it's fine."

He grinned. "Then why are you giving me the silent treatment?"

Kat drew in a breath and then said, "I don't need an escort."

He put his hand on her arm. "I never said you did."

She shook off his hand, acutely aware of how much she liked having him touch her, but reminding herself of the word "girlfriend." Trying to push desire away, she decided to focus on her earlier anger. "Yes, you did. You made it sound like I needed a babysitter to get home."

"No, I didn't. You just heard it that way. I offered to walk you home so Peter and Luke could go out without worrying about you. I figured I'd let them off the hook so they could go dancing." He grinned, trying to break the tension. "Besides, it was the perfect excuse for me, too."

"Meaning?"

"I was included in the dancing invitation, remember? No offense to anyone, but going dancing at a gay bar wasn't really what I was in the mood for this evening."

Kat looked at Alex and suddenly started to laugh. "You're right. The way you look *and* going solo? You'd be mobbed in minutes."

Alex smiled at the unexpected compliment. "So, can you forgive me, and let me walk you home?"

Cheerful again, Kat slipped her hand through the crook of his elbow. "Deal. It would probably sound stupid for me to say that I really *wanted* to walk through the city alone at this hour anyway."

Gratified by her change of mood, he quipped, "Especially looking the way *you* do."

***

The two of them chatted easily as they walked through the chilly streets. When they reached her apartment building, Kat hesitated for a moment. "Do you want to come up?"

Alex looked down at Kat, her eyes sparkling in the reflected streetlights, and knew he would accept the invitation despite the alarms echoing through his mind. "I'd love to. Just for a few minutes, though. I know you wanted to get some sleep."

In the apartment, Kat made tea, and the two of them sat on the couch, warming their hands on the mugs. Hours passed as they talked and talked, laughing so hard that Kat's sides hurt.

Finally, as they heard the mantle clock chime for the third time since they got to the apartment, Alex rose. "Okay, Kat, I need to go. You need sleep." At the door, he touched her cheek, "Thank you."

"For what?"

"For going to the opera tonight, and for letting me walk you home. I had a great time." His voice was warm. "I don't remember the last time I laughed so much."

Kat quickly rose on her tiptoes and kissed his cheek. "You're welcome. Thank you for keeping me company."

"My pleasure." He paused with his hand on her arm, suddenly nervous. "Kat, would you like to go out with me sometime? I mean, just us?"

For a moment, Kat fought the urge to jump up and down and shout *yes*. Then cold reality forced its way through. Her voice trembled a bit. "Alex, I'd love to, but…"

"But, what?"

With every ounce of her being, Kat wished she could have just said *yes* with a clear conscience. "Alex, as much as I don't want to be the one to bring this up, you have an umm…"

"A what?"

"A girlfriend, you have a girlfriend."

Alex felt relief rush through him. She wasn't turning him down because she didn't want to go out with him. "Kat, I don't have a girlfriend."

Her voice was suspicious. "Since when? She was supposed to be here last night, and tonight…"

Alex took her hand. "Kat, I broke up with her last night."

Her brow furrowed. "Why?"

He smiled, pulling her toward him a bit, "Because I thought it would be shitty for me to be saying that I'm still going out with her while I was trying to work up the nerve to ask you out."

A smile spread slowly across her face. "Really?"

"Really."

She squeezed his hand. "Ask me again."

"Would you like to go out with me sometime?"

"Yes." Her eyes clouded. "But I'm going back to college tomorrow, so I won't be back in the city for quite a while."

Disappointment flooded him as he understood the reality of their situation. "Oh. So, how about we say that when we both are in the city, we'll go on a date? And in the meantime, how about you call me sometime?" His voice deepened, quickly adding, "But I do realize how stressful the last semester of college is, so no pressure. I'll leave it in your hands, okay?"

"Okay. So, I should call you?"

"Please."

She paused, knowing how often she would be thinking about him until she called him, but still wanting to appear nonchalant, "This week will be insane with going back, figuring out classes, books, and all that crap. It probably won't be until later this week."

"Whenever works for me." He took a deep breath, "The ball is in your court, so to speak."

A notepad sat on a table in the foyer, and Alex bent over it, writing something quickly. "Here's my number. Call me."

Kat took the scrap, trying to hide her delight. "I will."

"If I don't answer, or I'm not there, leave a message. I'll call you back."

She grinned. "You promise?"

Smiling like a little kid, he started to laugh, "Cross my heart."

As Alex walked home, he tried to deny just how much he looked forward to hearing from her again.

Chapter One

Only a week into the spring semester, Kat's two best friends, Josh and Mariah shared horrified looks–as they waited in the hospital hallway. Mariah reached out a hand to squeeze his, so sad that all she could do was let the tears roll down her cheeks.

Finally, Josh sat up, squeezed her hand again and said, "We have to call her parents."

The idea of being the one to make that call made Mariah's heart sink, so she wanted to delay it if possible. "Shouldn't we wait until we know more?"

"What more is there to know? She's hurt, she can't go back to the dorm, and they're going to need to know sooner than later. Besides, *she* isn't going to call them. She can barely speak."

Just then a nurse came out of Kat's room, shutting the door carefully behind her. She walked over and looked at the two of them. "The sheriff is heading over to interview her. Have you contacted her parents?"

Josh shook his head. "No, we were just talking about it."

"You should give them a call now. With all likelihood, she'll be released tonight, so either she can go back to the dorm with you, or they may want her to go home with them for a day or two while this all gets sorted out."

Mariah's eyes widened. "What do you mean, all sorted out?"

The nurse shrugged. "Well, security has already faxed their report to the sheriff, and I don't expect that the sheriff will take too long here, as it seems to be pretty much a formality."

Mariah's voice was shrill. "Are you kidding me?"

Realizing the implication of the nurse's words, Josh put a warning hand on Mariah's arm. "Mariah, it's time for us to make the call." He turned to look at the nurse, consciously trying to look as adult as he could. "The sheriff can't talk to her until her parents arrive. Period. Do you understand me?"

"That's not the usual protocol. When they get here, they normally do the interview right away."

Josh's voice was firm, "Not this time. You'll wait for her parents."

Chapter Two

Five years later

Far too early, Kat was reluctantly awakened from a deep sleep by the buzzing of her cell phone on the table next to her bed. Pushing her hair off her face, she looked at the clock before checking the display on her phone. She stabbed 'answer' and grouched in Spanish, "What the hell do you want at this hour? I was at the convention until three this morning!"

The voice was firm, but not hostile. "I know you were up until three; I was too, but this is an emergency. Paco is in the hospital with a broken arm, and I need you to cover my interview this morning."

Kat sat straight up, her anger evaporating at her friend's words. "Is Paco okay?"

"He'll be fine. He was playing on the stairs early this morning. He took a header and broke his arm badly. They're going to pin his arm together in about an hour, and I need to be here with him. But I was supposed to do an interview this morning; it *must* be today, and I need you to cover for me."

"Where and when?"

Grabbing a notepad, Kat scribbled down the information. After hanging up, she showered quickly and pulled a lightweight maroon sweater over her head. She slid snug black jeans up over her hips and completed the outfit with black leather boots. As she walked out the door with her bag slung over her shoulder, she hooked golden hoops in her ears.

Kat strode quickly through the quiet streets, glad that her apartment on Madrid's Plaza Mayor was only eight blocks from the hotel where she would do the interview.

The April sun was beginning to glint off the windows of the skyscrapers, and a light breeze swirled through empty streets. It was going to be a gorgeous day, and as she walked, Kat began to make plans. If the interview went well, she'd be home and typing it up within a couple hours, and then she could spend the rest of the day on the final chapter of her latest novel.

At the Hotel Emperador, Kat pushed through the revolving door, approached the front desk, and smiled at the flock of housekeepers dusting every possible surface. It was reassuring that all good hotels in Spain did things in almost the same way, at almost the same time of day, every day. At the desk, the concierge quickly explained how to get to the hotel restaurant and told her where Mr. Tamaro was sitting.

In the restaurant, Kat looked around, spotting a dark-haired man sitting at a corner table as had been described. The man looked up, eyes widening as they both recognized each other. His voice clearly expressed his surprise. "Kat?"

He stood, and they hugged each other awkwardly. Kat tried to accept the realization that the same Alex she had been thinking of for the past five years was standing in front of her. "Alex? What the hell are you doing here?"

"I could ask you the same thing." He swallowed, struggling to wrap his mind around the fact that she was standing in front of him. "I'm waiting to be interviewed. Some guy named … Hell, I don't remember his name … is supposed to be meeting me here." He looked at his watch. "Now."

Kat's eyes widened in horror as she understood the meaning of his words. "I'm the guy."

He shook his head in confusion. "What? No, they specifically told me to look for a *big* guy."

Kat motioned for him to sit down again at the table. "My friend Secu was supposed to interview you today, but he had a family emergency, so he asked me to cover." She shifted uncomfortably. "Is that okay with you?"

"Of course." Alex's eyes narrowed. "Did you know you had agreed to interview *me*?"

Kat shook her head more vigorously than strictly necessary, face flaming in embarrassment. She felt even more uncomfortable that he'd thought, even briefly, that she might have maneuvered herself into interviewing him. "No. When we met before, I don't think I'd ever heard your last name. I mean, even when I listen to the band's CDs, I don't read the liner notes. And when Secu gave me a quick rundown on the background this morning, he must not have known the connection. I was still half asleep, and it just didn't occur to me."

Alex swallowed the brief hope that she might have known it was him and agreed to take the interview at short notice to see him again. Surprisingly disappointed, he fought the urge to ask why she'd never called him, not since she went back to finish her last college term. He cleared his throat. "Okay. Well, then…"

Kat answered his hint with her most practiced professional smile. "Let's order breakfast and get to work."

Over eggs and toast, Kat peppered Alex with standard questions using a small recorder to tape their conversation. Occasionally she'd jot a note down on her pad, to remind her of a question she wanted to ask. Surprised at how different she was in a professional role than the mercurial young woman he remembered, Alex watched her in fascination.

Kat turned off the recorder. "Thanks, Alex. That's it. I'll type a draft today, and if you want, I can give you a copy in English to look over before I send it to the magazine."

"Don't bother. I trust you." Hoping to see her relax now that the interview was done, Alex gave his most charming smile and poured more coffee into her cup.

"Okay, so now tell me about *your* life. Last I heard, you were about to pack up to go back to college, and now I find you here in Madrid."

Not quite meeting his eyes, Kat answered carefully, "I went back to college, and after graduating, I moved here."

He chuckled in disbelief. "That's it? I just gave you all the gory details of my life, and you wrap five years up in—" he paused to count "—eleven words? You moved to Madrid to do what? I mean, I gather you're a reporter here."

She nodded. "I'm a writer. I do some work for papers and magazines, and I also write fiction."

"And you live here full time? What about the house in New York? Peter told me you owned it together now."

"We do, but really, I live here."

"How often do you get home? Knowing how close you and Peter are, I can imagine it is pretty often."

Kat squirmed, knowing how strange it would sound to him. "My career is here. I go occasionally."

"Only occasionally? Your brother is there."

"We get together fairly regularly, here, there, or other places. Anyway, my life is here now."

To him, her voice sounded almost melancholy. "And you're happy like this?"

The corners of her mouth quirked in what could pass for a smile. "It's the way I want it."

To Alex, this conversation felt like pulling teeth. This Kat was so different from the one who'd captivated him at the opera. Just as beautiful, but now somehow so aloof and cold. Alex remembered the hours he had spent thinking about her then, and hoping that she'd call him. Now he was asking questions that should have elicited more than one-sentence responses, and she was giving the absolute minimum of information. She didn't seem angry with him, but he couldn't quite tell if the problem was that she wasn't comfortable talking about herself, or just didn't want to talk about herself *with him*.

They continued to talk for a while—or rather, Alex talked, and Kat listened. Finally, Alex looked at his watch. "Kat, I have to run over to the theater to make sure we're ready." He hesitated. "Would you like to come to the concert tonight? Then after, maybe we could have a drink together."

Kat's gaze was serious. She frowned slightly, then she slowly nodded. "I'd like that. I need to get some work done today, but I'd love to go to the concert."

Alex stood. "A ticket will be held at the box office." He paused. "I'd be happy to leave two tickets if you'd like to bring someone."

She shook her head. "One ticket will be perfect. I'll be alone." As the words came out of her mouth, she suddenly wished that she'd found a less pathetic way to phrase it.

Alex tried not to grin his relief. "One it is. It'll be at the box office under your name. The concert starts at eight."

***

Twenty minutes before showtime, Kat nervously entered the theater. Why was she going to this concert? She could have easily begged off, and now she was here all dressed up, and she'd have to hang around after until Alex was done, like some sort of friggin' groupie. Like the loser she'd been that night, years before, sitting around waiting for the damn phone to ring. Shit, she should have stayed home.

***

The concert was flawless. Despite her uncertain mood, Kat found herself mesmerized by the music and Alex's performance. At one point, Kat was grateful for the darkness in the hall as she realized that she had allowed herself to imagine how it would feel to have Alex run his fingers over her skin the way they flowed across the piano keys. No matter how much time had passed or how her life had changed, he still was so attractive to her that she could hardly think straight in his presence. How the heck was she going to get through drinks with him keeping her walls up?

After the concert, Kat wandered out to the lobby with the rest of the crowd. The times she had met Peter after one of his performances, she'd go directly backstage, but here that seemed presumptuous. She suddenly realized that she'd never gone to see their band perform live, just listened to the CDs Peter had given her. She made a mental note to try to see them play live in the next year. Feeling more and more uncomfortable, she slid to the side of the noisy crowd to stand next to the walls hung with tapestries. The crowd chattered happily as it left the theater, and Kat let their noise and movement mesmerize her.

When a hand touched her arm, Kat jumped, immediately defensive. A slight man dressed in the uniform of the theater stood next to her. The usher smiled apologetically before speaking to her in rapid Spanish. "I'm sorry, miss, I didn't mean to startle you. Are you Katherine Weston?"

Kat answered uncertainly, "Yes."

"Mr. Tamaro asked me to escort you backstage."

Bristling slightly over the idea of Alex presuming she would *want* to go backstage, Kat followed him silently. In the dressing room, Alex was just shrugging on a leather jacket, chatting happily with the small group of people in the room. He grinned when he saw her. "Kat, you made it!"

Despite her earlier irritation, Kat felt strangely pleased by his obvious pleasure at seeing her. For a moment, she was glad that she had spent so much time picking a dress that showed her best attributes. "Hi, Alex."

Always gracious, Alex shook hands quickly with the other visitors, while subtly moving them toward the door. When the last person had left the room, he turned back to her. "I'm so glad you came."

"It was a great concert, Alex. You should be proud. You wowed the Spaniards, and they love nothing better than to find fault with an American."

He was more pleased than he'd expected by her praise and inordinately glad that she'd obviously dressed so carefully tonight. The black dress skimmed her curves, and left her elegant shoulders bare. A black choker-style necklace emphasized her long, slender neck. "Thank you. I'm really glad you enjoyed it."

"I did. It was great to hear your solo music. I have to admit, I've never heard you perform anything other than your stuff with the band."

"Yeah, it is quite different, isn't it? Now, how about a drink? Where do you want to go?"

She thought for a moment. "There's a small bar near your hotel. It's usually pretty quiet."

"Sounds great. Do you want to walk or take a taxi?"

"Let's walk."

***

As they walked through the twilight glow of the streetlights, Kat described the histories of the places they were passing. They had walked several blocks when she slowed a bit. "Alex, do you mind if we stop quickly at my apartment? I forgot my cell phone at home, and I really don't like to be out at night without it."

"Of course, let's stop. You said you live on Plaza Mayor, right? Well, I only went there once in high school, and I don't really remember it at all."

They walked into the Plaza Mayor, streetlights reflecting off the windows and the statue in the center of the square. All around the square were small cafes, their outside tables mobbed with chatting people. Kat guided Alex down a narrow alleyway that he would never have noticed without her. As she stopped in front of an ornate cast iron gate, a small gray-haired woman came running from a room off the visible foyer and opened the gate before Kat could pull the key from her purse. The woman grinned happily when Kat introduced Alex to her, and warmly kissed his cheeks. In her apartment, Alex chuckled. "That has to be the sweetest woman I've ever met."

Kat nodded, throwing her purse onto a small chair in the entryway of her apartment. "Isn't she? If I don't see Marta for a day or two, she'll leave me a note in my mailbox that she's worried about me." She thought back, "I got really sick last year, and she made me soup and kept me company one night when my temperature got really high."

"Really?"

"Yeah. She was so worried that I was all alone and that I might fall or something. All I remember is that at one point I needed a drink of water really badly, and there she was with ice water and aspirin to bring the fever down."

Alex fought a surge of sadness at the thought of her sick and alone. Why the hell was she living here? Couldn't she write in New York, or at least in the United States? "That was really kind of her."

Kat motioned at the rest of the apartment. "I just need a minute to grab the phone and use the bathroom." She rolled her eyes, "You probably didn't need to know that, right?"

He grinned, seeing a blush stain her cheeks. "No problem."

"Anyway, before I started telling you about my bodily needs, I was going to say please feel free to look around."

While Kat was in the other room, Alex wandered through the small kitchen, dining room and living room before calling out, "It's a great apartment, Kat. How'd you manage to get it? It must be nearly impossible in this neighborhood."

Kat called out from the next room. "It belongs to a family who've owned it for generations. When I was in college, I dated one of their sons for a little bit. Now he's married and lives in Sevilla, so they lease it to me." She motioned toward the bedroom. "I'm just checking my messages."

"Sure." The rooms were warm and comfortable, but as Alex looked around, he realized that they were strangely impersonal. A few knickknacks were scattered around, along with several photos of Peter and Luke, a woman who looked a lot like Kat so was probably her older sister, another of that same woman with two small children, and a picture of her parents. Alex's eyes clouded for a moment, remembering how shocked and saddened he'd been to hear of them both dying in a car accident more than four years earlier. Knowing how close he still was to his own parents, he wondered how Kat had coped with their loss.

Alex was still looking for anything that would give him more information about Kat when she moved to stand in an open doorway, a neatly made bed visible behind her. She was tucking her cell phone into her purse as she walked into the living room. "Are you ready?"

"Whenever you are."

"Then let's go."

***

They walked the few blocks to the bar in almost complete silence. They chose a corner table, lit by a small candle. Alex looked at Kat quizzically. "Red wine?"

"That'd be great."

Once the bottle had arrived and been approved, Alex raised his glass. "To coincidences. I didn't know you lived here, you didn't know that I was playing here, and yet—we met again."

"To coincidences." Kat sat quietly, relishing the rich, smooth flavor of the wine. As they sipped, Alex attempted to get a conversation started but was frustrated again and again by her short answers and lack of laughter.

It might have been the wine or late hour, or the candlelight making her hair shimmer, but finally, Alex couldn't resist any longer. "Kat, what happened?"

"What do you mean?" Her tone was guarded.

He fumbled for the right words, "I mean, five years ago, the world was your oyster. You loved life, you loved to talk about *anything,* and you laughed. A lot. But I've spent several hours with you today, and you're happy enough asking me questions, but if I ask you one, you barely give an answer. And I don't think I've heard you really laugh even once today."

His words stung, but Kat kept her voice calm. "I don't think I've changed. Maybe it's your perception."

He shook his head, more and more convinced that he was right. Overwhelmed by the urge to make her admit how much she'd changed, how she'd faded to a shadow of the girl he remembered, he continued, "No, I don't think so. I looked around your apartment. Except for a couple of pictures of your family, it's about as personal as a hotel room. You don't want to talk about your life. Everything I try to ask, you deflect." He felt frustration building. "What the hell happened?"

Kat took a last sip of wine and straightened in her chair. Her stomach churned as she searched for an adequate response. "Nothing happened. I'm just me. As for my apartment, that's how I like it."

"And you are clearly almost alone here."

"What are you talking about? You have no way of knowing that."

Later, Alex would regret his next words, but at that moment he needed to make her understand what he saw. "No. I don't have any way except that on a Friday night, you didn't have a date, and I saw no sign of a romantic relationship at your apartment. There aren't even pictures of a man who isn't related to you. So, I can conclude that you don't have anyone in your life right now and probably haven't in some time."

Deliberately keeping her voice even, Kat responded, "Alex, you're making a lot of assumptions. But fine, I'm not dating anyone. Is that a crime? I don't need to have a date every Friday night to make my life complete. You're here in Madrid, and you don't have a date either, so does that mean that you're living like a priest?"

"Kat, I was here to do a concert, the last of a series of concerts. As I said this morning, I've been on tour for months now. Besides, we're not talking about my life; we're talking about yours. We've talked about nothing but me all day. Every time I try to get you to open up, you give me a polite non-answer. So, I'll say it again: something happened to you sometime in the last few years. What was it?"

Kat felt pressure building in her lungs as she fought back tears. There was no way she could let him see how much damage his words were doing to her, and she had to get out of there before she lost her composure. Taking a deep breath to steady herself, she responded as calmly as she could manage. "Alex, nothing has changed since the last time we saw each other. Maybe we both just remember those nights in an unrealistic way. They were great, and they will always stay that way in my mind. But it was a long time ago, and a lot of things have happened to both of us since then, and we've both probably sealed those evenings in our memories, making it more than it really was." She rose and dropped several folded bills onto the table. In a soft voice, she said, "I have to go, Alex. Have a safe trip home."

Almost knocking over the table, Alex stood hurriedly. "Wait, Kat. Don't go. Please, I'm sorry for what I said. Stay."

Swamped with a crushing fatigue that crashed over her in a wave, Kat shook her head. "You're not sorry for what you said. You meant it, and I'm sure with the best of intentions, but really, it's none of your business. So, if you'll excuse me, I'm going home to my life which is just the way I like it. Goodbye, Alex."

She walked out of the square without a backward glance.

***

Nearly a month later, Alex was finally back at home in California. As he sifted through the pile of mail that had inevitably accumulated in his absence, a small ivory envelope, addressed in metallic purple ink, slid through his fingers. Recognizing the king of Spain on the stamps, he tore it open immediately and pulled out a folded card wrapped around a smaller envelope.

The handwritten note was brief:

Dear Alex,

Please forgive my behavior when you were in Madrid. I greatly enjoyed your concert, and it was nice to see you. And again, I am sorry for the way I acted.

I hope you enjoy the performance – Katherine Weston

Alex opened the smaller envelope to find two tickets for the San Francisco Opera. He sat down on a stool in shock. Damn, he hadn't expected this. A pleased smile crossed his face; he'd spent the days since then thinking about Peter's beautiful little sister. Maybe she'd been thinking of him, too.

***

The phone rang shrilly, interrupting his reverie. Alex grabbed the cordless, tucking it between his ear and his shoulder. "Hello?"

"Hey, Alex. It's Peter. How's life in California?"

Alex grinned. "Hey, Peter. Life's pretty good. Always full of surprises." He looked again at the tickets. "Hey, I was just thinking about you."

"You were? That's weird."

Alex focused on the conversation, "Yeah. Anyway, what's up?"

"I'm calling about the wedding. You're coming, right?"

Having momentarily forgotten about Will's wedding, only two weeks away, Alex rubbed his forehead. "Of course I'm coming. I was thinking about flying out three days ahead and flying home two days after. That way I could go to the wedding and still have some time to hang out."

"Cool. But come earlier and stay longer. We can do the wedding shit and then have some time to plan for the fall, hang out, and relax a bit. Hey, do you want to stay with us?"

Alex already had hotel reservations, but staying with Peter and Luke sounded much more appealing. "That would be great."

"Okay, then the day before you come, give us a call with your flight number, and we'll pick you up at the airport."

"Great." As he looked again at the tickets, Alex wondered if his words could have motivated Kat to do more than just apologize; maybe she'd come back to the States sometime soon. Alex paused thoughtfully, wondering how to make his next words sound nonchalant.

"Hey, Peter. Did Kat mention that she interviewed me in Madrid?"

"Oh yeah, she did. She said it was great to see you again. And I don't know what happened when you were there, but maybe seeing a familiar face made her homesick."

"What do you mean?"

"Well, when she told me she'd seen you, she mentioned coming home for a visit sometime soon, which she hasn't done in ages."

"Really?"

"Yeah, I mean, when I brought up the idea of Thanksgiving, she didn't immediately tell me she was too busy. That's huge!"

"Really?" Alex had a thought. "What about the wedding? Is she coming home for it?"

"No, and it *really* hurt Mariah's feelings — which, by extension means that it really pissed her off. You know Kat introduced the two of them, right?"

"Yeah."

"So, she was invited to the wedding, but said she couldn't come home right now."

Disappointment flooded Alex. "Oh."

"Anyway, going back to an earlier discussion, you'll be here this fall for when we're recording. Just to plant the thought, you're welcome to have Thanksgiving with us."

The day was getting more and more interesting. "I'd love to." He tried to make his voice more casual. "Hey, Peter, she sent me a note, and I want to call her and thank her. Do you have her number handy?"

Ten minutes later, Alex sat looking at the number scrawled on the back of Kat's envelope. Taking the time difference into account, it would be relatively early in the morning in Madrid, but not obnoxiously so. Taking a deep breath, Alex dialed. After all these years, here he was the one calling her when their deal was that he'd wait for her to call him.

The phone rang five times, and Alex began to fear that Kat wouldn't pick up. He started to plan his voicemail message when a loud screech sounded just before a voice came on. "*Hola?* Hello?"

"Kat? It's Alex."

There was another screech. "Alex, hold on, I'm just getting off the metro so I can't hear you very well. Give me just a second."

Alex waited, hearing the now recognizable sounds of a subway station. Kat's voice came back on. "Hi, sorry about that."

"No problem." He tried to sound relaxed. "I just got your note, and I wanted to call and thank you. You really didn't need to apologize."

"Yes, I did. I was a bitch." She started to laugh. "Okay, I'm walking down the street speaking on the phone in English, and when I said that word, this old lady just tsked me! *That* word she knows. Anyway, I was a jerk, and you didn't deserve it."

"Well, I disagree that you were a jerk, but I still really appreciate the thought, and I love opera, as you know."

"Good. If you didn't notice, they're open-ended tickets, good for any show that still has seats. I figured that way you could pick the performance you wanted."

"That was really sweet of you. Anyway, I owe you an apology for the things I said. I was out of line."

"No, you weren't. As I said then, it was how you saw things. Besides, it's over. Let it go."

"Deal. How are things?"

Kat sighed. "They're really busy. I'm doing a series of pieces for a magazine, so I've been on trains a lot lately, going all around the country. But the good part is that I've visited a couple towns I've never been to before."

Abruptly, Alex realized that this was more information than she'd given him the whole time they'd been together in Madrid. Maybe what he'd said *had* made a difference. Or maybe she was getting used to talking to him.

Fifteen minutes later, Kat said, "Alex, this call is costing you a fortune. We should go."

Alex started to argue but decided to not end another conversation by putting Kat in a huff. "Okay. But, how about you send me an email occasionally?"

He could hear paper rustling. "Okay. I can do that. Hold on, I need to find a pen. What's your email?"

***

Not more than twenty minutes later, Alex's email buzzed. A new message had appeared in his inbox. It was short, but enough to make him smile. It read, *Hey, Alex. Thanks for calling. Send me an email when you get bored — Kat*

Chapter Three

A week later, the bleating of a garbage truck in reverse woke Alex from a deep sleep. He lay in bed, watching the morning shadows shift across the ceiling until he finally had to admit that he just wasn't going to fall back asleep. Casting a resentful eye at the clock, Alex dragged himself out of bed and into his clothes, determined to start the coffee and begin caffeine infusions as quickly as possible. When he stepped out to pick up the newspaper from the front steps, he saw a dark haze hanging over the morning half-light. Truck exhaust and the sweetish scent of garbage briefly dominated the familiar mélange of New York aromas.

Back in the kitchen, Alex hadn't progressed beyond scanning the headlines when Peter stumbled in yawning. "Damn, I really appreciate the city sending out its mobile alarm clocks on the day that I actually have the *option* of sleeping another couple of hours. Good thing nothing smells better than coffee, especially after about two hours of sleep."

Alex turned the page imperturbably. "It should be ready." He sent Peter a gently mocking look. "I hate to remind you, but we could've had more sleep if we'd left the club earlier."

"And miss the final set? I don't think so." As he spoke, Peter poured himself a cup of coffee and then reached for an orange.

"Save me a bite," Luke said from the doorway. He walked over to Peter, and the two men exchanged a tender kiss.

Peter tugged on the lapel of Luke's charcoal gray suit. "Nice. How come you always look better than me?"

"Because I go out and buy clothes. *You* root around in the rag box for t-shirts that haven't been turned into dust cloths yet." Luke's smile took any bite out of his words.

Peter held up his hands in mock surrender. "Okay – I give. Buy me clothes this weekend, please."

Luke claimed a section of his orange. "I will try to, either this weekend or next. But it's so much easier when Kat's around to shop with me. Too bad I can't wait for her to come home."

"*If* she ever comes home." Peter tried to keep the wistfulness out of his voice.

Alex was confused. "I thought you said she'd be coming home for Thanksgiving?"

Luke nodded, "Yeah, she said she *might* come, but every time we try to pin her down, she mumbles about getting back to us."

Peter inhaled deeply. "I just wish she'd move home for good." He gestured around the kitchen with one hand, "We own the house together, but other than paying her share of the insurance and tax payments, she hasn't actually stepped foot in it for over a year. A couple times in the last four years she came home for a few days, but then she headed out again and wouldn't talk about *really* moving back home." He realized that Alex was looking at him strangely and tried to change the subject. "How'd you sleep, Alex?"

Alex wanted to ask a hundred questions about why Kat had been away for so long, and why she wouldn't even talk about coming back, but Peter was clearly done with the subject. "Like a rock. It must be the clean air and quiet streets of New York City."

With a brief smile, Peter hit the 'play' button on the answering machine. "I forgot to check the machine last night, but I suppose it doesn't really matter since three a.m. isn't a great time to return messages."

Alex nodded, "And since we were gone all day yesterday..."

"It really doesn't matter. Anything major, people call our cells."

The machine beeped, and then a woman's voice came on. "Hi, guys, it's Mariah. It's around noon. I think I may have done something stupid or at least really obnoxious last night." The voice paused. "I had *way* too much wine to drink, and I started calling Kat, begging her to come home for the wedding. From my call record, it looks like I called her six or seven times. Anyway, I don't remember a whole lot about the conversations, other than being a crying, begging mess. But when I checked my email this morning, there was a message from Kat, telling me that she figured I must have a hell of a hangover and that she hoped my head hurt a lot. Which, for the record, it does. I feel like I got run over by a Mack truck. But, yes! She said she'd come home for the wedding. So, she may have already called you guys, but anyway, I wanted to give you a heads up that she's coming home. Love you. See you at the rehearsal in a few days."

The three men exchanged shocked looks just as the front door buzzer sounded. Peter stopped the message tape impatiently. "Who the hell could that be? And oh, my God, Kat's coming home!"

Luke rolled his eyes, "I'll get the door. You listen to the rest of the messages."

As he left the kitchen, Peter pushed "Play" again. Another beep sounded, and suddenly Kat's voice filled the room. "Hi, Pete, hi, Luke, it's me. Anyway, Mariah has probably already called you. I'm going to be coming home in the next day or so, basically just long enough to go to the wedding. I'm on standby on several flights today, but if those don't work, I'm booked on one tomorrow. I'll let you know when I get one and when I'll be arriving. Love you!"

Peter's eyes grew wide. "Oh, shit, that's her! She's finally coming home, and I didn't check the damn messages."

The machine beeped again. "Hi guys, you're still not answering either this phone or your cells. Please tell me again why you bother to have cell phones if you leave them off all the time. Anyway, it's three p.m. here, and I just made it on the next flight which is leaving in a half-hour. I will be getting into JFK at about three-thirty tomorrow morning on Avianca 1120. Don't be confused by the flight number; I'll be flying in from Bogotá since it's the connection from Madrid. Be there, please!"

Peter's face paled as he looked at the clock. "Holy shit! She should have arrived about four hours ago! And we're just standing here."

Just then their big black mutt skidded out of the kitchen and made for the front door, barking madly. Luke appeared in the doorway, with a huge grin on his face, "Hey, Pete, I think we should have checked the messages last night..."

Behind Luke, a feminine voice rose. "Max, get down. Damn it, Max, get out of the way!"

Peter lunged for the hallway as Kat and the dog came into the kitchen. He snagged the wiggling dog by the collar. "Max, knock it off. Kat, welcome home!"

"Hey, at least *Max* is eager to see me." Simply dressed in a white blouse and black slacks, Kat had restrained her strawberry blonde hair in a severe knot. She had several black travel bags slung over her shoulders. Dropping them unceremoniously on the floor, she crouched down to hug the huge dog. Smiling, she stood up and sent a stern look at her sheepish brother. "Hi, Pete. Remember me? Your darling baby sister? The one you keep begging to come home, and then you leave me stranded at the goddamn airport?"

Peter lifted her off the floor in an enthusiastic hug. "Welcome home! And why the hell didn't you call from the airport?"

Still held in Peter's arms, Kat whacked the side of his head with enough force to make him wince. "Duh. I don't have an American cell phone, and I didn't have any change for the pay phones, only a few bills for emergencies. It was going to take me longer to get change for a pay phone than it was to get a taxi to get here. Besides, I had this mistaken idea that my beloved brother would come get me."

"Okay, okay. I apologize, and I'll keep apologizing for the next few days. I'll make it up to you, I promise."

She grinned. "You bet your ass you will."

Kat suddenly glimpsed Alex sitting at the kitchen table, and could only stare at him in shock. His dark brown hair, waving to midway down his neck, was a bit longer than it had been in Madrid. She noted a few more sun streaks, which seemed to emphasize the hazel of his eyes and his golden skin. Realizing that she'd been silent too long, Kat blushed and fumbled a greeting. "Hi, Alex."

He stood quickly, offered an awkward hug. As his arms wrapped around her, Kat desperately wished she'd known he would be there so she could have made sure she looked and smelled better. For just a moment, she gave in to temptation and leaned against him, enjoying the sensation of his body against hers. Flinching slightly as she realized what she was doing, she gave herself an internal shake and stepped back, forcing herself not to look away.

Gazing down into her bright green eyes, Alex felt for a moment as if everything in the world had paused, and he didn't care if it started again... "Hi, Kat. Welcome home."

Abruptly aware that she was still staring, Kat spoke a little too quickly. "Thanks. I didn't know you'd be here. You didn't mention it in your emails."

Peter and Luke exchanged a quick glance. Since when were they emailing each other?

Alex answered cautiously, trying to judge from her tone of voice whether she was happy he was there. "Yeah. I came out for the wedding, and Pete and Luke invited me to stay here."

"Oh." Another silence, and then Kat noticed that Peter and Luke were watching them like the latest reality show. Narrowing her eyes at them in a warning glare, she turned back to Alex and offered her brightest guest-in-the-house smile. "I mean, that's great."

"It is." Alex was quick to pick up her cue. "And thank you again for the tickets." He swallowed some coffee, now less than hot. "I mean, there was no need for an apology, but I enjoyed the performance."

Kat felt like her brain had shriveled away, leaving her tongue thick and uncoordinated. "I'm so glad." She felt panic welling up inside her. What came next? "Well, it's nice to see you again."

Alex, pleased that she was at least trying to talk to him, sipped his coffee calmly.

At last, Luke took pity on them. Standing up, he pulled her favorite mug out of the cabinet and said, "Kat, you want some coffee?"

"That would be great."

He handed the steaming mug to her, and continued, "How was your trip? And how long are you staying? Can we keep you forever?"

"Nice to see that you're still so subtle, Luke." Kat started pulling pins out of her hair. "My trip was good but long as hell." She tried to smile. "I don't know how long I'm here for. I have an open-ended return ticket, but I should head back early next week. Anyway, the last few days have been insane since I was north up until just two days ago."

Peter tipped his head. "I knew you were out of town, but I didn't know that you were north."

Her face lit up. "I needed more info for an article on the anniversary of Ibárruri's death, but while I was there, I met a fabulous woman in the village. I spent hours and hours with her—she worked with the Basque miners during their uprising— so I have enough notes to carry me for a while once I'm done with my current draft. And I hit the apple harvest perfectly." As the last pin came out, her curls tumbled down, caressing her neck and shoulders. She grinned at Peter and Luke in self-satisfaction. "A case of *cidra* will arrive later today—I hired someone to deliver it rather than try to carry it by cab."

"Great!" Peter looked at Luke with a gleam in his eyes. "Luke forgot to check the machine last night, so we only just got your message. Why didn't you call us again?"

She rolled her eyes. "Nice try—blame it on Luke. You think I've forgotten that checking messages is *your* job? Anyway, I was lucky to get a seat on that flight since, obviously, I made my decision at the last minute. I mean, I had no intention of going to the wedding, but when Mariah kept calling and calling, I finally caved."

"I had just come back home to Madrid from the north. I mean, I haven't even done my dirty laundry. I just threw a few clean things into a bag. Then I called all the airlines and ended up going out to Barajas to get on standby. Finally, I got on the Avianca list for the flight. You know your options are bad when you feel lucky to be going to JFK via Colombia. But, even after I made the final list for the flight, we got delayed because there was a threat."

She shook her head in disgust. "I sat on my bags and waited. They didn't even check through our luggage for an hour until they had about a million troops at the airport to inspect them. So I played thirty-seven hands of Crazy Eights with some kid named Nicodemus. Why the hell would you name a kid Nicodemus? Talk about setting him up—with that name; e*veryone* is going to beat the shit out of him." As she spoke, she flipped her head upside down, briskly rubbing her fingers over her scalp. When she straightened up, the waves were in wild disarray. "It was a really long day or night, whatever it was."

Peter reached over and tugged on a curl. "Since when do you travel with your hair on top of your head instead of in a braid?"

She yawned. "I was at the Madrid airport for*ever* hoping for standby. A few hours in, I decided I had to get my hair *completely* out of my way or rip it out of my head. It kept sliding out of the braid, and it was driving me crazy."

She rolled her shoulders and circled her head around, deciding it was time to get herself out of the spotlight. "Anything new with you guys?"

Peter shrugged, swallowing coffee. "Nothing much. We've been busy as hell, but I can't say anything exciting happened. Oh yeah, Josh called a couple of days ago."

"He did?"

"Yeah, he's coming to the city either tonight or tomorrow, and he'll be at the wedding."

"Great! Is he staying here?" She sounded so happy, that for a moment, Alex felt a stab of jealousy.

"No. He's dating someone named Kim, so he's staying with her while he's here from Boston, and he's bringing her to the wedding." Peter scowled as he tried to remember the conversation. "He originally said something about stopping here to see you, expecting you'd come for the wedding. He was bent out of shape when I said you *weren't* coming so I just kept telling him that you told me you'd try to be home for Thanksgiving."

"I still don't know about Thanksgiving, but when 'Riah started to cry, I couldn't stand it anymore." She shrugged. "Besides, I sort of missed you guys." Kat stood up and stretched her arms overhead. "What are you up to today?"

Luke brushed crumbs off his jacket and looked at his watch. "I have to be at the gallery at nine-ish."

"Well, shit." Peter tipped back in his chair. "Since we didn't think you'd be here, we haven't been filling you in about anything. You probably have no clue about all the plans for this week and weekend." Kat shook her head and waited for him to continue. "Alex and I are heading out to the grocery store at some point this morning while Luke goes to the office. We planned on staying in tonight since we were all out really late last night, hence missing your calls."

Kat nodded. "Okay, then what?"

Peter ate another bite of orange. "Tomorrow, we're heading to the shore. We invited Sasha and Beth, and Josh and his date to stay with us. They'll come the day *after* tomorrow. Then on Friday, we have the pre-wedding final fitting crap. That evening we have the rehearsal, and rehearsal dinner, which you don't have to go to. Then the wedding is on Saturday. Sunday morning there's a brunch." He shook his head in amazement. "It's like a whole marathon wedding thing."

"And then? How long are people staying with you?"

He corrected her automatically. "With us." She rolled her eyes at him. "Everybody will be heading out either Sunday afternoon or Monday morning. Will that work for you?"

Kat thought for a moment. "That makes sense. Sure, the shore would be great."

Luke noticed the shadows under her eyes. "What are you going to do today? No offense, but you look like crap. You should get a few hours of sleep."

"I will. You know me, I can't sleep on a stupid plane. I thought I'd grab a shower, get into something clean, and then take a nap for a couple hours." She looked at all three men. "Who's making dinner tonight?"

"You are!" Luke and Peter yelled in unison.

Kat laughed and swatted at her brother with a dishtowel. "I'm the damn guest, and I have to cook?"

Peter scoffed, "You're not a guest. This is your house too. Besides, you cook better than we do."

"No, I don't. You're just hoping I'll make one of your favorites." She sighed, accepting that she would be in charge of dinner that night. "Okay, what do you want? You'll need to get the groceries for me."

Luke answered before Peter could. "Lasagna. Please Kat, lasagna. The only time we get it now is in a restaurant."

"Fine." Kat turned to look at Alex. "Alex, can you join us for dinner?"

"If it isn't a problem, I'd love you." Horrified, Alex realized his slip as Peter and Luke smirked. "I mean I'd love to." *God*, Alex thought, *I could have plans to dine with God, and I would cancel them in order to spend the evening with this woman.*

Kat chuckled in amusement. "I didn't realize I was so appealing when I haven't showered in days."

Peter snorted. "Don't let it go to your head, Kat— you look disgusting. Alex, please join us."

"I'd love to." He smiled at Kat. "Thanks for the invitation."

"You're welcome." Kat stood up to make her way over to the walk-in pantry. Looking around quickly, she jotted a couple things down on the back of an envelope she had pulled out of the recycling bin. Then she opened the fridge, poked around for a moment, and sighed. "You two really don't cook too often, do you?"

Luke shook his head. "No. I mean we cook sometimes, but usually, we wind up calling for take-out or going out. Your cooking is one of the reasons we want you to move home."

"Of course, it is." She squeezed Luke's hand. "And helping you put up with my brother. Anyway, here's what I need for tonight."

Peter looked at the list. "Fine. We'll get it all."

"Great." Kat leaned over and kissed the top of Peter's head. "Pete, will you bring some of this shit upstairs for me?"

Peter nodded as he gulped coffee. Wrinkling her nose at Luke and Alex, Kat grabbed the smaller bag, and a brown paper wrapped package. "See you later, boys."

Alex responded before he could stop himself. "Definitely."

***

Kat grumbled as she climbed the stairs. "Jesus. At this point, these weigh a ton."

"You have the small ones!" Peter said, huffing slightly.

"Yeah, but I'm delicate."

Peter's snort was audible even to Alex and Luke, who were still sitting in the kitchen. "Delicate, my ass. Why is your room on the top floor?"

"Because you claimed the bottom one, idiot. And as I remembered, we all agreed that several floors between us would give us the illusion of privacy."

"Who needs privacy? You're never here!"

Kat took a deep breath, trying to stay calm. "Let it go, Pete, before I start to feel badgered and head back to the airport."

"Fine, I'll stop." Once the siblings had reached the top floor of the house, Peter dropped the bags on the couch and hugged Kat quickly. "Glad you're back, Brat. I missed you."

"I missed you too." She leaned against his chest for a moment. "Thanks for bringing this stuff up for me. I'll see you tonight, if not sooner?"

"Bet on it."

Chapter Four

Around mid-day, Peter and Alex walked into the house laden with overflowing grocery bags. Casting his eyes toward the ceiling, Peter said, "The house is really quiet. Kat must have fallen asleep."

Alex nodded. "Good, she looked like she really needed it. Why doesn't she sleep on planes?"

"Kat hates to fly. No, really, it's not the flying so much as that Kat *hates* the noise of planes—she says it gets inside her skull. And even though she flies all the time, she still freaks out every single time the engine noise changes, and if she tries to sleep and the sound changes, she wakes in a panic. I mean a full blown, hands-sweating, dry-mouth, verging-on-hyperventilating panic. So, she reads or writes whenever she flies, and she has her iPod on to block it out as much as possible."

Alex tried to imagine it. "Really? I just can't picture Kat being scared."

Peter grinned. "Actually, it's pretty amusing to watch. She'll sit, iPod in her hands, ready to stuff those 'buds into her ears the *second* they say it's okay... And on a day like today when she has lousy flights and long layovers, she'll go for *days* without sleep, so as soon as she gets where she's going, she crashes hard for a few hours. But then, when any of the rest of us would still need more sleep, she bounces up like the Energizer Bunny. You just wait, when she gets up in a bit, she'll be irritatingly energetic."

"Why doesn't she take something to take the edge off her anxiety?"

Peter laughed, "Oh, we tried for years to convince her to do that, but she's afraid that if she does take something, and then something goes wrong on the flight, that she won't be able to respond the way she's supposed to." He shook his head, "She is the only person I know who reads the entire safety brochure every single time she gets on a plane, and she shushes people when they talk during the safety demonstration."

Alex tried again to picture Kat being that nervous. "Seriously?"

"Yeah. It's so tiring to fly with her that *we* take something instead for *her* anxiety."

***

Once the groceries were sorted and put away, Peter and Alex took Max for a long walk. On the way back to the house, Peter's cell rang. After a quick conversation, Peter hit the off button and said, "Hey Alex, Luke has a new painting at the gallery that he really wants me to see. Do you mind taking Max back to the house, and we'll meet you there in just a bit?"

Alex took the leash. "Not at all. Max and I'll head back and see if Kat's awake."

***

A surprising wave of exhilaration hit as Alex opened the front door, and he acknowledged to himself how much he was looking forward to seeing Kat again, even after their baffling interactions in Madrid. He unhooked Max and hung the leash on the hook next to the door. As he walked into the bright kitchen, he saw Kat standing dressed in black jeans and a dark green fitted T-shirt, her hair pulled back into a black scrunchie. He was amused to hear Twiddle blasting on the stereo, thinking that living in Spain would have kept her from learning about the new indie band. She hummed as she kneaded bread dough, her arm muscles straining, their clean lines seeming to beg for his touch. The smell of yeast filling the room welcomed him, and for a moment, Alex pictured coming home every night to her.

When Alex moved closer, Kat jumped, and a flash of fear crossed her face. Instinctively, Alex laid his hand on her arm to reassure her, the warmth of her skin sending a tingle of awareness up his arm. "I'm sorry, Kat; I didn't mean to scare you. I thought you'd have heard the front door."

Her eyes still showed her nerves as she reached over to turn the stereo down. "Don't worry about it." She lowered the volume some more. "It was too loud for me to hear anything." She looked around almost nervously. "Where's Peter?"

Was she as aware as he was that they were alone? Did it matter to her? "He went to the gallery to meet Luke to see some new painting. He thought they'd be back pretty soon." He looked around the kitchen. "Do you need help?"

"Not now. Once the dough's rising for the second time, there's a break." Inwardly, she groaned. Did she always have to sound curt with this guy? God, he must think she was such a bitch. Kat tried to soften her tone. "I could use some help later, though."

The idea of spending time with her sent a powerful surge of joy through him. "Great. Then if you don't mind, I'll go grab a quick shower."

***

When Alex walked into the sunroom after his shower, he found Kat sitting on the couch with the big dog.

At the sound of his footsteps, Kat's chin rose. Her eyes wandered up long legs encased in softly faded denim and a light gray T-shirt and lingered on the auburn highlights glinting in his damp hair. With a start, Kat realized he was watching her just as carefully, and she began to blush.

He sat on the couch across from her. "Am I interrupting?"

Her cheeks were red. "No. Max and I were just catching up. I really miss having a dog, so when I'm here, I tend to spend a lot of time talking to him."

"Does Max answer you back?" Alex asked teasingly.

"No, but he's a great listener. If I pet him, he'll listen for hours."

Before he could stop himself, Alex thought, *Max isn't the only one who'd listen for hours if you pet him.* He tried to cover his grin. "A good listener is hard to find, especially one who knows how to keep his mouth shut."

"Exactly! Give me a dog over a human any day."

Behind Kat, Peter and Luke quietly entered the room with a tall, handsome man with curly black hair. Kat was so focused on her conversation with Alex that she didn't hear the newcomer sneaking up behind her. Just as Alex was about to warn her, the stranger winked at Alex and bent down to kiss her neck.

A surprised squeak came rushing out before she jumped and quickly turned around to be wrapped in his arms.

Her voice was joyful as she recognized him. "Josh!"

The man chuckled as he held her tight. "Hi, Ducky, how are you?"

"Oh, I'm so glad to see you!"

After Peter had introduced Josh and Alex, Josh sat down next to Kat on the couch, their fingers entwining in a motion that was clearly familiar to them both. Alex tamped down a flare of jealousy. Who the hell was this guy?

Josh spoke gently. "So, you *finally* decided to come home?"

Luke quickly tried to change the subject. "Uh, Josh, how was your trip?"

Josh grinned. "Nice try, Luke. Always the peacekeeper." He turned back to Kat. "So, finally? Is this just a visit, or are you here for good?"

Kat sat straighter, moving away from Josh with a cold look on her face. "A visit. Enough."

Keeping his voice neutral, Josh tried to pull her toward him again. "Oh, come on, Ducky. Are we pretending that you live in Madrid just for work?"

Kat stood up, moving to the window and wrapping her arms around herself as if to ward off a chill, even though the room was warm. When she finally spoke, Alex was amazed that the tension in her body showed only in the shortness of her words. "Josh, my decision to move to Madrid was personal and professional, as you know. And my decision to stay is as well." Turning toward Alex, her face was tight with tension. "Alex, I'm ready to work on dinner now — are you?" She turned back to Josh. "Are you eating with us?"

Josh's face showed his anger, but his tone was civil. "No, Kat. I promised Kim I'd be there in time for dinner. I just wanted to stop by here first. So you're going to the wedding after all?"

She nodded. "Yeah, I finally caved, after a bunch of drunken calls from 'Riah."

That made Josh smile, "Alcohol always did bring out her phone addiction. Remember when we had to disconnect her phone?" He paused before moving toward Kat. "Kat, I'm sorry if I pissed you off by saying anything about Madrid. Truce?"

Kat's eyes stayed wary. "Truce. But we're done talking about it."

Josh's eyes narrowed. "We're done talking for tonight, maybe."

They could all see the angry glitter in Kat's eyes as she motioned toward the kitchen. "Josh, can I see you in the kitchen?"

Kat carefully closed the French doors between the kitchen and the sunroom, deliberately bringing them together gently, rather than slamming them as she was tempted to do. Taking a deep breath, she worked hard to keep her voice calm. "Damn it, Josh, you needed to bring this up in front of Alex? Jesus, he's a stranger. Thanks a lot! And to top it off, you call me 'Ducky' too?"

"I always call you Ducky, just like Mariah does." Josh thought for a moment, before admitting that she had a point. "Okay, so I should have waited until we were alone or at least until he wasn't there. Point taken."

"Thank you."

"But, damn it, Kat, you need to talk about it – to get it out of your system! And you hang up when I try to say anything over the phone. At least when we're face to face, you can't hang up on me." He reached out to touch her face, but she jumped back. "You need to get over it, Kat. Or at least deal with it openly, and move through it and go forward. And talking about it is the only way you're ever going to heal."

Her voice suddenly sounded young and confused, and painfully sad. "Why do I need to talk about it? It's not going to change anything. All it does is to re-open old wounds."

"Those damn wounds never closed, except that you keep pretending they did. Hell, you keep pretending they don't exist."

Sadness was instantly transformed into rage. "You want me to get it out of my system? I don't get to get it out of my system. It *is* my system. It is my fucking reality, twenty-four seven." She shook her head, so agitated she didn't care who heard her. "What the fuck do you want me to say, that it still hurts? Shit, yes!" She slammed her fist onto the counter. "Do you want me to admit that I still wonder what I should've done differently? Yes, I wonder every goddamn day. I don't ever get to walk away from that, ever. What the holy fuck do you want me to say, Josh, what? Tell me what to say that will make you happy."

Shocked by the intensity of her reaction, Josh shoved his fingers through his black curls. "Yes—no. I don't care what you say, just that you talk; to me, to Peter or Luke or 'Riah, or a therapist, or someone sitting on a goddamn park bench. I don't care who you talk to, or what you say, just that you let yourself express whatever it is that you truly feel. It's been destroying you for years, and yet you just keep saying that you're frickin' fine."

Kat's throat constricted as she felt the weight of his disapproval, so she instantly fought back even harder. "You son-of-a-bitch, you sit and judge me for not talking about it?" She jabbed her finger into his chest so hard he winced. "How dare you condemn me for wanting to try to keep it together the best I can? Don't you realize how hard I work to keep my shit together? But no, you give me a hard time for not doing it the way you think I should. Thanks a fucking lot, Josh." Her bitingly sarcastic tone carried into the other room. "Thank you for your kind understanding."

With his hands on his hips, Josh yelled as if that would help him get through to her. "Damn it Kat, listen to me! I do understand, as much as someone who didn't actually go through it can." Startled at his own volume, he took a breath and deliberately softened his tone. "What I understand is that you've driven this so deep inside that we're losing you. I'm fucking terrified that we've lost you for good, that you'll never come back the way you were. I'm afraid I'll never see you love again or laugh so hard you cry and milk shoots out your nose. You always kept things to yourself, I was used to that, but you still connected to the rest of the world. But ever since it all happened, you've shut down and never even refer to it, and now you only seem to connect with the stories you write, as long as you aren't a part of them at all, just an observer."

Her eyes widened, "So beyond being a nut job, I'm a shitty writer, too. Not putting myself into my stories? Fuck you!"

His voice rose again. "That isn't what I meant, and if you would calm down, you'd know that. You're looking for a fight right now."

"I am not. You're the one who started the entire conversation."

Josh took a deep breath. "Okay, let me rephrase my concern again." He stood for a second, trying to find the right words, knowing he had only seconds left before she would bolt. "Kat, it all had to impact you, and yet, no one ever even saw you cry. You didn't cry when it happened. You didn't cry at the funeral. And you didn't even cry when your parents died. You just plain shut down and shut us all out. I know you loved all of them with all your heart, but you just kept quiet and stoic, and then moved to Spain. And you keep saying you're fucking fine. But one thing you're not is fine."

She stood in front of him, unable to look at his face. Josh's voice softened. "Kat, if you won't talk about it, then write about it. Write about what you felt, what you feel."

He stepped closer and touched her face. She jumped as if his hand had burned her. "You're my best friend, and I love you more than I can express. All I want is for you to let it go and start to heal. And, no matter how much you don't want to hear me say it, you're not going to heal in Madrid. You can hide there, but you can't heal there. The demons are here. You need to face them and go forward. All of us will support you, do whatever it takes, but you can't heal there, and deep down, you know it."

***

Opening the French doors, Josh left Kat staring woodenly ahead. He shut the doors behind him before walking over to

Peter and Luke. "I'm not sure if I made things worse or better."

Only bits and pieces of the conversation had been audible in the living room, but Peter had heard variations on it often enough to be able to fill in what he'd missed. He met Josh's eyes calmly for a moment. "It needed to be said. Hopefully, you helped, but it certainly can't hurt. When I try to talk to her about it, she just walks away or hangs up." He shook his head. "But, you know, you could wait a whole five minutes after arriving before pissing her off."

"Why wait when pissing her off is so much fun?" Josh laughed. "Hey, somebody needs to cut through the crap with her. We all know exactly why she lives thousands of miles away, and we need an act of Congress to get her to come back for even a few days." He stuck out his hand toward Alex. "Alex, it was nice meeting you." He grinned wickedly. "Don't give up on her."

Alex looked confused. "What?"

"When we walked in, and the two of you were talking, you were sitting there looking at her like, as my mom would say, she's the cat's meow. Don't give up on her—she's worth it. Good night, guys. See you all at the shore."

The silence after Josh left was almost deafening, and then Peter asked, "Is he right?"

Alex shifted uncomfortably. "What do you mean?"

"As Josh put it, do you think she's the cat's meow?"

Alex rubbed his temple. "Damn, guys, I ..."

Peter chuckled. "Alex, I'm just giving you shit. I'm not serious."

Peter and Luke stood up, and Luke smiled warmly. "Alex, it's always amusing to watch someone else learn to deal with her." He motioned to the back stairs, "We're going to run downstairs and get cleaned up. We'll be back up in a few minutes."

***

Feeling like he was entering the lion's den, Alex walked toward the kitchen. As his hand touched the latch, he wondered what sort of state Kat would be in after such an intense conversation with Josh.

Kat was rummaging through cabinets, and occasionally slamming something on the counter. As she worked, she muttered to herself. Alex couldn't hear exactly what she was saying, only words and phrases: "Damn him..., *Madre de dios...*, *Pendejo...*, How dare he ..., Who does he think..., Stupid ass..."

Alerted by Alex's footsteps on the tile floor, she paused for a moment. The face she turned to him was ghostly white, her voice gratingly bright. "Can you cook?"

Alex tried to suppress a grin as he fought the urge to walk over and kiss her senseless just to bring some color back to her cheeks. Then he realized what she had asked. If only she knew of the countless hours he'd spent in kitchens. "I can manage pretty well."

Relieved as she was that she wouldn't have to show him what to do, Kat's stomach still twisted with nerves as she realized that she'd dragged him into another awkward moment. "Could you make a salad?"

Moving toward the wine rack next to the fridge, Alex's voice was calm. "Sure. I'll make one in just a moment; first I'm going to get a glass of wine. Would you like one?"

Kat sent him a searching look. "Do you like champagne?"

Alex thought a celebration was a bit odd considering what had just happened. "Yes."

She gestured toward the refrigerator. "In the back of the refrigerator, there are several dark green bottles of sort-of apple champagne from Spain. I should probably just call it sparkling apple wine. Anyway, if you want some, glasses are to the right of the fridge."

Alex looked at her carefully, "Why do you bring apple champagne back from Spain?"

Happy for a neutral topic, Kat tried to calm her nerves. "Apple orchards are everywhere in northern Spain, and they all make *cidra*. Everyone drinks it non-stop during the apple harvest while it's still fresh, then they bottle it for the rest of the year. When I'm there, I get the more refined type that can stay good either in the fridge or in the wine cellar." Careful not to bump into Alex, Kat went to the refrigerator herself and took a bottle out, gracefully holding it over her head. "Traditionally, you pour the fresh stuff from over your head into a glass held around your knee, and then you drink it like a shot, dumping the dregs on the floor or ground when you're done. But we serve it in wine glasses."

The strain left her face as she talked, and Alex watched in fascination as the color returned to her cheeks. He opened the bottle she handed to him and poured each of them a glass. After handing one to her, he raised his glass. "To friendship."

She smiled sadly. "To friendship." Taking roasted garlic from the oven, she took a deep breath before speaking, guilt rising like bile into her throat. Her voice quivered slightly as she said, "I owe you another apology. You must think that all I do is get pissed off since once again, I put you in an awkward position of being around while I go off."

Alex's voice was patient as he pulled salad ingredients from the fridge. "You never owed me the first apology, and you don't owe me one now."

His response irritated her, and her voice cut through the air. "Bullshit. You really must think I'm a wacko who goes around screaming at people all day long."

Alex couldn't understand how she could think that. *Couldn't she see the desire in his eyes?* Even Josh had noticed his interest in her. "No, I don't think you're a 'wacko,' as you put it. It just seems that I've managed to hit times when you've had a bad day or something."

She snorted. "How diplomatic you are. Anyway, I'm sorry."

"Stop being sorry. If you feel that badly, explain it to me. Tell me why he calls you Ducky. Then tell me why you live in Spain *really* and why Peter and Luke almost jumped out of their skin when Josh brought the subject up."

Kat chewed on her lip for a moment, thrown off by his directness, and unsure how to respond. With a sigh, she decided that she did owe him *something*. Taking a deep breath, she replied, "The Ducky part is easy. Mariah and Josh call me Ducky because in college I used to answer the question 'How are you?' with 'Ducky.' It just stuck somehow."

"And Spain?"

"About four to five years ago, I needed to get away for a while, to be somewhere else for a bit. I went to Spain because I love it there." She leaned back against the counter. "It never was supposed to be forever, but somehow, I've just stayed. I know that Peter and Luke want me to come back here for good, but they don't push me about it. But Josh has been my best friend almost forever, and he has never worried about whether I want to talk about something or not."

"Do you miss being here?"

Kat stared ahead for a moment, contemplating his question. "Yes." She shook her head. "No." She shrugged, "I don't know. I love being with Peter and Luke, I love being around some friends like Mariah, and usually Josh, but I don't like how I feel otherwise when I'm here. I don't mean here in this house, I mean here in the United States. It makes me feel like I don't fit in my skin." She looked at Alex with stricken eyes. "I really can't explain it. I'm sorry."

"Stop being sorry. You didn't have to explain anything to me, really."

She shook her head forcefully. "Shit. Yes. I owed you an explanation."

Her posture was painfully rigid. Alex balled his hands into fists as he fought the urge to wrap her in his arms and soothe her hurt and anger. "Kat. Stop." He moved closer, watching her carefully for signs of fear or discomfort as he put his hands on her upper arms. "Look at me, Kat."

Alex was shocked to see Kat's eyes filling with tears as she finally raised them to meet his. His voice softened even more. "Kat, let's make a deal, okay? I want you to stop apologizing to me. The night we met, as you reminded me, was a long time ago. In Madrid, I was an ass and too pushy. You apologized when you didn't need to, and I loved the opera tickets, but you've done nothing here tonight that you need to apologize for." He chose his words carefully. "And deep down, I know you know that Josh really did nothing more than be what he feels is a true friend."

Kat looked at him thoughtfully for a moment. Then she swallowed, and sniffed quickly, before taking in a huge breath. "Okay."

"Great."

***

Peter and Luke came into the kitchen, breaking the intimate moment. Alex and Kat moved quickly to finish the dinner preparations, and soon all four of them were sitting at the wooden table eating and chatting companionably.

When the plates were empty, Peter cleared his throat. "Okay, Brat. Since the two of you cooked, we'll clean."

She snorted. "You bet your ass you will. We'll just sit here and watch!"

While the other two rinsed dishes and cleaned the counters, Kat and Alex sat at the table. With a start, Alex realized that while he and the other men had been talking about the band they'd heard the night before, Kat had barely spoken. He touched her hand. "You okay? You're awfully quiet suddenly."

Kat shook herself, "I'm fine. It's just kind of nice to listen to other people talking. I'm having fun listening." She stood. "I'll be right back."

After she had left the room, Alex looked at the other men. "Did I say something wrong?"

Peter shook his head, "No. Kat's like that sometimes. She gets really quiet while other people talk around her, and then she needs a few moments to herself. She'll be back when she's ready."

Ten minutes later, the kitchen gleamed. Peter and Luke sat quietly on one of the couches in the sunroom as Max wrestled with a pillow in front of them. Kat walked back into the room and sat down on the other couch with Alex.

Peter stretched, "Hey you, there's some dessert in the kitchen if you want it."

Kat's eyes lit with hope. "Ben and Jerry's?"

"Yeah, in the freezer. We got a bunch of different flavors, so bring them all out. We can just eat out of the cartons and save dishes."

Alex followed her into the kitchen. "I'll get spoons."

Kat juggled eight pints of ice cream back into the sunroom. Dumping them on the coffee table, she kissed both Peter and Luke on the cheek. "Thank you, thank you! You got my favorite!"

Peter tugged her ponytail. "Yeah, we had them hand pack a pint for you."

"You are *so* good to me."

Peter rolled his eyes at Alex, who was clearly amused by Kat's enthusiasm. "She really likes ice cream, and *really* likes White Russian."

"Wow, I guess so." He raised an eyebrow at Kat, "Remind me never to try to sneak a spoonful; you look like you'd hurt me." Taking a pint of New York Super Fudge Chunk, Alex sat down on the other couch next to Kat, who was impatiently rolling the pint between her hands trying to warm it enough that the ice cream could be scooped without bending the spoon.

Peter looked at Kat. "Hey, Jess called earlier today, while you were sleeping."

Kat immediately sat up, visibly interested. "She did? Why?" Her look was stricken, "Shit, I should've called her to say that I was back. Was she mad?"

"No, she just called because she's coming to the shore on Monday after everyone leaves. She's bringing the kids down, and we're going to watch them for a couple days so they can have a little time alone. We figured we'd stay at the shore with them."

Kat's face lit with pure joy. "Oh, my God, I've missed the kids so much. I can't wait to see them! I can stay for a day or two for that."

Peter nodded, happy with her reaction. "Yeah, originally Luke and I had planned on staying there for the rest of the week, and you know, a mini-vacation." He turned toward Alex, "Alex, how long can you stay? Do you want to stay at the shore for a couple days after the wedding? Or, if you prefer, you can come back here. The house will be empty."

Alex checked his ice cream, which was still rock hard. "The shore sounds great. Right now, I'm booked on JetBlue on Tuesday, but I can change it to later in the week."

Peter grinned. "Cool. You'll like our sister, and her kids are amazing."

Happily eating her ice cream, Kat suddenly sat forward, "Luke, I almost forgot. I brought you a present."

This obviously caught Luke off guard. "You did?" Suddenly his eyes widened. "Please tell me it's what I think it is!"

"We'll see. It's on my bed, let me go get it." She started to leave the room, "I'll be right back."

***

Within minutes, Kat came back into the room with a paper-wrapped package, which she handed to Luke. "Here it is, and yes, it's what you wanted. You have to pretend to share it with Pete, but really the *cidra* is for him, and this is for you."

Luke looked like a little kid as he pulled the paper off the package, uncovering a small painting in a wooden frame. Clearly touched, he admired the delicate watercolor portrait of Kat sitting on a rock, writing. He held it reverently. "I love it. He captured that lost-in-space look you get when you're writing." He looked up, "And, oh my God, his skill is growing by leaps and bounds. This will be priceless at some point. And it is so fucking cool that it's a portrait of you, I mean, collectors have Tixi's work, but how many people have a portrait he did of a family member?" He held it so both Alex and Peter could see it before continuing. "Alex, Kat is good friends with Tixi Gonzalez, who's one of the hottest painters in Europe right now."

Peter looked it over appraisingly. "It's gorgeous, Kat. The earlier ones we have are good, but Luke's right, this is going to a new level." He paused, "You'll help us write him a thank you note? Maybe we can send him a gift?"

"Sure, Pete. We can do that this weekend."

Luke looked again at the painting. "He has a new show coming up, doesn't he?"

Kat nodded, "Yeah. In Barcelona, next month."

"Are you going?"

"Of course. I was going to ask if you wanted to come over and go with me."

His eyes lit up, "I'd love to. Has the catalog come out yet?"

"No. I think he said it'll be out next week."

"Great, I'll order one right away."

Kat looked at her brother for a moment, and then pressed her lips together, "Pete, I need to tell you something, and you have to promise not to flip out."

Peter turned his full attention to his sister. "Why would I flip out?"

"Because…" Her voice trailed off, "Because when Luke gets the catalog, and you look at it, you're going to see that several of the pictures in the Barcelona show are of me."

"So?"

Luke started to grin, knowing way more about the artist's work than Peter did, "Tell me you aren't part of his new emphasis."

Kat blushed and for a moment couldn't look Luke in the eye. "I am."

Peter was confused. "What does that mean?"

The sentence came out in a rush, "It means that in several of the paintings, I'm naked."

Peter's eyes widened. "You're what?"

"I'm naked. I mean, it's not like it was porn or anything. He painted me a couple times from the back, and one partially frontal, and I'm not wearing any clothes."

Peter's voice was dangerously high. "There are going to be naked pictures of you in Barcelona? Holy shit, Kat, Aunt Fran will *love* that…"

Kat put up a hand to cut him off. "Peter, I said not to flip out. Besides, this is art, nothing more."

"Bullshit! You're my baby sister, and men will be gawking at pictures of you without clothes."

Kat tried to add some levity. "Hey, maybe some women will gawk too."

Luke reached over to squeeze Peter's hand. "Calm down. This isn't a big deal."

Peter tried to smile. "Are you guys still, I mean…Is Tixi still married?"

"No, we're not *still*…Of course, he's still married. I told you I was staying with Tixi and Monce last week."

"How'd she feel about this?"

Kat rolled her eyes. "Tixi and I want nothing to do with each other that way, and Monce knows that."

Alex just sat and listened, as Peter narrowed his eyes. "His wife is okay with him painting naked pictures of a woman he dated for a long time?"

Kat's eyes began to glitter in irritation. "Pete, Monce has been my friend for as long as I've known Tixi. What happened in the past was past. She knew he was painting me, he painted her too, and he's now beginning to play around with self-portraits. Anyway, I just wanted you to know about the show before you saw the catalog and had a stroke."

Luke tried to lighten the mood. "Well, this will make the trip even more interesting. What does one wear to an opening when you are naked in the paintings? Have you thought about that at all?"

Kat snickered, appreciating his efforts. "I was thinking of wearing nothing at all, so they will recognize me."

Alex looked at her and smiled slowly. "Then, if that's the case, I'm going to the show too."

Peter took a deep breath, still agitated but trying to be reasonable. "Okay. I'm glad you told me. I know I'm supposed to be enlightened and all that shit, but I admit that I'm not thrilled about all of this, but it's your life."

"Thank you." Kat started to laugh. "Okay, Alex, you have to admit this is a unique evening. First, you get to sit awkwardly in the next room while Josh and I scream at each other, and now you get to sit through a conversation about naked paintings of me. Classy, I'm really classy."

Alex grinned at her, finally seeing a glimpse of the girl from five years ago. "I can honestly say I've never had an evening like this before."

***

Alex put the movie into the DVD player and sat on the couch again. Once she had finished her ice cream, Kat rested her hand next to Alex's. Was she trying to start something, or was it just an innocent gesture? Just as he was about to cover her hand with his, Max jumped up on the couch and snuggled between them.

An hour later, Peter and Luke announced they were exhausted.

Alex and Kat watched the rest of the movie in companionable silence. The movie ended, and Kat sleepily stretched beside Alex. "I'd better shut everything down for the night. C'mon, Max, last walk of the evening."

Alex stood up. "I'll go with you."

Kat shook her head sharply. "You don't have to. I can walk him alone. I still remember how to walk a dog in New York."

"I know you can walk the dog without my help—maybe I want to get some air."

***

They walked in comfortable silence. After they'd returned to the house, Kat gazed at him as she walked over to the staircase. "Goodnight Alex, I'll see you in the morning."

His voice was soothing. "Goodnight Kat, sleep well. Welcome home."

Chapter Five

The next morning Alex woke to find Kat already sipping coffee in the kitchen as she looked through the newspaper.

Her smile was rested and genuine. "Good morning. God, you must have had the house to yourself in the mornings, since Peter and Luke never get up before eight."

He chuckled. "Yeah, since I've been here, Peter and Luke haven't been up early ever, except yesterday, and that was because a garbage truck woke us all up."

Ruefully, she shook her head. "I know, they've always been that way."

"And you don't sleep late?"

"Don't I wish? I'm a complete insomniac, so I almost never sleep well, and then the time change is messing with my internal clock, too." She looked guilty. "Shit, sorry about my manners. Would you like some coffee?"

He gently put his hand on her arm. "Kat, don't worry about it. I'm here so often that I long ago got over the guest treatment. But thanks for the consideration, and yes, I'd love a cup of coffee."

As she handed him a cup, he smiled. "Are you ready for the shore?"

"I am." She took a sip. "I made the decision to come to the wedding on the spur of the moment, so I didn't think about much of anything, so going to the shore is a bonus."

Peter walked into the kitchen, clearly struggling to wake up. Automatically, she poured him a cup of coffee and handed it to him.

Peter pulled her ponytail. "Good morning, Brat. Thanks, I could smell the coffee coming up the stairs."

She swatted him. "You're welcome, and stop calling me 'Brat'."

Peter grimaced. "Sorry, kid." He poked his sister in the ribs. "We're leaving at two, remember?"

Her tone was patient. "I know, Peter. I'm ready to go. Frankly, I just kept everything in my bags yesterday, so I can just dump them in the car this afternoon. In a couple minutes, I'm running upstairs to get dressed, and then I'm running over to Leo's. But I'll be back and ready to go before two."

Peter looked confused for a moment. "Why are you seeing Leo?"

She sipped her coffee. "He called while I was at Barajas. And he really wanted to have a long conversation, and I hate talking to him with distractions like the announcements in the airport. I finally said I'd go see him this morning."

Alex was interested. "Who's Leo?"

Kat rolled her eyes. "My agent. He's a great agent, but so hyper it makes my head hurt. Since I'm rarely in the States, we do most of our business over the phone or through faxes or emails, so a meeting like this is unusual." She turned toward Peter questioningly. "Tonight, it's just us, right? Everyone else comes tomorrow?"

As he took a huge bite of a muffin, Peter nodded. "Yeah, they're coming up late tomorrow."

"Beth and Sasha are bringing beverages? Josh's bringing desserts?"

"That's what they said. Do you need me to pick anything up?"

She thought for a moment. "I can't think of anything, but if I do, I'll let you know." She motioned toward the cell phone on the counter. "Can I borrow your phone this morning in case something comes up?"

"Sure. I'll be home all morning, so if you need me, just call here."

"Thanks. What are you doing this morning?"

Peter refilled his coffee cup. "Luke is running to the gallery. I'm making sure we're ready here. And Alex has a quick meeting this morning too." He poked his sister, "Hey, how are you getting to Leo's?"

"I'll take a cab."

Peter motioned toward Alex. "Alex is headed in the same direction. Why don't you share a cab with him?"

Kat flushed. "Alex, is that okay with you?"

"Sounds great. I need to leave in about twenty minutes."

"Great." She rinsed her mug and put it in the dishwasher. "I just need to change. I'll be right back."

***

Alex went to his room to change as well, taking more care than normal. Fifteen minutes later, he walked into the kitchen, and stopped and stared. Kat wore a simple black suit with spiked black heels, her skirt showing off her gorgeous curves, a light gray lacy camisole peeking above the jacket. Trying to control his growing desire, Alex took a deep breath. "Wow."

Kat blushed. "Thanks, Alex."

Alex tried to make his voice sound light. "You dress like this for your agent? He's one lucky man."

Kat looked uncomfortable. "I wanted to make sure that I looked like a professional rather than some kid who gets paid to travel and collect gossip."

His voice was serious. "You're stunning."

Even Peter could hear a note of desire in Alex's voice. Kat's blood began to race as she looked at him, even though she tried to deny the feeling. "Thank you." Kat's facial muscles strained in an attempt at a natural smile. "Are you ready?"

"I am."

***

Sitting in the cab, Alex tried to keep his mind and hands off the crossed legs next to him. "What's your meeting about?"

Kat stifled a giggle, watching his eyes wander back to her legs. "I'm not really sure. I mean, I have a book in final edits before printing, and several articles recently published, and another book going, but he said this was about a new opportunity or something."

"Damn." He looked embarrassed. "I'm sorry, Kat. I knew you were writing professionally, but I guess I didn't realize how much or how seriously."

"There's no reason you should have known."

"What do you usually write about?"

Her answer was sure. "The socio-economic and political role of women in Hispanic countries."

Alex blinked, at a loss for words. "Wow. I don't have any idea of how to ask an intelligent question about that."

Kat laughed. "Most people don't. As I see it, my job is to interest people in a hidden and powerless population."

Alex was mesmerized by the conviction in her voice. "If anyone can do it, you can. What are you doing afterward?"

"I may do a quick shopping trip. I'm not really thrilled with the dress I brought for the wedding. Then I'll head back to the house."

Trying to keep his voice light, Alex asked, "How about meeting me afterwards for a late breakfast? Or an early lunch?"

Kat looked confused. "But you have a meeting."

"I do. But I should be done by around ten. We could meet somewhere, and have something to eat since you barely had anything this morning. And if you don't have time to shop before that, you could go shopping after."

Kat searched Alex's face for a clue of what he was thinking. "Are you asking me out?"

Alex could hear the note of worry in her voice, so he thought before answering. "Maybe."

Kat looked into Alex's serious eyes. Hesitation and fear clouded her eyes. Then the corner of Kat's lips lifted in a slight smile as her eyes cleared. "If it's a date, then I'm not interested. But if it's just as friends, I'd love to."

He didn't care how they phrased it if he got to spend more time with her. "Fine, we'll play this your way—just friends."

"Great. When and where?"

Alex was shocked and delighted that she had accepted so easily. "I don't know. How about the café in the Citicorp? It's close for both of us."

"Great. I'll meet you there at ten?"

"Sounds good. Give me the cell phone for a minute."

Kat pulled it out of her purse. "Why?'

Alex quickly punched in several numbers and hit the "send" button. Within seconds, a soft chime sounded from his pocket. "There. My number is the last one dialed, so if you need to call me, all you need to do is hit the send button. That way, if you get delayed or need to find me, you can."

Kat felt a thrill race through her at his thoughtfulness. "Thanks."

The cab pulled up in front of the office building, and she handed Alex several folded bills.

"What's this for?"

She rolled her eyes. "For the fare."

Alex held the money out to Kat. "I'll take care of it."

Kat pushed the money back toward him. "No. You asked me to breakfast, so you have to pay for that. I'll take care of this."

He tried to hand it back to her. "I'll take care of both."

Kat's tone was exasperated. "Alex, take the money." As she said this, she tucked the folded bills into his shirt pocket, trying to ignore the warmth of his skin through the fabric. "If you hadn't been around this morning, I still would have taken a cab and paid for it. Take the money."

Alex smiled and lightly ran his finger down the side of her face. "You win. I'll see you in a bit."

Without thinking about what she was doing, Kat leaned forward and kissed his cheek. "See you then."

Chapter Six

As Kat walked through the crowds on the sidewalks, she alternated between chastising herself for the kiss and thinking about seeing Alex again. *Why had she kissed him right after saying it wasn't a date?* Did he realize her confusion?

Entering the restaurant, she could see Alex was sitting in a booth gazing out the window. She knew she was at least five minutes early, and a small tingle ran up her spine at the thought of him wanting to see her that much. Stopping to fix her hair in the vestibule, she muttered, "Stop it. This isn't a date. Stop acting like an idiot and get your head on straight."

As she reached the table, Alex looked up. "Hi, you're early."

"So are you."

He beamed as she sat down. "I left early to make sure I got here on time. I figured I shouldn't be late for breakfast with a friend."

Kat knew he was baiting her. "That's right. Friends take priority."

"True. Besides, I got here early, then called the house to make sure Peter didn't need anything."

Her voice lost its joking tone. "Did he know we were having breakfast together?"

"No." His grin was devilish. "I just told him that I'd made friends with a gorgeous woman in a cab, and I asked her to join me for a late breakfast."

Kat rolled her eyes. "He's probably on the phone with Luke right now."

His voice lost its humor, hearing the note of concern in her voice. "Would that bother you?"

"What do you mean?"

Alex struggled for the right words. "Does it bother you that they know we're eating together? Or is it being here with me that bothers you?"

Kat touched his hand gently. "Alex, I wouldn't be here if I didn't want to be." She paused as she chewed on her bottom lip. "It's just that they'll think something is going on between us, and it isn't. We're just friends."

His voice was gentle and seductive. "You keep stressing the word 'friends'. Are you trying to convince me or yourself? As I remember, I never officially asked you out on a date, just for a meal."

In her heart of hearts, Kat had wondered the same thing. Walking over to see him, she'd found herself looking at her reflection in the windows, making sure she looked her best. Even at her meeting, at times she'd missed Leo's comments because she was wondering what Alex was doing at that moment. Shaking away her train of thoughts, her tone became impatient. "Oh, never mind. Let's stop talking about it. You promised food, and I'm famished."

***

Once they had ordered, Alex turned his full attention on Kat. "So, how was your meeting?"

Kat chewed her lower lip, unsure of how much to tell him. What Leo had proposed was so major, Kat wasn't sure if she was willing to talk about it with anyone yet. When he'd suggested it, Kat had almost refused on the spot. As the morning progressed, part of her brain began to play favorably with the idea

When Kat didn't answer, Alex looked at her strangely. "Kat, it was a pretty simple question. How was your meeting?"

Kat shifted uncomfortably in her seat. "It was okay. I mean, it was good."

"And what was the big idea he wanted to talk about?" Alex held up a hand. "You don't have to tell me if you don't want to."

"No, it's okay." Kat searched for a truthful answer that wouldn't give too much away. "He wanted to talk about the book going to print, and the one in progress. And he had some new ideas about articles. More than anything, he just wanted to make sure we had a shared vision for my writing future."

"Do you? I know my agent usually is about a million miles ahead of me."

"Yeah. I guess we do have a common view. It's just that I want to write more than anything, and I don't always remember to worry about the money part." She shrugged. "I guess it's because I can always survive if I need to off…" Her voice trailed off.

Alex's voice was gentle, realizing she was about to say she could live off her inheritance from her parents. "Sorry, Kat, I didn't mean to open a sore topic."

"You didn't. Anyway, my meeting went well. What about yours?"

At that moment, the food arrived, and as they ate, Alex regaled Kat with stories about making sure all would be in place for the recording sessions in the fall. As they ate, Alex realized that Kat had laughed more in that short time than she had in all their time together in Madrid. Again, he thought that maybe his comments in Madrid had done some good.

The plates had been cleared when Kat looked at her watch. "Shit, I didn't realize it was so late. I still want to run to look at a different dress."

"What's wrong with the one you brought?"

"It's not a dress for a wedding on the shore. It's more a dress for a city wedding." Working up her nerve, Kat swallowed. "Do you want to go shopping with me?"

"What?"

Kat tried to justify her idea. "We're both eventually heading back to the house. Bloomingdales is just around the corner. We could run there quickly, and I could find a dress, and then we could grab a cab home."

Alex didn't care what the reason if it meant she was inviting him to do something. "Do I get to express my opinion of the dress? Or do I just have to stand there and be quiet?"

Kat started to laugh. "You get the best of both worlds. I'll let you express your opinion, but I'm paying for the dress. How about that?"

"Sounds great."

***

At the store, Kat looked at the floor plan quickly before heading for the escalator. In the womens' department, she started flipping through dresses with the barest of glances at each one. While she did that, Alex looked around. Without saying a word, he slipped aside and pulled a dress from a rack.

His voice was firm. "Try this one."

"What?" Kat looked at the dress skeptically. "I don't wear pink."

He sighed. "You should. Just try it on, Kat. Please."

Kat took the dress and headed to the dressing room. Inside, she looked at her reflection and rolled her eyes. "Why the hell am I trying on a dress just because he wants me to? I can pick my own dress, and I don't wear pink dresses."

His voice floated over the door. "Kat, I can *hear* you. If you don't want to try on the dress, don't. But I think it would look fabulous on you."

"How do you know what size I wear?"

His tone was bordering on exasperation, "I saw what section you were looking in. If you don't want to try it on, just come out of the dressing room and pick another, but I think, just for giggles, you should try it on."

Kat couldn't help the sulky tone of her voice. "Fine."

Kat hung her jacket on the hook on the back of the door, before pulling the silk camisole up over her head. The short skirt slipped down her legs, and then Kat stood in front of the mirror, dressed in only her lacy bra, panties, and high heels. Looking at the dress, Kat realized she wouldn't be able to wear that bra under it, so she reluctantly unhooked it.

The dress Alex had picked was a deep rose color, and as Kat slipped it over her head, it seductively slid down her body. The draped neckline caressed her breasts; her arms were bare, as was most of her back. Even as much of a harsh critic of her own looks as Kat was, she knew Alex was right. The color showed off her hair and eyes, and the neckline and the back were, well, perfect. Damn, he was right! It was the perfect dress for this wedding. No, Kat chastised herself, it was more than the perfect dress for the wedding. It was the most perfect outfit for her she'd ever seen!

Kat stood looking at her reflection, part of her wanting to pretend that she'd never tried the dress on. This dress was one that she would have passed over without a second glance. But no dress in her life had ever made her look this good, this sexy, this grown-up, this...

A deep voice broke her reverie. "Kat, if you don't like the dress, or if it doesn't fit, be honest about it, and we'll keep looking."

Closing her eyes for a moment, Kat swallowed hard before opening the dressing room door. Leaning against the door frame, Alex was standing with his back to her. For a moment, Kat admired the way his broad shoulders stretched the soft blue fabric of his shirt; then she cleared her throat.

Alex turned around quickly, and in an instant, Kat saw by the look in his eyes that her perception of how good she looked in the dress was real. Before he could hide it, Kat saw naked desire cross his face, both exciting and terrifying her.

He let out a low whistle. "Shit, Kat. I'm speechless."

Kat tried to smile. "Thanks." Her mind screamed at her to be honest with him. "Thank you for suggesting this dress. I admit I would never have looked at it, but I really like it."

Moving closer, his hand touched her arm gently, "You look absolutely amazing. Thank you for trying it on."

"You're welcome." Kat tried to lighten the moment, "Okay, you can gloat now that you were right and I was wrong about this dress not working."

"Oh, I will. I plan to tell everyone at the wedding that I'm your personal dresser now."

Kat swatted him on the arm. "Perfect. That would be friggin' perfect."

Chapter Seven

When Alex and Kat returned to the townhouse, Peter and Luke were getting ready to leave for the beach. Kat quickly ran upstairs and came back down dressed in jeans and a snug black T-shirt.

The bags were stowed into the cargo area of the car with Max. Peter volunteered to drive, and Luke sat in the front passenger seat with Kat sitting beside Alex in the back.

Once out of the city, the conversation seemed to slow a bit. Kat found herself getting sleepy, and tried to keep from nodding off. Alex quietly reached over and unbuckled her belt, before whispering, "Slide over. You can fall asleep on me."

In her mind, Kat knew she should decline, knowing she was giving him conflicting messages, but she couldn't stop herself. "Okay." Sliding over, Alex rebuckled her and put his arm around her. Kat tried to stay awake, but before long, her head was nestled on his shoulder while she slept.

***

When Peter turned into a driveway at the shore, Alex was surprised. "This is the house?"

"Yeah, why?"

As he thought about how much a place like this would cost on the West Coast, Alex's voice was shocked. "It's huge! How the hell did you guys buy this place? It must have cost a fortune."

Peter shook his head smiling, completely comfortable with the question. "Nah. The original house belonged to our grandparents, who bought it when no one wanted to have a place out here. Then our parents added onto it, and the three of us inherited it. Luke and I use it more than the girls do, so we have kind of taken over."

After her nap, Kat's voice was a bit hoarse, which Alex found sexy as hell. "They sure as hell have! They've even taken over the master bedroom." Her gentle tone took the sting out of her words.

Peter chuckled. "Any time you want to move home and start coming here regularly, we'd be willing to talk about moving to another room, or renovating or something." He glanced back at Alex, "Anyway, we sure as hell couldn't afford to buy it now. Each year, people try to convince us to sell, but we all love it." He motioned to a small cottage next to the big house, "That belongs to the three of us, too. Our great-aunt built it as her summer home, and since she was a spinster, when she died she left it to our grandfather too. But we usually rent it out a year at a time, so like right now, there's an architect from the city who rents it for the whole year, but only comes up occasionally on the weekends."

***

The house faced the ocean with a full wall of glass. Inside, the main floor had lots of open space, the walls painted in soft, neutral colors. A staircase led upstairs, and from the bottom, Alex could see several doors opening onto a center hallway. Peter motioned up. "Alex, go look around."

Alex wandered up the stairs, finding five bedrooms with views of the open ocean. One room, clearly the master bedroom, had a private bath. On each side of the master bedroom, there were two bedrooms each, connected by shared baths. The staircase then wound up one more floor, and when Alex climbed the stairs, he found a small sitting room with windows in all directions.

On his return to the main floor, he helped Kat and Luke unpack groceries. "Guys, where am I sleeping?"

Peter came in from the car with more bags. "Well, Luke and I have the bedroom in the center, and Beth and Sasha have another. Josh and Kim will share the bathroom with them. So, I guess you'd be in the room next to Kat's." He grinned at his sister. "Be warned, she's a bathroom hog. I know; I had to share that bathroom with her every summer for years and years."

Kat threw a package of paper napkins at him. "Schmuck-face. You spent way more time on your hair each morning then than I did. You were trying so hard to catch the eye of the hotties that were lifeguarding."

He tossed the package back. "Yeah, I admit it, Baby Sister. Anyway, Alex, does that work for you?"

Alex nodded. "Fine with me, if Kat doesn't mind."

"Do you snore?" she asked seriously.

"I don't know. Why?"

"Because you can hear everything through the bathroom doors."

"I don't know. You'll have to tell me in the morning if I do."

Kat made a loud snort. "Morning nothing. If you snore, I'll suffocate you with a pillow."

"You'd do that to a *friend*?"

She rolled her eyes and turned away.

***

Everyone helped get a meal ready, and soon after dinner, Kat slipped upstairs to sit in her window seat and look at the waves. What was she going to do about the job offer? What the hell was happening with Alex? For a moment, panic started to swell, and Kat fought the urge to run back to the airport and get on a plane to Spain. It was so much simpler there. The few people who had known her before accepted that she was different since the death of her parents, and didn't push. She could come and go as she pleased, no one asking her much of anything. This was all too much. Too many people, too many options. *And Alex.*

Kat took a deep breath, trying to calm her mind. *Alex.* From an almost teenage crush to now, with all that had happened in between, there was no possibility of anything other than a brief fling with him, nothing more. Would that be enough? Shaking her head, no, that wasn't enough. But it was all that could be, so if that wasn't enough, she needed to make damn sure she kept her defenses in place. No more screw-ups like kissing him or falling asleep in his arms. And again, what the hell was she going to do with the job offer?

She tiptoed out of her room and sat down on the top step where she could watch the three men without being seen. Alex was stretched out on one couch. She moved closer to the edge of the step to see him more clearly, and he looked up and winked. Mortified, Kat ducked out of sight and sat in the darkness for a while. As she sat alone, she thought about him. What the hell was he doing to her? Now she was feeling all sorts of forbidden feelings and acting like a stupid teenager. Taking a deep breath, she knew she had to go downstairs and pretend like everything was okay.

When she walked into the living room, Alex's hand snaked around her wrist to pull her toward his couch. "Hey, come sit with me."

Kat blushed. "I need to check on something in the kitchen."

"What?"

Kat tried to think of a plausible answer. "I need to make sure I set the dishwasher to run later."

"I'll check it in a minute. Come sit down with me." He pulled her down onto the couch and turned to look at Peter and Luke. "Does anyone want a beer?"

Three voices answered simultaneously. "Sure."

Alex jumped up and grabbed beers for all of them. After twisting the top off one, he handed it to Kat and sat down on the couch.

Without realizing it, Kat began to rub the ball of one foot as she sat cross-legged. After a couple minutes, Alex nudged her arm. "What's the matter?"

"My foot hurts. I wore heels so long today on pavement that it hurts now."

His voice was completely nonchalant. "Put your feet on my lap."

"What?"

"Put your feet on my lap. I can help." Putting his beer on the floor, he pulled her feet onto his lap before Kat could fully realize what was happening.

Trying not to make a scene—or at least that was what she tried to tell herself—Kat didn't pull away. The four of them talked while Alex slowly rubbed Kat's feet. Damn, she was glad that she'd had a pedicure before leaving Madrid! The sensuous touch was so relaxing; her nervousness was replaced by a growing desire. Even as her mind recognized the feeling, she stuffed it down, refusing to explore it.

Finally, around midnight, Peter rose to set the alarm and then came back to rub Luke's shoulder. "Good-night, Sis. Goodnight Alex. Sweet dreams."

Luke planted a kiss on Kat's forehead. "See you in the morning, Sweetie."

After they had gone upstairs and closed their door, Alex turned thoughtfully to Kat. "You're lucky to have Peter and Luke." He smiled gently. "Then again, they're fortunate to have you."

Finally, a safe topic! "We are lucky. We've laughed about it a lot because Peter met Luke because I dragged him to the gallery one day. At first, they talked about it being luck, but it wasn't, it was fate." Her tone was envious. "They're one of the perfect matches in the world."

His long, strong fingers continued to caress her feet and ankles. "Did it ever bother you that Peter's gay?"

"No. Peter is Peter. Mom and Dad accepted it, and eventually encouraged him to bring friends home. Jess was the only one who had a problem with it for a while, but even she came around. I think it was more that he was dating guys better looking than she was. And for me, well, I never cared who he dated as long as he was happy." Kat looked intently at Alex. "Do you have brothers and sisters?"

He shook his head. "No, my mom had several miscarriages before having me, so I'm it. It's a shame. Mom wanted a huge family." He ran his fingers through his hair. "I'm not quite sure why they didn't adopt, but, I think part of it was that owning a restaurant is a difficult lifestyle."

"Do they still have a restaurant?"

"Yeah, there's a manager now, but Mom and Dad still go in every day."

Kat suddenly remembered their conversation while making dinner the first time, "And I asked you if you knew how to cook. You probably can cook like a pro, can't you?"

He shrugged. "I can cook pretty well." He lightly ran his fingertips over her toes, smiling as she shivered at his touch. "Why were you nervous when I was rubbing your feet at first?"

Kat was genuinely confused. "What do you mean?"

"You were completely relaxed until suddenly, you began to tense up like you were uncomfortable with me touching you." There was no censure in his voice.

For a moment, she tried to collect her thoughts before answering honestly. "I just began to relax more than usual, and frankly, I think we need to establish some boundaries. No offense, but you weren't touching me like just a friend."

"There's that 'friend' word again. You make 'friend' sound like a word to hide behind." He gently stroked her ankle. "This isn't a bad thing, Kat. I won't hurt you."

"What isn't a bad thing? There isn't a 'thing' here."

"Bullshit. You can say that nothing is happening, or going to happen, between us until you're blue, but it *is* happening, and you know it. Deep down, I think you almost felt it beginning in Madrid. I know I felt something when you walked into my dressing room after the concert, and believe me, I wasn't looking for anything to happen on that trip. Beyond that, something is certainly happening here. Tell me you didn't feel something when I just touched you."

Deep down, she knew he was right, and an edge of panic tinged her voice as she sat up, pulling her feet away and wrapping her arms around her knees protectively. "Alex, I can't do this. I can't. I don't want a romantic relationship. I just need a friend, nothing more."

"I am your friend." He stroked her arm, seeing her eyes darken momentarily. "But all I'm saying is not to rule out more than that. I won't hurt you."

Kat's voice showed no hesitation. "I know you wouldn't try to, but I'm just here for a couple days. If something were to happen, it would just be a fling, nothing more." In her mind, Kat hesitated after saying that, knowing the option now open to her. Kat yawned. "I'm exhausted. I'll think I'll go to bed."

"Me too." He paused. "You sure you don't mind me sharing a bathroom with you?"

"I'm sure." Kat rubbed her eyes tiredly.

Cautiously, he placed his palm on her shoulder, watching for resistance. "Do you want me to wake you in the morning? I can come in to get you."

Pointedly ignoring the comment, Kat gestured to the stairs. "Come on."

Once in his room, Alex changed quickly into his pajamas and realized that he hadn't heard Kat in the bathroom yet. She was probably waiting for him. Alex walked through the connecting bathroom and knocked on the door to her room.

"Yes?"

"Can I come in?"

"Okay."

When Alex opened the door, Kat was sitting cross-legged on her bed; her laptop open on her lap. Alex tried in vain not to notice how her breasts were so clearly visible through the black camisole, and instead decided to focus on the pattern of small flowers on her pajama bottoms. "I just wanted to see if you needed the bathroom first."

Kat looked up at him, trying to ignore her reaction to seeing him in a t-shirt and pajama bottoms. No matter how many times and ways she denied it, she still found him painfully attractive. For a moment, she wondered what it would be like to share a bed with him. Would he sleep in that shirt? Would he sleep in those pants? Did he have anything on under them? When he slept, did he wear anything at all? Kat swallowed hard, digging her nails into the comforter, trying to stop her train of thought. "I'm all set. I just wanted to add something to a chapter; then I'm going to get some sleep."

"Okay." He moved closer to gently touch her hair and one curl wound around his finger. "Sweet dreams. If you get cold, let me know, I'm right through that door." He leaned over and chastely kissed Kat on the cheek.

Kat turned red. "Good-night, Alex."

***

Several hours later Alex awoke hearing a door open slowly, and footsteps. Momentarily disoriented, he realized Kat was in the bathroom, but no light was on. "Kat, you can turn on the light."

Her voice was muted. "I don't need the light, thanks. Good night."

"If you say so. Good night." Alex rolled over in bed, pulling the covers back up to his shoulders, sleep pressing down on him again.

***

Alex awoke sometime later, feeling something was amiss. Walking almost silently, he went into the bathroom and got a drink of water. After shutting off the faucet, he turned to go back into his room.

The soft sound from Kat's room was almost obscured by the sounds of the water in the pipes. Without thinking, Alex opened the door to her room quietly, expecting to find her sound asleep in her bed.

Even in the dark, he could see the bed was empty. He looked around the room, finally seeing her huddled on the window seat, her arms wrapped tightly around her bent knees. His voice was quiet. "Kat, you okay?"

Kat didn't turn around to look at him. "I can't sleep. I'm fine."

"Do you want company?"

"No." Hearing how sharp her voice sounded, she tried to soften the tone. "No, thanks."

Alex stood helplessly in the doorway, knowing she was upset for some reason. "If you want to talk, I'm here."

"No thanks, I'll be fine. I'm sorry I woke you up." Her tone was cold.

"Sure you don't want company?" he said, confused by her iciness.

"I'm sure. Goodnight, Alex."

As Alex turned to leave the room, the moonlight reflected off a tear on her cheek, and Alex knew in his heart that no matter how much she insisted, she needed someone with her right now. Unless she yelled for her brother, he was staying with her!

Unaware that he was still watching her, Kat stared ahead. Her face was a mask of pain in the moonlight, tears slowly trickling down her cheeks.

"Kat?"

The sound of his voice made Kat jump. He sat down cautiously beside her on the bench. "Talk to me."

Her eyes radiated pain and sorrow as she finally looked at him fully. "Go back to bed. I'll be fine."

"You're sitting here in tears. I'm not going back to bed and leaving you here like this."

"Why do you care?"

"Huh?"

"Why do you care how I am? Take a hint, Alex, and leave me alone."

"Are we back to that stinking 'I just want to be friends' issue? Damn, you're stubborn." He took a deep breath. "You had fun today, and I could see it. Before you started to tense up, you enjoyed when I was rubbing your feet. But you fight it, and you shouldn't. All I want is for you to give us a chance." He paused. "Even if we never become anything more than barely friends, maybe I could still help with whatever's bothering you right now."

Kat's voice grew angry as tears glistened again in her eyes. She knew she couldn't tell him. Damn him for making her want to tell! No one had gotten her to feel that way in years. "No, you can't. No one can." Closing her eyes, she said tiredly, "Just leave me alone, please."

Unconsciously, Alex pulled Kat into his arms. She tried to shove him away, but he wouldn't let go, and finally, she buried her face in his shirt. Alex felt it become wet with her tears, as he rocked her until her crying stopped.

Kat raised swollen and combative eyes. "Go away."

He grinned, suddenly hopeful that she had let her guard down enough to cry in front of him. "Nope, you're stuck with me. Who knows, maybe you'll learn to like me, too."

"I never said I didn't like you. I just said I didn't want to *date* you. I don't want to date anyone. I just want to be left alone." Her voice broke again. "All alone. I just want to be left alone. I can handle things alone."

Whatever it was so close to the surface, Alex fought the urge to keep pushing, hoping to break through to her. But, she looked so fragile; he couldn't inflict more pain on her. "Someday I hope that'll change. Right now, though, please come to bed."

"I can't."

"What do you mean?"

"I can't sleep." Her voice sounded so weary and sad. "I shouldn't have come here. This is too much."

Alex's voice caressed her. "Why? Talk to me, Kat. Tell me why you need to stay in Madrid. When you were walking around Manhattan today, you looked happy and relaxed. Why don't you live here?"

Kat rested her head on his shoulder, for a moment wondering what it would be like to tell him all of it, but knowing how he would look at her in revulsion after. "I can't. I'm sorry, Alex, but I can't tell you." She swallowed, "There are things about my life that I can't tell you about."

"Okay." He paused, "Can we say someday? Will you tell me when you feel the time is right at some point?" He squeezed her hand. "Kat, whatever it is, it can't be as bad as you think."

Yes, it was just as bad as she thought. She'd seen the look on people's faces, even so-called friends. And they'd not known it all, just pieces. In her heart, Kat knew she could never tell him. Only her sister, Peter, Luke, Josh, and Mariah knew it all. And her parents. *Her parents.* A fresh wave of grief swamped her as she realized anew how much she wished she could see her mother and father one more time. *Just once more…* Trying to hold back tears, she realized that she could never, ever tell him. But he was being so kind. "Maybe." Suddenly, Kat yawned widely, exhausted from all the emotions swirling through her.

"Ready to sleep now?"

Kat gave a shadow of a smile, silently stood, and took his hand as he pulled her toward her bed. Without asking permission, Alex smoothed the blankets over her. "Good night again, Kat."

"Good night."

Chapter Eight

When Kat awoke, the sun was high in the sky. Moving quickly, she dressed in faded jeans and a black top.

No one was in the kitchen. Somewhat dejectedly, Kat poured a cup of coffee and walked outside to find the three men sitting on the porch, Alex and Peter reading the newspaper, Luke doing a crossword puzzle in ink as always.

Peter spotted her first. "Good morning, sleepyhead. I wanted to get you up earlier, but Alex wouldn't let me. He said you two had stayed up late talking, and you needed sleep."

Kat sat down on the step to sip her coffee. Cautiously, she looked at Alex. "Hi."

"Good morning." His smile was gentle, and Kat knew instinctively that he hadn't mentioned her nighttime behavior to anyone. "How'd you sleep?"

Kat felt her face flush. "Fine."

Sitting in the sun, Kat began to relax. Without realizing it, she kept sneaking glances at Alex, and every time, he was looking back at her with a warm little smile that made her skin tingle.

Finally, she stood up and brushed off the seat of her jeans. "I'm going to see if we have everything we need for dinner."

Alex's voice was hopeful. "Need help?"

"No!" Kat said quickly, frightened at the thought of having to make conversation with him. Her tone was short, and she knew it. "I mean, you enjoy the sunshine."

***

A half hour later, Kat came out on the porch and looked at the men, "Okay, I need to do something physical. Anyone want to go for a walk?" The four of them walked along the shore for miles, Max running freely down the beach, only seeing a few other people out walking.

The long walk tired everyone out, and so the group sat down on the sand and watched the waves. Kat sat to one side, barely talking. Peter and Luke were used to her silences, so they let her be. Alex watched her pensively, wondering if she was thinking about him as much as he was her.

***

As they walked back into the kitchen of the house, Peter's cell phone chirped in his jeans pocket. From the caller ID, Peter knew who was calling. "Hey, Josh."

"Hi, Pete. Is Kat there?"

"Yeah, hold on." He held the phone out to his sister. "It's Josh."

Kat took the phone, leaning against the counter. "Hey."

His voice was subdued. "Hey."

Kat's voice turned sharp. "What's wrong?"

"How do you know something's wrong?"

"Dipshit, I know your tones of voice. What's the matter?"

Josh swallowed. "Kat, I had to go to Tiffany's today."

"Yeah, Tiffany's, get to the point. You're scaring me." At her shrill tone, the three men in the kitchen all turned to watch her; unsure of what was happening, but sure that whatever it was, it was causing her great distress. Alex fought the urge to grab the phone away from her before Josh upset her more.

"Well, as I was paying, I heard my name called. When I turned around..."

"What? Who was there?"

"Nate was there." He paused, "Nate is coming to the wedding, Kat. I talked to him just a couple minutes ago, and he's here to go to the wedding."

Kat closed her eyes, feeling panic swamp her. "You're kidding, right?"

"Shit, Kat, I wish I was. But, it's true. I almost keeled over when I turned around and saw him. Then we did the nicey-nicey shit about how good it was to see each other. Even then, I thought it might just be that he was here on vacation or something, but when I asked him what he was doing here, he said he was going to Mariah's wedding. Then he reminded me that his brother roomed with Mariah's brother, and their fathers had roomed together before them. He was just picking up the gift, then heading directly out there."

Her lips pursed, Kat took in a deep breath through her nose, trying in vain to keep the little white panic dots from clouding her vision, sitting down on the stool before her knees gave out.

Josh waited for her to respond. "You okay, Kat?"

Kat shook her head mutely, unable to say anything. Suddenly she croaked, "Yeah, I'm fine. I have to go." Kat hung up, cutting off Josh's response, and buried her face in her hands.

Peter went to stand behind her to rub her shoulders. "Kat, what was that about?"

Kat took a deep breath as she looked up. Her face was ghostly pale, making her freckles stand out garishly on her nose. "Nothing. I'll be fine, Pete."

Peter pulled a chair up next to her, his voice gentle but insistent. "What the hell is going on, Kat?"

Kat looked at Peter, and sniffed, tears beginning to pool in her eyes. "Nate will be at the wedding."

As Alex watched, the shock of Kat's words impacted Peter. His look of disbelief was complete, before he barked, "What? Nate is going to the wedding? How the fuck did that happen?"

Suddenly, Kat stood up, almost knocking her chair over in her haste. "I have to get some air."

Peter stood up quickly grabbing her hand. "I'll go with you."

Her voice was desperate as she yanked her hand away from him, turning toward the screen door. "No. You can't. I really need some air, and I need to be alone for a couple minutes."

Peter started to argue, but Luke put a quieting hand on his arm. His tone was gentle but firm. "Okay, Kat, go. Here's my cell, call us if you want company, but I'll keep Pete here. We'll start dinner or something."

"Thanks, Luke." Kat almost ran from the room, the screen door banging shut behind her.

Peter turned on Luke, anger clear on his face and in his voice. "She shouldn't be alone right now! Why the hell didn't you let me go with her?"

Luke's voice was certain. "She *needs* to be alone for a minute. This shocked the shit out of her, and the last thing she needs right now is you being all puffed up in anger. She needs to breathe for a minute and figure out what she's going to do. Period."

Knowing he was right, Peter sat in sullen silence until Alex finally cleared his throat. "Somebody want to tell me what the hell is going on?"

Luke sighed, suddenly tired of all the secrecy around Kat. "Well, the short version is that Nate and Kat dated for a while in college, and toward the end of her time in college, he ..." His voice faltered as he tried to find a way to describe what Nate had done.

Before he could finish the sentence, Peter cut in. "The son-of-a-bitch completely and totally fucked her over."

Alex tried to figure out what Nate could have done to make normally even-tempered Peter so angry. "What did he do?"

For a moment, Peter wanted to tell Alex the whole story, but Luke interceded one more time. "Alex, we're not trying to hide anything from you, but, it wouldn't be right for us to tell you about what happened. Only Kat can do that when or if she feels ready."

Suddenly, Kat came back into the room. She was still pale but seemed calm. "I'm sorry, guys, I overreacted." Her voice was falsely bright. "I mean, what does it matter if he's here or not? That was a long time ago. Anyway, I'm here for 'Riah, nothing more. So what if we run into each other at the reception or whatever?"

Peter looked at her carefully, trying to gauge how much of an act she was giving. "Are you sure?"

"I'm sure. Anyway, I don't feel like making lunch. Let's go into town."

***

They drove into the village for lunch. Alex watched in concern as Kat barely picked at her salad. After lunch, Kat looked at Peter. "Pete, you said you had to go for a final fitting, right?"

"Yeah. I need to be there at two. Luke's going with me since he says I have no idea what I'm doing. I'll give you a ride back to the house first if you want."

She shook her head. "No. I need a couple things, and a walk would do me good." She looked at Alex for a moment, unsure of her feelings. "Alex, do you want to walk back with me?"

Was she volunteering to spend time with him? Alex tried to hide his delight. "Sure."

***

They wandered in and out of several shops, Kat barely saying a word. At one point, Alex took her hand, and she looked at him in surprise. Alex waited, expecting her to pull away, and instead, she stopped in the middle of the sidewalk. "Alex, you know I'm really messed up right now, right?"

He shook his head. "I don't think you're messed up. I think you got walloped by a shock this morning."

Without realizing what she was doing, she reached out to brush a small leaf out of his hair, her hand touching the side of his face. "C'mon," she said as she pulled him toward a bench. Once they were sitting, she looked him in the eye. "Alex, yeah, this morning threw me for a loop, but, frankly, that's just the tip of the iceberg as to how fucked up I am. All my 'I'm fine' comments aside, deep down, I know I'm a mess. I already told you, I don't date anymore. I'm no good at relationships, and I'm okay with that. I don't want to lead you on or anything."

He grinned. "Kat, I never realized we were in a relationship. I haven't even had any luck at getting you to go on a date with me. Every time I might ask you out, you tell me we're *friends*. Would I like to ask you out? Hell, yes. But, I'm realistic enough to know that right now we're on a mini-vacation, in an odd situation, and you live half a world away, and obviously, there's a lot about you I don't know." He touched her face, "But, I'd be lying if I didn't say that I'm interested in seeing where this goes."

Kat tried to ignore her immediate response to his touch. "And if it doesn't go anywhere?"

"Then no harm, no foul."

That sounded too relaxed. "You're not going to push?"

"I won't push. But you can't fault me for wanting to."

"Okay. Just as long as we understand each other."

***

Five minutes later, they walked into the drugstore because Kat needed sunscreen. Alex went to look for a pack of gum when Kat suddenly appeared next to him, her cheeks flushed, her eyes glittering. "Kat, what's the matter?"

Kat took his hand. "I need a favor, right now."

Whatever it was, she'd touched him first! "Anything."

She tried to keep her voice light. "You may regret saying that."

"What do you need?"

"You know how I don't date, and all that?"

"Yeah, we just had a long conversation about all of that, remember?"

"I don't have the time to explain, but I need you to pretend that you really, really"—her voice lowered with intensity— "really are my boyfriend, lover, whatever."

"Huh?"

"In about thirty seconds, we're going to run into people, including Nate. I can't stand having him think that I'm a loser going to the wedding alone." Her tone was desperate. "Please?"

Alex was trying to follow the conversation. "You need me to pretend to be your lover? Are we talking just right now, or through the wedding stuff?"

Kat looked behind her nervously. "I guess through the wedding stuff. They're all going to the wedding, so I can't be your lover here, then be alone at the wedding."

This could be fun! "On one condition."

Time was running out, and Kat felt panicky. "What?"

"That after the wedding is over, you go on a real date with me."

He was asking her out now? Shit, but she really needed his help in about two seconds, no matter the conditions attached. "Deal." As soon as Kat uttered the one word, she took a deep breath. "Ready? I'm going to walk down the next row, and in a few seconds, I need you to come down the aisle, and act all lovey-dovey."

"My pleasure." As she walked away, Alex fought the urge to tell her that it wouldn't be an act...

✱✱

Kat turned into the next aisle, feigning concentration in the row of hair products. As she looked at the bottles, she moved closer to the familiar figure looking at the shampoo. For a moment, she went back through time, to the countless times she'd run her fingers through his hair, or kissed his lips, or felt his arms around her. Anger at his betrayal warred with her mourning of an early love lost. Suddenly, she felt so old and sad but knew that she had to go through with all of this. Out of the corner of her eye, she saw Alex move to the end of the aisle, keeping his eyes on her. When she looked his way for a millisecond, he'd winked, and Kat fought the urge to giggle. At that moment, Kat picked up a bottle of gel, and turned away from Alex, knowing instinctively that he would be at her side when she needed him. Putting a bright smile on her face, she said in a surprised tone, "Nate!"

Shock was evident on Nate's face. "Kat." He swallowed. "What are you doing here?"

"I could ask you the same thing."

Alex started down the aisle, amused at the smooth tone of her voice. "I'm here for Mariah's wedding, of course. What about you?"

At that moment, a warm hand settled on her waist, and Alex moved to stand right behind her. Kat felt her body respond instantly to his touch. His voice was caressing, as he pointedly ignored the man standing in front of him, "Babe, did you find what you were looking for?"

Kat looked up at him adoringly. "I did." She turned toward Nate. "Oh, Nate. This is Alex. Alex, this is Nate.

We went to college together." Her tone was completely off-handed as if she and Nate had barely known each other.

Alex held out his hand. "Nice to meet you. I assume you're headed to the wedding too?"

"Uh, yes." In all the time Kat had known Nate, she'd never seen him at a loss for words, even when he'd sold her out. "Nice to meet you too. Anyway Kat," he stared at her. "Anyway, you look great."

"Thanks. So, I'll see you at the wedding? I'm sure we can catch up then…"

While Nate tried to formulate a response, Alex figured they'd better get away. With a sure arm around her shoulders, Alex said, "Kat, we should head back." His tone was sensual. "After all, we have the house all to ourselves."

Her smile said it all, and Nate watched in shock as Kat took Alex's hand. "We do, don't we? Nate, see you around."

***

After leaving the drugstore, the two of them strolled down the sidewalk, not talking. Once they'd gone a ways, Kat said quietly, "Thank you."

"For what?"

"For doing that. I know I sprang it on you."

Alex stopped on the sidewalk, and before Kat realized what he was doing, he'd pulled her into his arms. "Let's be clear, sweetheart, playing your lover was fun." He leaned down, so his lips were almost touching hers. "But I'd rather *be* your lover."

For a moment, Kat wanted to lean forward and touch her lips to his. With a sigh, she pushed him away. "Very funny."

***

Back at the house, Peter and Luke were starting dinner. "Hey Sis, Alex. How was town?"

Kat put her bags on the counter. "Fine." She washed her hands at the sink. "We saw Nate."

"What?" Peter was chewing on a carrot as he said it, and started to cough.

Kat whacked him on the back, laughing. "We were at the drugstore, and we saw Nate. So," she grinned at Alex, "I asked Alex to act like my boyfriend, and then we went over and said hello."

"No shit!"

Just at that moment, the phone rang, and Peter picked it up distractedly, still focusing on what his sister was saying. "Hello?"

"Hey Peter, it's Dan. I need a favor."

Peter was completely confused. "Sure, what?"

"Becky and I checked in the hotel earlier today, and all they had was a smoking room, and now her allergies are going nuts. Can we stay with you guys at the house?"

Peter's eyes widened. "Dan, shit. I'm not sure. I need to check and see what's going on. Can I call you in a couple minutes?"

When he got off the phone, he explained the situation. "But we don't have any more room. All the rooms are filled unless they sleep on the couches."

Luke looked around the kitchen, seeing how Alex was looking at Kat. A glimmer of an idea began. "Kat, you know how you just said you and Alex played lovey-dovey at the drugstore?"

"Yeah."

"Is your plan to keep up the façade through the wedding?"

She shrugged. "Yeah. I asked Alex if he would. I mean, as I said to Alex, I can't very well lie to Nate today, and then be at the wedding alone."

Luke tried to keep a devilish grin off his face. "So, Dan and Becky need a place to stay. And if you guys are really playing this romance thing, wouldn't you be staying in the same room?"

Kat felt panic bloom as she realized what he was suggesting. "I guess so."

"So, you guys move into Kat's room, and if you don't want to share a bed, the couch in that room pulls out. That way Becky and Dan can stay in Alex's room."

Peter looked at Luke in complete confusion. "Huh."

Luke continued to slice vegetables for a salad, keeping his voice neutral. "I'm just saying if the two of them are going to the wedding acting like a couple, wouldn't they be likely to be sharing a room?" He glanced at Alex, seeing by the look in his eyes that he understood the game Luke was playing and was enjoying every second. "Alex, I know you've shared rooms with women before, and after all, we've had conversations over the last few days about Kat posing naked for paintings, so I think everyone would think it was a bit odd if the two of you are all lovey at the wedding and then come back here after a friggin' wedding to sleep in separate rooms. I mean everyone gets horny at a wedding."

Peter frowned, but nodded. "Okay."

"So, I'm suggesting they sleep in Kat's room, and truly I don't want to know if the two of you end up sleeping in the same bed or not, since after all there is a pull-out couch. Then, they keep up the façade, and Dan and Becky have a place to stay too."

Peter nodded. "Sure."

Alex agreed. "It makes sense."

Kat turned to Alex with narrowed eyes. "Of course it makes sense to you. But what about how I feel about it?"

His voice was patient, but his eyes were twinkling. "Kat, you're the one who asked me to play along today, not the other way around. So, I'm just saying I'll make the sacrifice of sharing a room with you to make it all look real."

Before Kat could stop herself, she took offense. *"Sacrifice?* Sharing a room with me is a sacrifice? Fine, I'll share a fucking room with you!" With that, Kat flounced out of the room and slammed the door to the porch.

Once she left the room, Luke started to laugh openly, before pointing his knife at Alex. "You owe me!"

Alex chuckled. "We'll see."

"You better go make peace, or she'll stab you to death in your sleep."

***

Alex stepped out on the porch and saw Kat sitting on the bottom step staring out at the ocean. He sat down beside her. "I meant it as a joke."

Kat kept looking at the waves. "I know. I overreacted, but…"

"But, what?"

Her voice was small. "It hurt my feelings for a minute. I couldn't hear that you were picking on me, I heard that I was asking too much."

Alex put his arm around her. "Sweetie, do you remember that at least twice today we've had conversations about how interested in you I am? I was being a wise-ass, nothing more." Knowing he was taking a chance, Alex leaned over to kiss her hair. "I'm sorry I hurt your feelings. I was teasing you, nothing more."

She leaned against him. "I'm sorry I acted like an idiot again."

"You didn't. We are just getting to understand each other's senses of humor. It was too soon for a joke like that."

Kat slid her arms around him, and gave him a quick hug. "Thank you."

Chapter Nine

Around five o'clock, cars started to pull into the driveway. Josh, Kim, Beth, and Sasha came into the house with bags and suitcases. An hour later, Dan and Becky arrived. At dinner, everyone ate heartily and talked noisily, although Alex noticed that Kat avoided any chance of talking directly with Josh. Over coffee, Beth, Kim, and Luke decided to watch the news, Sasha and Peter decided to read the newspapers, and Dan and Becky decided to walk into town.

Kat disappeared outside. Alex slipped outside too and sat on the swing to watch her as she sat on the steps.

About five minutes later, Josh opened the screen door and walked over to sit down next to her. "Can we talk about Nate and what this means?"

Kat didn't look at him. "No."

His voice was insistent. "We need to. We need to talk about a *lot* of things."

"No, we don't."

"Yes, we do." Josh gently touched her hand as Kat woodenly stared at the ocean. "C'mon, Ducky. Look at me."

Kat turned her head slightly to look at him. "Happy now?"

Josh fought his frustration. "Stop being juvenile and really look at me. We need to talk about this."

Kat turned and looked at him fully for a second before turning away and saying, "No, we don't. Stop."

"Damn it, Kat." His voice sounded strained as he started talking. "Ducky, I love you more than I can express. I have loved you since that first day in the dining hall when I spilled orange juice on you, and you laughed and dumped seltzer on my shoes. The look on your face when you picked up the glass and poured it deliberately has stayed with me. You looked young and happy as if your only concern in life was making sure my shoes were soaked. And that look sealed our friendship forever."

His voice lowered. "I loved you so much. I still do." While Alex sat in the shadows, for a moment, he wondered where this conversation was going. Was Josh going to make a move on Kat suddenly? What the hell was he getting at?

Gently Josh ran his finger down the side of Kat's arm as she stared at the beach, noticing that she didn't react to his touch in any way, feeling slightly more optimistic that she didn't pull away. "That doesn't mean that I'm in love with you. Being in love with you was too much for me. I obsessed about you. I couldn't do anything but think about you." He started to laugh, "I heard a recovering heroin addict speak recently, and frankly, being in love with you was a hell of a lot like being a heroin addict." Kat turned and looked at him in horror. "Hear me out. When I was with you, the high was beyond description. When I wasn't with you, I would have sold my soul for a minute with you. When we were apart for more than an hour, I went into fucking withdrawal, shakes and all, dying until I could see you." Before she could interrupt, he continued, "It was too much for me. I needed to remember that I was in college to learn. My grades sucked when I was with you. Luckily I didn't have a merit scholarship because I would have been out on my ass." He took a deep breath. "Then we decided to be 'just friends.' Breaking up with you was one of the hardest things I ever did in my life. But, you said we could be friends. I honestly didn't believe we could go back to that stage, but we did."

He turned to look at Kat. "'Just friends' is such a shitty way to describe us. I'd do anything for you, and I know that you feel the same way."

Out of the corner of his eye, Josh could see Kat nod slightly. "But, I've lost you, and I know it, but it makes me sadder than you could know. Deep down, you know it too. You're lost to all of us. You're always in your head with your writing, but I'm used to that. You've always been that way, but this is different. No matter how hard you try to hide it, you're still letting all of it eat at you. You just hold it in, day after day, month after month, year after year. And I've tried to respect that and not push too hard, but you've become a shadow of the woman who dumped seltzer on me. And now Nate's here, and you're going to see him, and we need to know how to act." He paused. "I need to know what you need me to do."

Kat spoke quietly but firmly. "You don't need to do anything. Before you went on your tirade, I told you, we don't need to do or talk about him at all. I've already seen him."

His shock was complete. "What?"

Kat sat staring at the ocean. "After you called today, I wanted to go into town. Alex and I went for a walk after lunch, and at the drugstore, we ran into Nate."

"And?"

"And nothing. I went over and said hello. I decided that it was going to be on my terms, not his, and we played the game, and Alex and I walked away."

"What do you mean 'we played the game'?"

"I mean I walked over, started a conversation with Nate, and then walked away."

Josh's eyes narrowed. "And how does Alex fit into all of this?"

For the first time, Kat looked at him, looking deep into his eyes, her confusion clear in both the look on her face and in her voice. "I don't have the foggiest fucking idea."

"What do you mean by that?"

"I mean, he plays around like he's interested in me, and at the drugstore, I asked him to pretend to be my boyfriend while we're all here, and so he said yes, and now, well, we're…"

Josh started to laugh. "You're playing house, sharing a room. I noticed that when we all moved in today, but I didn't want to say anything in front of everyone." He nudged her with his shoulder, "Shit, Ducky, it took me almost six months to get an invitation into your bed, and he gets one almost immediately. The world is not a fair place!"

Kat whacked him on the arm. "Very funny."

Suddenly Josh's voice became solemn. "Kat, do you remember the night that we stayed up all night drinking wine coolers and talking?"

"How could I forget?" A ghost of a smile crossed her face. "Wine coolers still make me sick."

"Here's the thing. I think about that conversation a lot. We talked so much about how you loved me, and 'Riah, and liked a few other people, but other than your family and that small group, you didn't really want to connect with people. It wasn't that people didn't want to connect with *you*, I remember how you'd walk into the dining hall, and half the tables wanted you to sit with them. But you'd climb the stairs to the loft and eat alone with a book for company. I mean, you basically lived like a hermit in college. And as I've thought about it, I've concluded that deep down, I don't think you trust people all that much. Let me rephrase that. I know you trust me, Pete, and Luke. But you don't *need* us. If we weren't around, I think you'd keep going."

Exasperated, Kat's voice rose. "That's a shitty thing to say."

"I don't mean it that way. I mean it as a wake-up call."

"Calling me a cold, heartless bitch is a wake-up call? I'd call it an insult."

"No, it's not an insult. It's my perception, and it's time for me to say it like I see it, rather than trying to find a way to say it that won't piss you off. I love you enough to say it bluntly." He looked at her searchingly, putting his arm around her. "Please, let us in, let us help. Some of us know the whole story and still love you beyond belief, and maybe we love you even more than we did before. But, please, talk to us about it. Let it out. Let us all grieve together and heal together." His voice cracked, "Or if you still can't talk to *us* for whatever reason, talk to someone else. Anyone. Stop hiding from the truth."

Kat sat in silence so long that Josh started to give up that she would respond. Finally, sure that he'd pushed her too hard, he pulled back his arm and began to stand up. She pulled on his sleeve, pulling him back down next to her, then said timidly. "I don't know how to." She took his hand and held it tightly. "I don't know how to open that door anymore." Her voice was so small; it was hard to hear her, "I'm afraid of what's behind it. Maybe it would be too much. I don't know if I could handle it."

Josh was shocked that she would say so much. "We'd love you no matter what. We'd be there for you, Ducky, you know that, right?"

"I know." Her voice rose defensively, "I've made a pretty good life in Madrid."

His voice stayed calm, but he knew his words would infuriate her. "So you keep telling me."

Her voice crackled with anger. "What do you mean by that?"

"Are you living there or hiding there?" Hearing Josh's calm question, Alex's heart constricted, waiting to hear her answer.

It took Kat almost ten seconds to answer, and the pause seemed to take a lifetime. "I don't know. Six weeks ago, I would have said living. Now I don't know."

"What changed in the meantime?"

Kat sighed. "Did I tell you that Alex came to Madrid to do a concert, and after some strange coincidences, I ended up interviewing him?"

"Yeah. So?"

"So I went to his concert, and then we went out for a drink after, and he said some things about how I'd changed over the years, and I got pissed off..."

"Let me guess. You stormed out?"

She chuckled, amused in spite of herself. "Bite me. Yes, I stormed out. But I got to thinking about what he said. And then 'Riah kept calling, and she's my best female friend in the world, and I refused to be in her wedding because I didn't want to come home. And now I'm here, in a fucking bizarre situation, pretending I have a boyfriend when I don't, knowing that at best it can be a fling because I'm too fucked up for anything more, and shit, it all makes no sense. And no matter what, I know I need to get my life in real order."

"And Alex?"

"Josh, stop being such a fucking busybody. I don't know. He's gorgeous." In the darkness, Alex grinned, pleased to hear she felt *something* for him. "He makes me laugh. So far, he puts up with me being a nut case. He has great hands."

"Excuse me? You said you were just playing being together. How the hell do you know about his hands?"

"He gave me a foot rub last night that was borderline orgasmic."

"Wow, you are desperate. A foot rub gets you to that point?" He started to laugh. "As I remember, it used to take a lot more than that."

"Shut up! And anyway, in another world, in another time, I'd be doing everything I could to start something with him." Her voice got even quieter, so Alex almost missed her next words. "Like I tried to years ago."

Confused by her last statement, Josh focused on the earlier revelation. "Why not now?"

"Duh! I'm in a state of flux here. I'm fucked up beyond belief, and I need to figure some of this out. And he's Peter's friend, and they work together, so I can't screw that up, and let's face it, I completely totally suck at dating." She squeezed his arm, "I mean, you loved me, and I managed to screw it up to the point that you dumped me."

"Kat, listen, I broke up with you because it was too intense to last. You were a great girlfriend. I think you just need to find the right guy."

Kat snorted. "Josh, get real. I gave up on that dating shit. I'm no good at it."

He gently shook her shoulders. "Stop and really look at yourself one day. You're exceedingly attractive, smart, sexy, and funny."

Her voice was unsure. "Really?"

"Really, Ducky, really. But frankly, you scare the living hell out of most men. But I think if you didn't actively push him away, Alex would stick around."

Kat took a deep breath. "Josh, I love you. And I'm glad you came out here tonight. Right now, though, I need a break, so I'm going for a little walk."

Josh kissed her cheek. "I'll see you when you come back."

***

After Kat was far enough away from the house that she couldn't hear any conversation, Josh walked over to the swing in the shadows. Alex almost fell over in shock when Josh said, "Now that I've gotten her to admit that she's interested, why don't you get off your ass and follow her?"

"You knew I was here?"

"Of course. Why do you think I pushed several issues out here? I figure if you're interested in her, you need fair warning of the shadows in her life. Now, if you're still in the running, get going."

***

Alex slowly walked down the steps, following the footsteps in the sand. Kat sat on a dune gazing out onto the black ocean. The moon peeked through the clouds sending slivers of yellow light snaking down waves as they rolled toward the beach. Alex stood beside her, listening to the waves and the wind.

Kat stirred. "Hi."

His voice caressed her. "Hi. May I join you?"

"Seems like you already have," she said wearily. "Go ahead."

Once he was settled on the sand, Kat's voice was brittle with her emotions so close to the surface. "Don't you ever give up?"

He shook his head slowly. "No."

"Why not?"

"Because this is too important."

She sighed as she pushed her hair out of her eyes. "You're diligent. I have to give you that."

Kat shivered and, without thinking, Alex put his arm around her. Kat stiffened, and Alex felt like kicking himself. But then she leaned against him. Minutes later, he pulled her so that she was sitting in front of him, and he wrapped both of his arms around her, feeling her still shivering, but whether from cold or fear he couldn't tell.

Softly, he whispered in her ear. "I won't rush you. But I'm not just pretending here. This is real."

Her voice was tentative. "Okay."

"Okay? You're not fighting me on this?"

Alex felt her shake her head. "It doesn't seem to matter if I fight you or not. As you said before, it seems to be happening."

"Is that okay with you?"

Kat's voice caught her throat. "No, it isn't. I'm scared out of my mind. I'm completely fucked up, and I'm heading back across the Atlantic soon. But if you're okay with all of that, then…"

"I'm okay with that. Let's just see what happens." He nuzzled her neck. "You set the boundaries."

Kat gradually leaned back against Alex, relaxing into the protective warmth of his arms. They silently watched the waves for almost an hour before Alex realized they were cold and damp from the spray. "C'mon lady, let's go get warm."

Alex and Kat walked back to the lighted house, holding hands. As they climbed the steps, Kat began to pull away. Alex stopped. "Kat, remember that you started this. You know how I feel, but no matter how you feel, if you still want to keep up an image for this weekend, you need to play it through."

Kat stood on the top step, one step above his, so their eyes were almost level. "I thought we just decided we weren't playing."

For a moment, Alex didn't understand. "What?"

She leaned forward, and pressed the briefest of kisses to his lips. "I thought we'd agreed that we feel something, that this isn't just playing a game."

He reached up to cradle her face in his hands. "It isn't a game. It has never been to me."

His response took her breath away. "Okay then." Kat took his hand, and pulled him toward the front door, swinging the door open.

Six sets of curious eyes greeted them. Josh threw a pair of dice at Kat. "Hurry up; we want to play Trivial Pursuit, and we've been waiting for you guys. We pulled names out of the hat: me and Luke, Peter and Beth, Alex and Kim, and damn it, Ducky, you and Sasha."

Having caught the dice neatly, Kat grinned at Sasha. "Yes! C'mon Sash, we'll beat them *again*."

As the game progressed, Alex realized he hadn't had so much fun in years. The group yelled, competed mercilessly, drank copious amounts of wine, and laughed.

Kat and Sasha beat the rest of the competition easily and gloated mercilessly.

At the end of the game, everyone quietly shared a nightcap, the couples cuddling on the couches. Alex rested his hand on Kat's and smiled when she entwined her fingers through his.

Some time later, Kat excused herself to go to bed, squeezing his shoulder as she said goodnight to the others.

When Alex came upstairs, she was sitting on the bed. After closing the door to their room, Alex leaned against the door looking at her. "Hey."

"Hey." She chewed her lower lip, "I didn't know where you wanted to sleep. You can sleep in the bed, or the couch or I can, or whatever."

"What do you want?"

She shrugged. "I don't care." She stood up to go to look out the window. "This is stupid. We can sleep in the same bed, and have nothing happen, right?"

Was she asking him to share her bed? "Of course, we can." He came over to stand behind her, his hands on her shoulders, "Kat, let's be clear. I don't need to force myself on women." As he said it, he felt Kat's breath catch. "I can sleep in the same bed with you without making a move, I promise."

"Okay." Did he know? Is that why he mentioned forcing himself on her? Kat tried to sound normal as she turned around to face him. "Okay. I'm ready for bed then if you are."

They got into bed, Kat hugging the edge, keeping her body rigid. She tried to keep her breathing normal, making it sound like she was asleep.

Almost twenty minutes passed. "I know you're awake, Kat. You don't have to pretend."

Kat opened her eyes and turned over to look at him. "I'm sorry." Even in the moonlight, Alex could see her cheeks darken with her blushing, "It's been a really long time since I slept with someone."

Alex was confused. "What about Tixi? Is that his name?"

"Yeah. That was a long time ago. Years ago. We stopped being..." she paused, uncomfortable with calling him her lover, "intimate more than three years ago."

"Really? Peter made it sound like it was more recent than that."

"No." Suddenly Kat wanted to explain. "Tixi and I've known each other since we were in high school, and sometimes then we'd fool around a little bit. Then when I moved to Spain four years ago, we dated for a bit, then it was just that we'd get together sometimes. It wasn't a passionate romance; it was more like two good friends who occasionally..."

Alex started to laugh. "Scratched an itch?"

Kat gave his chest a shove, immediately aware of the feeling of the hair on his chest under her palm. "Such a tactful way to explain it."

"True?"

"True." She felt a giggle begin to bubble up, "And so I'm really bad at the sleeping part. I get all freaked out about whether I'm snoring or drooling, or my stomach is growling. And then I worry about whether I'm stealing all the covers. And it's exhausting! So, most of the time when I've been supposedly sharing a bed, I've pretended to fall asleep, and as soon as he's asleep, I've gotten up to write."

Alex lay beside her, delighted to hear her dismiss Tixi and laugh about her worries. "How about this, if you snore or take the covers, I'll give you a shove or steal them back. As for your stomach, if it starts to growl, we'll go have a midnight picnic."

"Deal." With that, Kat leaned back on her pillows and reached over to take his hand. "Thank you. Sleep well."

He leaned closer. "Sweet dreams." Gently, he kissed her on the tip of her nose.

"Good night, Alex."

Chapter Ten

In the middle of the night, Alex awoke and found that Kat was shivering in her sleep, keeping her body far away from his. Trying to not wake her, he moved next to her so he could wrap his arm around her and tuck her in against his chest. She stirred in her sleep. "Hmm."

He kissed her temple. "Go back to sleep. You're cold, so I just moved you over so you'd be warmer."

"Okay."

***

In the morning, Kat awoke completely entwined with Alex, her head pillowed on his chest. For a moment, she felt her stomach clench with nerves. Before she could get out of bed, his voice rumbled beneath her ear, "You know, for someone with so many worries about sleeping with someone, you're really good at it."

Kat pulled back to look at him, completely confused. "Huh?"

He grinned mischievously. "You don't snore or drool. I didn't hear your stomach growl even once. You didn't steal covers, and when I moved closer for warmth, you smelled great." His tone was wry. "I'd be willing to make the sacrifice of sleeping with you again."

With a shove, Kat started to laugh. "Yeah, well let me tell you about sleeping with *you*."

Before she could say anything more, from downstairs, she heard Peter yell, "Breakfast!"

***

Kat ate a light breakfast and then went for a long run. As she ran, she let her mind run free, thinking about the job offer and Alex. It seemed too simple to think that she could just take a job based in Manhattan, move home with Peter and Luke, and somehow have a relationship with Alex. Feeling anxiety begin to lick at the back of her brain, Kat started a second loop, knowing she needed to keep running until she had beaten back the fears. What if moving home made the anxiety worse? What if she gave up her life in Madrid only to find she hated the job? What if living with Peter and Luke now wasn't like it used to be? Could they all live together well? Peter and Luke had set their lives up just the way they wanted. Would her living there shift that balance? Would Peter be able to see her as an adult, or just his little sister? What about a relationship? Could she bring someone home there and have sex in the same house with them? What the hell was she doing thinking about *sex*? Even while running, Kat could feel her breathing increase at the thought of Alex naked. It had been a long time since a man made her think that way! Even Tixi had been more of it was nice to get together, have a few drinks, and have a real man-made orgasm. And the very few men since then had been short interludes, no real emotional connection at all. Kat felt her chest tighten as she realized that she was living in a dreamland if she thought that everything could work out with Alex. The best she could hope for was for a few fun days...

Kat finished her run, angry that even after such a long run, she felt more frustrated and sad than when she'd started. Usually the running gave her a chance to clear her head, and instead, she felt more confused than ever.

As Kat walked down the beach toward the house, her breathing began to slow. Alex was coming down the beach from the opposite direction, dressed in running clothes. As he came closer, he commented, "So, perhaps we should have mentioned to each other that we were going running, and we could have had company."

Kat grinned, suddenly hopeful. Instead of worrying about the future, why not just have a really good time now? "Company? I would have lapped you."

Alex laughed, thrilled to see her smile. "How about tomorrow morning? We'll see who laps whom."

She bounded up the steps. "You're on."

***

The rest of the morning and early afternoon passed in a blur. At lunchtime, all of them went over to a seafood restaurant to have a large and noisy meal. Afterwards, everyone headed back to the house.

After hanging out and talking music with Peter for a while, Alex went upstairs to find Kat sitting on the window seat, typing away. He stood in the doorway for a moment, admiring the way the sun glinted off her curls. When he cleared his throat, she looked up in surprise. "Hey. I didn't hear you come up."

"Would it be fair to say that when you're writing, an elephant could stampede through the room and you wouldn't notice?"

She stretched her back. "If writing is going well, that would be fair. If it isn't, I become hypersensitive to sounds and sensations."

"So, it's going well today?"

She nodded happily. "Last night I worked out a sticky bit, and now I can't type fast enough."

"Then I'll let you be." He turned to leave the room but stopped suddenly. "Kat?"

"Yes?"

"You know how I made you promise you'd go out with me?"

"Yeah." Suddenly Kat had a sinking feeling in her stomach that he wasn't going to hold her to that.

"I know I said after the wedding, but how about tonight? Peter and Luke will be at the rehearsal, and I thought we could go out to dinner."

Kat grinned. "I'd love to."

Alex felt his entire body relax with her words. "Okay. I'll make reservations."

"What time?"

"Seven?"

"Great."

***

In the early evening, Kat took Max for a long walk. When she got home, she found that Peter and Luke had left for the rehearsal, and everyone else seemed to have gone out as well. She sprinted up the stairs realizing that she only had fifteen minutes to get ready. Entering *their* room, she found Alex looking over a sheaf of music, mumbling to himself as he made notes on the pages. He looked up at her. "Fifteen minutes!"

"I know, I know! Go downstairs, so I don't have to worry about you seeing me naked."

He leaned back to look her up and down. "What if I want to see you naked?"

She rolled her eyes. "Get out, or I won't be ready on time."

In the bathroom, she hurriedly pulled off her shorts and T-shirt and turned on the shower. After soaping her body and hair, she turned the water to icy cold and then stepped out of the shower. Looking at her watch, she ran into the bedroom, grabbed a simple black sundress, and slipped it over her head. She pulled on her favorite black heels, and combed her hair, leaving it loose, so the curls cascaded down her back. Looking at her watch, she had just three minutes left. She quickly dabbed on Allure and mascara and put a pair of gold hoop earrings in her lowest holes and diamond studs in the other two holes on her left ear. She walked back onto the porch to find Alex sitting in a rocking chair, his feet resting on the railing.

"I'm impressed. I expected to be waiting for at least ten minutes. You look great." He was dressed in black jeans and an ivory linen Victorian peasant shirt.

"So do you."

Suddenly they didn't know what to say to each other. From inside the screen door, Max started barking, breaking the tension.

Just then, Peter's cell phone started ringing inside the kitchen, startling both of them. Kat picked it up. "Hello, Peter's phone."

For the next few minutes, Alex stood and watched as Kat spoke in rapid-fire Spanish, apparently arguing with the person on the other end of the phone line. Finally, she switched back into English. "Hello, Manuel. This better be damn good. It's Friday night, and I have a date." Kat looked at Alex and winked. "What's so stinking important that Pedro said you needed to talk to me today? Of course, I know who the Shining Path are. Yes, I know they're active again. No, I don't want to fly to Peru in two weeks. Manuel, I'm on vacation, and when I'm done, I'm heading back to Madrid, not Lima. No, I really don't want to hike around with a bunch of revolutionaries later this month. Why are you in such a rush? They've been there for years; they're not going anywhere tomorrow." Kat crossed her eyes at Alex.

"Yes, Manuel. I know, Manuel. Manuel, I'll make a deal with you. I need the next two weeks to finish some rewrites. If after that, you still want me to go, I'll think about it. Yes, I know you'd like me to commit, but I'm not going to today. That's my best offer. Final. Talk to you soon."

Kat clicked the phone shut. "Sorry, Alex. I forgot that I gave my agent Peter's cell as a contact number, and he gave it out."

"Don't worry about it. Are you ready?"

"Ready." Kat slipped a pashmina over her shoulders. Walking outside, they headed toward a restaurant visible down the beach, at the base of a lighted lighthouse. Once there, they were shown to a secluded booth in the back where a bottle of red wine was already waiting for them.

Kat touched his hand. "Ahh, a man with a plan. You called ahead."

"Of course." After ordering, they settled in with their wine and bread. After taking a sip, Alex looked intently at Kat. "Okay, tell me *your* version of your life story. I only know bits and pieces from Peter, and what I've picked up over the last few days."

Kat smiled as she took a sip of wine, suddenly feeling playful and hopeful. "Full name, Katherine Ann Weston. Age twenty-six. I'm named after my great-grandmother Ekaterina. When my grandmother felt I needed scolding, she used the Russian form." She rolled her eyes. "When I was eight, we moved to New York City. Dad had sold the family mill and instead, worked as a financial advisor. By the time we moved, Jess was away at college, so it was really just Pete and me."

"Was that a good thing?"

She shrugged, "Not good or bad. Jess is great, but she's so much older than me that we've only gotten close over the last few years now that we're both adults. When we were younger, I was always closer to Peter."

"And when did he come out?"

"When he was sixteen. But everyone already knew it. We just pretended we didn't."

Alex tipped his head slightly. "Your folks seemed amazingly supportive about it. I know the times I stayed with them, I never noticed the awkwardness of some of the families of other gay friends."

"They were. I mean, I'm sure they probably would've been happier if he'd married a woman and had kids, but they never rammed it down his throat."

"How'd he meet Luke?"

"Oh, I take full credit for them. Peter went to college for music." She grinned. "Duh, you know that. Anyway, on one of his summer vacations, I made him visit a new art gallery. When we got there, there was this really hot guy working as an intern. While I wandered around, they stood and talked. Suddenly Peter developed an interest in art. For years, I'd been trying to get him to go see shows with me, and he'd complain about how boring art was…" Her eyes grew misty. "I remember the night Peter told my parents he was in love. I will always remember that moment, just feeling his happiness, and Luke became part of our lives."

"Other than art and writing"—he paused— "and running, what do you like to do?"

"Wow, I don't know. I guess a lot of things. I love to travel…"

"But not fly."

"But not fly. I love to hike, ski, and cook."

"And after we met, you went back to school."

"I did. I graduated that May, and after that, I lived in New York for a while, then moved to Spain." Shaking her head, Kat turned to Alex. "Enough about me, it's your turn."

"Hmm, I'm thirty-two years old." He grinned. "I like all types of music, although some more than others."

"How'd you go into music?"

"My mother made me learn the piano when I was seven. What shocked the hell out of everyone was that I was good at it and loved it. One day I started writing my own music and soon I had a portfolio."

"How'd you form the band?"

"You know that Peter and I met in college. He answered an ad I placed on the board. Thirty other drummers came to audition, but he was the best, and we liked each other. Dave, I saw in a little bar in the Village. Will came along when our old bass player got pregnant.

"And the band's name?"

Alex laughed. "Before my first meeting with a recording executive, I called my father. I was so nervous I was actually throwing up. My father said, 'What's the American saying? You're a basket case over this audition.' I went to the meeting without a name for the band, and suddenly, when they asked me, I spouted 'Basket Case.' My father still gets a kick out of it."

"And you obviously still perform solo?"

"Yeah. Like Peter, I have the band but do other things too. The solo tour was something I'd thought about for years, and when the opportunity came up, I jumped at it."

Slowly, he sipped his wine. "Tell me about your writing. How did you get started?"

She thought for a moment. "I always wrote, even when I was a kid. In college, I needed a piece for an English class. So, I took a discussion I had with a Basque woman in Spain, and I turned it into a short story. Ironically, my professor was editing an anthology of short stories about women and asked if she could include my piece. Of course, I said yes, even then I knew I wanted to be a writer. And then the publisher called and asked if I'd like to turn it into a book. Duh, of course! I mean, even now, I'm amazed at how lucky I was. I basically walked into it."

"I know what you said about your topics, but what exactly do you write?"

"I generally write three different types of pieces. The first is non-fictional magazine and newspaper pieces, covering social or political changes or movements in Hispanic countries or cultures."

"Explain."

"Like I write about a female candidate in a Hispanic election, that sort of thing. I wrote a nonfiction book based on those pieces. I also write fiction loosely based on actual events or situations surrounding Hispanic women."

He thought back to the earlier phone call, "And the piece you were asked about tonight?"

"Non-fictional magazine article. They're looking for a woman to do something on the women of the Shining Path in Peru. I'd go and stay with them for a while and then write about the role and the lifestyle of the women."

"Is it dangerous?"

Her tone was nonchalant, "It can be. It can also be ordering room service in a lovely hotel in Buenos Aires before going to a cocktail party for a candidate."

"Why do you do it?"

"First, because these women have the right to be heard. Unfortunately, due to the macho social structure, women generally aren't allowed to have much power in Hispanic cultures. Letting those women have a voice is imperative. Getting down off my soapbox, admittedly I enjoy the thrill. I also do it because I'm good at it."

"Are you going to Peru?"

She shook her head. "I don't know."

***

Once they had finished their cappuccinos, Alex went to settle the bill. Looking at a clock, Kat was shocked to see that it was after ten. They wandered down the beach, taking off their shoes to walk in the sand, holding hands, seldom speaking.

As they walked, they could see the house was brightly lit, and music drifted over the sound of the waves.

To Kat's ears, Alex's voice was sad as he said, "Obviously, we have company."

She squeezed his hand, "Yeah." Inside, she struggled. Should she tell him she was disappointed too, or say nothing? "I had a great time."

He stopped, reached down to stroke back her hair, blowing in the wind. "Me too. It was over too soon."

She rested her head against his chest. "It was."

"Want to walk for a while more?"

"That would be great."

They walked far past the house, not talking. Finally, Kat realized that even with the pashmina, she was getting cold. "I guess we should head back."

Putting his arm around her, pulling her close, he said, "I suppose we have to let the world back in."

"We do."

***

At the house, they quickly joined the festivities. Music played, people laughed and chatted. Finally, around one, Kat stood up, unnoticed except by Alex, to leave the room quietly to go to their bedroom. Ten minutes later, he knocked the door. Her voice was muffled. "Come in."

He shut the door behind him. "You okay?"

"Yeah." She sat on the window seat, in her pajamas. "You know how I said that I don't feel like I fit in my skin when I'm here?"

Alex moved closer, to sit on the window seat. "Yeah."

"Sometimes it hits me, and I have to get away from everyone. I can't explain it; it's like suddenly everyone is too loud, and I don't have anything to say."

Alex picked up her hand. "Kat, it's okay. Sometimes everyone gets overwhelmed by a crowd."

She smiled. "Thanks."

"Ready for bed?"

"I am."

Chapter Eleven

The next morning, the house was crazy as people got ready for the wedding. Mid-morning, Alex came upstairs to get dressed and found Kat just coming out of the bathroom. Seeing her in the dress they'd picked out, now wearing high heels and makeup, her hair cascading down her back from a twist, took his breath away. "You look amazing."

She blushed. "Thanks."

He came close, to pick up her hand. "No. I don't think you really understand me. You are beautiful beyond words all the time, but in that outfit, you are absolutely stunning." He tried to make his tone sound joking, "I mean, Mariah may be pissed off that you're at the wedding because everyone will be looking at you."

Kat looked into his eyes and saw the naked desire there. "Thank you."

"You are going to stay by my side, right? I don't want some other guy trying to steal you away."

"Right by your side. To the point that you'll be ready to get away from me."

"Not going to happen."

For a moment, Kat leaned forward, resting her head on his broad chest, finding comfort in being so close to him. Her nerves were stretched to the breaking point. "Thank you." She sighed. "I don't want to go."

Alex put his arms around her, trying to ignore his reaction to the smell of her perfume. "Why?"

"I just feel funny about the whole thing." She half-whispered, "I'm scared."

"Of what?"

"Of being here, seeing people like Nate's parents, and of just not fitting in."

He rubbed her back, feeling the tension in her muscles, trying in vain to not react to touching her bare skin. "I'll be right there with you."

"Promise?"

"I promise."

***

Over the next hours, Alex never left Kat's side. Holding hands, they'd gone to the wedding. Even with her nervousness, she had to admit that she enjoyed being with him. After the outdoor service, they'd walked together to the reception.

Kat found herself seated at a table with Alex, Josh and Kim, and several people she didn't know. After introductions, the group ate the sumptuous meal, washing each course down with fine champagne. Throughout the meal, Alex kept her laughing, and at times, rested his hand possessively on the back of her chair. Once all dishes were cleared, the band started to play dance music, and Alex slid his chair back. "Dance with me?"

For a moment, Kat felt anxious at the thought of being that close to him after so much champagne. She knew her guard was down; maybe it wasn't a good idea to dance with him. She looked into his eyes and saw warmth and safety, and her nervousness evaporated. "Sure."

They danced and danced, never questioning that they would stay and dance the next song. Some songs were fast, and the younger couples danced energetically, while others were soft ballads, and everyone came onto the floor.

***

The band continued to play as the stars started to appear in the sky, turning to softer and more romantic songs. The music caressed them, and without meaning to, Alex pulled Kat closer and whispered in her ear. "Why didn't you ever call me after that night at the opera?"

She pulled back slightly, to look up at him. "I did."

He shook his head. "No, you didn't." Somehow, it was suddenly imperative to him that she tell him the truth about this. "I'm not mad, just asking why."

Her voice was certain, but for a moment Alex thought he heard an undercurrent of sadness, which confused him. "Yes, I did. I called you on Saturday night, January 21st. It was the Saturday night after the opera. Will answered, and I left a message. He said you'd be back in under a half hour, and would call me back. But you never did." Suddenly, Kat pulled away from him, "Alex, I'll be right back; I need to use the ladies' room."

Shocked by her certainty, down to the exact date, Alex didn't know what to do. "You did?"

"I did." She had to get away from him before she started to cry. "I'll be right back."

"Okay, I'll meet you over near the bar."

***

Quickly, Kat walked across the ballroom, waving hello to Mariah's parents but keeping moving. In the ladies' room, she stepped into the handicapped stall, pulled the door shut, and leaned against the wall, her eyes closed, trying to keep the tears back. Clenching her fists, she pressed her lips together so hard that she could feel her teeth beginning to cut into the inside of them. In vain, Kat tried to slow her breathing, and regain her composure. Just as she was about to leave the stall and leave the reception through a back hallway, and go home, no matter how much it would upset Alex, she heard voices coming toward her. "Have you seen Kat?" In her hideaway, Kat recognized Mariah's voice. "I'm trying to find her so we can take a picture of the two of us with Josh, you know, with the college banner."

An unrecognizable voice responded, "Shouldn't you include Nate since he went there too?"

Mariah's voice was sure, "No. The three of us were in a freshman hall together, not Nate."

In her stall, Kat smiled. Leave it to Mariah to find a simple reason not to have them be together. She stepped out of the stall to face her best female friend in the world.

Mariah looked at her searchingly. "You okay, Ducky?"

Kat chuckled at the nickname, something Mariah rarely called her anymore. "Of course. Why wouldn't I be?"

"Hmm, let's recap. Your friend called you shit-faced drunk to beg you to come home for her wedding, then your ex-motherfucking asshole snake in the grass boyfriend shows up, you hate crowds and social shit, and I just found you in a handicapped stall when you used to always go hide there so you could lean up against the wall for a bit. *That's* why I asked."

Love so strong it almost took her breath away filled Kat. "I love you, 'Riah. Yup, it's a bit much, but I love you, and I'm here and let's go do the banner thing."

Five minutes later, the three friends sat on the railing, the ocean behind them, holding the banner for the photographer. When done, Mariah handed each of them a glass of champagne, "To never-ending friendships."

"To never-ending friendships."

***

When Kat found Alex almost fifteen minutes later, her face was pale, but she smiled seeing him. He took her hand, "You okay?"

"Fine. I think I need to stop dancing for a while, okay?"

"Of course. Do you want to go out on the terrace to sit for a bit?"

"Sure."

As they walked across the crowded room, Peter caught up with them. "Alex, we're almost ready to play."

Alex smacked his hand on his forehead. "Kat, I forgot that we're going to play for a few minutes. Why don't you come over here near the band?"

For a moment, Kat thought of just running away, going home and getting away from everyone. Just as she started to make a comment about having a headache and leaving, she saw Nate out of the corner of her eye. Shit! He was just what she needed right now.

Alex saw him coming too and saw tension on her face. Without thinking, he pulled her to him, wrapping his arms around her, leaning down to whisper, "It's okay. I'm here. Just stay here with me, and when I'm done, we can head home if you want."

Feeling Nate's eyes on them, Kat took a deep breath, slid her arms around Alex, and leaned into him. "Thanks. Okay. But then can we go home?"

***

After watching them play for almost fifteen minutes, Kat needed some air. She leaned over and touched Luke's shoulder. "Luke, I'm going out on the deck for a moment."

He stood up immediately, "I'll go too."

She was touched by his unfailing loyalty. "I'm okay. You listen to the band."

Taking her hand, he pulled her to her feet. "C'mon kiddo, I'm not letting you go alone, so you either stay here or take me along. No arguing."

After standing on the balcony for a few minutes, enjoying the view and the cooler air, Kat leaned on the railing, rubbing her temple with one hand. Seeing her movement, Luke said, "Headache?"

"Yeah. It's been a long day, and"—she smiled—"let's face it, I'm not usually around this many people."

"I'll go get you a tonic water, and see if the bartender has any aspirin."

Kat started to argue, then stopped as relief from the pounding pain sounded so inviting, "That would be great." She motioned off to her left. "I'm going to walk down the balcony a bit, for a bit of quiet."

"Sounds good. I'll be right back." As Luke stepped into the glowing ballroom, he didn't notice that Nate was standing nearby.

Kat slipped further down the balcony, walking almost soundlessly. Once in the shadows, she leaned against the railing again and closed her eyes, hoping that the pounding in her head would stop. Why had Alex asked about the phone call? Why had she told him that she called, and why had she mentioned the exact date? Was she subconsciously trying to get him to ask more?

Kat was so wrapped in her own thoughts, she didn't notice Nate approaching. "Hi, Kat."

She gasped in surprise, then felt a wave of anger that she tried to ignore. "Nate."

"Alone at last. I hoped we might get a chance to talk." He stepped closer, and Kat suddenly realized from his slight stumble and his slurred voice that he'd had way too much to drink.

She tried to keep her voice calm and nonchalant, "Really? What would we have to talk about?"

"Well, first, how fucking hot you look tonight. And how we need to start spending time together again. What the hell do you see in the guy from your brother's band? He's a goddamn musician for God's sake, no offense to your brother."

As Nate made his last comment, Luke and Josh came out onto the balcony and realized what was happening. Luke started to rush forward, but Josh held him back. "Wait. Let's see what she does."

Kat hissed, giving in to the anger that he felt he could comment on her choices. "Really, Nate? Why do you care who I'm with?"

He ran his hand down her arm, not noticing when she stiffened at his touch. "Oh, come on, Kat. Let's talk about us. Let's talk about what we had."

Her voice was eerily calm. "Nate, you're here with a date."

"So are you. What does that matter?" Moving his hand back up her arm, he went to caress the side of her face, but Kat pulled away. He looked at her strangely. "Oh, I get it. You're still mad at me about that little misunderstanding."

"'*Little misunderstanding*?'"

"Yeah, you know the mix-up with Reid. You aren't still mad about that, are you? I mean, he's my DKE brother, I had to help him."

"So you lied about me?"

"I didn't lie. I just embellished the truth."

"You said I liked rough sex, and that I wanted to be hit."

He shrugged, "So I lied. You did let me tie you up that once with your silk scarf. So I made it sound like more. There was no way I could let Reid get in trouble." He rubbed her arm again, moving closer, looking like he might try to kiss her. "You understand, don't you, baby? Let's put it all behind us, get out of here, and go have some fun."

Luke started again toward them, but stopped as Josh whispered, "Oh, shit, I know that look on her face, and he should back the hell away from her!"

At that moment, Kat stood up straight, bracing herself on her feet more fully, then ran her hands up and down Nate's arms, enticing him. "Of course, I understand, Nate," her tone caressing him. As he looked at her in anticipation, thinking she was about to kiss him, she grasped his arms, and in a split second took a half step backward and jammed her knee into his groin as hard as she could. Shock and pain crossed his face, as he groaned and dropped to his knees, then rolled on his side and vomited off the edge of the balcony. Kat leaned over him. Her voice was low and threatening. "I understand fully, you fucking son of a bitch. I understand that you sold me out to a drinking buddy, and if you ever come near me again, I will make your life a living hell."

With that, Kat turned away, walked toward Luke and Josh, and asked conversationally, "Did you two enjoy yourselves?"

They both started to laugh, before saying in unison, "Sure did." Kat held out her hand, took the two pills from Luke, and swallowed them.

***

Back in the ballroom, Kat said under her breath, "Luke, please don't tell Peter while we're here. He'll make a scene. Please."

Luke squeezed her hand. "I won't tell him here, I promise."

***

Sitting back down at their table, Kat tried to focus on the band, and before long, she felt herself begin to relax and really enjoyed watching them. After almost an hour, including playing a new song Will had written for Mariah, their set ended, and the reception band started up again. Once they finished, Alex pulled Will aside. "Congrats again."

"Thanks, man, I can't believe she finally married me."

"What do you mean?"

"Shit. I've loved her for years, but she kept saying no." He grinned happily. "But she finally said yes!"

"Awesome, man, congrats." Alex took a deep breath. "Hey, this may sound like a really stupid question, but about five years ago, one night did Kat, Peter's sister, call me?"

Will looked at him like he was crazy. "What?"

No matter how hard he tried to keep calm, Alex's voice was impatient. "Did Kat call me one Saturday night about five years ago? It would have been in the winter."

Will's eyes narrowed as he tried to remember something so seemingly trivial from so long ago. "I don't think so."

"Are you sure?" Why would Kat lie about such a thing? "Are you positive?"

"Let me think." Slowly he nodded, "Wait! Yeah. She did. I remember it now because it seemed so weird that she would be calling you. For some reason, I remember I was eating sushi. I know why! It was because right before she called, I had a big bite of wasabi, and I really wanted to get off the phone and get something to drink. She just kept saying something like she was just calling to say hi. I think I told her you'd call her back when you got home." He shrugged, "I guess I sort of thought it was some sort of crush thing." He tipped his head. "Didn't I tell you about it?"

Alex tried to ignore the anger filling him. He'd spent months wondering why she'd never called and fighting the urge to call *her*. Now to find out that she had called, and he'd never known. He suddenly realized how hard it must have been for her to work up the nerve to call, and he'd never called her back. Had she thought he was ignoring her? Why hadn't she ever tried again? "Okay, Will. No biggie." He gave his friend a hug. "We're going to head out, but we'll see you tomorrow at the brunch."

Walking toward the table where Kat sat, he smiled as she looked up at him. Crouching down beside her, he stroked her arm, "Ready to go?"

She put her arms around his neck before leaning forward, so her forehead touched his. "More than you can know."

As they left the ballroom, Alex noticed that Nate was sitting down at the table, sullen and looking unusually pale.

***

Mariah and Will had planned every detail of the wedding, including having a fleet of cars and drivers available for anyone who needed a ride home. Kat gave the driver directions and sank into the back seat of the car next to Alex, her headache finally beginning to subside.

They rode in almost complete silence back to the house. After tipping the driver, they walked up the steps. Stepping into the house, Kat stopped and slipped off her heels. Without them, Alex once again towered over her. He smoothed a curl back from her temple. "Want a glass of wine? We could go sit on the porch, or sit in here."

She smiled broadly. "At this point, I think I'd like several glasses of wine. And let's sit on the porch so we can listen to the waves."

Kat pulled an afghan off a couch to wrap around her shoulders. The two of them settled in Adirondack chairs looking toward the ocean, and Alex opened a bottle of Merlot and poured two glasses. He raised his glass, "I know how much you didn't want to go, but you did it. Congratulations!"

She blew out a deep breath. "Thanks. I am so glad it's over. Thank you for being my date, for keeping me company." She looked down nervously. "I had a really good time with you."

He squeezed her hand, "Me too."

***

The two of them sat watching the waves, talking occasionally. Without fully realizing it, they kept holding hands. The bottle of wine was almost empty when Peter and Luke's car pulled up. As the two men got out of the car, Peter saw them sitting on the porch. His voice rang through the darkness with glee. "You kneed the son of a bitch in the balls and he puked? That is so awesome!"

Kat's voice was patient. "Geez, Luke, when I asked you not to say anything to him about it at the wedding, I thought you might wait until you were back *here*."

Coming up the steps, Luke leaned down to kiss the top of her head. "He knew something was up. As we were leaving, Nate stood up and had trouble walking, then glared at Peter."

Peter came up the steps and opened his arms to his sister. Laughing, she jumped up and hugged him tightly. He kissed her hair. "Wish I could have seen it."

She nodded. "You would have enjoyed it. I don't know what came over me."

Luke squeezed her hand. "Just before you did it, Josh knew what you were going to do. It was awesome."

Still sitting, Alex looked up at the two men, before turning his gaze to Kat, who had sat back down with her feet tucked under her. "What the hell are you talking about?"

Kat shrugged and smirked, and for a moment, Alex saw the girl from five years ago. "When I went out on the balcony to get some air, Nate followed me out. He came on to me…"

Before she could finish the sentence, Alex burst out angrily, "He hit on you? The asshole knew you were with someone!"

Kat picked up his hand, and squeezed it, oblivious to the interested looks from Peter and Luke. "Yeah, he came on to me. He likes you a *lot* by the way. So I politely declined his invitation by rearranging his genitals."

Chapter Twelve

The rest of the weekend passed in a blur. Everyone ate, drank, laughed, and talked. Alex tried to spend as much time with Kat as possible in the mayhem. On Sunday night, the group made a bonfire on the beach. In the firelight, Alex watched Kat. The light of the flames reflected off one of Peter's old Juilliard sweatshirts, just hinting at her curves underneath the heavy fabric. Moving closer, Alex put his arm around her. Kat sharply raised her head to look at him and then smiled tentatively before leaning her head on his shoulder.

With his other hand, he traced the silver ring on her middle finger, rubbing his finger over the piece of onyx. "That's a really interesting ring. Where'd you get it?"

"I bought it in Spain, years ago."

Hearing the intensity in her voice, Alex wound his fingers through hers. "Obviously, it's important to you. Why?"

"It made me feel invincible." She looked down at the ring and thoughtfully twisted it around her finger. "It still does."

"Tell me about it." His tone softened, "Please."

"It's kind of a long story."

Alex looked around at the other couples deep in their own conversations. He stood up, pulling her to her feet. "We've got the time. Let's go over on the dunes."

Kat followed him to where they could sit by themselves. Without thinking about it, Alex sat on the hill with Kat sitting in front of him. He put his arms around her. "Okay, now tell me about the ring."

Kat leaned back against him, loving the sense of safety and warmth in his arms, even as her rational mind screamed she was getting in too deep. "My parents sent me to summer school in Spain when I was sixteen."

"You were pretty young to be so far away and alone." There was no censure in his voice.

She nodded. "They said it was so I'd learn Spanish, but it was really to get me away from some of my friends."

"Why?"

"Because I was beginning to hang out with a group that thought partying was pretty cool."

Alex wanted to know everything about her. "Were you partying with them?"

"No. That's the funny part. My parents were worried about it, but I hung out with those kids because they were into art and theater, and they didn't think I was weird when I carried around my writing journal."

"So in some ways, it was guilt by association?"

"Yeah. It was really that they thought a change would be good, and I already knew I wanted to study Spanish in college, so I was okay with going."

"And the friendships? Did they stay intact when you returned?"

She shook her head. "No, by then they'd moved on, and when I came back, I didn't care anymore if people thought I was weird."

"Okay, sorry for getting off topic. You said you went to Spain."

"The whole start to the summer was surreal. When we got to Madrid, the airport had been bombed."

Her voice was so calm, he thought he'd misunderstood. "It had been *bombed*?"

She nodded. "Yeah, the Basques had bombed it just about the time we took off, so we landed on an outer landing strip way away from what was the airport, and walked all the way to the part that was still standing. It was so hot and dry; it was completely different from anything I'd ever known. It was almost like being reborn."

Trying to keep his voice light, Alex hugged her. "You were only sixteen, and you said you hadn't been doing anything wrong with your friends. How could you need to be reborn so badly?"

"I guess I don't mean literally. It was just such an amazing feeling. I was new."

"Go on."

"We got on buses to drive to the city. Everyone was so nervous; the air smelled metallic, it made my tongue feel funny." Her voice had a faraway tone as she relived the memories. "Hours later, we got there at sunset. I remember the ocean shimmering, and it was really cool because the ocean was on the wrong side to me. I'd never been to the West Coast of anything before, so my bearings were off. When the buses pulled up, there was a crowd waiting. There was a couple off to one side. The guy was really tall, with black hair shellacked into an Elvis-style wave, an oversized Dixie flag belt buckle, and a studded leather vest. The woman had a floor length black coat with purple paisley designs on it. They were awe-inspiring—a cross between the Dukes of Hazard and the Munsters."

"Let me guess?" His voice was amused.

"You got it. I remember my stomach rolling as I walked toward them."

Thinking of how young she'd been, his voice deepened, "You must have been terrified."

"I was so scared that I couldn't breathe. It was funny in a way because when I was little, I'd had an inhaler for asthma, but I'd outgrown it. But walking toward them, I really felt like I needed the inhaler again. Everyone else left with these nice preppie families, and I was left with Elvis and Morticia. Actually, I was only living with her and her parents in their small apartment. Her parents were awesome from the start, but, no matter how hard I tried to follow the conversation that night, it was like being in another universe. The only word I really understood at first was 'banana.' I was so thrilled to understand anything anyone said, that I said I *really* liked bananas. I don't. But to this day, every time I visit, they buy bunches of bananas for me, and I eat them."

"They wanted to make you happy."

"Yeah."

"So that night, after I went to bed, I lay there in the dark and cried and cried. I was so homesick. Once I was cried out, I began to look around. There were pictures of the young woman all over the walls. I remember staring at one, and suddenly I realized that there was only one other bedroom in the apartment, the parents' room." Her voice caught, "I was so upset. I suddenly realized that I was sleeping in the daughter's bed while she was sleeping on the couch. The next day, I tried to convince her to move back into her room, but she ignored me."

Alex rubbed her arms, sensing how embarrassed she still was about this. "That was her choice."

"I know, but I still feel guilty about it. Anyway, my second day, Ana, the girl, knocked on my door and invited me to go out with them. When I said yes, she did my hair and makeup and helped me dress, and when she was done, I looked completely different."

"What do you mean, helped you dress?"

"She picked out this tiny black miniskirt from her closet and pulled out this red silk men's pajama shirt that I had found in a thrift shop in the Village. And she had me wear them together with these tiny strappy sandals. I would never have put together an outfit like that."

Alex pictured her in such an outfit. "Damn, you must have looked incredible."

"I don't know, but it was just such a change for me. Remember, I was the baby in my family, and usually, my mom helped me pick out my clothes."

"How did you feel?"

"Like a split personality. Part of me still wanted to hide under the bed because I had been such a sulky little bitch, crying over scratchy towels while she'd given up what little privacy she had for me, and then I felt guilty for accepting her invitation and help after my behavior. But, the rest of me looked in that mirror and realized I could be whomever I wanted."

"And?"

"Javi and Ana introduced me to their friends, and we went to a fair outside the city. We got off the bus, a huge Ferris wheel glittered in the middle of the fairground, and loud music blared. I was so overwhelmed. They were all speaking Spanish a mile a minute, and I was lost. Luckily, Tixi was without a date, so he kept me company."

"The artist?"

"Yes. Anyway, that night at the fair, he explained words and gestures to me, so I wasn't so lost. Around two in the morning, Tixi lit a cigarette and offered it to me. I inhaled and almost choked to death. I mean, I'd never smoked before—you didn't *do* such things in my family. Tixi almost fell out of the seat laughing at me, and a great friendship was born. Sitting on the top of the Ferris wheel, I felt power and freedom. That was one of the most profound moments of my life when I became my own person."

"And he helped you become that person." Alex tried to keep jealousy out of his voice, struggling with the idea of this man being so important to her for so many years to the point that she would pose nude for him.

Kat looked up at him quizzically, trying to see if he was upset about something, "I guess you could say that. More than anything he was the linguistic conduit that helped me break the ice."

That seemed too simplistic. "Okay."

"So the next morning, I woke up with a purpose. After breakfast, I set out to explore. I walked into a store, picked out my ring, and carried on the conversation needed to buy it. It always reminds me of my independence and my need to try to think before I'm a bitch to someone." She blushed. "At least, it's supposed to make me stop and think."

Alex stroked the ring. "Wow, that's a pretty powerful ring."

Her tone was instantly defensive. "You asked."

"I didn't mean it in a bad way." He squeezed her shoulder. "I love it when you relax enough to talk to me. You're quite an interesting woman."

He leaned closer to whisper into her ear, the heat of his breath making her skin tingle. "And a beautiful, sexy, bewitching one."

Chapter Thirteen

The next morning, the other couples packed up to leave, and once they were gone, everyone pitched in to clean up the house.

As she was carrying towels and sheets down to the washer, Kat passed Alex on the stairs. "Alex, we need to talk about something."

He took the linens from her, "About what?"

"My niece and nephew are coming in a little bit, and well, they're going to think you're my boyfriend." No matter how much she tried not to blush, saying that word made Kat's face turn bright red.

"Am I your boyfriend?" Alex's tone was teasing.

Kat stood still and looked at him, "I don't know what you are. But they are going to want to know, and they are going to overwhelm you."

"Okay. So how about if they ask, we say we are sort of boyfriend-girlfriend?"

"That would work."

Alex looked at her, seeing how important all of this was to her. "Kat, would it be easier for you if we weren't sharing a room?"

The look on her face said that she hadn't thought about that at all. "Oh shit, they will think we're sleeping together."

"Uh-huh."

For a moment, Kat realized how much she would miss curling up beside him at night, waking beside him… "Probably." She looked at him with stricken eyes. "I'm sorry."

Alex dropped the linens so he could take her in his arms. "Stop being sorry. You know how much I want to keep sharing a room with you, you know how much I want to *be* with you, but I also understand that they are little kids."

Kat reached up to put her palms on either side of his face and kissed him. "Thank you."

"You're welcome. Now let's go move me out of your room."

***

It was early afternoon when a gray Volvo station wagon pulled into the driveway. Kat had been standing by the kitchen sink when she heard the crunching of the tires on the gravel, and Alex watched in amusement as she went running out the door.

"Aunt Kat!" a young girl's voice rang out loudly.

"Aunt Kitty-kat!" The other voice was a bit younger, but just as excited.

Moments later, Kat came back into the kitchen, carrying a little blond-haired boy on one arm and holding the hand of a blonde girl, both kids talking over each other to tell her things. Behind them came an amused couple, the woman bearing such a striking resemblance to Kat that Alex knew it had to be her sister Jess.

Kat quickly introduced Alex to her niece Lily, nephew Noah, sister Jess, and her husband, Brian. As introductions were finished, Luke and Peter returned from walking the dog.

That afternoon, most of the adults sat on the porch while Kat played in the sand with Lily and Noah. Just before dinner, Peter's phone rang. He shouted down to his sister, "Kat, it's Leo."

Kat quickly stood up and brushed the sand off her legs before coming up the stairs to take the phone. "I'll take it inside."

Peter looked at her quizzically. "Okay."

***

Inside, Kat moved as far from the porch as she could. "Hi, Leo."

"Kat. I thought I'd hear from you by now. What's your decision?"

"Leo, I told you that I need a few days to make one."

"It's been a couple days!"

Kat sighed, feeling the pressure of a decision looming over her. "Give me forty-eight hours, okay."

"Okay, forty-eight, but not more. You'll call me, or am I calling you?"

"I'll call you."

"Talk to you then. You should do this."

"Bye, Leo."

***

When Kat came into the kitchen, everyone was there. The children were oblivious, but all of the adults looked at her expectantly. She rolled her eyes, "For God's sake, he's my agent. We talk. No more to it than that."

Her sister looked at her, "Bullshit. He's calling you here? Something's up."

Kat shook her head, wanting to stop the conversation before they asked too many questions. "Nah. Just a normal check-in."

***

After dinner, Kat took her niece and nephew upstairs to read to them before tucking them into bed across the hall from her room. Coming downstairs, she sat down next to Alex, and her sister watched with great interest as they entwined their fingers. Jess sat quietly, listening to Brian, Luke, and Peter chatting, until she said pointedly, "Okay, Kat. Alex. What's the deal?"

Kat looked at her older sister and then at Luke, who was checking his watch and started to laugh. "Time, Luke?"

"Eight fifty-nine."

Kat pumped her fist, "Yeah! I win."

Jess looked annoyed. "What the hell are you talking about?"

"I bet Luke that you would ask about Alex and me before nine tonight. I won by one minute. Luke said it would take you until at least nine-thirty and several glasses of wine."

Jess started to laugh. "Well done. So, tell me…"

Kat looked at Alex and explained. "I head back to Madrid in a couple days, but we decided to have a fling while we are here."

Alex corrected her. "You said fling, not me."

Kat's eyes widened, oblivious to the others now watching this conversation with great interest. "We agreed that we understood the parameters."

"I agreed that you had your parameters. As I remember, I told you that we could take it as it came. Remember?"

Jess realized that she might have started something, and tried to regroup. "Okay, fling, not-fling. Just wondering. So, Luke, since you lost the bet, don't you need to go get us all some wine?"

As the conversation moved onto other topics, Kat sat in silence. She still held Alex's hand but seemed to pull further and further inside herself. Finally, around midnight, she stood up. "Good night, all. See you in the morning."

***

A few minutes later, she came out of the bathroom to find Alex sitting on the window seat in her room. He looked at her, trying not to notice the taut nipples pressing through the fabric of her tank top. "We need to talk."

She turned away to pull the covers back on the bed. "No, we don't."

"Yes, we do, and you know it."

She shook her head, still not looking at him. "I can't do this right now. Please, Alex. Not right now."

"No, Kat. Not this time. I'm doing everything I can to make you feel safe. But I'm not okay with a fling. I'm not." Her back was still toward him, "Damn it, Kat. Look at me."

Taking a deep breath, Kat turned to face him, and he was shocked to see tears in her eyes. He took two quick steps to wrap her in his arms. "I'm sorry, baby. Don't cry. It'll be okay."

Leaning against him, the tears started to pour out. "No, it won't be okay. This can only be a fling, Alex. Nothing more. It ends when I leave, no matter how we feel. It has to."

"Why, Kat? Why does it have to end? Unless you have a husband in Madrid, there is no reason for it to end, and at this point, the way I feel, I don't even really care if you *do* have a husband there."

Kat wrapped her arms around him, willing herself not to give in. "Because it does. No matter what, there are things that you don't know about me, things that will keep us apart. Please, Alex, please understand that I wish it were different."

As frustrated as he was, Alex could still hear that she wasn't saying that she didn't want to be with him. So he took a deep breath and started to rub her back without saying a word. He could feel her breathing change from crying to desire. "Alex, don't."

He smiled, his hands stroking her back sensuously. "Don't what?"

"Don't try to change my mind knowing how much I want you. That's not fair."

His body reacted immediately to her words, "You want me?"

"Of course I do. But this isn't going to work between us." Mustering all her willpower, Kat pulled back. "Good night."

Alex wanted to shout in frustration. "Seriously, good night?"

"Seriously."

Alex knew he had to leave the room before he said something he would regret. In his heart, he knew that she wasn't rejecting him, just the idea of them being anything more than a fling. "Good night."

***

In his room, Alex stood at the window, watching the waves, trying to calm his mind. What the hell had happened to her all those years ago? What could be so bad that no one would tell him about it? How could he get through to her?

A small sound made him turn. Almost soundlessly, Kat had entered the room and quickly crossed over to stand in front of him. "Don't say a word. Not a word." With that, she stood on her tiptoes, and kissed him with all of the pent-up emotion and desire she felt.

Alex felt himself immediately respond, and he pulled her into his arms hungrily. The kiss deepened within seconds, tongues teased each other, and hands roamed.

Minutes later, Kat pulled back and looked up at him, her face flushed. "That's how I feel. I don't know what to do with those feelings, but no, I don't want a damn fling either."

Alex smiled, "Okay, then."

"Okay, then." She chewed on her lower lip, "So, can I sleep with you? My room is awfully lonely."

"Of course you can." He leaned down to kiss her briefly. "Same rules, you set the pace."

"Same rules."

***

Just before daybreak, she slid out from under the covers and Alex struggled to wake up. "Where are you going?"

Kat kissed him briefly, fighting the urge to slide back under the covers and kiss him thoroughly. "The kids will come to get me soon."

"Grr." He held out his arms, "Come here for a second."

Kat sat down and leaned toward him. "What?"

Alex kissed her gently. "Good morning. Only because I love those kids am I not pitching a fit about you leaving."

"Good morning to you too."

Chapter Fourteen

After breakfast, Jess and Brian left, and the rest of the day was spent playing in the sand and waves. Peter and Luke offered to go get pizzas for dinner, and so Kat stayed on the porch with the children while Alex set the table for dinner. Kat was lying in the hammock when Noah came over and climbed up so he could cuddle with her. "Aunt Kitty, I really wish you could go to my soccer games. I'm really, really good. Sometimes I score goals."

"I know you're good, No-no. Mommy sends me videos, remember?"

"But I want you to go to my games, not just see the videos."

Lily was sitting on the porch, building a skyscraper with Legos. "Noah, remember, Mommy says to not ask Aunt Kat about coming home."

Kat's stomach clenched. "What do you mean, Lily?"

"Mommy says that asking you about moving back makes you upset, so we shouldn't ask about it."

The idea that her beloved niece and nephew were being coached not to upset her hit Kat like a ton of bricks. She could barely breathe as she hugged her nephew. "Lily, your mom is just trying to protect me like a good big sister, but you two can always ask me *anything*. I love you to the moon and back, and nothing will change that."

Noah snuggled in closer, oblivious to her pain. "Good, then I want you to move back and come to my games, and I could come over and have sleepovers with you and everything."

Lily seemed to decide this was now a safe topic. "Me too. Mommy doesn't get pedicures, and you do, and my friends go for pedicures with their moms or sisters, so I want you to move home so we can do stuff like that."

"I'd like that too." Kat tried to keep her voice calm. "Hey guys, I think the pizza is here. Go see if you can help Uncle Peter and Uncle Luke, okay?"

As the kids ran into the house, they also ran into Alex, who was coming back out onto the porch. He looked at Kat, then stopped. "What happened?"

"What do you mean?"

"What happened while I was inside? You are paper white. You okay?"

Kat sat on the edge of the hammock. Suddenly she felt so old and tired. "No."

"No what?"

She held out her hand to him, and when he came toward her, she rested her head on his chest, welcoming the feel of his arms around her. "No, I'm not okay."

"Why not? What happened?"

She sighed, "Noah asked me about moving back to New York, and Lily reminded him that they aren't supposed to ask." Her voice broke, "I'm such a whack job that my own sister has coached her kids not to ask me about things because it upsets me."

He hugged her. "Oh, baby, you aren't a whack job. She was just trying to protect you."

"She shouldn't have to. The world will tell them soon enough who they can talk to, how they can act, I'm supposed to be one of the people they can talk to about anything, and they are being taught not to upset me."

"I don't know what to say."

"How about I need to get my shit together?"

Alex leaned down and kissed her. After a moment's hesitation, she kissed him back. When he pulled back, he stroked her hair. "Okay. How about you get your shit together? Anything I can do to help?"

Kat looked at him, and her eyes filled with tears. "Don't give up on me, even when I tell you too."

Alex was shocked by her answer, and brushed the tears away. "I won't, I promise."

Just then the door banged open, and Noah yelled, "Dinner! Everyone get washed up for dinner!"

***

All through dinner, Kat barely said a word. After helping clean up, she walked over to Peter. "Pete, can I borrow your phone? I need to make a couple calls."

"You okay?"

She nodded. "Yeah. I just need to take care of a few things. I'm going upstairs to make the calls because I need to make sure I can hear."

As Luke walked by, he put his arm around her. "The three of us will take the monsters for one last walk, so you'll have some privacy."

***

In her room, Kat sat down at the window seat, looking out at the ocean, seeing Luke and Peter walking, swinging Noah between them, Alex giving Lily a piggyback. It was time to make the decision…

Fifteen minutes later, Kat came downstairs and pulled out some cookie dough from the fridge. When the group came back into the kitchen, she was making ice cream sandwiches with the warm cookies.

Within minutes, all were seated at the table enjoying the treat, dripping ice cream everywhere. Licking her fingers, Kat turned to Noah. "Okay, No-no, so when do you play soccer again?"

Through a mouthful of ice cream, his answer was a bit garbled. "Not 'til kindergarten starts. In the fall. You know, cause then I start real school."

"Oh. So would it be okay if I came to some of your games? I can't go to all of them, but I can go to some."

Noah was oblivious to the very interested looks Alex, Peter, Lily, and Luke were giving Kat, who kept her eyes on her ice cream. Lily finally spoke, her tone very adult. "Aunt Kat, to come to Noah's games, you'd have to be here a lot. Are you coming back for a vacation or something?"

Kat lifted her eyes to look right at her brother, her face flushed with nerves. "Lil, what I was thinking was that if it was okay with Uncle Peter and Uncle Luke, I'd move home to live with them again, so I should be around for some of Noah's games, and be able to get pedicures with you."

Peter inhaled so sharply, he started to choke on his cookie. "What the fuck are you talking about?"

Lily sounded shocked. "Uncle Peter, you said a bad word!"

"Yeah, Lil, I did, sorry." He looked at his sister. "What are you saying?"

"Is it okay if I move home with you guys? Really okay? Like not screw up your lives by living with you?"

Luke and Alex both looked on in total shock as Peter put down his cookie. "You're serious? You're moving home? Holy shit!" He jumped up and lifted her in a bear hug. "Yes, yes, yes!"

Mayhem ensued for the next few minutes as the kids and Peter and Luke hugged and danced around. Finally, Kat stood up, got a wet dishrag, and wiped the table down. "Okay monsters, now you need to go in the living room and find something for us to watch, okay?"

The two ran from the room, still talking about having Kat home to do things with them. When the kitchen was quiet, Luke looked at Kat. "Now explain the details. What the hell happened from your little tirade last night about moving back to Madrid and now?"

Kat sighed and sat down, without realizing it, she took Alex's hand and squeezed it. "So, when I met with Leo last week, it was because *Newsweek* was offering me a full-time role as their Latin America/Hispanic correspondent. In order to do it, I'd have to be based here in New York, but the deal they were offering is that my first loyalty would be to them, but I could still freelance at times and could keep writing books too." Then, she smiled at Alex. "It really hit me today that it's time to come home."

Peter stood up and kissed the top of Kat's head. "Champagne?"

She squeezed Alex's hand again. "Sounds great."

***

Hours later, all retired for the evening. Without asking, Kat came into Alex's room and sat on his bed. "We need to talk."

He had been waiting for this opportunity for hours, so he sat on the window seat so he could face her. "That probably would be a good idea."

She rubbed her temple, looking for the right words, "Here's where I'm at. I just agreed to take a job here, move back, and move in with my brother and his partner. My life just got turned upside down in a matter of minutes."

"Uh-huh."

"And…" Kat seemed unsure of how to go on.

"And what?"

"Shit. Alex, I really like you. I don't want just a fling. But, now I've turned my life inside out, and I need to make sure that I did it for the right reasons."

"Meaning?"

"Meaning that what I am asking is that we have this time now, then I have to go back to Madrid for a couple weeks to pack, etc., then I'll move here. Then I will need time to get used to my new job and living with Peter and Luke again, not just visiting them."

"Of course." Alex still wasn't sure where she was going with this conversation.

"What I am asking is if you'd be okay with us sort of ending this when I leave in a couple days, then like we talk on the phone or email and stuff, then maybe in the fall when you come back to record, we could see where we are at?"

Emotions raced through Alex at the speed of light. Thrilled that she was admitting to wanting more with him, frustrated as hell at the thought of having to be apart—all of it swirled around. "Kat, so what you're saying is that we take a break for a bit, while you get settled? Then we see where we are at?"

"Yes." It sounded better in her head than when Alex said it...

Alex stood up and held out his hand. Kat took his hand, and he pulled her up and took her in his arms. He leaned down to kiss her forehead. "So I get just a few more days with you, then you walk away, we do the phone/email thing for a while, then be back together in the fall? What about others? What about dating others?"

For a moment, Kat felt like someone had punched her and it showed on her face. Did he *want* to date others? "I don't know."

Alex leaned down and kissed her deeply, becoming painfully aroused as she responded with all of the emotion she felt. When the kiss ended, he looked down at her tenderly. "I saw your face. You thought I meant that I wanted to be able to ask someone else out with no strings attached. That wasn't what I was asking." He nibbled on her top lip, smiling as she tightened her arms around his neck. "Let me be clear. I don't like the idea of walking away from you in a couple days. I'd much rather get on the plane with you, help you pack, and get you back here as soon as possible. But I do understand your point and can put up with your plan with relative grace, but I want to be clear that this is a monogamous time. I'm not waiting to see if my feelings for you change, I'm waiting for you to get settled in enough to not freak out about my being in your life. And I'm not okay with this if I think you might be going out with someone else in the meantime."

Her relief at his explanation was clear on her face, "I wouldn't be going out with anyone else. I just need to get my life in order."

"Okay."

"Okay?"

He stooped slightly to scoop her into his arms and carried her to the side of the bed before laying her down gently. "Okay. We'll do it your way."

Alex laid down beside her on the bed. "A couple more days, then the long distance thing until the fall."

"Thank you." Her eyes clouded. "You know that there are still things I can't tell you."

He kissed the tip of her nose. "Kat, when and if you are ready to tell me, you'll tell me. I can wait, even if you never tell me, as long as you aren't pushing me away."

She wrapped her arms around his neck. "I don't want to push you away anymore. Just give me time, okay?"

"All the time you need."

Chapter Fifteen

Thursday night, back in New York, Kat organized her bag while Alex sat on the couch watching her. She looked up and saw him looking at her with a bemused look. "What? What am I doing now?"

"You've packed and unpacked the bag three times. Why do you keep changing it?"

She blushed. "I get so nervous, I need to have my stuff easily accessible, so I can get it quickly."

"I'd still go with you, you know."

She sat down next to him. "I know. And you know I'd really like you to go with me, but then it feels like the biggest reason I'm moving home is to be with you."

"And that would be such a horrible thing?" Alex tried to keep his voice neutral, knowing how quickly she would get defensive.

She touched his face. "No, it wouldn't. We both know that you are part of the reason I'm coming home, but to keep myself from freaking out, I need to feel like the biggest reasons are family and work. I'm not ready to say that I'm turning my personal and professional lives completely upside down over a relationship that is barely a week old. That's all I'm saying."

"Fine." He tried to lighten the mood. "How long do I have to wait after you get to Madrid before I'm allowed to call you?"

"I promise to call *you* as soon as I get there."

***

Kat had been back in Madrid only a couple days when Tixi called. "So, you're really moving back to New York?"

"You know I am. We've talked about this."

"What about the opening?" For a moment, Kat heard uncertainty in her friend's voice, "You said you'd go to the opening, but if you leave next week for New York, you'll miss it."

Kat rubbed her forehead, torn between her promise to go to the opening, the biggest of her friend's career, and getting started on her new life. "You're right. I *did* promise. I'll be there. Let me figure out the details."

After saying good-bye, Kat looked at flight options on the internet, then looked at the time and figured it was late enough that calling her brother wouldn't wake him up. She smiled when he answered the phone. His voice made it clear that she was *still* too early.

"What?"

"Morning, Pete."

He instantly sounded concerned. "You okay? What's wrong?"

"Nothing is wrong. I'm just wondering if you and Luke want to meet me in Barcelona next week for a couple days." She grinned. "I'll even spring for the flights and hotel."

"Barcelona, what the hell are you talking about?"

Later, Kat realized that Luke must also still have been in bed because he then grabbed the phone. "Barcelona, for the opening? Of course, we'll be there! I told you back when you were here that I'd love to go, but Pete would love to too."

Kat and Luke then chatted for a few minutes, agreed that Kat would send them the travel itinerary and make the arrangements, then promised to talk later in the day when all the details had been finalized. After hanging up, Kat decided a run would help her calm her mind, so she pulled on her running clothes and headed out toward the Retiro Park.

An hour later, Kat let herself into the apartment and found her message light blinking. "Kat, it's Luke. Just a thought, but what about inviting Alex to the opening too? If so, see if you can book us all on the same flight out of New York and we can travel together."

Kat dialed Luke's cell. "Would that be too much?"

"Hello to you too." Luke knew what she was talking about, "No. Kat, you know how he feels. He wanted to go to Spain to help you pack. You're the one who said no. Besides, I think he would think it was a romantic gesture."

"I guess I could ask or offer or whatever. I mean, he might not be able to, but at least would feel like I wanted him to come with us." Her eyes widened. "But Luke, what the hell do I do about hotel rooms?"

"Good Lord, Kat. Stop being such a friggin' prude. I know you aren't having sex with him yet, but you slept with him at the shore and when you guys got back here. Just share a room with him."

Kat leaned back in her desk chair. "But Luke, I mean, how long can I keep sharing a room with him without having sex?"

"I don't know. That's between you guys. I guess I'd say that when or if he has an issue with it, he'll tell you." Luke paused. "Don't you want to have sex with him?"

"Oh shit, Luke. I really do. But you know as well as I do that the past will be an issue at some point, and …"

Luke suddenly realized where she was going with her comment. "And if you get naked with him, he'll see your tattoo and ask about it, and then you can't keep it a secret then." He took a deep breath, "Kat, listen to me, Alex is a great guy. He really, really likes you, not just wants to jump you. You could tell him, and he won't run away."

She sounded so sad. "Luke, there is no way that you know that for sure. But, I do know that if this is really going somewhere, I will have to tell him at some point. But I'm not there yet."

Luke tried to bring some humor back to the conversation. "Or, you can just make sure the lights are off when you jump him."

She laughed. "Hell no, that man is gorgeous. If I'm going to jump him, I want to see him!"

"So, you going to ask him?"

"Yeah."

"Love you."

Kat's eyes suddenly filled with tears. "I love you too, Luke. Thanks for listening."

***

Kat sat at her desk, her phone in her hand. Should she call, or email? She wanted to hear his voice, but calling would put him on the spot. An email would allow him to think and respond without feeling pressured. Finally, she recognized the time difference. It would be awfully early in California for a phone call. Maybe she should look up flight information, work on hotel rooms, and then send him an email. She sighed, opened her laptop, and started looking at details. An hour later, she wrote an email.

Good morning— so I have an idea, and I wanted to send it to you this way so you could think about it without feeling pressured because I was on the phone with you waiting for an answer. I was wondering if you'd like to fly to NY, meet Peter and Luke, and come over to Barcelona next weekend for Tixi's art opening. I thought we could stay in Barcelona for a long weekend, see some sights, that sort of thing. I would buy your air tickets. Please don't feel pressured. I know it's a long way to travel for a long weekend, but I wanted to invite you.

Kat knew the email sounded awkward, but couldn't figure out how to fix it. Finally, she hit "send" and got up and grabbed her purse. She turned her cell off, and headed to the Prado to try to lose herself in the art.

***

Two hours later, Kat had to admit to herself that she was avoiding her apartment and cell phone because she was nervous about Alex's response. What if he said no? What if he said *yes*? Was she ready for the sort of commitment that having him fly across the ocean for a weekend insinuated? How long could she keep asking him to share a bed with her with no sex? Just thinking about him naked made her heart start to race. Shaking her head, she took a calming breath. "Okay, buttercup. You sent the damn email. It's time to see if he responded."

Opening her apartment door, she could see the blinking light on her machine. Three short blinks meant that she had three messages. Kat pulled her cell out of her purse and turned it on, and as soon as it powered up, her voicemail indicator and text tones sounded.

Kat sat at her desk, took a deep breath, and hit the play button. Peter's voice came on. "Hey brat, just wanted to say that I love the Barcelona idea. Can't wait to see you."

The second message was from the owner of the apartment, asking her to dinner before she moved out. Kat started to feel stupid that she had been so nervous when Alex hadn't responded yet.

Suddenly his voice filled the room, "Hey. Where are you? You send me an email, then disappear? I tried your cell, but it wasn't on, and now you're not answering here." He chuckled. "Call me."

Shit! He didn't give an answer. So she was going to have to talk to him about this after all. She hit play on her cell phone. "Good morning. Just got your email, trying to call you, but your phone is off. Call me." Grr. No answer there either. Kat opened the text message, and started to laugh. *If you want to know my answer to the invitation, you are going to have to call me and talk to me, not just wait for a text or voicemail.*

Kat dialed his cell and was shocked when it went to voicemail. He'd told her to call him; now he wasn't answering? She tried to keep her voice steady, "Hey, it's me. I got your messages, and I'm calling you—tag, you're it, call me."

Thirty seconds later, her cell rang. When she answered, he started to laugh. "I was just messing with you. I knew damn well that you were avoiding my calls this morning, so I figured I'd make you leave me a message."

Kat felt herself relax. "That is so mean!"

"Yup." His voice deepened. "Tell me, were you honestly nervous I'd say no? I practically begged you to let me go with you to Madrid to help you pack. Why wouldn't I come to Barcelona?"

When he put it that way, Kat realized how silly she'd been. "I know. But, I was overthinking, and got convinced that it was too much to ask."

"I would love to meet you in Barcelona, and, no, you aren't paying for my ticket."

"But I can order them together with Peter and Luke's tickets."

"Fine, and then I'll pay you back."

Kat smiled. "Okay. So I'll book the tickets in a few minutes, including you flying to New York the day before, and I'll get hotel rooms."

"Babe, let me take care of booking getting to and from New York. You do New York to Barcelona and back. How's that?"

"That works for me."

"As soon as you have that information, let me know, and I can book the rest." His voice got softer, more sensual. "So you are inviting me to an art opening to see pictures of you naked?"

Kat blushed, glad he couldn't see her face. "Yes, I mean no." He laughed, and Kat tried to get her thoughts organized. "Yes, I am inviting you to the opening. And yes, there are pictures of me naked in it. But no, I wasn't specifically inviting you to see *those* particular paintings."

***

Two hours later, Kat had all of the international flights booked, as well as two rooms in a seaside hotel, looking at the waterfront. She then emailed all the information to Peter, Luke, and Alex. Sitting there at her desk, she hugged herself happily, then dialed the phone. Alex answered on the third ring. "Hey."

"Hey. Are we all booked?"

"We are. You get there Thursday late afternoon if the flight is on time, and I will meet you at the airport. Friday and Saturday, we can relax during the day. The opening is Saturday night. Sunday, I thought we could go to the Sagrada Familia for a concert, then you all fly out mid-day on Tuesday, I'll go back to Madrid and finish up here, then I fly back to New York on Saturday."

"Do you want me to stay with you and fly home?"

Her voice softened, almost longingly. "I would love you to. But I'm not ready for that. It was a really big step for me to invite you to come to Barcelona, and …"

His voice caressed her. "Baby, it's okay. I understand. If you change your mind at the last minute and want me to stay, I would be happy to. Otherwise, getting to see you for a few days like this is an unexpected gift."

"I'm really, really glad you are coming."

"Me too."

***

On Wednesday, Kat took the train to Barcelona. That night, she sat alone on the balcony of her hotel room, sipping wine, looking at the twinkling lights on the waterfront. She poured herself more red wine, and put her feet up on the ottoman, and then her cell phone chirped softly beside her. "Hello?"

"I am sitting at your kitchen table, where are you? Why am I here without you?"

She pictured him there. "I'm sitting on our balcony, drinking wine, watching the waterfront." Maybe the wine made her bolder. "Thinking of you. Wishing you were here too."

"Less than twenty-four hours, and I'll be there." His voice softened. "Probably we need to eat dinner with Peter and Luke tomorrow night, but then, how about a nice bottle of wine on that balcony, just the two of us?"

"That sounds perfect."

***

The next afternoon, Kat almost cried when she received a text message from the airline saying the flight had been delayed by two hours. Finally, waiting at the gate, she saw the three men walking toward her. Her heart jumped, and she felt like a teenager again. Peter reached her first. "I don't care that I should let you kiss Alex first, I am so excited to see you, and he can wait." Peter picked her up in a hug, before putting her down next to Luke.

Luke hugged her quickly. "Thanks for the invite, Kat. So glad we could do it!"

Kat turned toward Alex, who was looking at her with a smile, his eyes darkening as he stepped toward her. "My turn?"

"Your turn."

He opened his arms, hugged her close, and then kissed her deeply. "Hi."

Kat was breathless. "Hi."

Peter laughed. "Okay, hotel, shower, beer, dinner, in that order."

***

Over dinner at a small seafood restaurant near the hotel, the men regaled Kat with stories of their last couple of weeks. Watching her brother and Luke, she suddenly realized how excited she was about moving home.

Alex squeezed her hand. "What?"

"What, what?"

"You looked like you just realized something."

She tipped her head looking at him. How did he know that? "I did. I just realized how excited I am to move back to New York."

"Good." His tone was gentle. "And me?"

How could she deny it? "And you." She paused, seeing his eyes light up. "You know…"

"I know. I know. Parameters and slow."

***

Back at the hotel, Peter hugged his sister. "Night, brat. We aren't setting an alarm, so if you get up early because you're on the correct time zone, and you want to go do something, no problem. Just leave us a message, and we'll catch up with you at some point."

"Sounds good." She looked at Luke. "Luke, Tixi asked if you wanted to stop by the gallery Friday during the final set-up. He thought you might like time to look without a crowd."

Luke beamed. "I'd love that. How about we plan that you and I will go there by ourselves on Friday afternoon, and these guys can amuse themselves."

"Sounds like a plan."

***

In their room, Alex smiled when he saw the bottle of wine and two glasses on the table on the balcony. "Ahh, a woman who thinks ahead."

Kat looked unsure for a second. "I just realized that I never asked you if you still wanted to sit on the balcony. You've been traveling all day, so if you're too tired, I understand. I mean, we can always do that tomorrow night, the wine would keep." Even to her own ears, she sounded like an idiot.

Alex put his hands on his hips and looked at her steadily. "Katherine."

The use of her full name got her full attention. "Yes?"

His frustration was clear. "Right now, I don't give a flying fuck if I've been up for three days straight, which, for the record, I haven't, when I have the chance to be alone with you, that's what I'm going to do." He took a step toward her. "And, baby, you need to stop worrying so much. If I want something, you are going to know. I want you to do the same." He reached out and put his hands possessively on her hips, pulling her toward him. "What I want right now is to kiss you senseless, then take a quick shower." He grinned suggestively. "You are welcome to shower with me if you want. Then I want to sit on the balcony with you and drink wine, and you tell me about Barcelona or anything else you want to talk about."

With that, he lowered his head and kissed her with all of the pent-up longing and desire.

When the kiss ended, Alex gazed down at her. "Now I'm taking a shower. The invitation still holds…"

Kat felt desire flow through her in a hot rush. She swatted at him. "Take your shower. I'm pouring wine, and if you don't hurry, I'll drink it before you come out."

"Then we'll order more."

***

The next day, Kat was awake early and took her laptop out to the balcony while Alex slept. Several hours later, a noise behind her made her turn, as Alex walked out onto the balcony wearing only his pajama bottoms. Kat tried not to react, but before she could stop herself, Alex saw the rush of absolute desire cross her face. Whatever it was that was keeping her from letting herself be with him physically, it certainly wasn't that she didn't want him. Alex leaned down over her from behind, putting his hands on her shoulders and rubbing them slowly. "Good morning. Have you been awake long?"

"Good morning. A couple hours." She smiled up at him. "How'd you sleep?"

"Really well, except for someone snoring next to me."

She grinned. "Oh well, shit happens."

Alex laughed. "Come here."

Kat looked up at him, "Huh?"

He walked around her chair, so he was in front of her and held out his hands. Sunlight glinted off the hair on his chest, and for a moment, Kat fought the urge to run her hands down his chest and abdomen. "Come here."

Kat put the laptop on the table and stood up. Alex pulled her toward him, wrapped his arms tightly around her, and kissed her deeply. Within seconds, her hands were grasping his back, holding on tightly as desire swamped her again. A noise in the hallway made them pull apart. Alex said ruefully, "Damn, just as it was getting really interesting…"

Kat straightened her clothes. "Good morning."

***

The rest of the day, they meandered around the old quarter of Barcelona, wandering in and out of shops, visiting galleries, and watching people. Mid-afternoon, they returned to the hotel to meet Peter and Luke, and the four of them went to the Picasso museum, then out to dinner.

The next day, the four went to the beach until Kat and Luke had to go back to the hotel to get ready to go to the gallery. In their room, Alex watched as Kat put in her earrings. She stared at him, seeing his serious look. "What's the matter?"

He tried to smile, looking uncomfortable. "You'll laugh."

"No, I won't." She walked over to him. "What's going on?"

He shook his head. "It sounds stupid, but I feel jealous."

Kat looked at him, confused. "Of what? Or who?"

He rolled his eyes. "I know you've explained and explained the relationship, but I'm still jealous as hell that you are going to the gallery to see Tixi without me." He flopped back on the bed, feeling like an idiot.

A wave of giddiness washed over her. She walked over to the bed, climbed onto it, and on her hands and knees, moved beside Alex. She put her arms on either side of him so she could look down at him. "Alex. Look at me."

He peered up at her, still clearly embarrassed. "That is the most beautiful thing anyone has ever said to me." Her voice softened, and he could see the raw emotion in her eyes. "I'm sorry you feel jealous, there is no need for you to be at all, but still, that makes me feel..." Her voice trailed off.

His hands went to her waist. "Feel what?"

"Like a princess. That you care that much is just amazing."

Alex's smile lit his face. "Thank you. And yes, I am pouting because I'm jealous. But if it makes you happy, I can live with it." He pulled her by the waist so that she was on top of him. "I want you here, with me. Just me." He kissed her, feeling her body relax down onto his. His arms tightened around her, his hands roaming down her back.

Kat felt her heart began to race, and without meaning to, she molded her body to his, feeling his manhood strain against her. With every ounce of her being, she wanted nothing more than to make love to him. With a groan, she pulled back to look into his eyes.

He could see the uncertainty in them. He rubbed her back comfortingly, trying to control his arousal. "It's okay, babe. I'm sorry I pushed."

She kissed the tip of his nose. "You didn't push. Alex, the thing is, I want you more than I can tell you. I just"—she struggled for words—"I'm not ready. I can't make love to you until I'm ready to tell you everything. And I'm not there, I'm trying, but I'm not there." She paused. "Yet."

His arms tightened around her. "You want me?"

She heard his need for reassurance. "Yes, I want you. So much it hurts at times."

"And you're okay with me saying that I want you just as much?" His voice deepened. "That isn't going to make you run?"

She grinned. "Yes, I mean, I'd prefer if you didn't bring it up at dinner with my brother, but otherwise, yes."

Moving with speed and grace, Alex rolled them so he was looking down at Kat. "Then let me assure you, I want you so badly that I'm taking a hell of a lot of cold showers. And yes, I can wait as long as it takes until you're ready." He kissed her briefly. "Know that nothing you tell me will change how I feel."

***

The next evening, Alex was tying his tie as Kat came out of the bathroom wearing a very simple sleeveless black dress with a low back and strappy black high-heeled sandals. His eyes widened. "Wow." He walked over to her, his tie hanging down. "You look amazing."

She grasped the ends of his tie, pulling his head down to kiss him. "So do you."

***

At the gallery, wait staff circulated with trays of champagne, wine, and hors d'oeuvres. Soon after arriving, Kat, Alex, Peter, and Luke were standing in the main gallery sipping wine when they heard a woman's voice call, "Kat, *aqui. Aqui.*" Kat turned and pulled Alex by the hand toward a very pregnant woman. Speaking in rapid Spanish, Kat hugged and kissed her before switching to English and introducing Alex to Monce, Tixi's wife. Peter and Luke then hugged and kissed Monce, chattering about the last time they had seen her.

Just then, the man who Alex recognized from the banner outside as Tixi strode over. For a millisecond, Alex felt hostility fill him, thinking of Kat being with the tall, dark-haired, and handsome man. The look of joy on Kat's face as she saw Tixi made Alex's jaw tighten. Tixi hugged Kat, kissed her on each cheek, then kissed her very briefly on the lips, and Alex wanted to hit him. Taking a deep breath, Alex tried to hold onto Kat's assurances that there was nothing more than friendship between them. And he was married. Alex couldn't hear fully or understand their conversation, but Kat was clearly congratulating him on the show. Kat then again switched to English, and reintroduced Luke and Peter, before pulling Alex forward by the hand. "Tixi, this is my boyfriend, Alex. Alex, this is my old friend, Tixi."

The word "boyfriend" took all of the anger out of Alex, and for a moment, he felt a swell of masculine pride. He held out his hand to shake Tixi's, but Tixi grabbed him and kissed him on both cheeks. In heavily accented English, Tixi said, "So glad to meet you. You're all Kat has talked about recently."

Alex was stunned by the comment, then almost stuttered, "So good to meet you."

Soon, Tixi had to move on to talk to other visitors, and Peter and Luke wandered off to look at the art. Kat and

Alex sipped champagne without talking. Finally, Kat raised an eyebrow. "So, are we going to stand here all night, or do you want to go look at the art?"

He grinned. "Do I want to go look at the art, or go look specifically at the paintings of you?" Alex wrapped his arm around Kat's waist. "You know which ones I'm looking for, but yes, let's go look at all the art."

As they wandered around the gallery, Kat realized that people were beginning to look at her with interest. She squeezed Alex's hand. "I guess they've figured out who I am."

The nudes were all in one wing of the gallery space. The first painting Alex saw was of a pregnant Monce seemingly getting dressed, pulling on a sleeve of a shirt. As much as Alex didn't want to be impressed by Tixi's work, he had to admit they were amazing. Turning a corner, Alex suddenly saw an almost life-sized painting of Kat standing atop a pile of rocks, looking toward a pond, her body facing away from the artist, but fully naked. His breath caught as he saw the beauty of the painting, the way the light danced on her skin, the shadows hinting at her coiled movement like she was ready to dive off the rocks into the water below.

Putting down his now-empty glass, he wrapped his arms around Kat from behind, pulling her into his warmth. "It is amazing."

"Isn't it? Not because it's me, but because he's so good at this."

He nibbled her ear, trying to control his reaction when her nipples tightened under the thin cloth. "Yes, his talent is mind-boggling, and it's also amazing because it's you."

Just then, Peter and Luke came up. Peter smiled, seeing Kat in Alex's arms. "Hey, Kitty Kat, so I admit it. This is amazing."

She grinned at him. "I told you so!"

***

The rest of the evening, they wandered the gallery and visited with Monce, Tixi, and the gallery owner. At one point, Alex excused himself to find the restroom. When he came out of the bathroom, Kat was standing in the hallway nearby. He walked over and brushed a curl from her face. "You okay?"

She ducked shyly. "Yeah. I'm better than okay. It's just…"

"What?"

She reached up to wrap her arms around his neck. "It's just that when you walked away, I realized that you've had your arm or arms around me all night, and it felt funny when you left." She looked down, and Alex could see a blush rising on her cheeks. "You've been almost possessive tonight, and I liked it."

Alex pushed her back against the wall so that their bodies were touching. "I'm trying like hell to not growl at men looking at you, and I almost punched Tixi when he kissed you. I love touching you, and there is no way on God's earth that I'm going to let the guys who are salivating over the paintings of you think they can come hit on you. You came here with me tonight, and …" He leaned close, so that she felt the heat of his breath on her lips. "And you're going home with me tonight."

***

It was well after midnight when the two couples left the gallery. Kat offered to get a cab, but the men were happy to walk back to the hotel, as was Kat. At the hotel, they said goodnight and went to their rooms.

While Kat changed her clothes, Alex stood on the balcony and looked out at the still bustling waterfront. How could he get her to trust him? What could be so bad in her past that she wouldn't talk to him about it? What could have happened that she was so afraid that he would run once he knew? He jumped as he felt a hand on his shoulder, not having heard Kat cross the room to him. He turned, towering over her in her bare feet. Her simple tank top and pajama shorts made her look so young, yet so sexy.

He cleared his throat. "Hey."

"Hey." She stepped forward, stood on her tiptoes, and wrapped her arms around his neck. "So, are you ready to sleep, or do you want to sit out here for a bit?"

"Sitting out here sounds great, you?"

"Perfect. Do you want me to order some wine?"

"Please. I'll go get changed."

Minutes later, as Alex came out of the bathroom, the wine arrived. Kat carried the tray of wine and a small plate of olives out to the balcony, and Alex poured them some wine. He raised his glass. "To the star of the show tonight."

She laughed. "Hardly." She smiled at him. "Thanks for coming over, and for going to the show. I know it was a weird thing to ask, but I'm really glad you're here."

"Me too."

They talked quietly, making plans for the next day, avoiding talking about what would happen when Alex left Barcelona. Finally, when all the wine was gone, Alex stood up. "C'mon, princess. Time to get some sleep."

***

The next morning, the four went out for a late brunch, then headed over the Sagrada Familia for a chamber concert. Leaving the cathedral, Kat turned her phone on and seemed surprised when a text message beeped. Kat looked at the message and shook her head.

Alex looked at her. "What's up?"

"Monce sent a message asking what we are doing tonight."

"Why?"

Kat rolled her eyes. "She's eight months pregnant, but she wants to go out dancing tonight and wants to know if we want to go with them."

Peter answered before Alex could. "Sounds great. How about we take them to dinner first?"

Kat stopped walking to look at her brother. "You want to go dancing?"

"Of course, well really, I want to hear the music." Peter looked at Luke. "What do you think?"

"Sounds like a great plan. Alex?"

Alex looked at Kat, then at the other men. "If Kat wants to go, I'm happy to."

She sounded exasperated. "Fine."

***

Back at the hotel, Kat stood at the balcony railing. Alex came up behind her and started rubbing her shoulders, feeling the tension in the muscles at the base of her neck. "Why don't you want to go tonight?"

She shrugged. "It's not that I don't want to go. They're my friends, and I love them, and I love being with them, and in a couple days, I'm moving away. But…"

"But what?"

Her words rushed out. "But I wanted to be alone with you tonight, not be with a crowd."

He wrapped his arms around her, rubbing her crossed arms. "Me too. But, we can go out, eat, dance, and then come back here and be alone."

She leaned back against him. "Okay."

He leaned down and gently kissed the side of her neck. "Besides, I get to dance with you, and holding you close for hours sounds like a great idea." He kept nuzzling her neck, feeling her breathing change.

She turned in his arms, putting her arms around his neck. "And what if the music is fast?"

Alex started dropping light kisses on her shoulder and neck. He could feel her nipples harden as they rubbed against his chest, and he fought the urge to stroke her breasts. "Then I'll pull you into a dark corner so I can kiss you as much as I want."

Kat tipped her head, allowing him easier access to the hollow at the base of her neck. When he kissed her there, she moaned softly and pulled back slightly. "Okay. Cold shower time."

Alex didn't let her go. "Why? I know the rules, and I agreed to them. So I'm not going to push this too far. I can control myself no matter how much I want you, so why not enjoy it."

Kat tightened her arms around his neck and kissed him deeply. When she pulled back, she looked up at him and said, "I know you won't push, but I can't say the same about myself." Alex looked confused, so she continued, turning bright red as she said, "I can't say that I can stop. But I know it's not right for this to go too far if I can't be completely honest with you. And no matter how much I'm trying, I'm not there yet."

He looked at her intently. "Have you lied to me?"

"No."

"Then what have you not been honest about?"

He could see her struggling to explain. "Maybe that's not the right way to say it. Maybe what I'm trying to say is that, until I'm ready to be open about my past, I can't do more than we are. And every time you touch me …" She looked down in embarrassment. "Damn, every time you *look* at me, I become a hormone-crazed idiot."

Alex grinned. "Hormone-crazed?"

She swatted at him. "Stop looking so smug."

"Hormone-crazed…"

***

Kat emerged from the bathroom ready to go out. Alex felt his mouth go dry. She was wearing a dark maroon dress, lower cut than some of her other dresses, and when she turned, he realized it was backless. He swallowed. "Shit."

She smiled and walked toward him. "I'll take that as a compliment."

He pulled her toward him and kissed her until they were both breathless. "Hell, yes. And I will kill any guy who hits on you tonight."

She put her hands on his chest, feeling his body heat through the fabric. "And how exactly is anyone going to hit on me when you said I was going to be dancing with you all night?"

"Just saying."

***

The two couples walked down to the waterfront and met Tixi and Monce for dinner. Alex had to smile when he saw Monce, so obviously very pregnant, was also in a slinky dress and high heels. After dinner, the six walked to a nearby dance club.

Over the next several hours, the couples danced, laughed, and all except Monce drank lots of wine. Finally, Monce pulled Kat aside to say something in her ear, then went to find the bathroom. Kat began to laugh before telling the men that Monce wanted to go to a local tango club. Peter started to chuckle. "She wants to tango at eight months pregnant?"

Kat nodded. "Yeah. You've seen her tango before. Besides, she's been dancing all night, and still, has more energy than the rest of us."

Luke nodded. "I'm game. Peter and Alex?" Peter nodded and looked at Alex, who also nodded.

As Monce returned to the table, Kat said, "Then let's go."

***

At the tango club, Peter, Luke, Alex, and Kat sat down on the comfortable couches facing the dance floor, enjoying the less raucous music. As soon as a new tango was ready to start, Monce and Tixi went dancing, and Alex was amazed at how graceful Monce was, even at eight months. Watching Tixi look at her, he fully understood what Kat had been trying to explain to him. The look on Tixi's face was raw with love and desire for his wife.

Finally, Monce pulled Tixi by the hand toward the table and sat down. "I'm done." She kissed Kat on the cheek, and said something to her in Spanish that Alex couldn't fully hear or understand. Kat shook her head. Monce said it again, with more vehemence. Kat shook her head and responded sharply in Spanish. Monce then turned to Alex, "Alex, you don't mind, do you? If Tixi and Kat dance once? Do you?" Before Alex could answer, Kat shot back a response that made Monce laugh.

Alex looked at Kat quizzically. Kat could tango? Well enough to dance with Tixi, who even to Alex, was a damn fine dancer? Seriously? Alex looked at Monce, "Of course not. I'd love to see Kat tango."

Kat's eyes widened at him, but it was Peter who spoke first. "Awesome! We haven't seen you dance for years. Go for it."

Kat squeezed Alex's hand and leaned closer to him. "You sure you're okay with this?"

He smoothed back a curl off her face. "Do you want to tango?"

Her smile was broad, and for a moment, he saw childlike joy in her eyes. "Yes."

"Another time and place, will you teach me to tango?"

"Of course."

His voice lowered. "Who is taking you home tonight?"

"You are."

"Then dance."

***

A few seconds into the dance, Alex felt like he'd been punched in the stomach. Nothing could have prepared him for the beauty and raw sexuality of Kat dancing the tango. It was obvious that she and Tixi had danced together often, but as Alex looked at Monce's face for any sign of jealousy, all he could see was joy in her face. Clearly, Monce felt completely safe in her husband's love and trusted her friendship with Kat. Feeling him looking at her, Monce slid over next to Alex, and put her arm through his and squeezed. "Don't they dance beautifully together?"

"They do."

Monce looked at him. "You aren't jealous, are you?"

Alex laughed at the blunt question. "No, because you aren't."

Monce tipped her head, focusing on him intently. "Alex, Kat and I are good. Better than good. We are old friends, who just happened to both have slept with the same man. Long ago we openly talked out the weirdness, and moved on." She rubbed her belly. "I felt so comfortable with it that I asked her to be in our wedding. Besides, I've never seen her look at a man the way she looks at you."

"Really?"

"Really."

***

Just then the song ended, and Alex fought warring emotions of wanting her to come sit with him and wanting her to continue to dance so he could watch her move. As she started to walk toward the table, Tixi grabbed her hand

and motioned back to the floor. Monce waved them both back to the floor, and they danced again.

The song ended. Kat kissed Tixi on the cheek and strode purposefully toward the table. Leaning down, she kissed Monce. "Thanks for letting me borrow your husband."

"My pleasure. Good to see you haven't forgotten how to dance."

Kat slid into the seat next to Alex and smiled when he wrapped his arm around her. "Aren't you full of surprises?"

"Huh?"

He kissed her ear, whispering, "So not only do I not know you can really dance, but you can tango like a pro? You were so sexy out there…"

***

The next morning, Kat tried to smile as she watched Alex put the last of his things in the suitcase. He stopped packing to look at her. "You look like you're going to cry."

Her voice trembled. "I don't want you to go."

"I told you I would stay."

"I know. But I need to go finish up in Madrid and get to New York. And if you stay, I won't be able to honestly say I'm moving back for family and work, it'll feel like it's *just* for you."

Alex tried to fight his frustration and keep it out of his voice. "And that would be such a bad thing? Moving back for me?"

Tears rolled down her cheeks. "Alex, I know I'm moving back for you, but it can't seem like the only or the major reason. Shit, I can't even work up the courage to tell you things, so it seems stupid to change my entire life on a *maybe*."

Alex sighed, rubbed his temples, and then sat down next to her, wrapping his arms around her. "Okay. I'll stay your *maybe,* and go home today. And in a month, I'll be in New York, and we can be together."

"You sure you're okay with this? I understand I'm making this so complicated. I'm sorry…"

With grace and speed, Alex suddenly pushed her back on the bed and looked down at her. "I've told you over and over. I'm not giving up on us." He leaned down and kissed her. "You're stuck with me."

Chapter Sixteen

Finally, at the end of August, Alex arrived from California. Kat met him at the airport, and as he came down the concourse, she could feel her heart race. Dropping his bags, he picked her up in a huge hug before kissing her deeply. When they pulled apart, he smiled down at her. "Have I mentioned how much I've missed you?"

"Once or twice." She stood on her tiptoes to kiss him again. "I've missed you too."

***

That night after dinner, Peter looked at Alex and Kat. "Hey, how about we go to the shore for the weekend? Summer is almost over, so we'll be closing up the house soon."

Kat looked at Alex, "Alex?"

"Sounds great."

***

The next day, all four of them got up early and packed. Once there, they laughed, read, walked, talked, and drank wine. Without realizing it, Alex and Kat were never more than a few feet away from each other. In all, it was a perfect weekend.

***

Soon after they got back to Manhattan, the phone rang for Kat.

Alex listened intently to her side of the conversation as Kat madly scribbled notes on a yellow legal pad. "Tomorrow? You want me to go tomorrow? You couldn't have said something before now? I was at the office on

Thursday. It would have been helpful to know about it then. Okay, yes, I know that I've been away for the weekend, but it can't wait?" She grimaced at the response. "Whatever. The flight leaves at six a.m.?" She paused in thought. "Okay, I'm on it. Fax me the information, and have a courier drop off letters and passes to the airport tomorrow morning. Good. Get me a reservation at a motel with air conditioning. No, no guard. They won't talk to me if I have a bodyguard. No, I'm not worried. Yeah, I'll fly back on Thursday, and I'll email you a final draft on Friday. You're welcome."

Kat hung up. "Well, I'm leaving for Brownsville in the morning. They have reports of witchcraft and Satanism among the women of the immigration detention camp."

There was silence as all three men stared at Kat. Alex sat shocked, fighting disappointment and anger that she was leaving so soon after he'd arrived. How the hell were they ever going to see if this would work if they didn't get time together?

Peter was the first to speak up, his voice strained. "I wish you hadn't refused a guard. Two years ago, when you went to Brownsville for El Pais, you came back with a bruised ribcage."

Her tone was patient. "If I have a guard, no one will talk to me." She shrugged happily, already focusing on the assignment in her mind. "Anyway, I'll be fine. I need to pack. Hey, will you guys order pizza?" Kat turned toward the stairs, humming cheerfully under her breath.

Sitting slightly apart from the others, only Luke noticed Peter's face contort with rage. As Kat passed him, Peter grabbed her and picked her up, so she was sitting on the counter, pinned by his arms. "Dammit, Kat, listen to me! Last time you were roughed up in that damn camp and your story was just about camp conditions. Do you really think you'll be popular looking into Satanism? This is nasty shit, Kat! Just once, could you think before you accept an assignment?"

Her face showed her shock. "Peter, this is my job. I don't interfere in your career."

"My career isn't a threat to life and fucking limb!"

She was confused. "Pete, I travel all the time. Why are you squawking about this now?"

"Because I'm sick of wondering where you are, or when you'll come back, and if you're safe. You finally moved home, and I stupidly thought it meant you might be taking better care of yourself. I love you, Kat, but I hate some of your work. It drives me crazy when you do these sorts of assignments. I hate letting you go like this."

Both Alex and Luke took in sharp breaths hearing the word 'let', knowing that Kat would hit the roof.

Kat's voice rose in disbelief. "*Let* me go? *Let* me go? Fuck, Peter, I'm an adult, you don't *let* me do anything. I can't believe we're fighting about this. I'm going to Brownsville tomorrow."

Peter whirled around and stomped away without speaking. Everyone else sat in silence in the kitchen. A minute later, the three people in the kitchen heard Peter angrily playing the drums.

"Son-of-a-fucking-bitch." Kat hopped down off the counter, marched out of the kitchen, and climbed the stairs to her rooms, stomping loudly.

Silence filled the kitchen as Alex and Luke looked at each other with shocked eyes. Then Luke shook his head and started to laugh. "Shit, there's nothing worse than sitting in a room while other people fight."

Alex nodded. "Yeah. I mean you can't say anything, but you also can't leave." He shook his head in confusion. "What the hell was that all about?"

Luke handed him a beer, then sat back down at the table. "Peter and I have been together for twelve years, and that's one of the only real fights I've seen them have."

Luke rested his chin on his hand. "Peter worries about her constantly, and when she travels like this, it makes him absolutely nuts. He hoped her taking this job would settle her and instead she's been on the road more than ever, and now that she's living with us again, it's in his face, and he can't do a thing about it."

Alex grinned wryly. "She does seem to be rather independent."

Luke snorted. "No, she's *fucking* independent. I mean, I know she's an adult and has every right to do what she wants, but she comes and goes with no thought of her relationships or her health."

"What do you mean?"

"Well, like last year she went to stay for a few weeks in a barrio in the middle of the drug zone of Medellin. For weeks, Peter and I had no way to reach her directly and had no idea if she was okay or not. And while it worries me, it makes Peter *insane*."

"Why's she like this?" Alex asked, dying to really understand her.

Luke's handsome face became serious, his dark eyes narrowing slightly. "I'm not sure, but I have a lot of theories. I think she doesn't want to need anyone."

"Why?"

"I don't really know. She was independent even as a kid." He laughed. "Remember the night you guys met, and she got angry because she felt you were insinuating that she needed a babysitter to walk home?" Alex nodded. "But now it's different. You know things happened between now and then." He swallowed. "I hate that I can't tell you all about it. But, know that I've told Kat that if she's really trying to be with you, she needs to tell you, and I think she's getting close to that point."

"I hope so. I just feel like there are so many mysteries about her." He shook his head. "And she was the one who put the brakes on us while she moved back and got settled, now I'm here, and she takes off. So I wanted to yell just as much as Peter." He sighed. "I just don't get her."

"I know. In some ways, I know Kat well. I can tell you what she likes to eat, and what she doesn't. I can tell you what size shoe she wears. Hell, from shopping with her, I know her damn *bra* size. But I can't tell you what she thinks about when she's alone, or when she wakes up in the middle of the night, or when she runs. In some ways, I don't know her any better today than the day I met her. I'm not sure if anyone *really* knows her."

Alex's voice was strong with conviction. "I'm falling in love with her."

"I know," Luke said, with a wide smile.

"Is it that obvious?"

"Well, yes and no. Anyone would notice that you're interested. But, I've known for a while that it was more than a passing interest for you."

"And you're okay with it? What about Peter?" Suddenly, Alex realized how much he cared about their opinions.

"Believe me, we've spent a hell of a lot of time talking about it. Truly, Alex, we're thrilled."

"I'm glad."

"Would you have stopped if we weren't okay with it?"

"No." He grinned.

"Good."

There was a sudden break in the drumming. Kat yelled from upstairs. "Peter, get up here."

Luke laughed, "I love it. They fight, and then the princess gives him an order."

Peter whacked a drum before he yelled, "No. I'm not climbing three fucking flights of stairs so you can tell me to mind my own business."

Kat stomped down the stairs. "Fine, asshole, I'll be the bigger person, *as always*, and come to you."

Luke grinned at Alex. "This could be interesting."

Over the next ten minutes, voices rose and fell downstairs, and then there was dead silence. Finally, Peter walked into the room, giving Kat a piggyback ride, and unceremoniously dumped her on Alex's lap. "Kat and I have reached an understanding."

Smiling at her brother, Kat was smug. "I'm going to Brownsville tomorrow, but I'll have my cell phone on and with me at all times, and I'll go out of my way to be careful. And I'll call home a lot. And I will try to be better about giving travel details and making sure I can be reached even when I'm traveling."

"And I'll stop playing mother hen." Brother and sister grinned at each other as Peter called for pizzas.

When Kat tried to climb off Alex's lap, he held her still. "You're not going anywhere—I like this arrangement."

Kat turned to look at him and stuck out her tongue. "Yeah, yeah, yeah."

Her gasp was audible as Alex gently kissed the back of her neck, but only she could hear his voice. "If you're going to run away for the next few days, at least you can let me enjoy right now."

Kat elbowed him in the ribs. "You're taking advantage of the situation."

"Well, since you won't let me take advantage of you ..." His voice softened, and her body warmed with the caressing sound. "What I'd really like to do is whisk you away for a bit, and convince you not to leave. To convince you to stay here with me, letting me ..."

He leaned closer, hidden to the rest of the room, and slowly ran the tip of his tongue from the neckline of her shirt up to the soft hollow where the riotous curls began.

"What was I saying? Oh, yeah, staying here, letting me kiss you, taste you, love you."

Kat jumped off his lap saying something about getting paper plates, but not before Alex noticed how her body had responded to his enticing words.

***

The pizzas arrived, and the four of them ate and laughed. Finally, Kat stretched and yawned. "Okay boys, I need to read the info that's hopefully up at the fax, and then I'd better get some sleep."

Peter ruffled her hair lovingly. "Will you accuse me of suffocating you if I ask to go to the airport?"

Kat winked at Alex. "Won't your boss be mad if you're sleepy because you got up at the crack of dawn to see me off?"

Before Peter could respond, Alex spoke thoughtfully. "What if the boss took you to the airport?"

Peter grinned innocently. "I could live with that idea. Then someone sees you off, and we get to sleep later."

"Alex, are you sure you want to traipse out there in the middle of the night?" Kat asked in an uncertain voice.

"I'm sure."

Kat looked at her notes. "I'm going to be ready to leave at four-fifteen."

"Fine."

She shrugged. "All right. Good night, big brothers. Petie, I love you even when you're an overbearing, protective pain in the ass. Luke, I love you all the time."

Peter reached out to hug her. "We love you too, monster. Be careful. Call us if you can."

***

At the airport, Alex carried her bag to the security gate.

Kat suddenly felt very shy. "Thanks for riding out with me."

"My pleasure. I'll see you Thursday?"

"Maybe sooner, if it goes well."

"I hope so. Be careful."

Kat looked at the security line, which was getting longer by the second. "I should go. Bye, Alex, I'll see you soon." She swallowed. "I'm sorry I'm leaving so soon after you got here. You know that wasn't on purpose, right?"

"I know." He stroked her cheek. "Go, do a great article, call me when you can."

"I will."

"Be careful." Alex leaned forward and lightly kissed Kat on the lips. "Remember, I'm only a phone call away."

"I will." Kat hurriedly stood on her tiptoes to kiss Alex and ran through the gate.

***

Monday, Alex walked home and found a message on the machine. Kat's voice sounded happy as she said, "Hi guys. I'm here. I'm safe, just checking in and I thought you might be home, I guess I should have called your cells. I'm headed out to do research, so I'll try you later or tomorrow." There was a pause, and then she said a bit more quietly, "Alex, I'll see you Thursday."

***

Tuesday, the day seemed even longer to Alex. Around noon, his cell chirped telling him he had a new text message. He smiled as he read it: "Hi, miss you. Waiting to do an interview so I can't call but wanted to say hi."

***

That night, the three men were sitting in the sunroom when the phone rang. Peter distractedly picked it up. "Hello? Oh, hey, Steve. She did what? No way. Yeah, okay, I'll turn it on, just give me a minute."

Peter rose and flipped on the radio. He fiddled with the buttons until a station came in clearly. "Thanks, Steve. I've got it now. Talk to you soon."

The announcer's smooth voice flowed into the room. "Hey, everyone. Tonight I'm doing something I don't usually do; I took a dedication. A friend of mine is hanging out in Texas tonight, and she's listening to country music because that's all they play down there. Anyway, this song is going out to Alex. Here it is, folks, the ultimate country love song, a true oldie about when you can't think about anything else but your lover, Patty Loveless' *I Try To Think About Elvis*, going out to Alex from Kat."

Peter and Luke broke into delighted laughter as Alex stared at the radio, looking like someone had just handed him a winning lottery ticket.

***

W ednesday night, the phone rang as the three men were making dinner. Peter grabbed the phone on the second ring. "Hello?"

"Heya, big brother."

Peter's voice rose in excitement. "Kat!" Hearing Peter's voice, Alex whirled around, splattering Alfredo sauce on the counter. "How are you?"

Her voice was tired. "Exhausted. Texas has to be my least favorite place in the entire world."

"Hey, at least you'll be on your way home tomorrow. What time will you be getting in? I thought I'd take a long lunch and go get you."

"Oh, Pete, that sounds great, but that's what I'm calling about."

"What do you mean, that's what you're calling about?"

Alex's stomach clenched, hearing the tone of Peter's voice. Peter leaned against the counter belligerently as Kat spoke. "Peter, I have to cross the border and go to Morelos to do research. I booked myself on a late flight tomorrow night, so I should be there when you wake up on Friday."

"Why the hell are you crossing the border?" Peter asked in a frustrated voice.

"Most of the women come from around Morelos, and I need some background."

"I hate when you cross the border there. I assume you're going alone?"

"Pete, please. I know how you feel, and I understand. But I'm almost done. I need this information to finish the article. I promise to be careful, and I'll be back soon in one piece, I promise." She sighed, and Peter could hear exhaustion and loneliness in her tone. "Pete, I really need to go there. The article would be half-assed if I didn't, and it will just take a few more hours. Please don't give me shit about this."

He could hear the quiver in her voice and immediately felt guilty. "Okay. I understand. You'll be damn careful? And you'll grab an international phone if yours isn't going to work?"

"I promise—I'll do both. Can I talk to Alex, please? I love you."

"Okay, call us if you need us. Hold on. I'll get him. Love you." Peter handed the phone to Alex.

Alex tried to sound joking. "Why do I think I'm not going to like this conversation?"

Her voice was strained, "I know. But I need to stay longer for more research. Peter will explain, but I should be back for breakfast on Friday."

"Oh. I really wish you were coming home tomorrow."

Kat ignored the longing that filled her hearing his comment. "I know, and I wish I were going to see you tomorrow too, but it's just one more day."

"All right. I won't give you grief about it."

"Thanks. I need to run and get ready for tomorrow. Tell Peter I'll call as soon as I get to the airport on Friday."

His tone was firm. "Call me instead."

"You want to run to the airport again?"

"To see you? Of course I do."

He could hear the smile in her voice. "I'll call you. Night, Alex."

***

Thursday morning, Alex got up and took a cold shower, trying to shake his bad mood. He rationally knew that Kat was working and that she wasn't trying to stay away, but no matter how hard he tried to be more even-tempered about it, he was grouchy, just plain grouchy.

Alex was surprised to find Peter sitting at the kitchen table. "Morning, Alex."

"Hey, Peter." Alex poured himself some coffee, in too much of a mood to even try small talk.

Peter grinned innocently at Alex, seeing the scowl on his face. "Well, I don't know about you, but I really wish my kid sister was coming home today. Although I don't know, the two of you seem to dislike each other so much."

Alex choked on his coffee, in no mood to be hassled. "Fuck you, Peter."

"Nasty, nasty. What, now you sort of like her?"

Alex took another sip of his coffee. "Yes, asshole. I like your sister. Happy now that I've admitted it?"

"Yeah."

Alex looked serious. "Peter, are you okay with this? I mean, I didn't plan to hit on your sister, ever. It was never just hitting on her. You know that, don't you?"

Peter picked up a spoon and stirred his coffee. "Relax, Alex. I know you already had this conversation with Luke, and he was telling the truth. Admittedly, at first I was most worried about what would happen to the band if it didn't work, but I got over that because I know that we could handle that. And then I heard the tone of her voice when she asked to talk to you last night, and, well, there was more longing and emotion in her voice than I've heard in a hell of a long time, like she's beginning to come back to life."

***

Friday morning, Alex was up early and dressed quickly, listening for the phone. As he put coffee on, Kat walked into the kitchen, dropping her bag on the floor as Max joyously welcomed her with loud barks and a furiously wagging tail.

Squatting down to hug the dog, she grinned at Alex. "Good morning. Did you make enough coffee for me too?"

His heart leapt. "Welcome home. Of course, I did." He pulled her toward him and bent his head toward her. As his lips touched hers, he wrapped his arms tightly around her and smiled as she lifted her arms to wrap them around his neck. The kiss deepened as they leaned against the counter, and Alex felt her heart race through her thin blouse.

Kat pulled back and looked at him. "Wow. Hi."

"Hi." Alex looked at her searchingly. "I'm glad you're home. You seem to be in one piece."

"Sure am. Other than the fact that I hate Texas, it was a piece of cake as an assignment. In fact, it was much easier than I expected."

"How are the witches?"

"Peachy keen."

"Are they witches?"

She rubbed her neck. "A few are, but mostly it's just the people reverting back to original 'pagan' beliefs, you know, things like believing in the sun god, stuff like that. I got a few good interviews, irritated some priests by suggesting that if the camps were better, people wouldn't have to search for ways to alleviate the pain and suffering, and came home. How are you?"

"Now that you're back and kissing me, I'm great. I missed you." As Alex said this, he handed Kat a mug of coffee, and lightly tugged on her ponytail. "I thought you were going to call me to come and get you."

"I was, but I decided that it would be quicker to get a cab. I figured by the time I called you to come out to the airport, I could already be here with you." She sipped the coffee. "Nice job. Peter always forgets how many scoops he's put in."

"Thanks." Alex moved to sit down at the table. "I really liked your surprise the other night. I meant to tell you that on the phone, but I got flustered because you weren't coming home."

Kat's face turned red with embarrassment. "I'm glad that you liked it. After I made the call, I panicked that it was a stupid thing to do."

"It wasn't. It made my day."

"And probably Peter gave you shit all the next day?"

"No. He just started playing the song when I walked into the studio. That was it."

"Good. Anyway, I missed you too. I almost called you last night just to say hi."

"I wish you had."

"It was really late here, and I didn't want to wake you." Kat stretched and yawned. "But, I haven't really had any sleep, and I really am grimy. I'm going to grab a shower and a nap. I'll see you later?"

"Count on it."

Chapter Seventeen

That evening, the three men walked back to the townhouse together. Peter whistled as he walked, looking in windows and smiling at everyone they passed.

Luke raised an eyebrow. "My goodness, your mood has improved."

Peter shrugged, unconcerned. "I called Kat at lunch, and she said she'd be home for dinner *and* she's making lasagna. What could be better than that?"

***

Walking up the steps, they could smell the lasagna, and inside, the kitchen gleamed. The table was set, a plate of cheese, crackers, strawberries, and grapes sat on the counter next to three empty wine glasses and an open bottle of Merlot. Music played softly, and Kat was perched on a stool, sipping a glass of wine and working at her laptop.

When she heard the door, she whirled around. "Hi!"

Peter rushed forward, almost knocking over glasses on the table in his hurry. He bent down to hug her. "Damn, I'm glad you're back!"

Moving more carefully, Luke came forward to kiss the top of her head. "Welcome home, cupcake."

"Hey, I thought you'd gotten lost on the way home. I've been waiting patiently for you to get here."

Pulling a cracker off the plate on the counter, Peter popped the whole thing in his mouth. Crunching, he ruffled her hair. "We know how patient you are. Is dinner ready right now or do we have time for showers?"

"Of course you have time. But don't take long, I'm hungry!"

***

Watching Kat smile at Luke and Peter as they left the room, Alex noticed the faint smudges of gray under her eyes. Once they were alone, he moved forward to put his hands on her shoulders.

Kat leaned against him and closed her eyes. Alex hugged her for a moment and then she opened her eyes to look up at him. His voice was gentle. "Hi."

"Hi, yourself. You know, I realized this afternoon that I'd never asked if you'd be here for dinner. So I just assumed." Kat bit her lip. "Is that okay? Were you planning on being here tonight?"

His fingers massaged the back of her neck. "I guess I assumed, too. So here I am, and I'd love to have dinner with you." Moving slowly, his hands moved to stroke her collarbone. "You should have just called or texted me."

Kat sat up, moving away from his hands. "I couldn't."

"Why? If you wanted to know something, just ask."

"And all I'm saying is that if I called you while you were at the studio, and it broke the session, the whole band would have a field day discussing whether we're sleeping together."

"So? Let them talk." He chuckled. "Besides, we are sleeping together, just not having sex."

She shook her head, suddenly very emotional about the whole discussion. "No! They don't need to gossip about us."

His voice was patient. "I wasn't saying I wanted them to gossip about us, all I was saying was that I don't care if they talk about us."

"Well, I do!"

"Why?"

"It's none of their business!"

Alex took several steps away from her, frustrated by her stubbornness about this. "Okay. I think we're at an impasse here. Do I have time to change?"

"You can change." Kat's voice was curt.

Alex started to say something and stopped, watching Kat through narrowed eyes. But then he realized he needed to say what was on his mind. "You seemed perfectly normal with Luke and Peter, but now I feel like you're ticked off at me for something, and I haven't the foggiest friggin idea what I did wrong."

Kat's shoulders sagged, and again Alex noticed how tired she looked. Pushing the laptop closed, she walked around the counter to him. Without warning, she leaned into Alex's chest. Her voice wavered. "I'm sorry. I guess I …"

Alex's anger evaporated. He put his arms around her and rubbed her back. "You guess what?"

"After this morning, I was all wigged out that I didn't know if you'd be here for dinner or not, and I couldn't decide if it was okay or not that I was assuming you would, then you mentioned calling you at the studio and I freaked out. I'm sorry. This is all new to me, and I seem to be really good at fucking it up."

Alex wanted to understand. "So you thought I was asking you to announce that we're in a serious relationship by calling me to check on dinner?"

She nodded. "Yeah."

He shook his head. "Damn, sweetheart. You complicate the simplest things. I brought up calling me because I hated the idea that you were stressed when you could've solved it with a simple call. That's it."

"Oh. Okay." Kat smiled at Alex, and he saw the uncertainty lift in her eyes. "I'm sorry for bitching at you."

He tugged a piece of her hair. "No harm done. Now, can I still change?"

"Yes." As Alex started to walk toward the stairs, Kat bit her lip again. "Alex?"

"Yeah?"

Quickly, she crossed the room. Standing on tiptoes, she put her hands on either side of his face and kissed him. Alex smelled her perfume, dinner smells, and her shampoo, and almost came undone. Wrapping his arms around her, he pulled her close and kissed her until they were both breathless.

In his heart, Alex knew he needed to pull back from the kiss, as he was getting more aroused by the second. With a sigh, he dropped a quick kiss on her lips. "I'm changing now. Then, I'm coming back to help you with dinner, and then I'm making sure that you get some sleep since I would guess that you haven't really slept since you've been gone, and I have plans for this weekend."

***

As Alex came back into the kitchen, the phone rang. Distractedly, Kat picked up the cordless from where it sat next to her computer, still typing with one hand. "Hello?"

Peter and Luke walked noisily into the room, arguing about something. Kat shot them a warning glance. "Hello?"

"What the hell is all the mayhem?" The voice on the phone came through clearly, even with the touch of an accent.

Kat's voice rose happily. "Secu! I've been leaving you messages everywhere! Where the hell have you been?"

"Darling, I've been busy. I just got back home, and Ana gave me your messages."

"Don't 'darling' me, I talked with Paco. I know you've been home." In the background, Kat could hear children playing. "Is he there? Let me talk to him."

"Hold on. I need to tell you something first." There was a long pause. "I got it."

Kat gulped air and grabbed her wine glass for a sip, her face suddenly bright red. "You didn't. You're lying."

"I'm not lying. Tuesday morning. I did it!"

Alex was trying to follow the conversation, only hearing Kat's part. Her distress was clear. "I still say you're lying. But, I'll play along. When, where, how?"

"I pulled some strings. I fly in on Monday, and I have two hours with him Tuesday morning, and then a bit of time to look around and meet with the opposition, and fly home."

She grumbled. "Fuck, Secu. I can't believe you did it. Congratulations."

Peter poured a glass of wine and took a long swallow leaning against the counter. "Hey Kat, the rest of us are dying here. What did Secu do?"

She looked at him, clearly trying to control her unhappiness. "He got the Somosa interview."

Peter's eyes widened. He grabbed the phone from her hand. "Shit, Secu. Congrats! Kat's been salivating over that one for months. Good for you."

Kat yanked the phone back, whacking Peter on the shoulder in the process. "Give me the phone, asshole." She spoke into the receiver. "So you called to gloat? If you're done, let me speak to Paco, you impossible ass."

"In a minute! I need a favor."

"What? You gloat and beg in the same moment?"

"Yes. I have no honor. You know that." He chuckled. "I need a complete set of your books, autographed to his wife."

Kat was shocked and immediately furious. "What? You shit. You get the interview, but you need *my* books as a hostess gift?" Her voice rose. "You used my name to get the interview. Now *I* need to provide the gift?"

His voice deepened. "Yes. And it would be a great help if you …"

Kat was going crazy with all the pauses in the conversation. "If I what? Jesus, Secu, get to the point."

"It would be a great help if you could get your skinny ass to Managua on Monday because we have to prepare for the interview."

"What?"

"You dope, I got his agreement only if we do the interview together. It was his condition that it be the two of us!"

Kat's eyes got big, and she swallowed hard. "We got it? We got it?"

"We got it. I can book you on a flight, and meet you in Managua. That is if you want to go."

Kat bounced off the stool, dancing around the kitchen. "Oh my God. Of course, I want to go! Book me on anything. I'll be there." She grinned at Peter. "Oh yeah, hold on, Secu. I have to tell Peter." She put the phone down. "Peter, I'm going to Managua on Monday, to do the mother-of-holy-God-friggin-God-damn-Somosa interview!"

Peter laughed and picked up the phone. "I pity you, Secu—she's so wound you'll need to lock her in a closet."

Minutes later, Alex watched in amusement as Kat spoke with the mysterious Paco in rapid Spanish. It was only after that conversation that Peter explained that Secu and Kat occasionally worked as writing partners on nonfiction pieces and that Paco was his eldest son and her beloved godson.

Dinner was loud and cheerful. Kat told the men about her trip. Her energy was contagious as she spoke about the women she had interviewed.

Later, Luke began to discuss a problem at the gallery. Alex sat watching Kat as she tipped her head to concentrate on Luke's depiction of the issue. Watching her ask questions, he was almost entranced.

Peter nudged Alex, and he realized that Peter was waiting for him to respond. "Did you say something, Peter?"

"No, I was just watching you get hypnotized by the two art fanatics. Aren't they amazing?"

"Damn, she never ceases to amaze me," Alex said in wonder.

Peter nodded. "Yeah, she is pretty amazing, but then again, I may be a bit biased."

"So am I."

***

After a nightcap, Peter and Luke excused themselves for the evening, and Kat and Alex cleaned up the few final dishes in companionable silence. Once the kitchen gleamed, they turned off all the downstairs lights. Standing at the window in her living room, Kat looked out at the dark street, then Alex wrapped his arms around her, gently resting his chin on the top of her head. "Will you go to dinner with me tomorrow night, just the two of us?"

Kat wrapped her arms over his, squeezing them, "Are you asking me on another date?"

Her tone made him smile. "Yes. An honest-to-God date. Our second official date, if you count the dinner at the shore since otherwise we always have a group with us. You know, a date, going out together, for the purpose of a romantic evening."

A grin spread across her face. "I'd love too."

"Be ready at five."

"Isn't that awfully early?"

Seriously, he traced her lips with his finger. "It's as late as I can stand."

Kat smiled at him. "I'll be ready."

Chapter Eighteen

The next day Kat and Alex smiled privately at each other at breakfast. As Peter watched the two of them, he said, "Kat, we decided to run down to D.C. to see a new exhibit at the National Gallery. We'll be back on Sunday. Is that okay?"

Kat shrugged. "We'll be fine, Peter. Don't worry."

"As long as you're sure..."

She leaned forward to pat his hand. In a patronizing voice, she said, "Peter, until a couple months ago, I lived completely alone. I can probably manage two nights without you."

"Okay, I just wanted to check after I gave you shit about being away so much." Peter stretched and yawned. "I have absolutely no energy for playing today. Maybe I better grab another cup of coffee to take with me. What are you doing today, Kat?"

"Back to normal schedule. Write, eat, write, run, and write."

"For someone who's self-employed, your life's a major drag."

"Tell me about it."

"Alright, I guess we better move our asses, huh, Alex? The guy we're working for is such a taskmaster." Alex was sitting sprawled out, slowly sipping coffee. He saluted Peter and laughed.

Peter stood up, and rubbed Kat's shoulders. "If you aren't out running, we'll see you before we leave tonight."

Alex stood up and walked over to her. He lightly touched her cheek with his index finger. "Five o'clock."

"Five o'clock."

***

Around three, Luke came home and brought her a seltzer. He sat in the lumpy old overstuffed chair in the corner next to her computer and watched her rub her eyes. "How's it coming?"

"Slowly. I had trouble getting back into the swing."

"Are you sure you're okay with us leaving for the weekend?"

"Luke, why are you both so worried about this weekend?"

Luke looked uncomfortable. "We're just worried about leaving you so soon after you came back from Texas, especially after Peter's hissy fit."

Kat grimaced. "I'm really okay with it, stop worrying."

"We just wanted to make sure you're okay."

"What do you mean?"

"Well, it seems like you may be wrestling with some stuff now, and we just want to make sure you're okay."

He didn't need to be more specific. "You mean you're wondering if I'll tell him anytime soon."

Luke heard the warning tone in her voice. "I didn't mean anything by the comment, Kat. Just trying to remind you that we are here for you, always."

Kat's anger evaporated as quickly as it had flared. "I know. I'm sorry, Luke, I'm really trying to figure out all of this."

"I know you are." Luke paused. "Kat, I know you're afraid to tell him, but I really think that he won't run away. You see it all as a failing on your part, but no one else does."

His love and support for her were a constant in her life. Her eyes filled with tears. "Thanks, Luke. I know you mean well. But, the truth is that neither one of us knows how he would react. So I can't go forward without telling him, but I'm so afraid to lose him that I can't tell him. It really sucks." She sighed. "I'm trying, Luke. I'm trying."

"I know you are, kiddo. Anyway, let me know if you need an ear." Luke rose from the chair. "I better go finish packing."

Chapter Nineteen

When Kat got back to the house after her run, she could tell that Luke and Peter had left. Sprinting up the stairs, she could see Alex at the piano, music spread out in front of him. "Ten minutes, I promise."

"Ten minutes."

Exactly ten minutes later, Kat walked down the stairs and stood in the doorway. "I told you."

Her cheeks were still flushed, whether from her run or from her awareness of Alex, he couldn't tell. "You look great. You ready?"

"I am."

***

The two of them walked through the relatively quiet streets, to a small cafe by the river. Alex held the door open. "I thought we could get a drink here, then go for a walk, then go for dinner."

"Perfect."

Later, when they got back to the house, Kat would realize that it was one of the most romantic evenings she'd ever experienced. Great wine, amazing food, candlelight, and the sensuous warmth of Alex's unwavering attention had made every moment special.

***

At the townhouse, Alex poured them each a glass of wine. She turned on the TV and sat down on the couch right next to Alex. He put his arm around her shoulders, and she leaned up against him. After they had watched TV for a while, Alex played with a curl near her ear, "What are your plans for tomorrow?"

"I'm writing from six until eight. Then I was planning to wander around the city, do some shopping, maybe check out the new show of Picasso's at MOMA." She looked uncomfortable. "I didn't ask you your plans."

"Would you like some company?"

She beamed delightedly. "I'd love some."

"Good, you can show me your favorite haunts in New York. I spend quite a bit of time here, but I never seem to have time to wander around like I did when I lived here."

"Make sure you dress comfortably. I'm not coming home because your feet hurt."

He grinned. "I was hoping you'd rub them if they hurt." His grin got wider. "Or anything else you'd like to rub."

"In your dreams."

The impish grin on her face made his urge to kiss her almost overwhelming, and he leaned toward her. "Damn, you are even sexier when you are being a smartass." He kissed her deeply, without realizing it, pulling her onto his lap so he could wrap his arms around her. Finally, he pulled back, struggling to honor her rules. Resting his forehead against hers, he said, "Okay, we'd better get some sleep."

"Alex, thank you."

"For what?"

"For tonight, for understanding."

"You're welcome, babe. I told you. I'll wait forever if needed."

Chapter Twenty

The next morning dawned crisp and clear. Kat was up at dawn and moved down to the sunroom to work on the final chapter. She worked diligently for almost two hours, until Max nudged her knee, pulling Kat back into the present. She looked at the clock and realized that it was already eight. Shutting down the computer, she ran back upstairs, hearing a piano playing in Alex's "old" room. Kat took a quick shower and dressed in a navy tunic, black leggings, and black Keds. Pulling her hair back with a bright pink scrunchie, she knocked on Alex's door.

"Come on in, Kat."

Kat grinned seeing how the room was filled with his presence, from the synthesizer set up next to the baby grand piano to the music spread all over the coffee table. Alex was sitting at the piano looking at a musical arrangement. He looked up when Kat entered and grinned at her. "Good morning."

"Good morning." Kat wandered around the room, unabashedly looking at his things. "What are you doing?"

"Well, I decided that if you were working, I should be too. So I've been going over music for Monday's session."

"Are you ready to go?"

"I am. Let's grab breakfast and go."

***

Outside, it was a beautiful fall day. Linking hands, Alex and Kat started up the street. As they walked, they admired everything while they talked and laughed.

As they passed one townhouse, there was a "Happy Birthday" banner above the front door. Alex looked at Kate. "When's your birthday?"

She blushed. "Why?"

"Because I don't know when it is."

"It's Friday."

"This week?"

"Yeah."

"Hot shit. So I'll be here for your birthday, and you should be back from your trip."

"Uh-huh." She squeezed his hand. "It's not a big deal."

"It is to me."

"When's yours?"

"At the end of September."

They kept walking. Kat took him into buildings where she liked the lobbies, cooking shops where she looked at the utensils, and tons of shoe stores. He thought they had probably gone into every independent shoe store in Manhattan. She exclaimed over styles and prices and complained about inferior workmanship. Then she took him into Tiffany's, and she looked at everything, from the baby rattles to the gorgeous place settings of wedding china. She looked at jewelry, sighing over beautiful necklaces, bracelets, earrings, and rings. Alex watched her face as she looked. He saw her eyes return again and again to a thin gold bracelet studded with a pattern of two white opals and then a small diamond. The bracelet was displayed on a cushion with other similar bracelets, with black opals and diamonds, diamonds, white and black opals, or patterns combining all three gems.

Gazing at the bracelets, Alex thought of how beautiful her wrists would look encircled by them. Suddenly he knew that he needed to get Kat out of the store before she could buy the bracelet, and then he needed to find a way to sneak back and buy it for her. He wanted to give her the whole set, but he knew she wouldn't accept them. But she might accept *one*.

Gently he squeezed her hand. "Kat, I hate to interrupt, but if I don't find a place to sit down and something to eat and drink soon, I may fall over."

"Oh, I'm sorry, Alex. I was so busy drooling, I didn't think. I'm sorry."

"You can make it up to me by finding me some food."

"We can go right around the corner. There's a great sandwich shop there."

"Lead the way."

They left the store and walked around the corner to the small but mobbed sandwich shop. Kat led the way to the food line. Alex tried to look tired and hungry, and Kat immediately offered to get him something to eat. There was a long line waiting for food, so Alex figured it would take her a couple of minutes to return.

As soon as she got in line, he quickly left and reentered Tiffany's. The clerk rapidly completed the purchase, and with the gift-wrapped bracelet hidden deep within one of the pockets in his jacket, Alex returned to the table just as Kat arrived with food.

They sat at the small table with their knees touching and ate ravenously. Alex sat thinking about the bracelet that was burning a hole in his pocket.

***

After lunch, Kat and Alex walked back out into the sunshine. Kat pulled Alex by the hand to the end of the block and excitedly pointed to FAO Schwartz. They passed the toy soldier at the door and entered the store.

"Oh Alex, look at the panda bear!"

Kat was looking at a panda bear who was sitting on a shelf next to numerous smaller pandas. He was about two and a half feet tall. "I always wanted a panda. I had tons of other stuffed animals, but never a panda. Dad always said he'd get me one..." A momentary sadness flashed over her face.

"Would you like a panda?"

"Huh?"

"Would you like a panda? It could be a really early birthday gift."

"Alex, you don't have to get me anything for my birthday."

"I know I don't have to. I want to."

She smiled delightedly. "I'd love a panda."

Alex sent Kat away to look at something while he paid for the larger panda. After they had left the store, Kat hugged Alex and kissed him lightly on the lips.

"Thank you. It's perfect."

***

Kat and Alex roamed the city for the rest of the day.

At dusk, they found themselves in Rockefeller Center. The sun was glinting off the windows of the surrounding skyscrapers. They sank onto a bench, and Alex put his arm around Kat. "I'm exhausted. When you offered to show me, New York, I didn't expect to see every single street and store."

"I always miss wandering around when I haven't done it in a while. So I have to reacquaint myself." As Kat looked at Alex, she felt the power of his gaze, and both of them were breathless.

"Kat," Alex spoke in a low and gentle voice. "We need to talk about us." He stroked the side of her face, "I've never felt like this before. I love spending time with you doing anything. Or nothing."

Kat touched his cheek and nodded slowly.

Her gesture gave Alex the confidence to continue. "Kat, I want us to be a couple, an official couple. I want to spend my time boring band members by telling them about us. I want to know it's okay to walk into the room and kiss you no matter who is there and tell you how much I've missed you. I want to know that I'm more than your *maybe,* as you put it before." He buried his hand in her hair, feeling the softness surround him. "I need to know how you feel about me, and us."

Kat stared at the reflection of the dying sun in the canyon of glass. Finally, when Alex was about to give up hope that she would answer, she began to speak. "Alex, when I came back for the wedding, the last thing I wanted or needed was a relationship. Then, suddenly, you came back into my life, and you're all I think about. And every moment I care more about you. And it still scares the shit out of me. You are more than the maybe I kept mentioning, and yes, I need to acknowledge it too, but I'm still scared..."

Alex stroked her hair, "I told you, I'll give you all the time you need, that hasn't changed. But, this is real, and I need to acknowledge it."

"Me too."

Alex gently put his hands on either side of her face and kissed her mouth. She put her arms around his neck and kissed him back. Alex was stunned by the intensity of the kiss. His heart soared as he felt Kat melt into his arms. After several minutes, a teenager whistled at them until they pulled reluctantly apart.

Kat straightened her hair. "Are you as hungry as I am?"

"Starved!"

"Do you want to go grab a cab, and go home and order takeout?"

"Chinese?"

"My thoughts exactly."

***

They walked to the street and flagged down a cab. When they got in, Kat started to give the address, but Alex stopped her.

"To the Citicorp building."

"Alex, why are we going to Citicorp?"

"You'll see."

The angled top of the Citicorp building came into sight. As the cab stopped, Alex paid the driver, and headed straight into the kitchen shop.

Alex found a clerk. "Excuse me. Could you tell me where I might find champagne glasses?"

"Certainly, sir. Go straight back, and you'll find them on the right after that picnic basket display."

Kat followed Alex in silence. He found the display and turned to face her. "Kat, tonight I want to go home with you and drink champagne. But I want to pick out champagne flutes with you, so they're *our* glasses. I want these glasses to signify the official start of *us*."

Kat looked up at Alex and her eyes filled with tears. Alex put their bags down and pulled her into his arms. "Oh, Kat, I'm sorry, I didn't mean to upset you. We don't have to get glasses."

Sniffling, she hugged him. "No! I want to get them! No one has ever felt that way for me before. I love the idea of us getting glasses."

"Well, I feel that way." Alex wiped Kat's eyes. "All I want to do is wrap you in my arms and keep the world away from us so we can just focus on each other."

"Let's get our glasses, and go home."

They kept looking until they found two very delicate flutes hidden at the back of a shelf. The flute was one piece, hollow to the base, gradually tapering from the wide opening to a tiny straw. Alex took the glasses to the counter and paid for them. They stopped at the liquor store next door, and found a cab to take them home.

Chapter Twenty-One

When they arrived at the townhouse, Alex put Billie Holiday on the central stereo while Kat listened to the messages on the answering machine. Once they ordered dinner, they both took showers. After his, Alex took the Tiffany's box out of his jacket pocket and put it in the pocket of his jeans. When he got back to the kitchen, he put the box on top of the refrigerator and unwrapped their new glasses.

On the low table in the sunroom, he put the ice bucket with the champagne and several small white candles. The doorbell rang just as Kat walked into the kitchen barefoot in maroon leggings and a black cashmere sweater. She opened the door for the delivery boy, paid him, and carried the large bag to the counter. She smiled at Alex, who was leaning against the doorway watching her every move. "What?"

"I get stupid when you're in the room. You're all I can see, and I just watched you pay for Chinese, and it was one of the sexiest things I've ever seen."

She started to giggle. "Then you may have trouble controlling yourself when I clean up the mess after."

He laughed and pulled her close. Kat rose on her tiptoes and kissed him. Without breaking the kiss, Alex stooped down and put his arm under her knees so that he could swing her into his arms. He gently placed her on the couch and went back for the food. "Would you like a beer with dinner? We could save the champagne for afterward."

"I think that's a great idea. Champagne doesn't really go with Chinese."

They sat on the floor next to the low table and ate from the cardboard containers with chopsticks. They talked about favorite foods, jobs, colors, vacations, books, music, movies, politics, old relationships, morals, dreams, and favorite clothes.

After dinner, they carried the rubble to the kitchen and took Max for a walk. When they came back, Kat ran upstairs to check her cell.

Coming back downstairs, she found Alex was in the sunroom with the champagne flutes. The candles flickered romantically on the table. Kat sat down next to him, and he rubbed her arms, still cold from the night air.

He opened the champagne and filled their glasses. "To the future, Kat."

She smiled. "To the future."

They touched glasses and sipped the champagne. Alex put his glass on the table and reached behind him to bring out the small box that he handed to Kat.

"What's this?"

"Your real birthday present. I know it's early, but I want to give it to you when we're alone."

"You already gave me a gift."

"That was a fun gift. This is your real gift. Open it."

Kat slowly opened the box and saw the bracelet. The diamonds and opals sparkled in the candlelight and were reflected in the tears in her eyes.

"Oh, my God, Alex. How did you know I wanted this?"

"I could see it in your eyes."

"Thank you. Oh, thank you. How?"

"While you bought us lunch, I snuck back." He picked up her hand. "Here, let me put it on you."

The band encircled her wrist like a band of shimmering fire. She leaned over and hugged Alex. He pulled her onto his lap, and gazed at her wrist. "It's almost as beautiful as you are." He kissed her with all of the emotion and desire that had been building up in him over the last few weeks. After a few seconds of hesitancy, Kat kissed him with equal fervor. When Max came to nose them apart, they were breathless.

Kat shoved Max away, and touched Alex's cheek. "Wow."

"Happy Birthday, Kat."

"Thank you for everything today."

Chapter Twenty-Two

Monday morning, Kat was awake long before dawn. Alex woke to her quietly picking up her bag from the chair in the bedroom. "Hey, leave that. I'm getting up. I'll bring it downstairs."

"Sleep." Kat leaned over him and kissed him. "You don't have to get up so early."

"Baby, I'm going with you to the airport. I'll be down in five minutes, with your bag. You make coffee."

Kat's desire to not put him out by making him get up early to go to the airport warred with her desire to have a few more precious minutes with him, no matter how excited she was about this trip. "Okay. See you downstairs."

A few minutes later, Alex came into the kitchen carrying her bag. She smiled at him. "How do you get ready so fast, and look so damn good?"

His hands on her hips were warm, even through her blouse and slacks. "Are you saying you find me attractive?"

Kat put her hands on his chest, loving the feeling of his firm muscles. "You know I do."

"Hmm." He grinned. "Still make you hormone-crazed?"

Kat blushed and laughed. "Stop being so damn smug about it. C'mon, let's get coffee, eat something, and get me to the airport."

"Okay."

***

The next four days passed in a whirlwind of activity for Kat. She couldn't remember a time when she'd both had so much fun doing an interview and simultaneously missed being with someone so much. Every minute of the trip was filled with the interview and research process, then with editing and revising. Kat loved working with Secundino, but she still looked for every opportunity to call or text Alex.

On her final night in Nicaragua, Kat sat at a cafe table with Secundino. When the waiter brought them two cold beers, Secu raised his bottle. "To what I think is our best damn interview and article together, ever."

She clinked her bottle against his. "To us. Damn, we're good together."

Secu took a swig. "So, *tia*, is Alex the one?"

Kat rolled her eyes, "Don't start, Secu. It's too soon to know that."

"Do you want him to be?"

Kat turned the cold bottle between her hands, the condensation wetting her fingers. Putting it down, she wiped her hands on her jeans. "Yeah. I do."

Secu looked at her searchingly. "So you'll need to tell him at some point. You know that, don't you?"

Kat sighed. "I know."

Chapter Twenty-Three

After her trip to Nicaragua, Kat was thrilled to come home to Alex. She got home late on a Thursday night, and was shocked on Friday morning to find the house decorated for her birthday. Throughout the day, flowers arrived from Alex, then that evening, Josh, Kim, Mariah and Will, Beth and Sasha all came over unexpectedly for a birthday dinner and cake. After they all had left, Kat came out of the bathroom, finding Alex already in bed. He smiled at her. "Did you have a good birthday?"

She nodded happily. "Yeah, I had a great birthday. For so long, I've been away on my birthday, so they've been really, really quiet. This was a great day today." Sliding under the covers, she kissed him briefly. "Thank you for making it so special."

"You're welcome."

***

It had been almost a week since Kat returned that Alex realized she was getting quieter and quieter each day. Finally, one evening while they were watching TV by themselves, he muted the sound. "Babe, what's going on?"

Instantly, her tone was cautious. "What do you mean?"

"For the last couple days, you have gotten quiet and more and more withdrawn. Is something bothering you?"

She shook her head but didn't look at him. "No, just having a down phase." She squeezed his hand. "I'm sorry, it happens around this time each year. Don't worry. I'll snap out of it, I promise."

Later that evening, she excused herself to make a phone call. Coming back into the room, she kissed Alex briefly. "I have to go to a meeting very early tomorrow, then do some interviews, so I will probably be gone all day."

Her tone sounded odd to him. "Everything okay?"

She smiled, but it seemed forced, "Oh, yeah. Just tired." She stretched. "We should probably get some sleep. Anyway, I'm not sure I will be back for dinner."

"Okay. Just let me know if that's going to change, and I'll wait for you to eat."

***

The next morning, Kat slipped out of bed long before dawn. Alex stirred as she came out of the bathroom, leaned down, and kissed his cheek. "Sleep. I'll see you later tonight."

He rolled over to look at her, blinking the sleep from his eyes. "Wait, I'll get up and have breakfast with you."

"Nah. I'll grab something on my way. I have to go." She kissed him, grabbed her bag, and left the room.

Two hours later, when Peter and Luke came into the kitchen, Alex was sitting drinking coffee. Peter looked around. "Where's Kat?"

"She left a couple hours ago. She said she had an early meeting, then some interviews, and that she wouldn't be back for dinner."

Peter's tone was concerned. "What? She's not going to be back at all today?"

"No. That's what she said. Why?"

Luke put his hand on Peter's shoulder, "No reason, just normally she doesn't make those decisions at the last minute, that's all."

***

Four days later, when Peter's cell phone vibrated in his pocket, he ignored it as he was so caught up in the music. When it started buzzing again seconds later, he knew he needed to answer it. Stopping suddenly, he stood up to pull it out of his pocket. "Sorry guys, I need to take this." Peter stepped out into the hall, "Yeah, Luke, what's up? I'm in the middle of rehearsal."

Luke's voice was quiet. "I know you are, but she's gone."

Peter was confused. "What are you talking about?"

"Pete, check your messages on your cell. I bet you and Alex both have half-assed messages from Kat saying she's gone on assignment for a couple days and that she won't have cell service during that time. I know because I got the message. She obviously just called the voice mail so she wouldn't have to talk to me. I immediately called home, and she didn't answer. Then I called her cell, and it's off. I can't reach her." He paused. "Pete, I came home and hit redial on the house phone thinking that might shed some light on what the hell is going on, and the last call was to West Brookfield. Tomorrow's the anniversary, Pete, I think she's gone to Massachusetts for whatever reason, and she didn't want us to know."

Shock shook Peter so hard for a moment the room started to swim around him, and he leaned forward, his forehead against the wall as he tried to think. At that moment, Alex came up behind him to lay a hand on his arm. Before Peter could say anything, Alex asked, "Everything okay?"

Peter just turned his head and looked at him, completely at a loss for words.

On the phone, Luke said, "Pete, you need to come home. If I'm right, we need to go too."

Peter nodded. "I'll be home in ten minutes. Get stuff ready." He looked at Alex and knew it was time. "No, let me rephrase that. *Alex* and I will be home in ten."

When he got off the phone, Peter looked at Alex. "We need to go home. Now."

"What? Is everything okay?"

"Yes. No. I'll tell you on the way home."

***

On the taxi ride home, Peter said to Alex, "Check your phone. I bet you have a message from Kat that says she's going away for a bit."

"What? We both saw her at breakfast, and she didn't say anything about going away."

Peter's voice was adamant. "Check your messages."

Both Alex and Peter listened to Kat's stilted message on their voicemails. Alex felt his heart sink as he heard her clipped voice, "Hi, Alex. It's Kat. I'm going on assignment for a couple days, and I won't be reachable by phone. I'll see you on Thursday or Friday. Have a good week."

Alex looked at Peter. "What the hell is going on?"

Peter sighed. "You know how Kat has a secret?"

Alex was tired of the secrecy, and his voice showed it. "Yeah, the great big secret that you all know and I don't, but you all dance around like it will explode or something."

"Well, all I can say is, it's a safe bet that you're going to find out about it in the next twelve hours." Peter paused. "Frankly, Alex, if Kat doesn't tell you in the next twelve hours, fuck it, *I* will."

***

At the townhouse, the three men packed overnight bags quickly and headed out to the Jeep. As Peter started to climb into the driver's seat, Luke stopped him. "I'll drive."

"No, I'll drive."

Luke stood firm. "No, no offense, but you're getting more pissed off by the second, and there's no way you're going to drive that way. I'd like to live through the day, not get killed in a road rage incident."

Peter thought about arguing, and instead climbed into the passenger's seat and sat in sullen silence.

***

Just over three hours later, they pulled into a long winding dirt driveway, and through the trees, Alex could see sunlight reflecting off a large lake. At the end of the driveway, a white lodge with a wraparound porch faced the lake.

Peter got out of the car, as an older woman came out on the steps. "Peter, it's so nice to see you! I haven't seen you in years, probably since..." her voice trailed off.

Peter walked over to lean down and kiss her weathered cheek. "Mrs. Wyman, it's so good to see you again. Thank you for finding room for us on such short notice."

"Of course, dear. If Kat had mentioned you wanted a cabin too, I would have made sure to have the one you've used before. But, at least you're next to Kat." She smiled. "Or I should say, your cabin is the closest one to hers. She always rents the one on the point."

Peter tried to smile, "Mrs. Wyman, we can't wait to say hello to Kat. Where is she?"

"Katherine? Oh, when she comes, she always goes shopping for a bit and then has some sort of a meeting. Usually, she gets back somewhere around six. But she always tells me she'll take care of feeding herself dinner."

"Shopping?"

"Yes, she heads over to Auburn."

"To the mall," Peter paused. "Our grandmother used to take her shopping there."

Luke and Alex saw the color start to rise in Peter's face, but his voice was calm. "Geez, Mrs. Wyman, I guess I'm feeling a bit stupid here, but I can't remember, how many times has Kat come to stay here by herself?"

She didn't realize that Peter was fishing for information. "Oh, just the five times. This is the fifth. She has a standing reservation for three nights, the same nights, each year. And she always asks for the same cabin, you know, the one on the point. She says the privacy there does her good."

***

As the men carried their bags to the cabin closest to Kat's, both Luke and Alex tried to engage Peter in safe conversation, but he didn't even answer. At the cabin, he dumped his bag on a bed, and then turned toward them suddenly. "I'm moving the car over here, so she doesn't see it."

Luke's voice was gentle. "Peter, she's not trying to get away from you. For whatever reason, she needed to do this each year, and…"

"And what? She's been flying home from Spain for the last *four* years, and never bothered to even tell us she was in the country?" He stopped. "I'm moving the car, and then I'm going outside. I'll wait for her there."

Alex stood in his way. "No, we'll all sit on the porch. We're in this together."

Peter glared at him, wanting to start an argument with anyone to vent his rage, but Alex was staring back calmly. "Fine! *We'll* sit on her porch and wait."

***

An hour later, a small black rental car drove slowly past the lodge, and the men could see it coming closer to Kat's cabin. By this point, Luke and Alex sat in the rocking chairs on the porch, while Peter stood leaning against the railing, coiled like a rattlesnake. A car door could be heard closing, and suddenly, around the corner of the building walked Kat, so deep in thought, she didn't see the men waiting for her. She turned the corner of the walkway, and suddenly glanced up at them.

As Alex sat watching her, he saw raw panic cross her face. The color drained out of her face, and he saw her body clench, ready to flee.

Before she could turn and run, Peter's voice cut through the air. "I have your license plate number, and if you try to run, I will call the fucking state police and say you stole the car."

Luke's voice was a warning. "Peter, stop."

"Why, why the hell should I stop?" He glared at his sister. "So help me, Kat, you run this time, and I will call the police."

Kat swallowed and asked in a timid voice, "What are you doing here?"

Sarcasm made Peter's voice even deeper. "We could ask you the same thing since we all got lame messages about you being on assignment."

For a moment, anger flashed across her face, but her voice was relatively calm. "What I do is my business, Pete. Period."

"Bullshit."

Alex realized Kat was wearing a severe black dress with a white scarf with red roses on it, and spike heels, seemingly out of place for shopping at the mall. But, then he remembered that the older woman had mentioned a meeting. What kind of meeting had it been?

Kat closed her eyes for a moment. "Anyway, now you know where I am, do what you want. I'm going inside to change, and then go get some food. If you want something, let me know, and I'll order something for you too."

"Of course you will, as you obviously know exactly how to get dinner around here since you've been doing it for *four* years."

Before their eyes, Kat seemed to shrink into herself. "You know?"

Peter exploded with rage. "Yes, I fucking know! I get a lame message from you, and then we drive all the way out here, worried as hell, to find out that you've been doing this for years, and you never had the decency to tell us." He pointed his finger at her. "You never told us! Did you think we wouldn't support you? Did you ever think we'd try to help?"

Alex and Luke waited for her to erupt in matching anger, but her voice just got quieter and sadder. "I know that you'd try to help, but that's exactly what I *didn't* need. I needed to do this on my own! On my own, Pete. This is my burden, and mine alone. I have to do it alone!"

Still standing on the porch, looking down at his sister, Peter yelled, "It never was your burden alone, Kat. Never! We all bore it in our own ways. All of us. Mom, Dad, Luke and I. Jess in her own way. I was there, remember? I was the one in the room with you when you first saw her, when you first held her. I was the one holding you when she…" Peter's voice broke. "I was there too. So help me, it almost killed me too. How fucking dare you take this on alone? How dare you act as though none of the rest of us felt anything? I think about her every day too. I think about what could have been. And I know what tomorrow is because it still haunts me too. Damn you, Kat, how dare you shut me out!" He looked at Luke, "How dare you shut *us* out of this."

"I know you were there, both of you were there. I couldn't have survived it without you both. I know it impacted you too, but…"

"But what, Kat? Why all the fucking secrecy? Did you think we'd think less of you?"

As Alex and Luke watched in fascination, Kat's shoulders sagged. "I…"

"What, Kat? What?" Peter's voice rose again.

Her voice broke. "You all kept telling me that I had to go on, that I needed to find my peace and go forward, and …" Tears slid down her cheek in the twilight. "And I can't! And I couldn't tell you that. I couldn't tell you that all of you kept telling me to go forward, and not let it destroy me, and it *is* destroying me!" With a sniff, she wiped at the tears angrily. "How could I say to you that I can't let go? That I spend every day wondering what I could have or should have done differently, and what it would be like now if I'd done things differently. That I wake up at night and sit with my guilt, knowing it is all my fault."

Even in his anger, Peter wanted to protect her, and make her see the truth. "Kat, it wasn't your fault. None of it was your fault!"

Her voice rose in frustration, "Yes it was! If I'd not gone to the party. If I'd not had anything to drink. If I'd not gone in the taxi that day. All of it was my fault! All of it." She started to cry in earnest. "And I miss her, Pete. I miss her so much. I wake up at night, and all I want is to hold her again. And Mom and Dad, too. I miss them so, so much. And it's my fault, all of it. So I stuff it down, and pretend that I don't think about it, and then once a year, I let myself come here, and I let myself feel it, and I let myself cry. Because I'm afraid if I let myself cry other than when I'm here, I'll never stop." Kat suddenly turned on her heel. "I've got to go. I've got to go," and she ran into her cottage before the men could react. The sound of the lock clicking into place cut a divide in the silence.

The three men sat in shock for several minutes, all of them reeling inside. The silence was so thick, it was overpowering. Peter looked at Luke in surprise. "Holy shit."

A ghost of a smile crossed Luke's face, "Holy shit, indeed." He stood and took Peter's hand, "Less angry with her now?"

Peter rubbed a shaky hand across his face, "Shit. I didn't mean to…"

Alex's voice cut through the air. "You didn't mean to do anything. You were pissed off, and you said what was on your mind."

"Yeah, but I didn't expect her reaction."

Luke said, "How could you? We had no idea she was coming here, how could we have known how much it was eating at her?"

Alex felt frustration fill him. "What? Could somebody finally tell me what the fuck is going on?"

A small voice said from behind him, "I will." Kat came back onto the porch, barefoot, in jeans and a thick cardigan sweater. She looked at all three men. "It's time, I guess."

For a moment, Peter wanted to stop her, knowing how much it would hurt her to say it all. "Kat, are you sure?"

"I'm sure." She smiled sadly at Luke. "Mr. Psychology over there will say that subconsciously, I probably wanted you to figure out where I was, to force the issue." She swallowed. "After all, I've kept my trips secret for all this time. I sure as hell could have done a better job hiding this one, couldn't I?"

Peter walked over and put his arm around her. "Yeah, it wasn't your best effort."

She elbowed him in the ribs. "Asshole." She looked at Alex, "Ready?" She sighed. "It's a really long story. We might as well go inside and be comfortable."

As she turned to go inside, Peter made a move to follow her. She held up a warning hand. "Pete, this is the time for me to tell Alex. If you come inside, you need to shut up and let me tell it."

He held his hand up in promise. "If I interrupt, you can kick me out."

"Okay." Inside the cabin, Kat walked over to the gas fireplace and lit it, providing the only light in the room.

Before she could sit down, Alex walked over to her, took her hand, and pulled her into the small kitchen without a word. Once they were alone, he pulled her stiff body into his arms, wrapping his arms around her. For a moment, she seemed like she would pull away, but then suddenly she leaned against him. He kissed her hair. "Kat, you don't have to do this."

Her voice was muffled against his chest. "Yes, I do."

"No, you don't. It doesn't have to be right now. It can be another day." His hands stroked her back. "Or never, if you're not ready."

She wrapped her arms around him, and hugged him fiercely. "It has to be now. You're here, and it's time." She looked up at him, tears glistening in her eyes. "Alex, kiss me, please."

He leaned down to kiss her slowly and deeply, feeling her desperation, and sensing her saying good-bye. With a sigh, she pulled away and looked up at him. She cradled his face in her hands. "Alex, I have to tell you that after you hear all of this if it's over between us, I understand."

"Kat, whatever this is, it's not going to change my feelings for you."

She shook her head sadly. "You don't know that." Suddenly she pulled away and opened the kitchen door. "It's time."

"Kat, wait."

"I can't."

Chapter Twenty-Four

Back in the living room, Peter and Luke sat on one couch, leaving the other couch empty. Alex sat down, assuming Kat would join him. When she went to sit on the hearth by the fire, he held out his hand. "Come sit with me."

"I can't." She gazed at him sadly. "I can't touch you and tell you. This is hard enough." She looked nervously at Peter and Luke. "Pete, there are some things you don't know."

For a moment, irritation crossed Peter's face, and Kat saw it instantly. "Pete, please don't be mad."

Seeing her fear, Peter smiled at her gently. "I won't, Kitty Kat. I promise. I love you, and all I want is for you to be happy."

"I know." She pulled her knees up to her chest and wrapped her arms around them. Tipping her head, she looked at Alex, taking a last moment to savor him. Then she took a deep breath. "Alex, I want to try to tell this in the right order, but I only ever *told* anyone all of it once, and that was in a sort of odd situation, so I'm sorry if some of it doesn't make sense."

"It's okay."

She took another deep breath and focused on Alex, suddenly ready to lay the truth out, no matter the consequences. "So when I was in my first year of college, I had a roommate. The college makes all freshman have a roommate that they pick for you. It was the only year I had one, but Kelly was okay. I mean she was completely different than me. She was tall and gorgeous, and dark haired and made guys crazy. And our freshman year, she started dating a guy named Reid. She thought he was amazing, but I don't know why he always made me uncomfortable. But they dated from like October on, and even dated the next year."

"They broke up in May of our sophomore year. After we stopped sharing a room, Kelly and I had breakfast together once a week, so I knew what was going on between them. And that summer, I stayed on campus to get ready to move to Madrid, and Reid stayed on campus too because he was getting ready to go to Russia. And that summer, he asked me out a couple times. And I kept saying no, and it made him really unhappy. But then I started dating Nate, who was going to be going to Russia too. And we sort of dated through the rest of the summer, and when we came back for our senior year, we really started dating."

Alex was trying to follow, knowing that whatever had happened was at the end of college. Why the need for all the history? "Okay."

"And then we broke up around Thanksgiving of my senior year, and soon after, Reid asked me out again, and I still said no. And then I came home for Christmas, and…" Even in the dim light, Alex could see her cheeks darken. "And I met you over that break."

"When we went to the opera," he said gently, "And then we stayed up way too late talking that night."

"Yeah."

"And you called me on January 21st, right, isn't that the date you said? You called my apartment while I was out running errands."

Peter's voice cut through the room. "What did you say?"

Kat looked at him sharply, "Peter, I told you, some things you don't know, and I really need you to be quiet now."

Alex continued. "And I never called back because Will never gave me the message."

Peter realized the implications. "Son of a bitch…"

"Pete, shut up!" Kat closed her eyes for a moment, and when she opened them, naked pain radiated from them as she looked at Alex. "And you never called me. And the thing was, well, it was *really*, really hard for me to get up the nerve to call you. I really liked you. Looking back now, I had a hell of a crush on you, then you gave me your number and said to call, but I wasn't sure that you really meant it. I kept telling myself that you hadn't really wanted me to call, that you were just being nice. But then I decided that the only way I was going to know for sure was to man up and call you. And so that afternoon, it was a Saturday, I made up my mind to call you."

She rubbed her forehead. "It sounds really stupid, but after I decided, I took a shower, and did my hair, and got dressed up, and put on makeup and perfume." She buried her face in her hands for a moment, then lifted her head. "I was so nervous about calling you that I needed to make sure I looked really good before calling like you'd be able to see me or something."

Out of the corner of his eye, Alex saw the pain on Peter's face, but he knew he needed to focus on Kat. "I'm sorry I didn't call you back, Kat." He smiled at her, trying to convince her he was still there for her, "Kat, I kept hoping and hoping you'd call. I promise if I'd gotten the message, I would have called you back."

She sniffed. "I know you would have. I mean, I know that *now*. But, I didn't know that then. But after I called, and Will said you'd be back in about a half-hour, I sat and waited. Actually, I didn't sit. I paced, and I cleaned my bureau." She stopped. "That's funny, I'd forgotten that part. I was so wound I cleaned all the drawers in my bureau trying to kill time." The amusement left her face as quickly as it had come. "But after an hour, you still hadn't called. And so I got up to use the bathroom, and when I was out in the hall, I ran into Kelly and her friend Kaitlyn." She grimaced. "They invited me to go to a party, and I said that

I was busy, and anyway, Kelly kept pressing until I said that I was waiting for a call, and she asked how long I'd been waiting, and when I told her, she told me to get a life and go out for a change. And I suddenly got mad at you for not calling me back," Kat's face showed contrition. "I'm sorry I got mad at you, Alex. I didn't know you didn't get the message. I just thought you were blowing me off."

How could she apologize for being upset that he hadn't called her back? He should be apologizing, not her! "Kat, you don't have to apologize for that!"

She looked down at her hands, rubbing her fingers like she did after writing for too long. "So I went out with Kelly and Kaitlyn, and we went across campus to Deke."

"Deke?" Alex knew he'd heard it mentioned before at the wedding, but couldn't remember the context.

"One of the frats. The one that Reid and Nate belonged to. And when we got there, there was a band, and purple punch and everyone was drinking."

Alex remembered their first meeting, "And you didn't drink because you were still underage."

She shook her head ruefully. "No. Life would have been really different, maybe, if I'd been so virtuous *that* night. I didn't drink with you guys because I wasn't legal, but somehow on that night, my morals left the building. So I drank a cup of purple punch, which was basically all vodka, rum and a little bit of grape juice. And then I danced for a while, and then Reid came over and asked me to dance, and I said no, and it really pissed him off, and he called me a cold bitch, but then he came back over a few minutes later, and apologized, and offered to get me a drink to show there were no hard feelings. And by that time, the punch was already making me stupid, so I said yes, and he came back a few minutes later with a cup, and I drank the punch for a while."

Suddenly, Kat stood up. "I need something to drink."

Peter jumped up. "I'll get it. What do you want?"

She shrugged, "I don't care. Water, Diet Coke, seltzer." A smile flickered across her face. "Hemlock tea." While Peter went into the kitchen, Kat turned and stared at the fire silently. As Alex watched her, he realized he'd never seen someone farther inside themselves than her at that moment. Pain radiated from her hunched shoulders.

A minute later, Peter returned with four cans of seltzer and handed them out. Kat turned around, took the can, took a long swallow, then sat back down. "And so if the first punch made me stupid, the second was worse, especially since it had been laced. But I didn't know that then."

With a sinking heart, Alex suddenly knew what was coming. Before he could say anything, Kat continued, "And a while later, Reid asked me to dance again, really nicely, and I said yes, and then, the next thing I remember is waking up in his room, most of my clothes gone. And when I woke up, he was raping me, and I tried really hard to stop him, and he hit me several times, and I passed out again." She paused, took a sip. "Then I came to again, and he was raping me again, and I remember trying really hard to get him off me, and he was saying things about how I deserved it after all the times he'd asked me out, and that I was a tease showing up at the party dressed like I was, and I kept trying to get him off me, and finally I got enough leverage that I nailed him in the groin with my knee, and he punched me in the head at least once, I remember one, but in the end, I had a bunch of bruises, so I don't know how many times he hit me. And I woke up half-naked, bruised, and in the back stairwell of the frat house. There was this back stairwell that no one used unless it was to toss bags of garbage from a party." She closed her eyes. "I guess I was sort of like a bag of garbage at that point."

Alex searched for something to say, nauseous at the thought of what she had gone through. "Kat, I'm so sorry."

"You have nothing to be sorry for." She took a deep breath. "So I remember getting up, trying to make sure I was covered, and I remember it was so cold, and I didn't have my coat anymore, only some of my clothes. Luckily, my room key card was in my skirt pocket. So I walked back to my room, and called the only person I could think of who could help. I called Josh. And he came over with Mariah and took me to the hospital, and they examined me, and they couldn't do a rape kit because they were out of them. They had plenty of the stupid plastic bracelets, but they didn't have a rape kit." She swallowed a sip of seltzer. "And while I was doing that, Reid was clearly figuring out what he'd done, and by the time the police were called to the hospital, he'd already gone to the college security, and thrown himself on their mercy, saying we were a *couple*"— she spat out the last word— "and that it had gotten out of control, and that he was so *worried* about me. The security came over to the hospital, and literally, the woman told me how lucky I was to have such a nice boyfriend."

Shock made Alex's voice harsher than he intended. "You can't be serious."

Peter couldn't keep quiet. "It gets better."

Kat shot him a warning glance. "And so Josh called Mom and Dad, and they came right up, and took me home for a couple days. But in the midst of it all, we never stopped to think that the hospital never gave me the morning after pill. And in the meantime, the local police investigated, and Deke brothers gave affidavits about how I'd been dressed that night, and how I'd taken a drink from Reid, and how I'd danced with him. And one swore he heard me begging for Reid to, quote, 'Fuck me hard.' Another said the bruises were from when I tripped and fell when I was so drunk. And Nate…" Kat stopped, so tired and sad that she didn't know if she could continue.

Luke stood up, crossed the room, and squeezed her shoulder. "Kat, enough. The rest can wait."

She looked up at him, seeing his concern. "I've gone this far…" Kat looked at Alex. "And it's time he knows it all."

"Are you sure?"

She shrugged. "I might as well say it all. If after I say it's over, it's over."

Luke felt his heart swell with pride at her bravery. "Okay." He moved to sit down next to Peter again.

"And Nate gave a sworn affidavit that when we were together that I'd liked rough sex. He even said I liked being hit. Which, for the record, I don't. I didn't then, don't now, never ever." Alex ached looking at Kat, suddenly understanding her reaction at seeing Nate last summer. "And meanwhile, Reid's father was contacting the college, making a deal to pay for a new student center. So after a week at home, I came back to college, thinking that maybe someone other than Josh and Mariah would support me, and everywhere I went, people stopped talking and stared. And then the phone calls started, and each night I got calls over and over with guys saying things like how much I'd liked it when Reid had 'done' me, and how they'd listened to me moaning. And maybe I could have made it through all of that, but then the local police notified me that they weren't going to press charges, since Reid had admitted having sex with me, but it was all a romantic evening that had gotten out of control. And I completely fell apart." Kat leaned back against the wall. "And I came home, and Dad made arrangements with the college for me to finish my senior year as an independent study so I could still graduate. And even then, the phone calls didn't stop until we unlisted our phone number. One of the last ones, a guy told me the drink had been laced, but that I deserved it. In the meantime, the college released the news that the Morgan Family Student Center would be started the day after graduation, completely and totally paid for by Reid's father."

Alex closed his eyes for a moment. "Jesus, Kat, I'm so sorry."

"Oh, it wasn't over." Alex looked at her, trying to imagine what more could have happened to her. "When I came home, I just wanted to hide and lick my figurative wounds, and then two months later, I..." Kat hugged her knees closer. "My periods had never been regular because I ran too much, so I never knew when they were going to come or not. So at the end of March, I suddenly realized that I was queasy a lot, and my favorite jeans weren't fitting right." Alex suddenly realized what she was saying, and his eyes got wide. "And so I went to the doctor, and found out I was two months pregnant, from the rape. I'd had periods since Nate and I had broken up, so it was the only possibility. And so I had to figure out what to do. My parents"—she looked at Peter and Luke adoringly—"and Pete and Luke and Jess were wonderful. And Mom and I spent many hours trying to figure out what to do, and finally, I decided to have an abortion. On the day it was scheduled for, Mom had strep throat and was really sick, so Dad took me. I knew he wasn't happy about it, I mean, he was a pro-choice guy, but not pro-choice when it was his little girl, but he never said a word to try to stop me. But I knew how he felt. Probably if he had said anything, I would have gone through with it to prove I was an adult, but when we got to the clinic, he just said he loved me no matter what, and when they asked me if he was coming in with me, he said he would, and I said no, that I was going in alone. Knowing how he felt, I couldn't ask him to hold my hand through it." Alex tried to imagine her father's pain, how much it must have hurt him to see her walk through that door. "So he stayed in the waiting room, and I went in, and just before they were going to do it, I had them stop. I couldn't go through with it. And so I came out and went home, and we all figured out how I was going to have a baby, and how we were going to make sure as a family that the baby never knew anything but love." Suddenly Kat looked at Peter with eyes filled with tears. "She never knew anything but love, did she, Pete?"

His gentle voice was certain, "No, Kat. She was loved through and through. That is certain." His voice broke. "She still *is* loved. That never changes."

Alex's brain reeled as all the pieces began to fit together. When Kat had said earlier how much she missed 'her,' he'd assumed she meant her mother. But now, he suddenly knew.

Kat's voice trembled. "And so I came home, and over the next months, I got really pregnant." She paused.

When she resumed, her voice seemed stronger, "Anyway, we figured it all out. I was going to have the baby, and stay in New York with Mom and Dad, and once the baby was old enough, I'd think about working, and we even made the room off my room into a nursery. And then, Dad got contacted by Reid's father, that they wanted to give me a financial gift, not as an assumption of guilt, but because I had obviously misunderstood what had happened that night."

Alex needed to know something, "Did Reid or his father know that you were pregnant?"

"No. We never told them."

"Did you accept the money?"

She shook her head. "I didn't want to. I wanted nothing more to do with any of it, just make a life for me and my child." She looked at Pete. "Remember how she used to kick at night when we'd watch TV?"

For a moment, the pain left Peter's face as he smiled, thinking back. "She packed a wallop. I remember watching your stomach move as she'd dance around."

"Especially when you'd play the drums."

"Yeah. That was the best." He gazed at Alex, suddenly so relieved to be able to share the memories.

"And I'd play, and then after, I'd feel the baby just dancing up a storm."

"And Pete was my birthing partner. So he'd go to baby class with me." She grinned. "Remember when that bitch CeeCee yelled at you?"

Peter chuckled. "Yeah." He turned toward Alex. "After class one night, I told Kat that as soon as I took her home, I was going out dancing." He looked at Luke. "After all, Luke was being so cool about all of this, but we wanted to go out. This woman heard me and went off about men who get women pregnant and then don't stay around to help. Kat just burst out laughing and told her I was her brother, not the father, and the woman almost swallowed her tongue."

Kat looked at Alex. "But you asked about the money. I refused, but Dad convinced me otherwise. He convinced me that by taking their settlement, the baby would always have financial stability. He convinced me that I could take it and put it in a trust fund. So I did." She looked embarrassed. "Reid's father paid me a million dollars. Then it seemed like a huge amount, but frankly, he'd spent eighteen million dollars on the stupid student center, so it was nothing to him. He sent the money, and we put it in a trust fund."

Her face clouded. "And then, in late September, I was beginning to be really uncomfortable. I was supposed to go to my doctor's appointment, and I decided to take a cab because it was hot, and I just was too tired to walk." Her shoulders sagged. "My cabbie was in a huge hurry because his wife had called and he was supposed to pick up his son at school, and so he was driving like a bat out of hell. He came flying up a side street, and the light was yellow, and instead of slowing down, he gunned it, and as we went through the intersection, a Ryder truck plowed into the side of the cab." Her voice trembled. "I got thrown against the driver's side wall of the cab, fracturing three ribs, and it caused the amniotic sac to rupture, and suddenly I was in labor, and being rushed to the hospital."

Kat sat up straighter, leaning against the wall in exhaustion, her face ghostly pale. "I got to the hospital, and they almost immediately put me in a labor room because she was ready to be born. And Pete got there, and they had to figure out how I could naturally deliver this premature baby with broken ribs. And then, several hours later—"

Peter interrupted. "And incredible pain on Kat's part." He smiled at her with tear-filled eyes. "And you never complained."

"Several hours later, she was born. Five years, four days ago, Rose Belle, our Rosie, three pounds, one ounce, and seventeen inches long."

Alex couldn't help himself from interrupting. "Four days ago, when you took off for the day?"

Kat nodded, "I needed to be alone for the day. It was the best excuse I could think of, I'm sorry." She wrapped her arms around her knees again, trying to keep from crying. "Five years, four days ago. But she was so little, and the accident had made her be born too early. But she tried so hard..." Kat laid her head down on her knees, and her shoulders shook with silent sobs.

The three men sat in silence. Alex looked up at Peter and Luke and saw tears running down their cheeks too, and suddenly realized his own cheeks were wet. Peter swiped at his eyes. "Kat?"

For a few seconds, there was no response, but then she lifted her head and looked straight at Alex. "But no matter how hard she fought, or how hard we all tried, or how hard the hospital tried, it was too much for her little system. And five days later, she died." The last word was so softly spoken, Alex barely heard her.

He tried to convey his sadness. "Oh, Kat...."

It was as if she didn't hear him. "And so three days later, we came here, and had a private ceremony to bury her." She looked at Peter, "And this is the rest of what you didn't know, and I'm sorry for that, Pete."

His voice was so low, it was hard to hear his words, "It's okay, Kitty, tell me now."

"That night after the funeral, we came back here. And I was supposed to go to sleep."

"We sedated you. You needed to finally get some sleep."

"You thought you sedated me. But you didn't."

"Of course we did. I sat there while Mom gave you the pills. I remember being mad because she made you show her your mouth after you swallowed like you were a child again." Peter suddenly grinned, remembering something from years before. "It was like the Ritalin, wasn't it?"

Alex's confusion was clear on his face. "Huh?"

Kat grinned, for a moment pleased with herself. "When I was little, I was considered a problem child in school, so the school recommended I be medicated so I would be calmer. So, Mom and Dad had a doctor prescribe Ritalin for me, and every time they'd give me a dose, I'd put it in my cheek and spit it out later. Finally, they gave up. So, yes. I cheeked the sedative."

Peter raised an eyebrow. "And?"

"After you were all asleep, I climbed out the window and walked back to the cemetery."

Peter's voice showed his horror. "It's over three miles! You'd just been badly injured, had a baby, and the trauma of her death, and then you walked back there?"

Her voice was small. "I couldn't let her be there all alone that night. I couldn't. I know it sounds stupid, I know now that she was gone. But I couldn't let her be there alone. In my mind, all I could think about was she would be afraid in the dark, all alone. And probably, frankly, it was the first time since she'd been born that I was alone even for a moment. And I could say the things I needed to say."

"We would have taken you." Peter corrected himself. "I don't know if Mom and Dad would have taken you, but I would have. Or I would have walked with you or something."

"I know, Pete. I probably knew that then, but I couldn't tell anyone. I needed to do it alone. She was *my* daughter, the little life that I had at first so dreaded and resented, and then been so excited to welcome. I needed to be alone with her, to talk to her alone. So I got there, and I sat next to the grave, and I started talking to her. And then about an hour later, a man came out of the shadows toward me."

Luke was shocked. "Jesus!"

Kat continued, "Remember how the day Rose was buried, there was another funeral there?"

Both Peter and Luke nodded.

"It was for a twenty-five-year-old boy, named Jacob White. Jesus, listen to me call him a boy. He was almost five years older than me. He'd been hit and killed by a drunk driver as he crossed the road near the post office the same day Rosie died. Anyway, it was his father who'd been sitting at his grave, for the same reason I was there. The two of us sat for hours and hours, talking. We'd both lost our children on the same day, and buried them on the same day. We were both alone. His wife had died two years before from cancer, and Jacob was his only child. He was there because Jacob had never really left home. He'd gone off to college to become a kindergarten teacher, and then he'd moved home while he found a job, and had just sort of stayed. His dad said that every night that Jacob was home, that he and his dad would sit together, have a Molson Golden, and talk about the day. He said that after all the people left his house after the funeral and reception, that he couldn't stand the thought of Jacob being alone, so he took the beer to the cemetery. So we sat between the two graves, and drank a couple beers, and cried and cried, and laughed, and shared our life stories. And when the sun started to come up, he drove me here, and I snuck back in."

Peter's voice was incredulous. "We never knew."

"You weren't supposed to. It was my secret." She was desperate for her brother to understand. "Pete, at that point in my life, you and Mom and Dad in particular, and Luke and Jess to a lesser degree, knew every possible thing about my life, down to having to talk about my sex life with Mom and Dad in the room. In having that few hours, I wasn't on display. And so when Mr. White drove me back here, we made a pact."

"What?"

"Every year, on the day they died, we'd come back together. That night when he dropped me off, he made a joke about how I'd bring dinner, and he'd bring the beer, and we do. Tomorrow, I'll go pick up a pizza that I have a standing order for, and I'll meet him there at dark, and we'll let ourselves mourn, catch up on the year, talk about what could have been, and then we can go forward again."

"Okay." Peter tried to assimilate all of this new information, still reeling from all of his emotions.

Luke leaned forward, suddenly realizing something. "Kat, if you're meeting him tomorrow, why do you come up the day before, and what is the meeting that Mrs. Wyman says you go to each year?"

Kat took a deep breath. "I…"

"What?"

She looked down at her hands, suddenly afraid they wouldn't like her answer. "I started a foundation with the money. I come up each year and go shopping for the local battered women's shelters, and then each year, I give them a donation from the foundation." She swallowed, and her voice was small, "This year each of four shelters received fifteen thousand dollars each. I'm sorry I didn't tell you. I just wanted to make sure that her life stood for something. I give the gifts in her name." She stood up, rubbing her arms as if cold. "Guys, I really need a moment. I'll be back, but I need some fresh air. I promise I'll be back."

Almost silently, she walked away, fading into the darkness away from the fire.

Peter looked at Alex, seeing the sadness and shock on his face. "Sorry, Alex, I..."

Alex shook his head. "You don't need to apologize. If anything, I owe you one." Peter looked confused. "I'm sorry, Peter. And Luke. I'm so sorry that I wasn't there to support you during all of this. I'm sorry." He stood. "I need to go find her."

Chapter Twenty-Five

The front door of the cottage was ajar. In the quickly fading light, Alex could see her standing by the shore, staring out at the black water. Walking quietly, he approached her, unsure of what to say.

When he stopped beside her, she didn't look at him, but quietly said, "You don't need to say anything. It's okay. No matter that it changes how you feel about me, it was time to tell you. Probably deep down I knew that leaving those messages would make all this happen."

Her certainty that he would walk away from her, from *them*, almost ripped Alex's heart in two. Without saying a word, he moved to stand in front of her, reached out to gently cradle her face in his hands, and leaned down to kiss her, willing every ounce of his love for her into the kiss.

At first, Kat held herself stiffly, not touching him, not responding to the kiss. When Alex continued to kiss her, he felt her move closer, then, tentatively raise her hands to wrap her arms around him. Suddenly, the kiss deepened, as passion erupted between them. Tongues danced, hands roamed, until Alex reluctantly pulled back, finally needing to speak out loud. "I love you."

Kat stared at him in disbelief. "You what?"

"I love you. I've loved you probably since the first night at the opera, almost certainly since you interviewed me in Madrid, but definitely since the wedding weekend. I loved you then, I love you now, and after what you just shared, I love you even more."

Kat stepped back, looking at him warily, her arms crossed in front of herself protectively. "You can't. You can't love me. I just told you that I was raped, knocked up, and my child died. And the part I left out is that I fell apart so badly that my parents had to take care of me, then they went away for a weekend for a break, and were killed by a drunk driver. So, in effect, I killed my own child and parents. You can't love me. You just feel sorry for me right now, so you are saying you love me."

Strangely, her words filled him with hope. She hadn't said she didn't love him; she just tried to justify why someone wouldn't love *her*. He smiled and pushed a strand of hair away from her eye. "Nope. I love you."

Her voice became more strident. "You can't."

"I can." He rested his forehead on hers. "I love you, and I love you although right now, I don't think *you* can love you. But I love you enough for the two of us, and now that the truth, the huge, life-shattering secret is out in the open, we can go forward."

"You think that now. But in the cold light of day, you will realize that you don't love me."

"No, I won't." He hesitated before asking, "Do you love me?"

Even in the darkness, he could see her eyes glisten with tears, "Oh, God, yes, Alex. I love you."

His arms wrapped tightly around her and kissed her forehead. "Then I love you, you love me. All the rest we can figure out."

She started to cry, and Alex picked her up, cradling her close to his body as he moved them over to one of the Adirondack chairs. He didn't say a word as she cried, just rubbed her back. While she wept, he tried to imagine her pain, fear, and sadness, and without meaning too, his arms tightened around her hoping she could feel his love for her. Finally, her breathing slowed, and the sobs quieted. She sniffled. "Your shirt's all wet."

He was amused that would be what mattered to her right then. "Yup. And it will dry."

She pulled back a bit to look up at him. "I love you."

He smoothed her hair back and brushed away the remaining tears from her swollen eyes. "And I love you. Nothing is going to change that."

Suddenly her eyes filled again. "Shit, Alex, I miss her so much."

His own eyes immediately filled with tears too, seeing her pain. "I know, baby, I know." He stroked her cheek. "I wish I had met her."

Just then they heard the porch door swing open. Kat took a deep breath. "That's Pete, being as patient as he can. I guess we have to go back now."

"If you're ready to. Otherwise, he can wait." Even Alex could hear the protective note in his voice.

"Ahhh." Kat's voice sounded more relaxed.

"Ahhh, what?" He nuzzled her cheek.

"You sounded possessive again. Protective."

"Is that a good thing or a bad one?"

"A very good one." Kat shifted on his lap, then stood up. "We have to go back." She held out her hand. "C'mon."

***

As they got close to the cottage, Kat dropped Alex's hand and suddenly ran up the stairs to run into Peter's arms. Alex watched as brother and sister hugged, cried, and held each other. He could only hear bits and pieces but heard Rose's name several times over the next couple of minutes. Finally, Peter stepped back a bit, his arm still protectively around his little sister, and looked out at Alex. His words were directed at his sister, but his eyes never left Alex's. "You two okay? I mean, really?"

Kat tipped her head looking at Alex, and then a slow smile lit her entire face. "Yeah. We're good, really good."

"Well then, shit! Let's have dinner to celebrate!"
***

The four of them discussed getting take out or going out for dinner, and Peter and Luke were surprised when Kat wanted to go to a local diner, one that the family had gone to regularly before Rosie's death. After a dinner of burgers and fries and local draft beer, the four went back to the cottages. At the steps of Peter and Luke's cottage, Kat paused. "Pete, Luke, Alex is going next door with me. But we'll see you in the morning, okay?" Her voice broke. "I am so glad you guys came up today, and I love you more than I can tell you."

Peter's voice shook. "Kitty Kat, I am so glad too. And I am so glad that we can finally talk about it. I feel like, for the first time in almost five years, I can mention her name, talk about her, and acknowledge the feelings, without being afraid of driving you away."

Kat looked down at her feet, suddenly afraid to ask a question that had been on her mind for the last couple of hours. "When we get home, would it be okay if we put the picture of all of us up in the sunroom?"

Peter immediately knew what picture she meant. "Of course. We would love that."

Kat stood on tiptoe and kissed her brother on the cheek. "Night, Pete. Night, Luke."
***

Alex and Kat walked in silence to their cottage. Inside, Alex lit the fireplace, as the room was cool. Standing back up, he put his arm around Kat. "What picture?"

"Do you want to see it?"

Alex was surprised that she would have the picture with her. "Of course."

Kat left the room and came back a minute later with a wooden box. The top of the box had a rose engraved on it, with a birth and death date under it. Reverently, Kat put the box on the coffee table and sat down, and motioned for Alex to sit next to her.

She opened the box. On top was a soft green baby blanket. "I knitted this for her. I knitted a couple of them; one was buried with her, and this one I kept." She picked it up and held it to her face. "I can still almost smell her." She set the blanket aside with trembling hands. "This is the first picture of her."

Alex looked at the framed picture of an absolutely perfect, tiny baby girl, held in Kat's arms. Even in the picture, he could see the bruises on Kat's face and arms, but the look of joy and love on her face was so clear. "She was absolutely beautiful, Kat. And you looked so happy, so full of love."

Over the next half hour, Kat took item after item out of the box, explaining them to Alex. At the bottom of the box was a framed photo of Kat, Rose, Peter, Luke, Jess, and Kat's parents. The tiny baby was held protectively in Kat's arms, with all the others wrapped around the two of them. "This is the picture I meant." Her voice broke. "It was the last picture we had taken before she died." She wiped her eyes. "They told us there wasn't anything more they could do, that her organs were failing, so they recommended that we hold her and talk to her and sing to her, and let her know how much we loved—" she corrected herself "—love her. And we did. And she died in my arms, with my whole family around us."

Alex pulled her close and kissed her hair. "How beautiful, Kat."

Kat leaned against him tiredly. "I am so glad you know. Now I don't have to pretend anymore."

"Me too. So many things make sense now."

"What do you mean?"

"Like when you said you get down this time of year. Or why you reacted when I asked why you hadn't called me." He paused. "Kat, I am so sorry."

"For what?"

"For not calling you back. Maybe if I had, it would have all been different. For not being there as you were going through hell. For not being there to help your brother as *he* was going through hell. For being so intent on my feelings for you that I missed some pretty obvious signs about all of this."

Kat sat up and turned so she could look at him fully. "Alex, don't apologize. The thing is, I finally began to figure it all out recently. I wish I hadn't been raped, of course, I do. But I will never regret getting pregnant and having Rosie. Even with what happened, I wouldn't give up having those days with her, having my pregnancy with her. I'm her *mom*, and I wouldn't change that for the world. I've hidden that part of me for so long, stuffed it down, and I can't—won't do that anymore. I want to put up pictures of her. I want to say her name. I want to finally let myself *feel* it." Her voice broke. "I will live, for the rest of my life, every single day with the guilt of the responsibility of getting in that cab that day. The would-haves, could-haves, should-haves. If I hadn't gone in that cab, and walked, she might be here now. I can't change that. I have to live with that guilt. I have to live with the guilt that if I had handled it all better, my parents would have had an easier time, and might not have gone away, and might still be alive."

"Their deaths, all three of them, aren't your fault." How could she blame herself? "Kat, truly they aren't."

She stroked his face. "Alex, on that we have to agree to disagree, okay?"

Maybe in time, he could help her let go of the guilt. "Okay."

There was a quiet knock at the door. Alex went and opened it, and on the doorstep was a bottle of wine and a bottle of champagne, with the note, "Love you both."

Standing behind him, Kat chuckled. "Peter and Luke strike again."

Alex carried the two bottles into the kitchen. "Would you like something?"

"Wine, please."

When Alex came back into the living room, Kat was standing by the fireplace, gazing into the flames. Alex handed her a glass. "To the future, Kat."

"To the past and to the future." Kat took a sip, then looked at Alex searchingly. In a tentative tone, she asked, "You really love me?"

With lightning speed, Alex put his glass on the mantle, then took hers and put it there as well. He turned to Kat, and pulled her into his arms. "I love you more than I can express. I think I've loved you for more than five years, but I know for certain that I've loved you since you looked like you bit into a lemon when you realized you were going to interview me in Madrid."

"I did not!"

"Yes, you did. And it was one of the sexiest things I ever saw. You, all prissy about the interview, looking fine in those black jeans, asking all your questions without letting me know anything about you. Then we went out after the concert, and I can promise you, my hope was that you were going to come back to the hotel with me that night." He smiled. "I felt a bit guilty that I was about to hit on my friend's baby sister."

"That's not love, that's horniness."

"Uh-unh. I fully admit that you turned me on, just like you do constantly, but I wanted to make love to you, sleep with you, wake up and have breakfast with you, not just jump you." His voice deepened. "After all the years, when as far as I knew you'd never called, I thought it was the universe giving us a second chance, and I wasn't going to screw it up again."

"Oh."

"And then there was dress shopping with you. The nervous look on your face when you came out of the dressing room made me want to beat up the world for you." He nuzzled her ear. "Yes, Katherine, I love you to the moon and back. I love you, I like you, you turn me on, I want to protect you, sometimes you make me insane, but more than anything, I love you."

The final hesitancy in believing him dissolved. Kat reached up to pull him down to kiss him and did so with all her love. For the first time, Alex didn't feel any hesitation from her and knew somehow that he needed to let her take the lead. She pulled him back toward the couch, and laid down beside him, not breaking the kiss. She tugged his shirt free, needing to feel his skin on hers.

For long minutes, they kissed, hands roamed, tongues teased each other. When she started to unbutton his shirt, Alex stopped her hands. She pulled back, and he saw the instantaneous look of uncertainty on her face and kissed her lips softly. "I'm not stopping you, but I promised you that I'd follow your parameters. This is going farther than we have before." He grinned and nipped at her bottom lip, "And as much as it is killing me to stop you right now, I need to know what you want."

Kat was no longer afraid he was rejecting her. "I want you to make love to me." Her eyes glowed. "Please."

Alex stood up, then reached down to take Kat in his arms. "Then we are moving into the bedroom. I damn well am not making love to you for the first time on a couch like some teenager."

In the bedroom, a small lamp lit the corner of the room. Alex placed Kat gently on the bed. Kat reached up to unbutton two more of the buttons on his shirt, suddenly nervous. She whispered, "Alex, would you please make love to me now?"

"Are you sure?"

"Yes," Kat looked straight at Alex. "I'm sure."

Silently, he laid down next to Kat and caressed her face with his fingertips. Kat's breath caught as desire overwhelmed her. Still, a little voice inside nagged at her. "Alex, wait. I need to tell you a few things. Obviously, I'm not a virgin, but I have a clean bill of health."

"I do too."

"I'm on the pill too, so we don't have to worry about me getting pregnant." Kat blushed. "Well, damn that was really romantic."

Alex's voice was almost fierce as he replied. "Stop putting yourself down, it needed to be said." Stroking her hair back from her face, Alex kissed Kat deeply. He smiled as her tongue came to stroke his in a tantalizing dance. Alex rubbed her back, and then slid his hands under her cardigan. Kat was naked under the sweater, and her skin was softer than he had imagined.

Kat's hands wandered over Alex's chest until they came to the buttons on his shirt. With shaking fingers, she undid the rest of the buttons until her fingertips brushed over the curling hair on his chest. Alex gasped at her light touch. At the sound, Kat stiffened. Pulling back from the kiss, Alex looked into her eyes, seeing her hesitation. He slowly nibbled on her lower lip.

"Kat, I love you. If you want to stop, you just have to tell me. I won't be mad."

"I don't want you to stop. I'm just..."

"What?" He stroked her face. "Tell me."

"It's been a really intense day. My head is spinning."

"Do you want to take this slow?"

As he asked, Kat was running her fingertips over his chest. She suddenly realized how much she wanted to touch every inch of him. "No, if anything, I can't take much longer." She smiled. "Yes, I'm feeling hormone-crazed."

"Well, then we should probably do something about that…" He ran his hands lightly down her sides, feeling her breathing change, "Hormone-crazed? I think I like it when you are hormone-crazed…"

She giggled, and Alex realized it was one of the sexiest sounds he'd ever heard. Still giggling, she undid the rest of his shirt buttons with fumbling eager hands. Alex stopped to unbutton his jeans, while Kat stood up to pull hers off. When she turned, she wore only her unbuttoned cardigan and her silk bikini panties. Blushing, she tried to get under the comforter quickly, but Alex kicked it out of her reach as he lay beside her wearing only his unbuttoned jeans. Reverently, he traced a line from her rapid pulse in her neck to the shadow between her breasts. Pushing the sweater aside, he took a sharp breath as he saw her perfect shapeliness for the first time. Looking into her shining eyes, he kissed the shadow and murmured, "Kat, you are more beautiful that I imagined, and I've spent a lot of time imagining lately." Suddenly he saw the small tattoo on her left breast. He traced it gently with one finger, "A rose for Rosie. That's why…"

Kat knew what he was thinking. "That's part of the reason. If you'd seen the tattoo before knowing, you'd have asked about it, and I'd either have had to tell you, which I wasn't ready to do, or lie to you, which I didn't want to do." She blushed. "I also couldn't make love to you with a secret like that, even if I could have made sure you didn't see it."

Alex rolled over to turn up the light so he could see it clearly. The small red rose rested in a heart, with two dates on either side, dates he now knew represented the life of that beautiful little girl. He traced the heart with one finger. "It's beautiful." He looked uncomfortable. "Is it going to weird you out if I touch it when we…?"

Kat blushed but didn't pull away at the intimate words. "No, it won't weird me out at all. Alex, please take off your clothes."

"With pleasure." Alex stood and pulled off his jeans with fluid grace, and Kat lay on the bed watching. She had seen him naked from the waist up, but seeing him totally naked for the first time made her heart race. His body was perfect in her eyes. Once he was naked, he leaned over and kissed her parted lips. "Do you need help with the rest of your clothes?"

Biting her lower lip, Kat shook her head. With trembling hands, she pulled her sweater off and then slid the wisp of black silk off her hips. Totally naked, she laid back on the bed never taking her eyes from his. The bed moved as Alex came to lie beside her and then he kissed her deeply. Where their bodies met, Alex could feel Kat's racing heart. Murmuring words of endearment, he began to lightly kiss Kat's face and neck. Slowly he kissed her shoulders and arms, smiling as Kat gasped when he kissed the hollow of her collarbone. Without stopping, Alex kissed every inch of her until he reached the swollen, rosy peaks. Lightly kissing them, he ran his fingertips over the sensitive skin until Kat began to move restlessly. His tongue flickered out to tease them as she unconsciously arched upward to give him easier access. Slowly, Alex continued kissing her smooth stomach and then stopped. For an agonizing moment, Kat thought Alex was through, and that her reaction had turned him off.

Then she saw the loving look on his face. He looked at her with passion and hope as he intertwined his fingers through hers. "Say it, Kat. I need to hear you say it."

With complete understanding, Kat looked into his eyes and firmly said, "Please make love to me Alex, please."

With the smile of a conqueror, Alex softly kissed the mound of reddish-gold curls. Lightly licking and nibbling, Alex became unbearably aroused listening to Kat's gasps, until he heard her say, "Alex, please, I need to feel you inside of me now."

Alex slowly slid into her warmth. All of the months of agonizing desire built up in him as soon as she wrapped around him. He braced himself on his forearms as he looked down at her face. Her cheeks were flushed, and her eyes glowed in the lamplight. Slowly, he moved in and out, watching her look of wonder. He leaned closer so that he could lightly lick her ear. Her intake of breath made her tighten her muscles around him.

"God, Kat. You feel so good." He slid back, so they were barely in contact. Kat bit her lip and opened her eyes. The fear in them made Alex pause. "Baby, what is it? What are you afraid of?"

"I don't know. I don't feel in control anymore. This is so different. I don't know what to do."

"Good different, or bad different?"

"Good different."

"Then enjoy it. Stop thinking so much, and just feel us together."

Alex leaned down and lightly began to stroke her lips with his tongue. When Kat opened her mouth so he could slide his tongue inside, he whispered, "Let go, Kat. Nothing that happens between us is wrong. Let yourself go and just feel. This is right. This is love."

Slowly she ran her hands down to his waist and pulled him closer. Alex watched the emotions on her face as he began to move again. Kat closed her eyes, and her lips parted as her muscles tightened around him and her breathing became ragged. Alex felt her fingernails dig into his back as she constricted around him with a passionate "Alex. Oh God, Alex." Smiling, Alex lost himself to the tide of passion as he poured into her.

Neither one of them knew how much time passed before Alex stirred. "Oh, baby, I must be crushing you."

Kat tightened her arms around him. "No, you aren't. Don't move. I don't want this to end."

Gently Alex untangled himself so that he could pull Kat into his arms. "Don't want what to end? My crushing the breath out of you?"

"No." Kat smiled shyly. "Our making love. I don't want it to end."

Alex kissed her hair. "I have to admit, I've spent an amazing amount of time fantasizing about making love to you, but it was better than I ever thought it could be."

Kat stroked his chest. "It was like I was being drawn to the edge of a cliff and even if I had wanted to, I couldn't have turned around. Suddenly, the whole world was swirling around me, and it was like freefalling, and then I felt you come with me."

Alex kissed her gently. "You just needed to trust us."

"Trust and love. I trust and love you." Tears glistened as she looked at Alex, "Oh, Alex. Thank you so much."

Alex caught one tear on his finger. "No, baby, thank you. You trusted me. That means more to me than you can know."

"Do you think we could do that again?"

Alex raised an eyebrow. "Try and stop us."

Chapter Twenty-Six

Kat woke up slowly, and as she rolled over, she felt a little sore from their activity last night. She stretched, realizing that she had slept through the entire night, something she had not done for a very long time.

Just then, Alex started to kiss her shoulder blade from behind, gently placing kiss after kiss, moving up toward her neck. Logically, Kat knew it was probably time for them to get up, but the sensations were so good, she couldn't have pulled away for anything. Slowly, his arm wrapped around her, sliding up to slip under one breast, holding her close. He whispered, "Tell me you aren't thinking of getting out of bed right now."

Kat rolled over, pressing her breasts against him, feeling his arousal. "I was, but then you started kissing me."

"Hmm. What are you thinking of *now*?" As he asked, Alex's hand slid from her upper thigh, up over her hip to slide up her ribcage. She shivered in anticipation.

"You." She stretched so he could stroke under her breast. "I'm thinking of you."

He grinned, his fingertips lightly brushing her nipples. "What about me?"

She arched her back, wanting him to continue. "At the risk of swelling your ego, I think that if you don't make love to me now, I may scream."

"Really?" In one fluid movement, he rolled her on her back, gracefully resting on his arms above her, looking down at her lovingly. "So, you want to make love with me again?" As he said it, he rubbed against her tantalizingly.

Kat's fingernails bit into his back, "Damn it, Alex. Yes. Now." She thought she'd lose her mind in her need to feel him inside her again. She reached down to his lower back, pushing him toward her, urging him to enter her.

"Do you love me? Still? In the cold light of day?" Kat looked up at him, remembering her words from the night before.

Her tone was certain. "More than I can tell you."

"And do you believe me that I love you too, and nothing will change that?"

Kat nodded. "I do. Now can you please, please make love to me?"

With a smile, Alex slid into her, hearing her sigh of pleasure.

***

An hour later, Kat stirred, her head resting on his chest, listening to the reassuring sound of his heartbeat. "Okay. I think we have to get up now."

"Probably right." He stroked her back, even now feeling both of their bodies respond. "What do you want to do today?"

She pulled up to lean on one elbow so she could look at him. "I don't have the foggiest idea. If I was alone, I would have worked today, gone for a run, and then gone to the cemetery."

"Do you still want to do that?"

"No." She blushed. "Maybe we could all go to the shelters, so Peter could meet the people I work with on this stuff. And maybe we could show you where our grandmother lived, and take a walk before we go over to the cemetery."

"That sounds great."

***

Several hours later, Luke drove the Jeep into the driveway and smiled at Alex as Kat and Peter almost jumped out of the car. He waved to Peter. "You go ahead. We'll be right there."

As they walked away, Luke said to Alex, "It's like now that her secret is out, she can't wait to show it all."

Alex nodded. "I think she held it in so long, that now she can share it, she wants to show you both, especially Peter, that she made a plan, followed it, and tried to make good."

As the two of them walked into the shelter, Kat happily introduced them to the directors of five women's shelters from around Massachusetts. The men sat stunned as the directors told them of her generosity to their clients, both financial and in terms of time and personal attention. Peter's eyes brimmed with tears as one director talked about how Kat had become close to a rape victim, and that she had even come back from Spain to go to court with her to confront her rapist.

***

Afterward, they went out for a late lunch, then back to the cottages. Sitting on the porch, Kat looked at her brother. "You really okay with this? I'm going to go get pizza, and go to the cemetery to eat dinner there. This isn't too much?"

Peter looked at her seriously. "Brat. My head is fucking spinning as it is. There is no way it could spin more. Pizza and a beer at the cemetery don't even sound remotely weird at this point."

Kat laughed. "Okay." She stretched. "I'm going to go lay down for a bit. Meet here at seven?"

Peter and Luke nodded, and Alex looked at her quizzically. She blushed. "Seriously, Alex, I mean I'm taking a nap, but if you want to join me…"

***

In their cottage, Kat kicked off her shoes, then stretched out on top of the comforter. Alex came over and laid down next to her. "Sleepy?"

She smiled and reached up to tangle her fingers in his hair. "Sort of. More than anything, I'm just sort of fried emotionally, and I needed a break."

"Do you want some time alone?" He caressed her face. "It's okay if you do."

"No. I want you here." She looked so vulnerable. "Could you just hold me for a while?"

"Of course." Kat snuggled into his arms, much like a child, and Alex just held her and stroked her back, trying to make her feel as safe as he could. How painful all of this must be. No matter how cathartic this all was, how draining for her. He suddenly realized that her breathing had slowed as she had fallen asleep.

While Kat slept, Alex tried to put together all the pieces of information from the last twenty-four hours, as well as think about his very physical reaction to her very presence. He'd certainly had enough lovers in his life, but none of them had ever made him feel like Kat did…

Two hours later, he stroked her hair and whispered, "Hey, Sleeping Beauty. It's time to wake up."

Kat woke slowly, blinking her eyes. He could see when she realized where she was, and what time it was. "Hey." She sat up. "I need a shower."

Alex stood up, stretching the arm that had been around her for hours. "Okay. I'll just head over to visit with Peter and Luke if that's okay."

"Sure." Kat stood up and pulled clothes from a drawer. She started to walk into the bathroom, clearly far inside herself. She stopped, turned around, and looked at him through stricken eyes. "I don't mean to shut you out. I don't. I don't know how to do this any other way than alone."

Alex crossed the room, and hugged her. "I don't know how or what to do at all. So we'll figure it out together. I'll just give you a few minutes to yourself." He kissed her hair. "I love you."

"I love you too."

***

Next door, Peter and Luke sat on the porch, Luke reading a book, Peter staring at the lake. As Alex walked up the steps, Peter looked at him. "Did she sleep?"

"Yeah, for about two hours."

"Good, she needed it."

"I know." Alex sat down in the empty rocking chair.

Peter turned back toward the lake, but his voice was insistent. "You need to know this. I have no idea, no fucking idea at all, how she has kept going. The shit those assholes did to her after the rape, the calls, the comments—they would have destroyed most women. Then she found out she was pregnant, and after she had decided to keep the baby, she was like a friggin' train, she plowed ahead, doing everything she was told to do for the baby. If they said to walk three miles a day, she did it faithfully. She didn't drink a drop of alcohol or caffeine. When they recommended antidepressants for the issues with the calls, she refused because some research said it might hurt the baby. The doctor said to do yoga, so she did yoga, she read books, she listened to Mozart by the fucking hour because the doctor said it might help the baby. And talk. Shit, she talked to the baby constantly. You'd hear her washing the dishes, and she'd be talking to the baby. She called her 'Bubba' because she didn't want to know the gender, but you'd hear her telling Bubba how much she loved her, all the things they were going to do together. When she was in the accident, she was so badly injured herself, and it was like she didn't even realize it, all that mattered was Bubba.

They wanted to sedate her and take the baby by C-section because of her own injuries, and she knew that because of Bubba being born too early, the meds she would need for a C-section might hurt Bubba, so she refused and gave birth naturally, with no meds at all." His voice cracked. "Shit, watching her push, with fucking broken ribs, even the nurses were crying in sympathy." He looked at the lake, no longer seeing Alex as he remembered. "Then, for those five days, I don't think Kat slept one minute. I think somehow her soul knew that Rosie wasn't going to survive, and she wasn't going to miss a minute with her. She held her, nursed her, talked to her, sang... She made up songs about how much Mommy loves Rosie. When she died, Kat wouldn't let them take her away. She just sat holding her, didn't cry, and just held her. I had heard the words 'broken heart', but I swear I actually saw her heart break in two. Then, when Mom and Dad tried to make the arrangements for the funeral, she refused and planned it herself. And fuck, now we know how much she went through here, after the funeral, all alone."

Alex tried to find the right words, realizing that Luke had put down his book, and was just watching the two of them. "Pete, it had to be alone." He thought back to his own parents, "My parents lost several babies before I was born. My mom once said that the reason their marriage had survived it all was because they were the only two people in the world who shared the exact experience, that they weren't alone in their grief. You all were there, loved Kat as much as anyone in the world, loved Rosie, but ultimately, Kat was the only parent. She had to do it alone to a certain extent."

"Maybe. Then when we came home, she became invisible. She stopped eating, stopped running, and stopped writing. She would sit in the rocking chair in her room for hours. My parents worried that she was suicidal. I don't think she really was. I think it was just that the grief was so profound that she went into a sort of dormant state. But they didn't leave her alone for as much as a minute. When they needed to go do something, they would call us or Jess, and we would come over. She was in hell, and our parents were in the hell of watching her fall apart, mourning their grandchild, and mourning that their baby had been raped and treated the way she was."

"What happened with your parents?" Alex shook his head. "Damn, Pete, I am so, so sorry that I wasn't around when they died. I remember getting the call when I was in Italy, but I couldn't get back in time for the funeral."

"Six months after Rosie died, Jess and I convinced them to go to the shore for a long weekend. You know, get away, sleep for a night, and not watch Kat constantly." He rubbed his face. "Luke and I were living together by then, in the apartment, and we said that we would go stay at the house with her because our dad especially couldn't stand the thought of her not having someone with her all the time. So we were staying there, and it was a pretty good weekend. Then Mom and Dad called to say they were going to get some dinner on the way home. From what the police said, they were just leaving the restaurant when they were hit. The only blessing was that they were killed instantly."

"The other driver was drunk, right?"

"Drunk and high. Turns out he was driving without a license too."

"Then what happened?"

"You mean with Kat?"

"Yeah."

"We all planned the funeral together, came back here to bury them. Then Luke and I moved into the house with Kat. It had been left to Kat and I equally. Jess inherited an equivalent amount of money, so we moved in. And Kat still was invisible, but frankly, no matter how much we might have wanted to be with her every minute, we couldn't. So I guess you could say we all sort of limped along for three months. Then, we came home one night, and there was a suitcase in the hall. Kat was sitting in the kitchen and said she needed a ride to the airport. She was moving to Spain that night. And until you came back into her life, she never really came home again."

"You mean she literally up and announced she was moving to Spain about two hours before she did it?"

"Yes. She literally was sitting there with her bags packed, waiting for a ride to the airport. I think if we'd been late coming home that night, we would have just found a note on the counter."

Just then, the three men heard the door of the other cottage open. A few seconds later, Kat came around the corner. Pete took one look at her and jumped to his feet. "You've been crying! Are you okay?"

Kat smiled tiredly. "Calm down, Pete. This was what I was trying to tell you when you got here. This is what I do when I come here at this time of year. I cry, sometimes I yell, sometimes I throw rocks. Regardless, for a couple days, I let myself feel it fully, let it out, then try to put myself back together to face the world. So, yes, I just cried, a lot. And it's okay."

Alex could see Peter trying to stomp down the urge to protect his little sister from any sort of harm. Finally, he sighed and held out his arms to his sister. "Okay. I just want to help."

She hugged him tightly. "I know you do. And I love you. And I'm trying to let you in like if I'd come out wearing sunglasses, you probably wouldn't have known that I'd been crying." Letting go of her brother, she moved over to stand next to Alex, picking up his hand without realizing it. "Are you all ready? We need to go."

In town, Peter pulled into a parking space in front of the only pizza place. Kat started to get out, and Peter said, "I'm going too."

"You don't need to. I can carry the pizza."

"I need to."

Together, they walked into the restaurant, and the owner looked up happily. "Kat! Always good to see you." He suddenly realized who was with her. "Pete, shit, it's been years!" Coming around the counter, he hugged Kat, then hugged Peter.

Peter started to laugh, suddenly realizing how much he'd enjoyed coming here summers as a kid. "PJ, great to see you too!"

PJ took three boxes off the oven, "So that's why the larger order, you have company this year." He rang up the order. "Thirty-three sixty, Kat."

Kat put forty dollars on the counter. "A tip, PJ. Same date next year, not sure of the order amount."

"Sounds good, darling. See you then. Pete, great to see you. You should come by more often!"

***

As they drove through the cemetery gates, Alex could feel Kat get apprehensive. "Are you worried your friend will be upset we're here?"

"No. He'd never get upset. It's just different."

Suddenly, Alex could see a sedan parked on the side of the roadway. Kat's voice sounded stressed. "He brought someone." For a moment, Alex heard a note of jealousy in her tone. "He brought someone, and he didn't tell me."

Luke turned in his seat. "Kat, so did you. Breathe. It's okay."

Peter parked the car, and Kat looked at her brother in the rearview mirror. "Can you guys wait here for a minute?"

"Of course."

Kat got out of the car, seeing a woman in the passenger seat of the sedan. Mr. White was nowhere to be seen at first, until Kat suddenly saw him over at her parents' graves, on his knees, pulling weeds. "Mr. White?"

He stood slowly, and turned toward her, his face breaking into a huge smile. "Katherine, you made it!"

The men in the car watched as the two of them almost ran toward each other, tears running down their faces, and hugged and hugged. From the car, they couldn't hear all of the conversation, but it was clear that the two of them were explaining bringing guests and something that Mr. White said clearly pleased Kat immensely. Kat turned and waved to the jeep, "C'mon! Pete, Luke, Alex, come here!"

Over the next few minutes, introductions were performed, and Kat shared that Mr. White's guest was his fiancé, Dotty. Dotty got out of the car, and Kat's joy in meeting her shone clearly on her face. Mr. White then held Kat's hand. "Okay, Katherine. Now you take them to see little Miss Rosie for a few minutes and visit your parents. We'll set up for dinner on the hill."

Peter wrapped his arm around his sister, and together they walked ahead of Luke and Alex. The tiny headstone was beautifully engraved with a simple rose, and underneath were the words "Rose Belle Weston, beloved daughter, granddaughter, niece."

Kat knelt down. "Hi, Rosie. We're here. Mommy brought Uncle Peter and Uncle Luke and Alex." Tears started to roll down her cheeks. "We love you, Rosie, and we miss you."

Peter crouched down and looked at the small stone. "Hi sweetie. I miss you an awful lot. I sing your song a lot because I know you can hear me."

Luke knelt down and brushed some dried grass off the stone. "Hi, Rosie, we love you, always."

Kat stood up and wrapped her arms around herself. "We'll come back again in a bit. Let's go see Mom and Dad."

Peter and Luke stood up and started to move toward their gravesites. Kat gazed at the small headstone, holding herself stiffly. Alex moved forward and wrapped her in his arms from behind. For a moment, she continued to hold rigid, then leaned back against him. He kissed her ear. "I wish I'd met her."

"Me too."

"I love you."

Those words made Kat come undone. She turned, hugged him convulsively, and started to sob. Alex held her tightly, silently. Finally, her crying slowed. Pulling back, she wiped her eyes and her nose on the crumpled tissue in her hand. "Okay, let's go with Peter and Luke."

***

Later, the six of them sat on a hill, ate pizza, and drank Molson Goldens. They toasted to the memory of Jacob, Rose, Mr. White's first wife, Dotty's first husband, and Kat's parents. Then Mr. White and Dotty told Peter and Kat about how they'd gone to high school with their mom and regaled them with stories of her. As the moon rose, the group had cried and laughed together.

After picking up the trash, Kat and Mr. White walked together hand in hand to the graves of their two children. As they walked, Mr. White looked down at Kat. "I like him."

"Who?"

"Alex. I like him. I've been waiting for you to find the right man. He's it."

"I don't know if he's it, but I like him a lot."

"You told him everything?"

She nodded. "Everything. Start to finish. Other than you, I'd never told anyone the entire story."

"Good." He squeezed her hand. "And you promise you'll come back for the wedding?"

"I promise."

Chapter Twenty-Seven

Back in New York, they unpacked, and Alex offered to make dinner. Kat sat on a stool and watched him cook, saying little. After dinner, all four went into the sunroom, and when Kat started to yawn, Alex pulled a throw pillow onto his lap, "Lay down." Kat laid her head on the pillow, and as Alex stroked her hair, she fell asleep.

***

Hours later, Kat awoke in bed, realizing that she'd fallen asleep on the couch, but was now tucked in bed beside Alex. She rolled over, trying to be as quiet as she could, and started to stroke his chest. Alex stirred. "Hi."

"Hi." Kat's hand moved lower, as she reveled in touching him. Alex moved to stroke her arm, and Kat stopped his hand. "No. It's my turn to play."

His voice deeper than normal from just being asleep, he asked, "Really?"

"Really. I want to touch you all over. You have to be patient, and can't touch." With that, Kat rolled so that she could kneel next to him, her hands roaming to touch his shoulders, his legs, hips, her fingers just skimming the surface of his skin. In the dim light coming through the window, Kat could see how aroused he was becoming. She bent down, her lips and tongue then tasting everywhere her hands had just been. Alex took a sharp breath in as she slid his boxers down his hips, then took him in her mouth, "Jesus, Kat."

She paused. "You want me to stop?"

"Hell, no, baby. Just let me touch you too."

"Not yet." Kat continued to taste his skin, licking, nipping at times, and sometimes just barely running the tip of her tongue across his skin.

Finally, she leaned back to pull her tank top off, then moved to straddle him. His hands came to rest on her hips. "Unh-uh. Patience." She pushed his hands back to his sides. Slowly, she rubbed against him, feeling him strain against her.

"Kat, enough. I want to touch you too."

She leaned down, her hair cascading down around them like a veil. She kissed his lips briefly, still rubbing against him. "Why? You aren't enjoying this?"

He growled, "Yes, I'm enjoying this. It's just…"

"What?" Kat teased him by slowing moving her hips.

Alex couldn't take it anymore, and his hands grasped her hips possessively. "In this case, patience is not one of my virtues."

Moving so that he could slide inside her, Kat started the rhythm, loving every moment. Within seconds, passion overtook them, and conversation stopped as Kat continued to move.

***

Later, as their breathing returned to normal, Alex stroked her hair. "I don't know what I did to deserve that, but thank you."

She laughed, tightening her arms around him. "I just wanted to touch you." She suddenly sounded tentative. "You don't mind, do you?"

Alex shifted so he could look down at her, "Babe, I love touching *you*. I love you touching *me*. You can wake me up anytime you want."

***

Monday morning, Kat was sitting sipping coffee when Alex came into the kitchen. He kissed her forehead. "Why didn't you wake me?"

She smiled. "You seemed to be sleeping so peacefully, I didn't want to disturb you."

He leaned down, pulling aside her hair so he could nibble on her neck. "Yeah, somehow mind-boggling amazing lovemaking makes for deep sleep."

She blushed. "Really?"

He poured a cup of coffee, and looked at her. "What are your plans today?"

"Editing. I need to get a revision to my editor by Thursday, so it's going to be a rush for the next couple days. You?"

"Planning session today, tomorrow rehearsal. Wednesday and Thursday we're recording if all goes well."

She sounded sad. "So we are back to reality, busy, busy."

"But we're together."

"Yeah." She still didn't look up.

"Kat, you okay?"

She sighed. "Yeah, I'm fine. It's just… it feels like we just had so much change in our lives over the last few days, now it's back to the mundane."

He stood up to come over and pull her to her feet, wrapping his arms around her. He kissed the top of her head. "I know. But, we'll make the evenings special, I promise."

***

As the week went on, Alex had an idea. On Thursday morning, he asked Kat, "So, done editing?"

"Just about. It'll be done by noon today."

"Then what?"

"Then I can get back to writing for a bit."

He tried to sound nonchalant. "Any work plans for tomorrow?"

"Just normal writing, why?"

"Just wondering."

***

Friday morning, Alex kissed Kat goodbye in the kitchen. "What are you doing today?"

"Writing, running. Why?"

He pulled her close. "How about stopping by the studio around ten this morning?"

"Why?"

"I have a surprise for you, that's why."

"And I have to go to the studio to get it?"

"Yes."

"Tell me now."

"No." He grinned, his eyes twinkling. "You have to come there, or no surprise."

"I'll be there."

***

Kat walked through the studio door exactly at ten. When Alex saw her, he stopped the band and came out to kiss her deeply. When he pulled back, she smiled. "I guess that falls under the category of making sure that everyone knows our status."

He stroked her arm. "I love you. That's what it means."

"So? My surprise?"

Alex pulled her into the hall, mostly out of sight of the rest of the band. "So…if things had been different in how we got together, before we started basically living together, I would have tried to convince you to go away with me for a romantic weekend in a hotel. So, how about going away with me for the weekend?"

Her eyes sparkled. "I'd love to, where?"

"Here. New York. We have a corner suite at the Plaza for the weekend."

Her eyes lit up. "Really?"

"Really. And you have your travel bag in the office over there, and then a cab is going to take you over to the hotel because our suite is ready. You have a pedicure appointment at noon, a massage at one, and I'll be there at three." He ran his hands down her sides, resting them on her hips. "You, my lady, are going to go be pampered for the day, then we are going to have an entire weekend to ourselves."

"You arranged the whole thing?" She sounded almost childlike in her delight. "That sounds so, so good."

"It does, doesn't it? When you sounded so down on Monday about going back to the mundane, I wanted to do something special."

Oblivious to the band watching what was happening, Kat stretched up to wrap her arms tightly around Alex's neck before kissing him deeply. His hands were warm as they slid up her back, pulling her to his chest. They both started as Peter whacked a drum.

Alex turned, laughing, to stick his head back into the recording studio. "Fuck off, Pete."

"Hey, that's my sister, remember?"

Kat slid under Alex's arm to enter the studio, and went over to hug Peter. "I kissed him first."

Peter rolled his eyes. "Whatever. Don't you have somewhere to be?"

"You know?"

"Of course, we've been in on the secret all week." He kissed her cheek. "Go, have fun, see you Sunday night for dinner. Love you."

***

Alex walked Kat outside, carrying her overnight bag. A cab was waiting by the curb. Putting her bag inside, Alex turned and kissed her one more time. "I will see you at three."

"At three." Kat squeezed his hand. "Thank you so much."

He pulled her close. "I love you—it was my pleasure."

"Love you, see you at three."

At the hotel, Kat checked in, and a bellhop carried her bag to the suite. After tipping him, Kat walked around, delighted by the beautiful rooms looking out over the city. Stepping into the kitchenette, she opened the fridge, finding it fully stocked with wines, beer, cheeses, fruit, and chocolate. Damn, he had planned ahead! The dining table had a bouquet of perfect long-stem red roses, with a card leaning up against the vase. Kat opened the card.

Kat,
This is your day, your weekend. As I said, you have a pedicure appointment at noon because you said you wanted one, and a massage at one because I thought you might enjoy it. If either doesn't appeal, just call the front desk and cancel. As for clothes, I grabbed your travel bag, but take the card and go shopping if you want.

I love you, can't wait to be with you. See you in a bit.
Alex

Behind the note was a gift card to Bloomingdales. Kat started to laugh. Looking at her watch, she realized that if she left right then, she could go shopping before her pedicure. Something slinky would be perfect for tonight...
***

At five minutes after three, Alex was in the elevator of the hotel when his phone buzzed with a text message. Reading it, he smiled. "By my watch, it's 3:03, where are you?"

Two minutes later, Alex slid his key card into the lock. Opening the door to the suite, the first thing he saw was a very sexy black negligee draped over a chair in the foyer, with a deep rose one on the next chair. A folded note card rested on the table between them. Opening the card, Alex's eyes widened. *I couldn't decide which one to wear tonight—your choice.*

At that moment, Kat appeared in the doorway, barefoot, wrapped in a white hotel bathrobe. She frowned playfully. "You're late."

Alex dropped his bag to gather her in his arms, kissing her hungrily. Finally, he pulled back. "Sorry I'm late, and damn, you know how to get my attention."

"Thank you."

Picking up his bag, Alex took her hand, pulling her into the living room. "How was your afternoon?"

"Perfect, absolutely perfect."

"Good. That's what I wanted it to be." He looked around, then looked down at her, "Room okay?"

She swatted his arm, "It's perfect, as you damn well know."

"I'm going to take a shower, then, your wish is my command."

"Nope."

Alex was confused. "Huh?"

Her tone was sure. "I want you. Now."

Alex moved toward her, his hands on her hips. "Baby, I want you too, but I need a shower first." He nuzzled her neck. "You smell amazing, and I smell like the studio. Five minutes is all I need."

Kat growled, "Fine."

"Thank you." Alex turned, grabbed his bag, and took it into the bedroom. As he walked into the bathroom, he called back, "Five minutes."

As soon as Kat heard him shut the shower door, she slipped out of her robe and quietly entered the bathroom. As she walked toward the glass shower door, she could see Alex washing his hair, suds cascading down his tanned, muscular back. Kat opened the shower door, smiling as Alex startled. "Hi."

Alex smiled, pushing his wet hair out of his eyes, "Hi yourself. Decided you needed a shower too?"

Kat moved forward, relishing the feeling of the warm water on her bare skin, "No, I told you, I want you. Now."

Alex rested his hand on the shower wall, the other hand slowly caressing her breasts. "Really?"

Kat arched her back. "Really."

Alex picked her up so that she could wrap her legs around his hips, sliding inside her. "Damn, I love you."

"I love you too." As Alex slowly made love to her, the two of them murmured words of endearment.

***

After, Alex gently toweled Kat dry. Tying the belt of the robe around her waist, he smoothed back her hair. "You are full of surprises."

She sat on the chair, watching him towel off. "Sorry, no patience." She looked down at her hands, suddenly quiet.

"What's the matter?"

"Nothing."

Shrugging on a robe, Alex tied the belt before crouching down in front of her so that he could look her in the eyes. "What's going on?"

Her cheeks grew red. "I'm sorry."

"For what?"

"I couldn't wait. I needed to know that you needed me as much as I need you."

Once again, her vulnerability floored him. How could she be apologizing for this? How many men dreamed of someone like her walking into the shower? How could he make her understand? Alex stood up and pulled the other chair over next to her. "Let me understand. You're apologizing for joining me in the shower?"

Kat still couldn't look at him. "I told you I wanted you, you said you wanted a shower, and I still went ahead."

Alex put a finger under her chin, tipping her chin up so he could see her face fully. "Look at me."

Kat looked at him, and he could see the uncertainty in her eyes. "Katherine, listen to me carefully. I felt like a damn teenager in the cab on the way here, I was so crazy for you. The little lingerie show in the hallway did nothing to cool my desire. I would have happily taken you standing up in the hallway, on the couch, on the damn kitchen counter, anywhere and anyhow, but when I kissed you, you smelled so good, that I felt like a grub, nothing more. I wanted to shower just because I felt like my touching you when I smelled like that wasn't fair to you." He rubbed his thumb against her lower lip, smiling as he saw her eyes darken with desire. "Kat, unequivocally, I want you as much or more than you want me. I struggle with keeping my hands off you. You turn me on so much it boggles my mind. You walking into that shower was amazing, sexy beyond belief, and just the sort of things that I dream about at night."

"Really?"

"Really."

Alex pulled Kat by the hand into the living room, over to the huge windows. He wrapped his arms around her, resting his chin on the top of her head, amazed at how much just being near her impacted him emotionally and physically. They had made love only minutes before, and already he could feel the pull of his desire for her again. "Okay, love of mine. What do you want to do? We can stay here, and order dinner. We can go out to the hotel restaurant or someplace else. We can go get a drink and come back and eat here. What do you want to do?"

Kat felt so loved and protected, wrapped in his arms. "I don't know. I'm so happy right now that I can't think of anything beyond the next couple minutes."

"Then we don't need to make a decision now." Without warning, he scooped her up in his arms and carried her over to the huge overstuffed armchair looking out the window. Settling into the chair with her still held in his arms, he said, "We can sit here all night if you want."

Kat smiled. "No, you know me. I'll get hungry at some point."

Alex gently brushed a curl off her temple, then stroked the side of her face. "Do you understand how much I love you?"

"Yes, I do."

Kat leaned forward and kissed him, and within minutes, their desire had blossomed again. Staying in the chair, Kat untied both of their robes with shaking hands, sliding them open. Their lovemaking was gentle, slow, and sweet, punctuated by endearment and ecstasy.

***

Later, Kat stirred. "Okay, so now I want to get dressed, go down and get some dinner, then come back here and drink wine and watch the city."

"Sounds like a perfect plan."

***

An hour later, while waiting for their entrees to arrive, Kat excused herself to use the ladies' room. Coming back toward the table, she saw two very attractive young women in very slinky dresses approaching Alex. Even from a distance, she could hear their giggles, and then heard one of them ask, "You're Alex Tamaro, aren't you?"

Alex had been watching for Kat to return, so he was surprised by the intrusion. "Yes, I am."

"We are huge fans of yours." One shoved the other, "Could we get pictures taken with you?"

"Sure." Alex stood up and stepped away from the table, finally seeing Kat coming toward him. "I'd be happy to."

Kat came back to the table and sat down, not saying a word. Alex patiently stood with each woman while the other took a photo of them, both women clearly vying for his attention. After the photos, Alex thanked them, "Thanks so much for your support ladies, now please excuse me, but I am on a date."

"Oh." The taller woman looked at Kat with a haughty air, "Oh, we didn't realize you were with someone." She nodded at Kat. "Anyway, Alex, thanks for the pictures."

As they walked away, Alex picked up Kat's hand off her lap and kissed it lingeringly. "Don't you dare look intimidated by them." Kat looked at him, shocked at how quickly and accurately he could read her thoughts. "I love *you. You* turn me on. *You* are the woman I want to be with. *You.*"

***

Back in their suite, Alex sat on the bed and smiled at Kat. "As I remember, I had a choice to make about what you were going to wear tonight."

"You do."

"The rose one."

Kat picked it up. "I'll go change, and you go pour us some wine."

Minutes later, Alex felt his mouth go dry as Kat walked toward him, clad only in wisps of rose silk, barefoot. He walked to her, traced the neckline, trying to keep his voice light. "You have amazing taste in clothes."

"Thank you."

Going over to the chairs by the window, Kat smiled seeing the glasses waiting for them. "Perfect."

Alex sat in the chair across from her and handed her a glass. "To us."

"To us." She raised her glass. "I love you. Thank you for planning all of this for us."

"My pleasure." Alex pulled a small box from the side of his chair. "This is to go with your outfit."

Kat looked at the small Tiffany's box. "Alex, you are spoiling me rotten, you know that, right?"

He took her hand and kissed her palm. "I'm not spoiling you." He grinned. "I'm *accessorizing* you."

Kat laughed and opened the box. Nestled on the blue velvet were four other bracelets, the rest of the set to match the one he had already given her. "Oh, Alex, they are gorgeous." She looked at him. "You shouldn't have. All this, you didn't need to do all of this."

Alex stood up and came to kneel in front of her, reaching up to hold her face in his hands, "I didn't *need* to do anything, and I *wanted* to do this. I love you, and I had more fun planning this for us than I've had in a really long time, maybe ever." He stroked her lips with his thumb, and saw her body respond through the thin silk, "Figuring out the details of this was a blast." He picked up the bracelets, "And every time you wear these, it makes my day. The bracelets were the first part of my plan this week." He slid them onto her wrist, then looked at her with twinkling eyes. "Unless you don't like them."

Kat leaned forward and kissed him passionately. Pulling back, she looked at her wrist. "I absolutely love them, thank you."

"Okay then."

***

The rest of the weekend passed in a blur of luxury and passion. Saturday morning, they'd gotten up late and ordered room service for breakfast before taking a long walk through Central Park. Saturday night, they'd ordered room service and watched a couple of movies on TV, cuddling in the king-sized bed. Sunday morning, they both awoke early, made leisurely love, then went out for breakfast before coming back to the hotel.

Walking back into the suite, Kat's voice sounded wistful. "So I guess we need to think about heading home."

Without speaking, Alex pulled her toward him and kissed her hard. Her immediate reaction was a wave of desire, and within seconds, both of them were shedding their clothes as they headed toward the bedroom one more time. Afterward, Alex kissed her hair, as both of their heart rates began to return to normal. "*Now,* we have to think about going home..."

Chapter Twenty-Eight

Two weeks later, Alex returned to California. Back at home, his house echoed with emptiness, and he found himself calling Kat constantly just to hear her voice.

One night he wandered into his parents' restaurant. After kissing his mother and hugging his father, he grouchily pulled out a chair. His mother raised her eyebrow. "And to what do we owe this honor? I've called you twice this week for dinner, and now you blow in looking like a thundercloud."

Alex's father scolded his wife, "Oh, Maria, leave him alone. He obviously needs some real food to improve his mood."

Alex smiled at his father, then turned to face his mother. "Right now, I need some company. I think I'm bored."

"Hmm. Seems to me you weren't bored when you were in New York."

Alex bit into a breadstick. "The good thing about you is that you're predictable, Mom. The Inquisition has started."

"I didn't ask anything. I was just stating the obvious. Now, are you going to order or do you want us to?"

"You do it. I really don't care what I eat."

Ruffling his hair, his mother quickly stood and walked into the kitchen. While she was gone, Alex's father poured him a glass of wine. "I would've thought you'd be happy to be home."

"I thought so too, but I'm not."

"Who is she?"

"How do you know there's anyone involved in this? Maybe I'm just bored."

"You've never been bored. So, I figure there's a woman."

"Oh, Dad. I miss her so much."

Maria sat down at the table just in time to hear the comment. "Who do you miss so much?"

"Kat. Her name is Katherine, but everyone calls her Kat. She's Peter's sister."

Alfonso looked at his son, "And does Katherine miss you too?"

Alex nodded. "Yeah, I think so. If the four phone calls today are any indication."

"Then, my beloved son, what's the problem?"

"She's there, I'm here, and I don't know what to do about it."

"When do we get to meet her?"

Alex grinned unexpectedly. "How about this weekend?"

***

Alex called Kat when he got home. The phone rang and rang. Just as he decided that the machine would pick up, a sleepy voice said, "Hello?"

"Oh shit, Baby. I forgot about the time difference."

"Alex?"

"Yeah. Hi. Are you mad at me for calling so late?"

"Of course not. What's up?"

"Oh, jeez, Kat, I'm so sorry for waking you. I'll call you in the morning."

Exasperated, Kat said, "Alex, for God's sake, I'm awake now. What's up?"

"What are you doing this weekend?"

"I don't know, why?"

"If I send you a ticket, will you come out here for the weekend?"

"Of course I will—you don't even need to send the ticket. What's up?"

"I really miss you, and I really want you to meet my parents."

"Whoa. This's kind of out of the blue, isn't it?"

"No. Come on, Kat, I know all of your family. I want you to know mine too."

"And they're okay with meeting me?"

"Kat, they can't wait. My entire life they've waited for me to introduce them to a woman I love, and you're that woman."

"You've never introduced anyone before?"

"No."

"Wow."

"Kat, I love you. I had dinner with my parents tonight because I've been moping around for days. I thought maybe a good dinner would snap me out of it, but I realized as I was talking to them that what I really want is for you all to meet."

"What if they don't like me?"

"Kat, I don't think anyone has ever not liked you. Please. For me?"

There was a long silence; Alex sat on his end of the phone line, suddenly nervous. He had never thought that she might hesitate. Finally, he heard her sigh. "Just what does one wear to a meet the parents' event?"

Alex laughed. "Anything you want. How about you pack some stuff, and then we'll go shopping when you get here too?" Kat heard a hesitant note in his voice. "Maybe though, you might bring some stuff that could stay here. Then it's like your house too."

"I'd like that."

"You would?"

"Yeah." She yawned. "Baby, I'm falling asleep. I'll find a flight that will get me there either Friday night or Saturday morning. I'll call as soon as I know when."

"Thank you. I can't wait. I'm really sorry I woke you up."

"Don't worry about it. I can't wait to see you."

"Say hi to Peter and Luke. I love you."

"I love you, too."

"Only four days."

"Only four. Good night."

***

When Kat's alarm rang at six, she hit the snooze button. Finally, at seven, she showered and dressed in ripped jeans and a "Question authority" sweatshirt. When she walked into the kitchen, Peter and Luke looked up from the paper.

Peter smiled. "Well, good morning, sleepyhead. I don't suppose sleeping late has anything to do with your phone ringing at two this morning?"

Kat poured a cup of coffee. When she plopped down at the table, she grimaced. "It has everything to do with the phone. Alex forgot the time difference and woke me up. We talked for a while, and then I couldn't get back to sleep."

Sipping his coffee, Luke gazed at Kat. "Must have been pretty important if he called that late."

"Yeah. He wants me to come out this weekend and meet his parents."

Peter chortled. "Hot shit. Next thing you know Luke, we'll be going with Kat to Tiffany's to pick out china."

Both men gasped as Kat slammed down her mug. "Thanks a fucking lot, guys. I need your help here, and I get jokes." Her voice got high as she looked like she would cry. "I don't know if I'm ready for this."

Luke wiped up the spilled coffee. "What are you scared of? They're only human."

"I'm not really scared of them. I'm scared of the whole idea. The joke about the china, well, I thought that too. And I'm not ready. I love Alex, but this is more than I'm ready for."

"We understand how you feel, kiddo, but what are you going to do about it?"

"I'm going to go meet his parents. This is important to him, so I have to."

Luke's voice was thoughtful. "What if you went a few days early so that you could spend some time with Alex alone? Then your whole visit wouldn't revolve around his parents."

Kat nodded enthusiastically. "That's a really good idea. Maybe I could leave on Wednesday, so I'd have part of Wednesday, and all of Thursday and Friday alone with Alex." She got up and kissed Luke and Peter. "I think I'll keep my early arrival a surprise."

***

Wednesday morning, Peter and Luke drove Kat to the airport. At the gate, Luke hugged Kat, "Good luck kiddo, call us if you need anything."

"Thanks, Luke. I will."

Peter handed her a leather tote. "You can do this. We love you. Say hi to Alex."

She hugged him tightly. "I'll tell him. Thanks, guys."

***

As Kat walked out of the airport hours later, the sunshine blinded her. Suddenly, she knew the weekend would be great, and smiled as she hailed a cab. When the driver pulled into the driveway, Kat was thrilled to see a car already there, and she could hear Alex playing the piano inside the house.

Minutes later, Alex was surprised to hear the doorbell. He opened the door, and his eyes widened in shock and joy as he realized that Kat was standing on his top step. "Kat!"

"Hi."

He pulled her inside, taking the bags before he kissed her. "What are you doing here?" Rather than letting her answer, he leaned down to kiss her again, but she stepped back.

"Are you mad?"

He was confused. "Why would I be mad?"

"That I'm here early."

"Oh, Baby, I'm *thrilled* you're here. I wanted to ask you to, but I didn't want to fuck up your schedule." He ran his hands down her sides, resting them on her hips, seeing her immediate reaction to his touch, "What other surprises do you have in store for me?"

Trying to look devious, Kat burst into giggles. "Well, I was planning on stealing all of your clothes ..."

Alex nuzzled her neck, becoming increasingly aroused as he watched her nipples harden. "That sounds like a really good idea." He kissed her mouth, ending the conversation.

Kat quickly helped him undress, before he pulled her dress up over her head and threw it to the side. Then he picked her up and strode down the hall to his bedroom. She was as aroused as he was when he slowly slid into her warmth. Bracing himself on his arms, he watched her bathed in sunlight from the windows as he eased slowly in and out of her. When they reached the pinnacle of their passion, Kat looked straight into Alex's eyes and saw the love and amazement she was feeling mirrored in his eyes.

Afterward, Kat slept in Alex's arms. When she awoke, he was stroking her hair. She stretched. "Hi. Did I sleep long?"

"No, only about an hour."

"Did you rest?"

"I didn't sleep, I just relaxed. I'm so glad you're here. Why didn't you tell me?"

"I wanted to surprise you. I felt bad about how I reacted when you called to ask me."

He raised one eyebrow. "This is a pity visit?"

"God, no. I know I didn't respond the way you expected, and Luke suggested that maybe some extra time together would be a good thing for us."

Alex stroked her face. "Well, I definitely need to thank Luke. Why are you so wigged out about my folks?"

"It really isn't them, I just suddenly was overwhelmed by nerves."

"Why?"

Kat reached for his hand and laced her fingers through his. She squeezed his hand before answering. "Because, I mean, in some ways it seems so soon to meet them." She tried to find the right words. "In some ways, we've been together for months and months, but in other ways, we just became a couple. So, it got all confused in my brain, and I got worried that meeting them was pushing it too fast."

"Oh sweetie." He rolled onto his side so he could look at her. "Do you still feel that way?"

"No, that's the funny thing. On the flight, I had a stomachache, but when I walked out of the airport, I knew it would be fine. That this is right."

"It *is* right." They kissed lovingly until Alex's phone alarm beeped.

"Alex, why's the alarm going off?"

"I was supposed to meet friends tonight for a concert in Golden Gate Park. I should let them know I'm not coming."

"Why not?"

He kissed her uncovered breast. "Because, I plan to hibernate with you."

"Can you get an extra ticket?"

"Probably, why?"

"Well, you're right. You know everyone in my life, but I don't know anyone in yours. Will you take me to the concert?"

His smile encompassed his whole face. "I'd love to. Let me call and get a ticket, and then let's order a picnic to take with us."

"Any food in your fridge?"

"Yeah, lots. I stocked up for your visit."

"Okay, then while you find me a ticket, I'll make us a picnic."

"You don't have to. You must be tired."

"No, I'm not. Now, get going and find me a ticket."

"As you wish."

While Alex called to order an extra ticket, Kat quickly packed a picnic. As she was standing in the kitchen sipping seltzer, Alex snuck up behind her and wrapped his arms around her.

She leaned back against him. "Did you find a ticket?"

"Sure did. Did you find everything you wanted?"

"Definitely. But now I should probably find a shower."

"Sounds like a great idea, how about some company?"

"Lead the way."

***

The shower turned into a long session of making love. When they finally dried off and dressed, they had to hurry into the car to head for the park.

Looking out the window, Kat commented, "It seems funny how almost everyone in California seems to have a car."

"I know. I don't really miss driving when I'm away, but I always enjoy it when I'm here." They pulled into a parking space, and Alex carried the basket as Kat carried their blanket.

At the park, they quickly found Jonathan and his wife Kelly, and Richard and Mica. All three couples spread their blankets on the grass and quickly shared their picnics. After eating, they laid back with glasses of wine to listen to the symphony. Kat gazed at the stars and felt truly relaxed. She liked Alex's friends.

Alex watched Kat daydream on the blanket. He had seen her relax as she met his friends, and as he stroked her hand, he could almost hear her purr.

He leaned close to her ear. "This feels so right. Going out with friends, and then going home."

Kat turned to look at him. "It does, doesn't it?" She seductively whispered. "Home, soon?"

Alex immediately became painfully aroused. "Jesus Kat, how can you make me react like that instantaneously? I want you now."

"Me too."

Alex looked at the program. "Only one more piece, and then quick good-byes."

"Deal."

The anticipation rose as they waited for the concert to end. Finally, when the thunderous applause started, Alex and Kat said farewells, and darted for the exit. By the time they reached the car, they were almost running. As Alex tried to unlock the doors, he pressed Kat against the car so he could kiss her. "Damn, I wish we didn't live so far away." The door unlocked, and he opened the door for Kat. Quickly, he slid into the driver's seat.

"Drive fast."

He smiled at her excitement and raced for home.

As they got out of the car, they intertwined, leaving the picnic basket in the car. By the time they reached the front door, they were peeling off jackets and shoes. They left all of their clothes in a trail to the bedroom. Falling onto the bed, Alex gasped, "Kat, I'm sorry, I can't wait any longer."

"Please, Alex, now!"

**

Afterward, they lay together and talked. When they got hungry, Alex found ice cream that they ate in bed, and then they fell asleep locked in each other's arms. Alex dreamt of lying in the shade next to the pool with Kat beside him and a small child running up to them, yelling, "Mommy, Daddy, look!" Smiling, Alex awoke to find Kat no longer in bed with him. Instinctively sensing that something was wrong, he went looking for her.

Kat was curled up on the couch, watching Home Shopping Network. From the look on her face, she was terribly unhappy, and Alex immediately went to her side. "Baby, what's wrong? Why aren't you in bed?"

She looked at him sadly. "I couldn't sleep."

Alex sat down next to her and put his arm around her. "Why couldn't you sleep? You seemed to drift off pretty well."

"I did. Then I woke up." She looked at him with teary eyes. "I didn't feel well."

Alarmed, Alex asked, "Are you okay? Do you need me to call a doctor?"

Kat almost chuckled, and then tears started to flow, "No. It's just that I got my period." She laid her head on his chest.

"Oh sweetie, are you okay?"

"I'm fine. Sort of. I mean, I feel like shit, but now our romantic weekend is shot to hell."

Finally, Alex understood her unhappy face. "Oh, Kat, nothing is shot to hell."

"Yes, it is. I mean the last time I got my period was months ago, and we weren't even having sex then, so it didn't matter. And then I came out to spend extra time with you, and now we can't make love."

Looking serious, Alex leaned toward Kat, "Kat, is sex the only reason you came out here early this week?"

"Of course not. I came because I wanted to be with you."

"Do you trust me?"

"Of course I do. Why?"

"You need to listen to me on this. I love you. I loved you when we weren't making love, and I love you when we are. I will always love you, and if we're together as a couple, we need to adjust to life. Don't sweat it. I promise I can wait until you're able to again, and until then, I still love sleeping with you and being with you. And tomorrow we're going to wander around my city, and at the end of the day, we're going to come home and soak in the hot tub. And then go out to dinner. And maybe go see a movie because, love of mine, I have your complete attention while you're here and I'm not going to let you out of my sight for more than a minute." He watched her face relax, and her eyes no longer swam with tears. "Now, do you feel better?"

Kat launched herself at him, and hugged him tightly. "I love you so much."

Scooping her into his arms, Alex strode into the bedroom and lay down on the bed with Kat still in his arms. He pulled the comforter over them. "I love you too. Now, I want you to go to sleep, so you're ready to walk around tomorrow."

"Yes, sir."

***

The next morning Kat slept late. She awoke to find a rose on the pillow with a note saying, "Good morning, love. I'm out on the deck, come join me." Smiling, she showered and dressed, amazed at how relaxed she felt this morning.

Stepping onto the deck, Kat smiled at Alex, who rose to kiss her. "Good morning. I thought you were going to sleep the day away."

"Good morning. I was so comfortable, I couldn't seem to wake up. Have you been awake long?"

"No, just long enough to make us some breakfast and read the paper." He stroked her stomach. "Feel better this morning?"

"Yeah. I felt better as soon as I talked to you last night."

"You'd be amazed at what talking can do. Come on, sit down and eat so we can go exploring."

***

They spent the day wandering around the winding streets of San Francisco. They laughed and talked, and at the end of the day, they wandered into a small pub for dinner. Kat was quiet on the way home.

"Kat, are you okay?"

"I'm really good. I just realized that I had fun today. I know that sounds stupid, but I really had fun today, and I don't remember when I last had fun for a whole day."

Alex squeezed her fingers. "It doesn't sound stupid. I feel the same way."

"Alex, would you go to Spain with me?"

"Huh?"

"In January, would you go to Spain with me?"

"For what?"

"Just for a vacation. I thought that maybe we could go for a week and just visit. You could meet my friends, stuff like that."

"I'd love to."

Kat seemed not to hear him as she rambled. "I know that's a long time in the future, and so I understand if you don't want to make a commitment yet..."

"Katherine! I'd love to go. I'm not worried about making plans a couple months ahead of time. I know we'll still be together then. I'd absolutely love to go."

"You mean it?"

"Of course I do. Tomorrow we can pick dates and start planning."

***

The next morning, they poured over date books until they decided on a January 9th departure date. Kat started making arrangements for the trip. Alex listened delightedly, sensing how important this trip was to her. Most of the day they lounged and talked, and together they made dinner.

Saturday, Kat asked Alex to go shopping with her, and with his input, she found the perfect dress for dinner. When she had showered and dressed, she came out of the bathroom, and Alex gasped. The forest green dress made her eyes look even darker. One shoulder and her neck were bare, and the full skirt fell almost to her ankles.

"You look absolutely gorgeous."

She smiled shyly. "Thank you."

Kat was quiet on the ride to his parent's restaurant. Turning up a sharp hill, Alex drove to the top and parked. As Kat got out of the car, she was able to see all of San Francisco spread before her.

"It's so beautiful here."

"Isn't it?"

Holding tightly onto his hand, Kat let Alex lead her into the busy restaurant. They had barely stepped through the door when an older version of Alex bustled up.

"Hey, Dad." Alex hugged his father. "Dad, I'd like to introduce you to Katherine Weston. Kat, this is my father, Alfonso Tamaro."

Alfonso pulled her close to kiss her cheeks. "What a pleasure this is, Katherine. You are even lovelier than Alex led us to believe. Please excuse my wife; she was so nervous about meeting you that she went to check her hair again. Come, let's sit down."

They were just entering a private dining room when a small, dark haired woman almost ran to meet them. "Oh, Alex, I'm so sorry I wasn't there when you arrived."

Alex kissed his mother fondly. "It's okay, Mom. This is Katherine. Kat, this is my mother, Maria."

The two women looked at each other searchingly. Finally, they nodded at each other and Maria pulled Kat into a hug. "It's wonderful to meet you. Alfonso and I have waited all week for this moment. We know and love Peter, but you have a special place with us. Please, come sit down."

As the men walked ahead into the dining room, Maria took Kat's hand. When Kat looked at the older woman, she was shocked to see pain and longing in her eyes, "I think you and I have more in common than you know. I know about your dear parents and their death. And I too always bear the guilt of a parent's death, as my mother died giving birth to me. And I know about your beloved Rosie, and I too lost little ones. And we both love Alex very much. So perhaps, neither one of us had such a reason to be so nervous these last few days, hmm?"

"How did you know?"

"Know what? About your parents and Rose? Alex told me. About being nervous? I saw you take a deep breath after we were introduced, and I did the same thing."

Kat kissed her cheek. "Thank you. I was so scared."

"Of us? Posh. And Alex says you cook so well, so come, tell us what you think of our restaurant."

Standing across the room waiting for the women to join them, Alex and his father watched the exchange. "Well, son, they seem to have found a bond."

"Yes, they do. Maybe someday they'll tell us what it is."

The foursome ate and talked until late in the night. On the way home, Kat fell asleep in the car. Alex carried her into the bedroom without waking her. He lay next to her watching her sleep for hours until he fell into a restless sleep.

When he awoke, Kat was lying with her head on his shoulder, stroking his hand.

"Good morning. I must have fallen asleep in the car since I have no recollection of how I got in here."

"You were sleeping so peacefully that I didn't want to wake you. Did you have fun last night?"

"I did. I really enjoyed both the food and the company. Your parents are wonderful."

***

After breakfast, Kat began to find her scattered belongings. Alex played the piano for several hours as Kat wrote. Just as Kat was shutting down her computer, Alex abruptly stopped playing.

"Kat, where are we going with this?"

"With what?"

"With us. Where are we going with our relationship?"

"I don't know what you mean."

"I mean what's the status of our relationship?"

"We're a couple. We try to be together as much as possible. You visit me. I visit you. We talk on the phone constantly. We're monogamous."

His voice rose, "I need to know if this is all you see for us, this commuter relationship. Do you see us doing this forever?"

"Alex, *forever* is a really long time. Right now, I know only that I love you, and love to be with you. I don't know any more than that. We've only really been a couple for a month and a half. We can't make life decisions yet."

He nodded slowly, looking unhappy. "I guess you're right. But, I feel so helpless thinking that you're going back tonight, and then we'll be apart again."

"I feel the same way. But you and I both have huge things coming up soon. I have the new book, and you and Peter leave on tour in February. We're going to Spain in January. We're spending Thanksgiving together. We need to keep things as simple as possible."

"What are we doing for Christmas?"

She thought. "What if we invited your parents to come to New York?"

Alex grinned. "That would be okay with you?"

"I'd love it."

"Great, we'll work that out. What if I fly out several days before Christmas to help you get ready? That way I can also get some work done with the band."

"That sounds great. But, that means we will be apart for almost three weeks now. I'll miss you."

Alex pulled Kat onto his lap. "I'll miss you too. I guess we'll have to settle for the phone and email until then."

Chapter Twenty-Nine

A week and a half before Christmas, Kat woke up late, stretching slowly in bed, trying to figure out what she was going to do with an entire day alone, as Luke and Peter were in Boston for the weekend. Pulling on jeans and a sweatshirt, she opened the door to the stairwell and was shocked to find the stereo playing. She walked downstairs assuming that her brother's plans had changed, only to find Alex making coffee in the kitchen.

With a shout of joy, she raced to him. "What are you doing here?"

"Well, I just happened to be talking to Peter yesterday, and he said he was going to be away tonight and tomorrow night, so I decided to surprise you. Is that okay?"

She kissed him passionately. "Of course it's okay. God, I missed you."

"Me too." He handed her a cup of coffee. "Come cuddle with me, we'll worry about food later."

Sitting on the couch, they watched the snowfall outside.

The phone next to the couch rang, startling both of them. Alex reached over and picked up the phone and handed it to Kat.

"Hello? Heya, Beth. What's up? No. No. I'm not quite up to running out shopping today. My man just arrived, and we are vegging out on the couch. We even have the house to ourselves, since Peter and Luke are in Boston for the weekend. Alex, Beth says hi."

Alex smiled before shouting, "Hi, Beth."

"No, I'm not really sure how long Alex is here for. I'm going to enjoy every moment until Monday. All right, I'll talk to you sometime tomorrow. Say hi to Sasha."

Alex nuzzled Kat's neck, and gently bit her ear. He laughed as she immediately shivered and her nipples hardened under her shirt. He pulled her onto his lap and began to kiss any exposed skin. Between kisses, he asked, "What happens on Monday?"

"I fly to Madrid on Monday."

"What?" He suddenly stopped kissing her and straightened up, almost dumping her off his lap onto the floor. "Why didn't you tell me?"

"Because I didn't know until last night, and you didn't call last night."

"I was on my way *here*."

"I'm sorry. I didn't know you were coming, so I thought I had time to make this trip before Christmas."

"Couldn't you have talked to me about it before you made plans?"

"I didn't know until yesterday that the only serious female presidential candidate is willing to talk to me. She'll see me Wednesday morning, and I need at least one day to do some research there."

"You're going to Madrid on Monday, and I only found out about it because I happened to be here when Beth called? Beth knew before I did?"

"Alex, I told you, I found out about this last night, and we didn't talk last night."

"Because I was flying *here*!"

"How the hell was I supposed to know that? Anyway, Beth stopped over last night to drop off a dress she had borrowed, so I told her then."

"So basically, I'm the last one to know?"

"No, you aren't the *last* one to know. You're the *second* one to know. Why are you so angry about this? I'll be back next Friday, so I'll have four days to prepare for Christmas."

"Why are you going for so long?"

"A friend is getting married. I didn't think I could go. Now I will be there anyway, so I can be at the wedding."

"Why didn't you invite me?" Alex knew he sounded petulant, but he couldn't stop himself.

Kat's temper flared, and she stood up to face him. "Jesus Christ, Alex. You keep telling me how busy you are, and how many details still need to be ironed out for the tour. I didn't want to make you feel guilty about not being able to go, so I just didn't ask. Why are you being this way? This isn't a major deal."

"It is to me."

"Why? I don't blow up every time you tell me you have to go somewhere. Now I'm saying I need to go to Spain because of my job, and you're upset. I don't understand."

"I don't understand why you run off to these places. You certainly don't need to work. Even if you didn't have money, you know I'd support you. You could stay in New York or California and write. Or do something else if you wanted to."

Kat's eyes widened. "So basically my writing is my hobby, while your music is a career?"

"No, that's not what I mean, but you don't have to race all over the globe. You could stay here or in California."

Kat's voice became shriller. "Are you saying that I should basically become your kept woman? Stay home, have a cute hobby, and be here for you when you find it convenient. God forbid I not be here when you need servicing."

"I can't believe you said that. I never said I wanted to, as you so nicely put it, keep you. All I want is for you to stay in the same country with me, and work on your writing that doesn't take you into Godforsaken countries."

"Spain isn't exactly a third world country. I'm just going for less than a week. I didn't know that you were coming, and I didn't think you'd mind. I'm sorry if this bothers you, but I've already committed to the trip. I'd love it if you wanted to go with me."

"Oh, now that we're having this discussion, suddenly I'm allowed to go with you? If I hadn't been here when Beth called, what would you have done? Left a message on my machine on Monday, saying 'I'll be back in a week. Don't call me, I'll call you?'"

"No. I was planning to call you today and tell you."

"It would be nice if we talked about things before you made decisions."

"Did you ask me how I felt about your being on tour for February and March? Did you ask if I might want to come along? No. You just assumed that I wouldn't want to."

"That's why I'm here! I came out this weekend because I wanted to talk to you about our getting an apartment together. I am tired of living alone without you. I want us to live together, and I want you to go on tour with me."

"You came here planning to throw the idea of living together at me? You never brought this idea up before, and you accuse me of not talking to you about things!"

"I'll do anything I damn well please. You sure do."

"You can't be serious! You're mad because I made a decision last night and hadn't told you yet, and you show up here to ask me to move in with you? You're doing exactly what you are accusing me of doing!"

"I am not. I'm here to have a conversation about this, I didn't lease us an apartment or anything like that. This is completely different. You made a decision about being away, *again*, without talking to me. I am just a spectator in our relationship, not a part of it. And I can't do this."

"What are you saying?"

"I'm saying that I need us to be together, whole-heartedly, or not. I can't do the commuter, half-assed thing."

"Are you giving me an ultimatum?"

"No." His voice became more certain, "Yes. I guess I am."

"Alex, Jesus, how can you do this? We aren't at that point in our relationship."

"I think we are. And if you are hesitating, I know what your answer is."

"Don't do this."

"I have to. I love you, but I need to know we are together or aren't. I can't do this shit of having you make major plans without even talking to me. Clearly I'm more invested in us than you are."

"I can't believe you would say that." Kat stood up and grabbed her jacket and keys off the coffee table. "I'm going to Beth's house. You are welcome to stay here until you can get a flight back home later today." She walked over and put her hand on the side of his angry face. "I'm sorry. I love you more than I can express, but I will *never* be dependent on anyone, and I will never ask permission for anything. My career is just as important to me as yours is to you. I won't determine everything in my life according to whether or not it makes you happy. Goodbye, Alex."

Chapter Thirty

Kat walked out the front door and hurried through the quiet streets to the subway station, getting on a southbound train. She held herself together until she reached Beth's door. Once Beth opened the door to her apartment, she gasped, "Jesus, Kat, what's wrong with you?"

"Alex and I just broke up."

"You did what? I just talked to you an hour ago, and you two were fine. What happened?"

"We broke up. He was angry that I had decided to go to Spain without talking to him about it. And then I yelled back that he made decisions without talking to me. Then he told me he had come to ask me to move in with him, and I accused him of double standards, and he told me to give up assignments that take me on the road, and I walked out." Suddenly tears began to pour out of Kat's eyes. Beth hugged Kat as she led her into the kitchen, where she poured her a stiff shot of brandy.

"Drink this."

"I hate brandy."

"I know, but it will help."

"Help what? To kill me?"

"Just drink it."

Kat downed it and shuddered violently. Beth poured her a cup of coffee. "Okay, the brandy will calm you down, the coffee will keep you from getting a headache."

Kat started to cry. "Shit, Beth. I fucked up. I didn't talk to Alex before accepting the assignment. Now he feels like he doesn't matter to me." She shared every bit of the conversation with Beth, who sat in stunned silence.

Beth's look was pensive. "Okay, kiddo. Here's the thing, looking at it from my old married woman standpoint.

You should have told him as soon as you could that you were offered the assignment, but he shouldn't expect that he can decide whether you take an assignment or not. He can't expect you to be sitting here waiting for him when he unexpectedly decides to pop in for a visit. So, as I see it, both of you need to figure out what the hell you want out of this relationship, and work together on it or break up for good."

"What do I do?"

"No clue. Either you decide to not go on the trip because it's a big deal to him…"

"Not happening, it's too big of a deal to have gotten the interview. Besides, if I cancel, that will get around and hurt my chances of future interviews."

"Then you try talking to him, tell him that this is important to you, but that you blew it by not talking to him about going *before* you booked the flights, that sort of thing, and that you'll try to be more considerate in the future."

"So, you're saying I screwed up?"

"Yes, you did, and so did he. Somehow, text, email, voicemail, you should have let him know as soon as the trip came up. Right now, his ego is hurt because I knew before he did. But he should have told you he was coming or at least understood your point of view before blowing up at you."

"Should I call him?"

"You told him he could stay at the house until he could find a flight. So, he might still be there. I'd suggest that you go home and talk face to face. If he's gone, *then* call him."

***

At home, Kat opened the door unsure of what would be worse, to find out that Alex had left, or that he was still there. As soon as she opened the door, she could see his keys and a piece of paper on the counter.

Dear Kat,

I don't know how to say everything I want to. We both said awful things to each other this morning. I love you. I will always love you. You're right. I was expecting you to live by a code I wasn't willing to follow. I thought I was being romantic by surprising you with the idea of living together, and instead, you saw that I was trying to control you and our lives as a couple. Maybe I was. I don't really know. For me, the bigger issue is that I was here to ask you to live with me, but I realized that what I really want is for us to get married. I want us to be joined, not just in our hearts, but legally, and to have a complete life together, kids, dogs and all. But, right now I feel like this can't work, and it's breaking my heart. Ultimately, I think we both need time alone, time to think about us. We moved pretty quickly, and maybe I rushed you too much. I guess what I'm suggesting is that we take some time to think. Now, you know what I want for us, please look in your heart and see if you want it too.

I love you. ALEX

Kat picked up the phone and dialed his cell which went right to voice mail. With a trembling voice, she said, "Alex. I just got your letter. Please call me when you get in. Please. I love you."

***

Mid-afternoon the phone rang.

Kat's heart lurched as she picked up, "Hello?"

"Hi. It's me."

"Hi."

"I got your message."

There was a pause. Kat took a deep breath. "I love you."

Alex closed his eyes and sighed. "I love you too."

"I wish that you had stayed here, so we could've talked this out."

"You told me to get out!"

"And you believed me?"

"You took off to Beth's instead of staying to talk it out with me."

"So once again, it's my fault."

"No, in a relationship, people talk. You should have talked to me about all of this."

"So, once again, we're back to my inadequacies as a partner. You were here to talk about moving in, and you accuse me of not sharing?"

"Yes, I was. But you were planning to leave the country without even telling me. I was trying to be romantic."

"And I was trying to be supportive of your career pressures by not putting more pressure on you right now. It was never that I didn't want you to know about the trip. I was planning on telling you."

"But you didn't. You told Beth first. That's what it boils down to, Kat. I need to be first in your life, and I'm not. I come in a distant second or third to your writing and other people."

"Alex, I need to go. I can't handle this conversation right now. I love you, but I'm leaving to go to Spain on Monday."

"I know that now." Alex's voice cracked. "I love you. But I can't go on like this."

"I know. Goodbye, Alex."

Chapter Thirty-One

Kat wandered around aimlessly over the weekend until she flew to Madrid on Monday. The interview went well, and then she traveled north for the wedding.

Throughout the festivities, she stayed outwardly cheerful. The large group of friends celebrated until the sun started to rise. Silently, she left the reception and went to sit alone on the sea wall, looking at the cold ocean. A noise made her look down, and she saw Secundino climbing up.

He sat down next to her and lit a cigarette. His pockmarked face scanned the ocean as he quietly said, "Okay, *tia,* we need to talk. Are you going to tell me why your smiles haven't reached your eyes today? Or, why not only is Alejandro not with you, but you won't even talk about him? And suddenly, you've canceled your trip with him."

Kat said tiredly, "Fuck off, Secu, you busybody. I'm fine."

"You're always fine, lovely. But recently, you softened, opened up. When we were talking about setting up the interview, you were human. Now, you're back to shutting everyone out. Why?"

Sighing, Kat looked at the ocean before speaking. "Oh, Secu. I fucked up big time." She closed her eyes, and shook her head sadly. "I've never really been in love like this before, and so I didn't think about how to make sure Alex doesn't feel left out. He came to visit last weekend, and I hadn't yet told him I was coming here because I didn't want to put pressure on him to come with me when he's so busy. So, he got angry that he hadn't known. Then I got angry because he was angry, and before I knew it, we were screaming at each other, and I left."

Secundino raised a questioning eyebrow at her. "You love him?"

"Of course I do."

"Then you should have stayed and talked it out."

"I know!"

"Have you called him?"

"No. Not since the afternoon after the fight. I called him, and he was still so angry that I gave up."

"Why haven't you called him again? Doesn't this matter to you?"

"Of course it matters to me! I haven't called because he recommended some cool off time and I agreed."

Secu snorted. "You need to start trusting him and your relationship."

"What are you talking about?"

"You need to trust that his love is strong enough that you can each make concessions."

Kat was genuinely confused. "What?"

"Right now, you need to each start giving some. You need to start asking if you need or want something. If I do something Ana Lucia doesn't like, she screams at me. And when I get mad at her, it works the same way. We work it out. But you two are so afraid of upsetting each other that you would rather lose Alex than stand your ground and fight it out. You would rather lose him than honestly tell him that you were deep down afraid to ask him to come with you because you're afraid he doesn't love you enough to rearrange his schedule."

Kat reached over and took a drag from his cigarette. She blew a perfect smoke ring and quietly asked, "All right Mr. Know-it-all, what do I do now?"

"My, my, asking for help. You are softening."

Her voice was imploring as she asked. "Really, Secu, what do I do?"

"Call him. Just start with hello. Come on. I'll walk you to the Telefonica because the cell service here is awful."

At the phone office, Kat cautiously punched in Alex's home phone number. As it started to ring, she hung up.

Secundino rolled his eyes. "Why did you hang up?"

"It's the middle of the night. I didn't want to wake him."

"And you have never awakened him before, perhaps to …?"

Kat's blush told Secundino the answer. "Call him now."

She resolutely dialed again, and on the third ring Alex answered in an annoyed voice, "Hello?"

Kat slammed down the receiver.

Exasperated, Secundino picked up the receiver. "Now, *hija,* you've hung up on him twice. Call him back and at least let him know it's you."

This time he answered on the second ring. "Whoever you are, I hope to hell you know what time it is, and I really don't appreciate this hanging up shit."

"Hi."

"Katherine?" With the use of her full name, Kat's heart sank.

"Yeah. Hi. It's me. It was me before too. I'm sorry I hung up, but..."

"But what, Kat?"

"But, I just wanted to tell you I got here safely."

"I'm glad." There was a long pause. "However, if we'd gone together, you wouldn't have needed to call, I would've known firsthand."

Hurt showed in Kat's eyes. "I know. I'm sorry, but I did what I thought was best."

His voice softened. "I know you did. But you need to think about what's best for us as a couple and talk to me, rather than making decisions based upon what you *think* I want or need."

Kat's voice hardened. "Alex, I'm not the only one who screwed up. Anyway, I just wanted to hear your voice, but I guess this is too soon. Goodbye, Alex."

"Kat, wait!"

"No, Alex. I tried, and you aren't ready to meet me halfway. Now the ball's in your court."

"Kat..."

"Goodbye Alex."

Kat hung up and turned to a shocked Secundino. "I tried Secu. I tried..."

Chapter Thirty-Two

Once back in New York, Kat fell back into her normal schedule. Every time the phone rang, she hoped it was Alex, but she didn't dare call him again.

Peter, Luke, and Kat had decorated the house for Christmas before she left for Spain. After she got back, Kat shopped and baked, but couldn't really get into the holiday spirit.

Meanwhile, Peter hadn't told Kat that Alex had been in New York finishing up the cuts, staying in a nearby hotel. Peter and Luke planned their annual Christmas party at the house, and they invited all of her friends, hoping to cheer her up.

The night of the party arrived. Guests poured through the doors, and Kat welcomed people as they arrived.

As the crowd grew, someone asked Kat for glasses for tequila shots. She climbed up on the counter in her bare feet and had her back to the room as Alex walked in. He had agreed to come to the party only because Peter had begged him, but the view of her perfect legs as she reached into the cupboard took his breath away.

Alex was filled with hurt and jealousy as a strange man walked over and carefully lifted her and the glasses off the counter. He turned to leave just as Josh grabbed him by one arm.

"Come on Alex, let's talk." Josh tugged Alex by the arm into the fairly quiet mudroom, as it was the only room not teeming with people.

"What's there to talk about?"

"Your reaction to Kat's being lifted down, for starters. Second, the fact that you obviously still love her.

Third, she's going crazy missing you, but is afraid to call you again."

Alex just stared at him.

Josh continued, "She loves you so much it's amazing, but she's afraid you'll reject her. Why don't you get over the silent act and talk to her?"

"She seems happy enough without me."

"Oh, screw you, Alex, you know Kat. You could be about to slit her throat, and she'd comment about the nice weather. Talk to her."

"Why?"

"Well, she's one of my best friends, and I've lived through most of her relationships. She has never loved anyone like she loves you, and she's going crazy trying to figure out how to make things right."

Alex refused to give in. "I'll think about it."

"Damn, you're even more stubborn than she is." Josh stalked off and left Alex alone.

The Christmas tree glowed in the corner, and Alex thought about all of his fantasies about waking up on Christmas morning and making love to Kat before showering her with gifts. Never in his life had he ever felt that way, and the realization made him take off his coat and lay it on a chair. He walked back into the fray and realized that many of the people had moved to the sunroom for dancing. He saw Kat dancing with the man who had lifted her down, and before he realized what he was doing, he stalked over. "This dance is over."

The man looked shocked and immediately got defensive. "What?"

"I'm going to dance with Kat now."

"Maybe you should ask her first."

Alex turned to Kat, who was standing in stunned silence. "Kat, may I have this dance?"

She looked at him searchingly before quietly nodding, "Yes."

As they stood there looking at each other, a new slow song started, and Alex cautiously pulled Kat toward him, waiting for any sign of resistance. Alex wrapped his arms tightly around her and sighed contentedly as Kat tentatively returned his embrace.

When the song ended, Alex gazed down at her. "It feels so good to hold you again."

She smiled sadly. "I know."

"Please, can we dance again? This is the first time in two weeks that we haven't ended up hanging up or walking out on each other."

"Alex, I've always been the last one to want to talk, but we need to."

"We will. Later. Please, just dance with me."

Kat nodded slowly as he pulled her close again. They danced the next three songs, and then Alex pulled Kat by the hand toward the food. Kat went willingly, beginning to feel a shimmer of hope. Standing by the buffet table, Dave slapped Alex on the back and said, "Wasn't the last remix a bitch yesterday?"

"It was. I thought we'd never finish."

Dave nudged Kat. "Hey lady, we've missed you around the studio lately. What, you too famous to hang out with bums like us?"

Kat grinned at Dave, "Nah. I just..." She stopped in mid-sentence. "You guys were remixing yesterday? Alex never told me anything about a remix."

"Hell yes, we finished it up late last night." He sounded apologetic. "Hey, my gorgeous date is waiting for me on the couch. See you later."

As Dave sauntered off, Kat turned to Alex with narrowed eyes. "You've been remixing? You've been in town?" Before Alex could answer, she yanked his hand toward the stairwell. "We need to talk, now, upstairs."

"But, Kat..."

"Now!"

In the relative quiet of her sitting room, she pointed to the couch. "Sit down. I have some questions for you."

"Kat..."

"Don't give me 'Kat' bullshit right now. I want answers. How long have you been in town?"

Alex looked uncomfortable as he squirmed on the couch. "Basically on and off since I came to see you. I flew home for a couple days for my mother's birthday party, which was when you called me from Spain. Then I came back to New York."

"Where have you been staying?"

"At a hotel."

"And I assume that Peter and Luke knew?"

"Of course they did. Come on Kat, let me explain."

"Wait a minute. Now it's my turn. You've been here over a week, and you never told me? You've actually been here almost two weeks, and you never told me? I bet you didn't think I'd be here tonight, did you?" His silence gave her his answer. "You accuse me of not telling you things, then you're here in town, and you avoid me to the point that you come to my house only because you thought I wouldn't be here?"

"Kat, wait..."

"No, *you* wait. I've had it. I made the effort of calling you to apologize. I didn't question when you showed up tonight. Shit, Alex, you came to ask me to dance, and I began to hope that you were trying to meet me halfway. But now I find that it was just another game, another fucking power trip. In other words, *you* do what you want, and *I* do what you want. What part of this did you think was so good for the *us* you were harping about?"

"Kat, listen to me!"

"No. Goddamn it. I'm through listening. I've taken the blame for the problem between us. I admit I screwed up about the trip to Spain. I admit it. But, now this isn't my fault. I tried to make amends. I tried to call and apologize.

But you're playing by different rules, Alex. It's not okay for me to make decisions but it's okay for you to do it. Do you have any idea how much it would've hurt to run into you on the street? Jesus Christ, I've been wandering around Manhattan for a week, most of the time around the studio. I'm trying to deal with missing you. Just trying to get through each day. And now I find out that I could've bumped into you looking at the Christmas windows. It would've absolutely destroyed me to run into you like that." With her fists clenched, she looked at him. "It would've hurt almost as much as it does now. Do you care?" She turned to face the windows for a moment, before turning back to look at Alex. Her voice softened, "God, Alex. I love you so much it's inconceivable. But..."

As Kat stood poised to finish her sentence, Peter knocked on the door and strode into the room. "Hey, Alex. Sorry to interrupt, but we're ready to play downstairs, and we need you."

Alex sat looking alternatingly at Kat and Peter. Before he could speak, Kat coolly answered, "He'll be right down. We're through here." She looked pointedly at Alex. "And I do mean *through*."

Peter raised his eyebrow. "What's your problem?"

Kat's control snapped. "You are such a motherfucking shit that you neglected to tell me Alex was in town!"

"Kat, we just..."

"Don't say anything right now, Peter. Get the hell out of here now." She turned back to Alex. "Now you need to go downstairs and play. I'm not leaving tonight. But I'm warning you, Alex, stay the fuck out of my way, or I'll make an unholy scene that will forever tarnish that sensitive guy image you have."

"Kat, please let me explain."

"No. Not now, maybe not ever. I'm tired of this game, Alex. Get away from me and stay away from me." Alex stood helplessly in front of her. "*Now*, Alex!"

Slowly, Alex followed Peter downstairs.

Kat stood silently and stared out the window. Finally, she walked into the bathroom to repair her makeup and fix her hair. Belligerently, she looked at her reflection, unbuttoned another button on her blouse, and adjusted her skirt to show more of her legs. Then she took a deep breath and walked down to the party. She mingled with friends, pointedly ignored Peter and Alex, and tried to avoid any deep conversations. With malice in her eyes, she danced with men in front of Alex, who stood at his synthesizer looking like he was about to explode. Finally, around midnight, Kat kissed friends goodnight. As she stood at the edge of the room, looking around one more time to make sure that she had said goodbye to everyone, Alex approached.

Imploringly, he held out his hand to her. "C'mon Kat, just let me explain."

"Did you miss the part of the conversation where I said that if you got anywhere near me, that I'd raise holy hell?"

"No. I heard every word you said, which is more than I can say for you. You won't even let me have a chance."

Kat took a deep breath, and shoved a finger into his chest. "Alex, I've listened to you since we had the fight, more than you've listened to me. And I was all ready to try here tonight, but I got screwed." She smiled cruelly. "And I don't mean in a fun and dirty way, I mean screwed over. You made me feel like shit, and goddamn it, I am not willing to put myself in the position to be treated that way." She ran a finger along the side of his face, "I love you more than I can tell you, but right now I need you out of my space, and we need to be apart. Maybe we can work this out once we've both had a chance to cool off." She rose on tiptoes to kiss his cheek. "Good-bye, Alex."

***

At dawn, Peter knocked on the door holding two mugs of coffee, surprised to find her sleeping on the couch. Shrugging off sleep, she sat up and motioned him in.

"Are you still pissed at me?"

Her eyes were swollen and red as they looked at him sadly. "Yeah. But, I don't know what to do about it."

Peter sat next to her and handed her one of the mugs. "I'm so sorry, Kat. Alex couldn't really take off after he arrived to see you. We needed him for sessions. And so he moved into the hotel. And you went away, and then he asked me not to tell you because he said you wanted him out of here. And I didn't know what to do. I thought I was helping. And then I thought you two could work it out if he came here last night." He looked helplessly at her. "I seem to have made it worse. I'm so sorry."

"You didn't really do anything wrong, Pete. It's just I needed to trust someone, and I felt like you set me up last night. And I still don't know if we can work this out. It doesn't seem like it right now." She picked up a pillow and swatted at him. "I was really ticked at you last night."

"I gathered that."

Her eyes filled with tears as she leaned against him. "Oh, Pete. I miss him so much. I don't know what to do."

He hugged her close. "You wait and see."

***

Christmas morning, Kat awoke to find the world covered in snow. She pulled on a thick coat and went for a long walk with Max, and then came home and hopefully checked the answering machine. Peter, Luke, and Kat exchanged gifts and made a complicated lunch. At four, Kat was curled up in the deep armchair in the sunroom, when the phone rang. Peter answered, "Hello? Oh, hi. How are you? Merry Christmas to you, too. Let me get her." He turned and held out the phone to Kat. "Kat, it's Alex's mom."

Slowly, Kat got to her feet, "Merry Christmas, Maria. How are you?"

"Merry Christmas, sweetheart. We wanted to tell you how much we loved the gifts you sent us. The pictures of Alex are spectacular, and the tea set is perfect."

"Oh, Maria. I'm so glad you like them. Thank you so much for the sweater, I love it." Kat looked down at the beautiful hand-knit sky blue Aran sweater. "I have it on right now."

"Good. Sweetheart, Alfonso and I were so disappointed that we couldn't spend the holiday with you this year."

Kat sat down and sighed. "Oh, Maria, I was so looking forward to the holiday with you both and Alex."

"Well, love, perhaps next Christmas. True love always wins, even if it takes a while. Well, I must go. Alfonso sends his love. Merry Christmas, Katherine."

"Merry Christmas, Maria, please send my best to Alfonso."

As Kat hung up, she looked at the men. "Pete, Luke, I'm going out for a while. Okay?"

"Sure, do you want company?"

"Nah. Just some time to think."

Kat and Max wandered up and down the streets, watching couples and families exchange holiday greetings. Windows glowed brightly in the dusk, and finally, they started home.

Peter greeted her at the door. "Alex called."

Her smile was blinding, "He did?"

"About fifteen minutes ago. He said there should be an email for you."

***

Kat raced up the stairs.

Kat,
Merry Christmas. I love you more than anything. That I
know. That part is easy. It is the rest that is so hard. I feel
like you don't want to commit to me, only be part of my life
when it's convenient. I want more than that. But, maybe
with time, we can both compromise. I don't know how yet.
But, I wanted to let you know that more than I ever believed
possible, I love you.
Alex

Kat immediately dialed Alex's home number and got a recording saying, "Hey, Happy Holidays. I'm not here, as I've taken off for a few days of creative space. I'll be checking my messages occasionally, so leave one if you want."

Kat listened for the beep, "Hi, it's me. I got your email, and I just wanted to say I do understand, and I will wait forever, hoping." Her voice wavered. "And I will always love you. Always. Merry Christmas."

Out in California, Alex closed his eyes against the pain of hearing her voice as he listened. Then he picked up his bag and left the house.

Chapter Thirty-Three

After the holidays, Kat's life settled into a monotonous routine. The last week in January, Kat received a call from a lawyer she knew in Madrid. The woman was heading up a conference on the role of Hispanic women. She called to say that the keynote speaker had broken her leg skiing, and they wondered if Kat would travel to Madrid to give the speech during the second week of February.

Kat packed excitedly and left for Madrid to have time to prepare. She was to give the speech the night before the opening concert for their tour, and then fly home with just a few hours to spare before the concert. She felt in her bones that she'd be home in time to see the concert, and she so hoped that she and Alex could work things out on that night.

An hour before the speech, a bellboy knocked on her door with a bouquet of multi-colored tulips and a Hershey bar. Attached to the flowers was a note. *Hey, the flowers are to wish you luck, and the chocolate is to give you a rush before your speech. We are so proud of you. Good luck -- see you at the concert. Love, Peter and Luke.*

The speech went beautifully. Afterwards, she rushed to the airport only to find that her flight was delayed. Kat sat for two hours before she realized that she'd never make it home in time. Luckily, she had the number of the fax at the stadium, and she dialed there, praying someone would give it to Peter in time.

Peter got the fax just an hour before the concert. His disappointment was tangible as he handed it to Luke. Peter paced nervously as Luke watched him. "Peter, calm down, this certainly isn't your first tour. Why are you so wound?"

"I've never been on tour before without Kat here for the first concert."

"You've never been on tour with this band, so stop overthinking the significance of her not being here."

"You know what I mean!"

"I know, but you read the fax, she got delayed. She'll be back tomorrow before you actually go on the road. Relax." Just as Luke was comfortingly rubbing Peter's shoulders, Alex walked into the room. He looked around hopefully. Luke immediately understood. "Alex, she's not here. She got delayed. She should be back tomorrow."

Alex flopped into a chair. "Damn. I really hoped to see her tonight to make things right."

The phone rang, and Peter pounced on it. His face lit up as the connection crackled. "Hey! Where are you?"

"Madrid. Shit, Petie, I'm so sorry. My flight has been indefinitely delayed, and there isn't any other option, so I won't be there for the concert."

"I understand. You did the best you could."

"Hey, but I'll be back tomorrow. How about lunch?"

"That sounds great. I miss you."

"I miss you too. Knock 'em dead tonight."

"We will."

There was a pause. "Peter, is Alex there?"

"Yeah, I'll get him." He handed the phone to a shocked Alex.

"Hello?"

"Alex? Hi."

"Hi."

"Good luck tonight. I really wanted to be there."

"Me too."

Mockingly, she asked, "You really wanted to be there tonight?"

"No. I mean I wanted you to be here. Where are you?"

"In Madrid."

"Why?"

"Why what?"

"Why are you there?"

"Because I gave a speech."

"Oh. I didn't know."

"I didn't tell you. How could you have known?"

"I should've asked Peter."

"Alex, relax! You don't need to know everything."

"Yes, I do! I do need to know everything about you. And maybe if I had asked, then we could've worked out something for tonight."

"What do you mean?"

"So you could've been here tonight."

Kat spoke slowly and carefully, enunciating each word but trying to keep the anger from her voice. "Listen carefully, Alex. As much as I love you, I just was the keynote speaker at an international conference on the role of Hispanic women. I was not over here doing my nails. I would not, repeat *not*, have given up the opportunity to speak even if I'd known I would miss the concert. This is not my hobby—this is my career. Until you understand that, I don't see the point in talking. I have to go. Good luck tonight."

"Kat, wait. I love you."

"I know, and I love you too. Let's see what we can do with that."

Chapter Thirty-Four

The concert was a rousing success. Peter and Kat had lunch together the next day before the band left for a concert in Saratoga. Peter left the next morning, and for the next week, Kat and Luke moped around. At the beginning of the third week of February, Kat again got a call inviting her to go to Peru to report on the Shining Path. After starting the process to go, she went downstairs to the kitchen to have dinner with Luke. Partway through the meal, she took a deep breath. "Hey Luke, I'm going to Peru three days from now."

Luke almost choked on his seltzer. "You're going where?"

"To Peru, to work with the Shining Path. I was offered the assignment again."

Luke considered his next words carefully. "This has nothing to do with showing Alex that you're in control of your own life?"

"No!" she said forcefully.

"Bullshit, Kat. This has everything to do with you saying that you're in control." He gently rubbed her hand. "Make sure you're picking the right reason to go on this trip. They aren't exactly a vacation tour group."

"I know, Luke. Believe me—I'm going for all the right reasons."

The next weekend she flew to Lima where she met Secundino. Except for one call to let Luke know that she had arrived, she didn't contact anyone for the next three weeks. When she flew home at the end of the second week of March, Luke was shocked at how thin and tired she was. Her long braid was gone, and her hair now barely covered her ears.

Her first night home, she called Peter at the hotel in Amsterdam. After their conversation, Peter spoke to Luke. "She sounds exhausted."

"She looks it. She even said she was going to take a few days off."

"Wow, that's not like her. Was the trip more than she bargained for?"

"I don't know. But she looks absolutely beat, and she says she got blisters at one point, and they still hurt. Hopefully, a few days of rest will snap her back to normal. Did you tell Alex she went?"

"No. Kat insisted that I not volunteer any information. Did she say anything about him?"

"No. She looked through her messages and then just sat there."

***

At the beginning of the third week in March, the band landed in London and got ready for the two concerts they would play in England. The first concert was absolutely perfect for both the band and the crowd. It was late when the limo finally sped with them back to the hotel. Peter was so quiet in the car that Alex finally nudged him. "Hey, what's the matter with you?"

Dave snorted, "Oh, he's just lonely. He hasn't seen Luke in almost two weeks."

Looking serious, Peter shook his head. "No, this has nothing to do with Luke. I don't know. Maybe it's just some nasty form of jet lag, but I feel jumpy."

Alex smiled at him. "As my mother would say, a good night of sleep will cure what ails you."

"Yeah, I'm sure it will."

As they entered the hotel, the night clerk motioned to them. "Excuse me, Mr. Weston, you have a message. You were asked to call this number as soon as you came in."

Peter's face grew grave as he took the message slip and sprinted toward the elevator.

Alex put his hand on Peter's arm as he went past, "Who's the message from?"

"Luke. Alex, I've got to go."

Alex removed his arm, as Peter slipped onto the elevator and the doors closed.

***

In his suite, Peter called the number, which was Luke's cell phone. Luke answered on the first ring. "Peter?"

"Yeah. What's the matter? Where are you?"

"I'm at Cedars. Kat's in the critical care unit."

"What the hell happened?"

"As far as I can tell, she came home with blisters on her right foot from hiking. She'd been real quiet for the first two days she was home, and yesterday, she kind of closeted herself in her room. She came down at dinner time, but barely said anything and only picked at her food. From looking at the fridge, I figure she's had about three bites of food since she got back. Then she went to bed. Today, when I came home from work, I went up, and she was lying in bed barely conscious. She was burning up with fever, and when I pulled the covers off her, her right foot and leg were swollen like a watermelon. I couldn't even get her up to walk down the stairs. I carried her down the stairs, and got a cab. I took her to the emergency room here, and they admitted her to the critical care wing immediately. The doctor says she has some kind of major infection. They may have to operate on her foot. And they had to put her under sedatives because she was so insistent that I not call you and have you come home." Luke's voice cracked. "And, I'm sitting in the fucking waiting room because she can't have visitors until they stabilize her situation. Fuck, Peter, I don't know what to do."

Peter's throat constricted in fear and worry. "Are you okay?"

"No, of course not! I can see her through a window, but I can't even sit with her. She was down in the emergency room crying because she didn't want to fuck up your tour, and then she started screaming that Alex wasn't to know anything about this. They had to have an orderly come in and hold her down while they injected a sedative. And once that started kicking in, she started crying for your mother. Fuck, Peter, she sounded like she was a little kid, she was thrashing around on the stretcher calling out for Mommy."

"Oh, Luke, I'll come home on the next flight."

"You *can't*. I promised Kat that you wouldn't. I wasn't even supposed to call you. I called Josh, and he should be here momentarily, and Jess and Beth are on their way. We're covered."

"She's my sister, I'm coming home! They can either go on without me, or cancel the next couple shows."

"Listen to me, Peter. I want you here as much as you want to be here. But, number one, I think it'll flip her out even more, and if you come home tonight, Alex will have to know. Please, please, just stay put tonight. Let's see what happens with the antibiotics. If it's not improving in the next couple hours, *then* come home."

"When's the doctor going to talk to you again?"

"She said she'll check in with us in a couple hours if not before. For now, they've all sorts of antibiotics, painkillers, and lots of other stuff dripping into her. Once she's stabilized," his voice shook, "I can stay in the room with her. The doctor says if they can bring the fever down and get a hold of the infection that they won't have to operate. Luke was silent for a moment. "Peter, the doctor said they have to get the fever down because there is the possibility of brain damage if they don't. Shit, I should've kept a better eye on her."

"Oh, Luke. You did everything right. She'll pull through this, we know how tough she is." He rubbed his forehead, "I really want to come home."

"I know, but I promise I'll call you as soon as I talk to the doctor."

"Sounds good." Peter thought for a moment, "What the hell am I going to tell Alex? He was there when I got your message."

"Tell him it's none of his fucking business."

"Whoa. Why are you so ticked at Alex?"

"You haven't spent the last month watching Kat eat herself alive with missing him. And he can't be bothered to send a fucking postcard. I know he's angry with her, but, give me a break." He took a deep breath. "What if you tell him my sister got sick? Then you aren't really lying since Kat's the only sister I have."

There was a knock at the door, and Alex poked his head into the room. Peter motioned him to the couch and then stood up to look out at the balcony.

"Yeah. That will work. Luke, I'm really sorry you have to go through this alone. I really appreciate all you are doing." His voice thickened. "Sometimes I forget to tell you how much I love you."

"I love you, too. It's okay. I love her, too."

"I know you do. And that makes this bearable. Can you give..." he looked over his shoulder at Alex, "your sister a message for me? Tell her I love her, and I'll be home in a minute if either one of you wants me to."

"I'll tell her. Oh, here comes Josh. Good luck with Alex."

"You'll call me as soon as you hear something? Don't worry about the time difference."

"I promise."

Alex sat with a worried look on his face. Peter saw the shadows under his eyes and knew the problems with Kat hadn't been easy for him either. The idea of lying to his friend made Peter's heart ache, but his love for Kat came first. He flopped into a chair.

"Peter, is everything okay at home? Is something wrong with Luke?"

"He's fine. His sister is in the hospital with a massive infection. She's in really bad shape."

"Jesus. How's Luke holding up? Do you need to fly home?"

"He's doing all right. Obviously scared out of his mind, but he's getting through it. They'll know in the morning if everything's going to be all right."

"Well, let me know if you need to go home. Is there anything I can do to help?"

Peter shook his head. "I guess, just pray. We need her to get well. She's so important to...Luke."

Alex left the room, and Peter sat and stared ahead, feeling helpless.

It was almost two hours later when Peter's phone rang. "Hello?"

"Hey, it's me." Peter could hear the exhaustion in Luke's voice. "We are just about to go in to sit with her. Things have stabilized some, and so Josh and I can sit with her. She's out, but at least we will be able to see her."

"Have you seen the doctor?"

"Not yet." Luke yawned. "I've gotta go, but I promise to call you as soon as I have news. Get some sleep."

"I'll try. Love you."

***

At dawn, Peter rose to stand on the balcony. As the sun rose over the horizon, he tilted his face up and closed his eyes. "Please, let her be okay. We need her. Please, just let her come through this."

Two doors down, Alex was stepping out of the shower, and the view of the sunrise awed him. Without realizing it, he copied Peter's actions, and quietly said, "Thank you for not letting it be Kat who got sick."

After he'd dressed, he knocked on the door and found Peter sprawled on the couch, flipping through the channels on the television.

"Any news?"

"Not really. I talked to him about four hours ago, and things had improved a bit. The doctor should be checking in with them in the next few hours."

"Do you want to go wander around? We could kill some time that way."

Peter jumped up. "Sure, anything beats sitting here on my ass."

The two of them wandered around, but Alex realized Peter was getting increasingly agitated as it got later. Finally, they returned to the hotel, and the clerk waved a message as they walked through the door. "Mr. Weston, a message for you."

Peter picked up the message, and Alex looked over his shoulder at the neat script. "Luke called, sister is better. Call immediately." Peter hugged Alex and dashed for the elevator with Alex in pursuit.

In his suite, Peter dialed Luke's number. Again, Luke answered on the first ring. "Peter. Hi. She's okay. She's going to be fine."

Peter started to laugh. "What happened?"

"We'd been sitting in the waiting room all night. Suddenly, around four hours ago, the nurses said the fever started dropping, and so they let us go sit with her. I was sitting holding her hand, and then about two hours ago, the doctor came in to check on her. Kat seemed to be coming around. The doctor walked in, started calling her name and asked Kat if she knew who she was, and Kat opened her eyes and said, of course, she knew she was Katherine Ann Weston, and if the doctor thought some, exact quote, 'motherfucking blisters' were going to kill her, she was sorely mistaken. And then Kat informed the doctor that having some water to drink would help the fever go down."

"No shit!"

"Honest to God! The doctor thinks it's the funniest thing. She's still really sick, but the doctor says if she keeps going like this, she should be home in a few days with crutches, but she shouldn't have lasting problems."

"Thank God. I was so scared. How are you?"

"Tired. Josh and Beth sat with me all night, which helped. How are you?"

"So excited I can't stand it. Can I talk to her?"

"Yeah, the nurses said to come down when you called, and they'd let me in for a minute. Hold on." Peter could hear Luke walking down the hall, and a door opening. He stood up, walked into his bedroom, and shut the door.

A weak voice came on. "You weren't supposed to know."

"I know. But Luke couldn't *not* tell me. He made me stay here, but I knew something was wrong. How do you feel?"

"Like I got run over by a truck. I guess I was really sick. I don't remember."

"Yeah. You were. Do you want me to come home?"

"No. I'll be fine with Mommy Luke. You finish the tour. You'll be home soon enough." She yawned. "Peter, I need to go. I'm glad you called. I love you."

"I love you, too. So much. You listen to the doctors. Please."

"I will. Call Luke later, okay?"

"I will."

Peter bounded out and grinned at Alex. "She's going to be fine. Just fine. Let's go find lots of food."

Chapter Thirty-Five

Three weeks later, Peter and Alex and the band were playing a concert in Barcelona. Alex had been especially melancholy since they had arrived in Spain, but the concert went well. As the band was relaxing backstage afterwards, a tall man with a pockmarked face strode in with a press pass.

Peter jumped up to greet him with a hug. "Secundino! I didn't know you were covering the concert. God, I would've made a point to see you before."

Secundino scoffed. "The day I cover concerts is the day I shoot myself in the head." He grinned. "No offense. I just swiped the pass so I could see you."

Peter laughed. "It's good to hear honesty." He blushed, "Oh, damn, my manners. Secundino, this's Alex. Alex, this is Secundino, a friend of Kat's."

Alex stuck out his hand and raised his eyebrow as Secundino belligerently crossed his arms. "Hello. It's nice to meet you."

"I can't say the same. So, you're the asshole who didn't know what he had in Kat's love? I'd hoped to meet you with Kat back in January, but she canceled."

Peter jumped in before Alex could respond with the anger that was clear on his face, "Secu, how was the trip? I only spoke briefly to Kat about it, what with all of the confusion. And, why are you here? Don't you have a new arrival coming?"

"Yes. Ana Lucia is as big as a house. About to deliver number four. That's why I need to head back to Madrid tonight. She gets really cranky if she goes into labor when I'm away. Anyway, I really just wanted to see you, and meet this one here," with a nod toward Alex. "The trip was pure hell. I didn't see Kat for weeks on end as she was hiking farther in than me. That woman can move when she wants to. Must be all the running and not smoking." He lovingly rubbed the pack of cigarettes sticking out of his pocket, "Did she tell you about her hair? Is she walking without crutches yet? I tried to call her yesterday, but she didn't answer the phone. I hate her machine, so I didn't leave a message."

Alex couldn't sit quietly any longer. "What the hell are you talking about? What trip? What about her hair? And why does she need crutches?"

Secundino looked at Alex with narrowed eyes. "Oh, so suddenly you care? You couldn't be bothered to contact her lately. A lot has happened." Jabbing his finger into Alex's chest, he continued. "Did you know that your woman has been in Peru for the last month, hanging out with the remnants of Shining Path? Did you know that her braid got caught in a tree, and she got so angry that she had one of the women cut it off with a bayonet? That the blisters from hiking got so infected, that when she got home she had to be put in the hospital for days and they were worried about lasting brain damage?" Seeing Alex's pale face, his voice softened. "*Tio*, you have a woman most men would kill for, and you're too stubborn to call and talk to her so you would've known some of this."

Peter gently put his hand on Alex's shoulder. "She's okay now, Alex. Luke stayed home with her when she got out of the hospital until she could walk relatively comfortably. The doctor said her immune system was so run down from overexertion that she couldn't fight the infection."

Alex jerked away from Peter as his voice crackled with anger. "How the hell can the two of you sit there and act so relaxed about this? For God's sake, don't you think it would be better not to encourage her to take assignments like that? Damn it. I wish she'd stop being so stinking cavalier about her safety."

Secundino raised an eyebrow. "She won't stop taking them, *tio*. And if she did, she'd no longer be the woman you love. This is part of her. I love my wife. We have three beautiful children, and one on the way. But I have my career, too. Ana Lucia understands that, and that's how our love survives." He looked almost kindly at Alex. "Have you ever read her books?" Alex shook his head slowly.

Secu continued in a sure voice, "Read them. Pick one up and read it." He shrugged. "I'm a good writer. Some days very good. Never outstanding. I'm too lazy, and I don't have a true gift. Kat does. Her stories are so alive you can smell and taste them." He touched Alex's arm, "Read one, see that this isn't a hobby to her. It is who she is. And who she *will* be." Secundino stood. "Anyway, I must go. Peter, it was wonderful to see you again. The concert was fabulous."

At the door, he stopped and looked quizzically at Peter, "Are you going to watch the event tonight? Her email said it was going to be streamed online. And what about the house?"

Peter nodded, uncomfortable in his knowledge that Alex knew nothing about what they were referring to, and that he would be furious. "Yeah. I figure I'll get back to the hotel with about twenty minutes to spare to make sure I have the connection. And the closing is next week. The architect has already been to meet with her."

Alex felt frustration building again, knowing they knew something about Kat that he didn't know. "What? What the hell are you talking about?"

Secundino turned to look at him, his voice calm. "In about an hour, she will be presenting at a conference at that goddamn college about her rape."

Alex's shock was clear. "What the hell are you talking about? She's going *public*?"

Peter nodded, "Reid Morgan contacted her a couple weeks ago to make amends for what he did and invited her to a symposium tonight on drugs and alcohol at the college, and she agreed."

Secundino opened the door. "Anyway, I'm leaving."

Peter spoke. "Bye, Secu. Thanks for stopping by."

***

After Secundino had left the room, Peter took two bottles from the buffet table, and handed one to Alex who was pacing around the room. Then he sat down with his own beer, figuring Alex would explode soon. Alex twisted off the top and took a long swig. Peter watched Alex start to talk several times. Each time he stopped as he tried to get his anger under control.

He turned toward Peter, his arms crossed. "Why didn't you tell me she was going to Peru?"

Peter calmly sipped. "You didn't ask."

"Damn it, Peter, now you sound like Kat and that self-satisfied prick, Secundino. You should've told me."

"Once again, I'm going to turn it around. You should've asked me."

"What, I should ask on a daily basis if your sister is running off to play with revolutionary crazies? I didn't realize this was such a commonplace activity for her."

"It isn't. But, yes, she does go off to some strange places, and some of them are dangerous. Last year she studied the women of ETA, the Basque liberation group. They're not exactly a day in the park either." Peter took a deep breath, trying to see the situation from Alex's point of view. "I wasn't saying that you should've asked if she was in Peru, just that if you were interested, you should've asked how she was. In the months we've been on tour, you haven't mentioned her once. Shit, you've so blatantly ignored her existence that I'm afraid to mention her at all. If you cared, you could've asked what she was doing in the last several months. Did you expect that she's been sitting home doing her nails? She gave up the trip to Peru to be with you in the fall, and then you left. The opportunity arose again, and she couldn't pass it up." He smirked. "Our career path leads us to cushy hotels, and hers leads to the jungles of Central America and the mountains of Spain. That's just who she is."

"Jesus Christ, Peter. How can you sit there and act so calm about this? How can you care so little about her safety?"

Even though Peter knew Alex was striking out in his own pain, he wasn't going to take that comment without responding. "Wait one goddamn minute, Alex. Don't you *dare* make any fucking comments about my lack of concern for her." Peter's eyes blazed. "I'm tied in knots every time she leaves on assignment, but I don't control her, just as she doesn't control me. Control isn't love." He took a deep breath. "Yeah, I admit it, sometimes I wish that she'd picked a nice, safe career, but she didn't. Her career is talking to women who don't have the chance to do much besides live and die without any voice. I can't stop her."

"How can you let her go do things like that? Shit, why don't you at least try harder to convince her to stop?"

"Weren't you there the night we fought about 'letting' her do something? Kat's a grown woman, and as Secu said, what she does is who she is. It's part of her. She's good at it. She loves it. It makes her the woman we love. Did you ever stop to think about the importance of the fact that she was asked to be the keynote speaker at that conference the night of the first show? She's recognized by others in the field as being important. She's not even thirty years old, and she is world-renowned in her field. She's recognized as being an *expert*. That's so awesome. Did you ever congratulate her on that? She's worked hard to get there. And I'd never dream of stopping her. Deep down, I would never want to. She always comes back, but taking her writing away from her would strip her soul. Just like if you or I stopped playing."

Alex stopped pacing to face Peter. "Why didn't you tell me she was sick?"

"Indirectly, I did. I told you Luke's sister was sick. She's Luke's sister, too."

"Don't play word games with me, Peter. Why the fuck didn't you tell me it was Kat? I would've flown back to be with her."

"That was the point. She didn't, and doesn't, want you to race back unless you're ready to understand her life." His eyes became slits. "She felt so strongly about it, she had to be sedated because she was screaming at Luke not to let you know, that she didn't want your pity." He raked his hair back from his face. "Alex, you have to understand her system of beliefs. She'd rather be without you than with you for the wrong reasons."

"You had no right to not tell me she was sick."

Peter's voice was icy. "I had all the right in the world. She's my sister, and she was screaming that you weren't to know. I will *always* protect her rights first."

Alex took a deep breath, and rubbed his face. "Tell me about her foot."

"Just as we said. She was hiking up to twenty miles a day and got huge blisters. Sometime during the last week, some of them got infected, and they didn't get treated. She made it home, and I guess she tried to take it easy but didn't get medical attention for them and a couple of days after she got home, she collapsed with a fever of over one hundred four. Luke rushed her to the hospital. They put her in intensive care until the fever came out of the danger zone. She was there for four nights, and then went home.

The doctor says she'll be fine, but the foot will take a while to heal. Luke has stayed with her constantly."

"Why didn't you tell me? I should've known. I could've done something."

"She was okay, Alex. I was constantly in contact with Luke. And then she specifically told Luke to tell us not to come home. When I finally spoke to her the day I got the message that everything was fine, she insisted that we stay and finish the tour."

All of Secu's comments were swirling around in Alex's brain. "And the event tonight at the college?"

"As I said, a couple weeks ago, Reid called her saying he is a recovering alcoholic, and that he needed to make amends for what he'd done to her, and took full responsibility for the rape and for getting out of it. Then he said he was going to be speaking at a symposium on addiction and substance abuse and the treatment of women at the college and asked if she would go to hear him speak. She met him there yesterday; they talked privately, he invited her to join him at the symposium, and she agreed."

Alex's voice rose. "She met with him? How the hell could you let her meet with her fucking rapist? Why the fuck didn't you stop her from getting anywhere near him?"

"Alex, I'm trying to not go for your throat right now, but stop being a prick." Peter tried to keep his anger at bay. "Luke, Josh, Jess, and Mariah are all with her. They went with her to the meeting and sat outside the room while they spoke, and they are there with her tonight. She wasn't happy that Luke told me it was happening, but when we talked before she went to Vermont, she insisted that I stay here. If I had known she was going to speak, maybe I would have gone anyway, but by the time I found out, it was too late." He took a deep breath. "She didn't want you to know at all. I wouldn't have told you if Secu hadn't brought it up."

"Are you kidding me? You wouldn't have told me? Fuck, Peter, I thought we were better friends than that. Thanks a lot!"

Peter was reaching his breaking point in the conversation, but he knew he had to stick it out. "Alex, you are my friend. One of my closest friends. You also happen to be my sister's lover, or were, whatever. But, at the end of the day, every day, I will protect her first over our friendship. Do I wish the two of you could work this out? Of course I do. But as for this event tonight, that was *her* decision to make, and it was *her* decision to make regarding if you and I knew, and if we went. *Her* decision only." He rubbed his forehead. "I'm just glad, I guess, that we can see the broadcast online."

Alex struggled with his reaction to Peter referring to him as Kat's lover in the past tense. "They're broadcasting it? Why would they do that?"

"My understanding is that there was a Title 9 violation of some sort, and as part of the program of corrective action, the college has to do things like this."

"Oh. And we can get the website back at the hotel?"

"Yes."

"Can I watch with you?" Peter heard the note of uncertainty in Alex's voice.

"Of course."

Alex suddenly remembered something else Secu had said. "What about a house? What the hell was that about?"

Peter took a deep breath, wishing he was anywhere but there right then, "Kat is buying Jess and I out of the little house next to the beach house, the cottage. She's renovating it and adding on to it so she can move there next fall."

This shook Alex to his core. "She's bought a house? And she didn't tell me?"

"Technically, she already owned it. She just bought us out, so it's her house now, and she's not going to rent it out anymore, and is instead going to live there." He looked at his watch, "We need to move if we are going to watch this live."

Alex grabbed his jacket, too stunned to speak, and followed Peter out the door.

***

In Peter's room, the two of them pulled the laptop over to the coffee table. Peter walked over to the fridge. "I'm getting a beer, do you want one?"

"Yeah."

They opened the website and saw the link to the symposium. Clicking on the link, they could see a long table with people sitting at it, but the picture was blurry.

Ten minutes later, the symposium began. The picture became crystal clear as the president of the college stood to make introductions, "Welcome. Good evening. To all of the trustees, students, faculty, alumnae, staff, and community members here tonight, we are so glad you could join us for this very important event."

"Tonight's symposium serves two very important functions. First, as some of you know, there have been questions raised lately regarding the treatment of women at our esteemed institution. While I do not feel the accusations are warranted, I support the discussion of how we can treat *all* members of our community better. Secondly, we also have struggled at times with the use of alcohol and other substances, and we want to address that through this symposium. Therefore, I am pleased to announce our speakers for tonight, in the order they will speak. First, I welcome Chaplain James, who will talk about the need for civility and tolerance on campus. Second, Doctor Edmunds, head of mental health services at the college will speak about the services open to all of our students. Third, head of Security Jim Stearns will speak about how we look to keep all members of the school community safe at all times. Then Reid Morgan, of the Morgan family, will speak about his addiction and recovery. Finally, which was not announced in the brochures, we are thrilled to be joined by Katherine Weston, well-known author and expert on Hispanic women's issues, who will speak in a more global context about the treatment of women. After each of our panelists has spoken, we may have time for a few questions from the audience."

Alex was shocked seeing Kat for the first time in months, seated at the long table. "She looks so different! Her hair. It's great, but she looks so thin, so fragile."

Peter nodded. "Yeah, Luke said she lost a lot of weight when she was sick. He says she's still really weak, and tires easily."

For the next hour, the two men sat in almost complete silence watching the first three speakers talk. Finally, it was Reid's turn. Looking at Kat briefly, Reid smiled at her before standing up but stayed at his place instead of moving to the center podium like the other speakers had. "Hello, my name is Reid Morgan, and I am a recovering alcoholic and drug addict." They could hear the murmur of the crowd after those words. "I also am an alumnus of this college. My addiction really started here, but I started using long before coming here. I started drinking pretty regularly in prep school, then started using some prescription drugs when either I needed a boost or needed to sleep. By college, I was drinking almost every day, drinking a *lot* most days. It was part of the frat culture and our behaviors when drinking were appalling, especially in how we treated women, but we got away with them." He turned to look at Kat, and both Peter and Alex were shocked when she reached out to squeeze his hand. "But that's not really what I came here to talk about today."

Reid took a sip of water from the goblet in front of him. "On January 21st, 2010, I was at a party at DKE, my frat, and we were all drinking purple punch as we always did at such parties. We'd had a keg for brothers before the party started. There was a woman at the party that I had asked out a lot over the last years, and she'd turned me down each time. You need to understand that 'no' is not a word I had heard often, and it really pissed me off that she kept turning me down. On that night, she was there, she'd had a drink, and I asked her to dance, she said no, so, I made the choice to drug her punch. We, as a frat, had ketamine powder, which had been used before with other women. I offered to get her a drink, she said yes, and I gave her laced punch. When it took effect, I took her to my room, barely conscious, and she passed out in my room. I raped her once while she was unconscious, then she started to come to as I was raping her for the second time, and I hit her in the head, and she passed out again. Later, I raped her again, as she started to gain consciousness, and she fought me for all she was worth. I hit her again, really hard, and she passed out. Then, when I was done, I carried her to the back stairwell and left her there."

He took another sip of water, "Then before I was even sure that she'd awakened, I called my dad and told him that'd I done something stupid with a woman, and that I needed him to help me clean it up. My dad told me he'd take care of it, and that we'd figure it out as a family and talk about what I'd done later, and he hung up to make some calls. Before long, Campus Security came to my room, and I gave them a bogus story about dating the woman, and that we'd had too much to drink, had rough sex, then had a fight. By then, I knew she was gone. Around the same time, the college got a call from the hospital saying that a woman was there and that she was saying she'd been raped. So, I kept lying, saying that she was saying that because she was mad at me. After Security had left, my frat brothers and I had a meeting, and we'd agreed what we were all going to say. One of my friends had dated her, so he offered to say she liked rough sex so it would sound more plausible. And so we all lied to Security, and later, some of us lied to the police, and my dad worked with the college on donating the money to build the student center, and for me, all of the possible legal ramifications went away. The woman went away for a while, then when she came back, my frat brothers systematically harassed her. They made phone calls, left notes, made comments when she passed until she dropped out of college. We *actively* worked on destroying her because she'd had the backbone to say that she'd been raped."

He took a deep breath. "For me, while all this went on and every day since, what I did to that woman has eaten me alive. My drinking went from somewhat recreational to a necessity. It was the only way I could get through the day. I started taking prescriptions regularly, then started using illegal drugs, all the time maintaining the outward look of prosperity and success. I made over three million dollars in trading bonuses in my first full year of being an analyst, by the next year, it was five million. And all the while, I hated myself and was using anything I could to drown or at least quiet the self-hatred. I would wake at night, seeing her face when she was unconscious, and I would get up and drug myself to sleep. This downward spiral kept going until the only person in my life who ever tried to hold me accountable for my actions, our housekeeper Maria, told me I had a problem and I needed to get help. The next day, I checked myself into a rehab for six months, and I've been clean for almost eighteen months now. Finally, in that process, I had to face what I'd done, and own it, and try to make amends for it. *That's* why I'm here today."

Alex looked over at Pete, seeing the tears slowly running down his face. "I'm here today to publicly take responsibility for the fact that on January 21st, 2010, I knowingly planned, drugged, and repeatedly raped a woman on this campus, and then worked with my family, college administration, and my frat brothers to not face the consequences for my actions."

Reid stood up straighter, pulled his shoulders back, and looked out at the audience unwaveringly, "On that day, I raped Katherine Weston, who, God knows why, agreed to meet with me yesterday and talk about this, and then agreed to be here today. There is no clearer example of the role of drugs and alcohol and how it impacts the treatment of women on this campus than what I did to Katherine, and here in front of all these people, including my family and frat brothers, I take full responsibility for what I did."

He turned to Kat. "As I said to you yesterday, there are not enough ways for me to say how sorry I am for what I did to you, and how much I wish I could undo it all." Both Peter and Alex realized that tears were streaming down Reid's face as he finished the last sentence.

The audience was silent, but Pete's phone buzzed, he looked down to see a text from Luke. "Holy fuck, if you're watching this, you should see the look on people's faces."

Kat looked up at Reid, and her smile was gentle. She reached out her hand and took his, and pulled him down toward her and hugged him. She then patted the chair next to hers and motioned for him to sit down.

Kat pulled the microphone closer to her, still seated. She looked around the room. "I wish you could all see the looks on your faces." She chuckled, "Especially those of you who are administrators of this college and trustees. You didn't expect Reid to say what he just said, and I'm sure several of you are now about to hyperventilate about what I'm going to say."

She took a sip of water. "Please forgive me for sitting while I speak to you. Recently I had a health issue that makes it very difficult for me to stand, so I will speak to you this way." She lifted her chin and looked out over the entire audience, scanning until she could see Luke, Jess, Josh, and Mariah, and looked at them for just a moment.

"As you know, my name is Katherine Weston, and I am a graduate of this college. Note, I did not say *proud* graduate. To my professors sitting in the audience, I am so thankful for the education you gave me, you are amazing. But, I sit here tonight as a woman who has traveled the world to report on the role and treatment of women, and yet, a place that should celebrate and inspire women has allowed for their systematic mistreatment, abuse, and degradation, and then has celebrated the men who have done so."

She turned to look at Reid. "Reid and I met yesterday to talk privately. I will never condone what he did, obviously, but I forgive him for what he did because while he made a personal choice, he also was shaped by this environment. He has to live with what he did to me for the rest of his life, period, but I have told him that his taking the responsibility here makes amends to me in my mind." She swallowed. "But, having said that, I do not, nor will I ever, forgive this institution for what it allowed to happen, and for the way in which *I* was vilified and victimized again by the institution itself instead of being supported. *I* was the one who had to leave the school instead of the person who had assaulted me. And, I know that I am not the only woman who has been assaulted here, or been victimized in some way, and has known either implicitly or explicitly that she had to keep quiet because the institution itself would not help her." She sat straighter in her chair. "As for me, you can see the very, very visible symbol of how the college chose the institution over my wellbeing, in the fact that *I* was sold out for an eighteen-million-dollar student center."

She shook her head. "For a long time, what happened here destroyed my mental clarity, made me doubt myself, made me question what I had done wrong to be treated this way. For years, I was afraid to have a relationship, afraid of what the person would think of me when they knew I said I had been raped, but that the police and college had instead said it was a *romantic disagreement*. I'm not willing to stand in the shadows anymore, taking the blame for what happened."

She looked down the table at all of the presenters, then turned back to the audience. "This symposium was called for the right reasons—the need to look at both substance abuse and the treatment of women at this college. But, unless something drastic changes here, this will be just another example of how this institution will give public lip service to an issue, but not really fundamentally change anything."

"On January 22, 2010, the president of this college spoke repeatedly by phone with Reid's father about the student center, and about Reid having had a *little misunderstanding* at a party." She swallowed.

Watching, Peter's eyes grew wide, "Holy fuck, I know what she's going to do!"

Alex was so stunned by what he was watching. He couldn't imagine what would happen. "What?"

"Watch!"

Kat's voice was strong. "Over the next few days, the president of this college talked to security and the local police, assuring them that it was all a misunderstanding and that there wasn't anything more that needed to happen about all of this. If the trustees of this institution truly care about changing the culture, it is time to give a message loudly and clearly, that such behavior is not what is wanted here, and call for the president's immediate resignation." Her voice rang through the auditorium. "A leader who would sell out a student for a student center is not the role model we want for our community. I'm sure I'm not the first who has been sold, nor, if he is allowed to stay, the last." She turned to look directly at the trustees. "*You* have the power to change this."

She turned to look back at the general audience. "And for the women out there who have been victimized, and have suffered in silence because you knew how it would be received, take back your lives. Stand up for yourselves, make a big public stink if you need to." She swallowed. "I wish I had then. I was too sad and tired to fight, but I'm not now. If you are sitting here tonight, knowing someone has hurt you, please reach out to someone, stand up, and don't let this continue. Thank you."

The applause was deafening, as the crowd surged to its feet. Finally, as the chaplain tried to get everyone seated again for questions, a line of women, only women, formed at the two microphones for the audience. The first woman stepped forward. "Katherine, thank you for being here tonight." Her voice wavered. "I'm standing up right now because I too was raped on this campus."

Over the next ten minutes, thirty women stepped forward, openly admitting to having been assaulted on campus during their time at the school. At that point, while there was still a long line of people at the microphones, the head of the trustees came forward to the podium and held up his hand. "Ladies and Gentlemen, at this time, we are going to conclude the symposium." The crowd erupted in boos. "No, not downplaying anything. The trustees will be meeting tomorrow, and this will be the *only* topic. We will develop a way in which every single victim can be heard and helped, and make a plan about how to make sure it doesn't happen in the future." He turned to Kat. "I promise all of you, but especially you, Katherine, that *I* will not let this be swept under the carpet. You have my word."

Kat nodded, then gestured that she wanted to say something to the audience. "I will hold you to that."

Minutes later, the live feed ended, but not before Alex and Peter could see the long line of people still going up to see Kat.

***

Peter stood and took the empty bottles to the recycling box. "Shit. What a night!"

Alex shook his head. "I can't believe she had the balls to do that."

"I told you before, in Massachusetts, that I didn't know how she'd survived what she did. When she decides to fight, she's unstoppable."

Alex put his head in his hands. "Fuck, Peter, what the hell have I done? I love her more than anything, but I've fucked this up so badly that she didn't even want me to *know* about this tonight." His shoulders slumped. "How the hell do I fix this?"

Peter gently put his hand on Alex's shoulder. "Alex, she loves you more than anything or anyone, including me, but, if you love her, you need to really love *her*. As Secu said tonight, this is who she is, and there are things about her I'd like to change, but then she wouldn't be *her*. You have to decide how you can live with what she does and how she does it, instead of trying to make her into what you want her to be."

"I love her. You know that."

"I know you do. But I'm not sure you really *get* her. I was thinking about what Secu asked when he asked if you'd read her books."

Alex shifted uncomfortably. "What about it?"

"You haven't read her stuff. Think about how you'd feel if she'd not listened to your music. You want her to be around, to stay where you are, to have a normal life. Maybe at some point, she'd have agreed to that. But she's come far enough to say that she can't give up her soul for someone else, and has found her fire again." He smiled. "We just saw her call for the resignation of the president of one of the finest colleges in the country. I'd say she's spunky." He paused. "Do you think you really love her, not just what you want her to be?"

"More than anything."

"Then I guess you'd better figure this out."

Alex stood up and grabbed his coat. "Oh shit, Peter. What the hell am I doing with my life?"

"You're living it. Some days are better than others. We'll be back in New York in two weeks. See what happens then."

At the door, Alex turned. "Do you think I should call her? To tell her how awesome that was?"

Peter shook his head vehemently. "No offense, but every time you get on the phone with her lately, it goes really badly. If you want to say something to her, I'd text or email her instead."

"Good point." He swallowed. "Sorry for being such a dick to you earlier. I know you were just protecting her."

"No problem. Go get some sleep."

Chapter Thirty-Six

In his room, Alex stood looking out the window. He needed to reach out to Kat somehow. Suddenly, he knew what he needed to do. He pulled open his laptop and got on Amazon, and within minutes had ordered a set of all of Kat's books to be overnighted to him at the next hotel. Then he pulled out his phone and texted Kat. "Hey, it's me. I saw your speech tonight. You were amazing. I love you."

Two hours later his phone buzzed. He'd been lying in bed, trying to no avail to sleep, hoping she would respond. Her text was brief. "I love you too, forever."

He sat up, and texted back. "Are you awake? Can I call you?"

"I'm texting you, of course, I'm awake. Yes, call."

She answered on the second ring. "Hi. It must be super late there. Why aren't you sleeping?"

"I was waiting to hear from you."

"Oh. Good thing I responded tonight, then."

Alex took a deep breath, trying to formulate what to say. "You were amazing tonight."

"Thanks."

"I know you didn't want me to know about it, but Secu came to the concert, and I heard him talking with Peter about it."

"Oh. What else did he share?" Alex could hear a defensive tone creeping into her voice.

"He told me that you've been sick, and that you were doing this tonight, and that you've bought a house."

"Oh." He could hear the nervousness in her voice, "Alex, I never didn't want to tell you about those things, it's just, well, we have exactly been communicating well lately."

"I know. I just wish you'd told me."

"And I wish that Secu had kept his mouth shut so I could have told you when I was ready."

"And when were you going to be ready?"

Kat felt a flash of anger. "Alex, don't start, okay?"

"Start what?"

"Start about my deficiencies in communicating with you, okay?"

Alex felt like kicking himself. "I didn't mean it that way. Sorry, Kat. I just wanted to tell you that I love you and that I was so proud of you tonight, that's all."

"Thank you." She sniffed, and Alex realized that she'd started to cry. "Let's leave it at that then, before we end another call in a fight. I love you too."

"Will you come to the last concert, please?"

"I'll be there."

"Love you, see you in two weeks."

"Love you."

"Kat?"

"Yes."

"Would it be okay if I texted you between now and then? Just so maybe we could communicate without fighting?"

She paused. "I'd like that. I'd like that a lot."

"Okay. Good. Sleep well, I love you."

"Love you too."

***

The next morning, Alex finished brushing his teeth, then picked up his phone and texted Kat. "Good morning, hope you have a good day."

Three hours later, his phone buzzed. "Sorry, remember the time difference. Now good afternoon to you. Hope the concert goes well tonight."

That night, as Alex was walking back to the hotel with Peter and Will, his phone buzzed with a text. "How was the concert?"

"It was great. Great crowd. How was your day?"

"Busy, still going. We drove home today. Just got to the house."

He tried to think of simple questions he could ask, just to keep the conversation going. "What's for dinner?"

Before she thought about his reaction, she typed and sent, "Don't know, not hungry. You?"

Alex remembered how thin and fragile she'd looked in the broadcast. "I think I want fish tonight. Please eat something, please."

"Don't start. I eat when I'm hungry. Gotta go, love you."

"I didn't mean to upset you. Love you."

Chapter Thirty-Seven

The next two weeks passed in a blur. The band finally returned to New York, and Alex stayed at a hotel, unsure of how Kat would feel about him staying at the house.

Three hours before the concert, he texted Kat. "Will you be here tonight?"

"I'm trying. Not sure."

"Where are you? Can I help get you here?"

"In D.C. Trying to get back as fast as I can."

Alex was so desperate for her to be with him, he texted, "I'll send a plane if that helps. I have a friend with a private jet here."

"I'd love that, but I can't fly."

Alex felt irritation grow, thinking she was refusing because of nerves. "Why not? You fly all over the world."

The capital letters showed her anger. "I'M NOT TRYING TO BLOW YOU OFF -- I CAN'T FLY FOR AT LEAST ANOTHER MONTH BECAUSE OF MY FOOT AND THE DAMN BLOOD CLOTS. I AM FUCKING TRYING TO GET THERE AS FAST AS I CAN, BUT I'M IN THE MIDDLE OF SOMETHING IMPORTANT RIGHT NOW."

"I didn't know. I'm sorry."

"Stop assuming that I don't want to be there with you. I'm trying."

"I'm sorry. I love you."

"Love you too. Hope to see you at the concert, or at least after."

***

Once at the stadium, he looked around for Kat but didn't see her. Peter realized what he was doing. "Alex, she had something come up. She thinks she'll be here later. She said if she gets back to New York in time, she'll come to the concert even if only for a little bit."

"Yeah, she said she's in D.C. I don't understand why whatever it is she's doing couldn't wait for a day or two."

Peter looked interested. "She didn't tell you what she's doing?"

"No. Why?"

"Never mind. She can fill you in when you see her."

***

The concert was a rousing success. Still no Kat. He hoped she'd be at the party after the concert.

At the townhouse, Alex looked around for Kat but still didn't see her. Finally, he collapsed on the couch in the sunroom and chatted with friends, trying to be heard over the music.

At a few minutes after one, Peter flashed the lights for quiet. "Excuse me. Silence please." The group kept chatting, so Peter raised his voice, "Shut up, everyone! Now that we have had a chance to unwind a bit, I would like your attention. Josh taped something tonight on the news that I want us all to see." He walked to the DVR, "Ladies and Gentlemen, I give you my baby sister, Katherine."

Alex watched in shock as the newscaster's smooth voice filled the room, "Today, local writer Katherine Weston appeared before a Senate sub-committee about the role of the CIA in Central and South America. They were specifically interested in her research on the treatment of women in Central and South America, and possible CIA involvement in that treatment." Alex watched in amazement as a clip of Kat appeared, with her sitting at a table in front of the committee. He took in the serious looking gray suit, with a rose blouse peeking from underneath.

The newscaster continued, "After her hearing, Ms. Weston was invited to a tea given at the White House, and then a closed-door conversation with the President and First Lady, which we assume centered around Ms. Weston's recent trip with the Shining Path." Alex watched with an open mouth as the President greeted Kat, who he now saw was wearing a short skirt and high heels. As she walked toward the President, there was still a pronounced limp, but her grasp was strong as the President said that his wife had read her novels for years, and they were looking forward to a pleasant conversation before a more serious policy discussion. As the recording ended, everyone in the room burst into applause.

Peter beamed. "Unfortunately, Kat wasn't able to get home in time for the concert or this party, especially since she can't fly yet. But, you know, when you're famous..." Everyone laughed, and the music started up, people started chatting again.

Suddenly, Max started barking madly. A bolt of anticipation ran down Alex's spine as he heard Kat's voice yell, "Max, Goddamn it, get down." She pushed her way into the room as Peter ran to swing her around in a hug. All of the guests welcomed her like royalty as Kat tiredly smiled back. Alex sat in the sunroom watching her, although she couldn't see him.

Finally, she pulled Peter aside and whispered, "Pete, I really need the bathroom and to change my clothes. I'll be back down shortly."

He hugged her again. "Sure. Take your time. It was so cool to see the clip. I'm so proud of you. Oh, by the way, your hair looks awesome."

"Thanks. It's the latest thing, haircut by bayonet."

Not even realizing that Alex was watching her, she turned away. As she wearily started up the stairs, Alex thought about following her, but decided to wait, knowing she would be back down soon.

In her bathroom, she looked in the mirror and saw the shadows under her eyes. Slowly, she dressed in a pair of leggings, and a long tunic sweater. Even she could recognize that she'd lost so much weight that it hung on her, but it was warm and comfortable, so she didn't care. Her foot hurt too much for shoes, so she padded downstairs in bare feet. She quickly got a beer and visited with Josh and Kim, still oblivious to Alex. A short while later, she stood up, and walked into the kitchen, and leaned against the counter, pulling her injured foot up, so she wasn't putting weight on it. Alex stood in the doorway watching her for a minute, debating whether or not to say something to her before going over to her. As he watched, she stretched up, trying to reach the aspirin in the cupboard.

Moments later, warm hands settled on her waist. "I'd bet if I looked in that fat file folder from Cedars that's on the counter, it says that you still shouldn't be on your foot a lot. Right?"

Kat leaned back against him, so glad to be near him that she couldn't will herself to pull away. "You know me, I'm really good at doing what I'm supposed to."

"Yeah, right." Taking a chance, he kissed the side of her neck. "How about you go sit down, and I'll get it for you?"

For a moment, Kat wanted to argue, to show she didn't need him to take care of her, but the pain was too much to refuse his offer. "Okay."

As she said it, Kat turned to look at him, and up close, Alex was shocked at how fragile and tired she looked. "Where do you want to sit?"

Something in his eyes made Kat suddenly feel hopeful. "Upstairs."

"Upstairs?"

"Yes."

Alex cautiously put his arms around Kat and pulled her close. Without warning, he scooped her up and carried her toward the stairs. "Alex, what are you doing?"

He grinned, "Keeping you off your feet."

"Oh."

Once Alex reached the sitting room in Kat's room, he placed her gently on the couch, "Put your foot up. I'll be right back with the aspirin."

He could see the look on her face that she was going to argue about his telling her to do something. "Kat, if your foot hurts enough that you were getting medication, you probably should put it up."

Even to her own ears, her voice sounded sulky. "Fine."

Minutes later, he reappeared, and he locked the door at the top of the stairs. "I don't want interruptions."

"Okay." Kat swallowed the pills with the water he'd brought.

Alex paced in front of her, speaking quickly before he lost his nerve. "I need to know how you feel. I need to know if there's any hope for us. I need to know all about everything you've done in the last three months. I need to know how your foot is. I need to hear about your haircut. I need to know about what happened with Reid. I need to know why you bought a house. I need to be part of your life." He pushed his fingers through his hair in an impatient manner. "I need to know how to make this work. I can't stand living without you. Every time the phone rings, I pray for it to be you, but I'm afraid to call you because I keep fucking this up. I'm an asshole to my friends. My band hates me. I'm writing depressing music. I wake up at night reaching for you, and you're not there. I finally got it tonight, Kat. Everything that you kept trying to tell me about your writing, everything Peter and Secu kept telling me. I finally understood that I wanted to be the most important thing in your life, and I was so fucking jealous of your writing that I couldn't stand it. So, I kept acting like it was a little thing, and that you should be willing to give it up if you loved me."

Lovingly, his eyes roamed her face. "But then, watching that tape, I suddenly realized that I was so proud of you that I couldn't stand it and that Secu and Peter were right when they said it was part of you. And suddenly I ached because I realized that I was being such a shithead that I never said congratulations about the conference, or Congress, or anything. I just kept putting it all down. And I'm sorry." He looked at her sadly. "I'm so sorry. I should've been your biggest fan, not your critic."

He turned and walked to the bookcase. "Secu told me to read one of your books. So, I did. I read them all. And he was right. I was blown away. I had to admit that I couldn't trivialize what you do anymore."

Crossing the room quickly, he sat across from her, "Now that I finally figured that out, I realize that if we love each other enough, it doesn't matter if we have to be apart for our careers, our love will still be there, growing." His voice grew desperate. "But, it's been so long since I really talked to you, I don't know how you feel any more."

Kat leaned forward and reached up to smooth his hair back from his face. "How do I feel? I feel like I'm caught in a black hole. I miss you so much I find myself looking for dumb excuses to go to wherever the band is, just to try and catch a glimpse of you. I can't write. I listen to your CDs over and over, pretending you're playing for me. I tell Max all the things I want to tell you. I wake up each morning, depressed because I have to pretend to be cheerful and happy for another day when I really just want to lie in bed and cry. I went to Peru thinking that it would make me forget, and it made it worse. There's now a whole bunch of soldiers in Peru that know all about our relationship. When I got sick, I couldn't have you come back because you didn't understand what I was trying to tell you, and yet I wanted you so badly it was killing me. And since then, I keep trying to figure it out. And I keep wondering how to keep up this facade, when all I want to do is call and beg you to take me back, no matter what the conditions. I don't care anymore; I'm ready to do anything you want just so I can be with you."

Alex's smile lit up the room. "I don't want you to give up anything. I just want us to be together. I never really wanted you to give them up, just to include me somehow. I understand that I can't go on some of the trips, just include me in the planning, or let me help you look up research, anything. I just need to be part of your life."

Kat's voice was firm. "You are part of my life, the most important part. I want to go with you on tour. I want to be involved in *all* of your life. I can write anywhere."

"But, if you feel that way, why'd you buy a house?"

She suddenly was nervous that he wouldn't like her response. "I bought it for us." She stood up and pulled a roll of papers from next to the couch. "These are the blueprints. I had them plan an addition on the house that would give you a studio and me a writing space." She smoothed the papers open. "See. I had it planned so you could play, and even record some, right there. Peter helped me figure out what you'd need for space." She looked down at her clasped hands. "I thought that with me doing this, you'd see how much I love you, and how much I want to be in your life." Her face showed her nervousness, "I thought we could keep your house in California, and have this one here."

Alex looked at the drawings, his heart racing. "You did this for me?"

"For us."

"Oh, my God, Kat. That's amazing." He looked at her in awe. "Could we go tomorrow and look at it together?"

"I'd love that."

"And I get to pay for it too."

Kat smiled, "Of course. But I get to pick the colors for the bathrooms."

Alex started to laugh, then reached out to pull her into his arms, kissing her hungrily.

With his arms wrapped tightly around her, Alex pulled back and sighed. "Okay, love of mine, I need to go now."

Kat was shocked. "What?"

"I need to go." He kissed her forehead. "Here's the thing, I love you more than I can tell you, and I don't want to fuck this up. We've gone from being a couple to barely being able to talk to each other to being back together, but, I need to do this right."

"I don't understand."

"There is nothing I want more in the world right now than to make love to you, to stay here with you tonight. But"—he looked at her, emotion clear in his eyes—"I want us to go about this the right way this time."

"How do we do that?"

"Do you want to live with me?"

"Alex, I bought a house for us. Of course, I want to live with you."

"Then I'll pick you up here tomorrow at two, and let's go see the house."

She sighed. "Damn, now I understand how frustrating it must have been for you when I kept saying we needed to go slowly."

He hugged her. "Hear me clearly. I am not rejecting you or us, just the opposite, but it's important to me to do this the right way."

"Okay." She stood on her tiptoes. "So what do we do now?"

"Well, we can go downstairs for a bit, then I'm heading out, and I'll be back at two."

"Okay."

***

A half-hour later, Kat walked Alex to the door. He kissed her deeply, his hands warm and possessive on her hips, sliding up under her sweater. "I will see you at two."

"You promise?"

"I promise." He caressed the side of her face, "I love you now and forever, and I will see you in a few hours."

"Now and forever."

***

At just before two, Peter walked into Kat's sitting room as she came out of her bedroom. "Hey, Kat. Alex called while you were in the shower. He said he's running behind, and asked if you would meet him at the house instead of him coming here to meet you. I said I was sure that was fine, and that you could take the jeep to drive out there."

Peter watched in shock as Kat's eyes filled with tears. "He's not meeting me here?"

Peter put his arms around his sister. "He's running behind, that's all. He thought you could meet there instead of him coming here first." He smiled at her. "C'mon, Kat, this isn't a big deal."

Luke walked in at that moment. "What's not a big deal?"

"Alex wants Kat to meet him at the house instead of him coming here."

"So, what's the big deal?"

Kat's voice trembled. "The big deal is that this is supposed to be the day when all of this works out, and he can't even come here to meet me. I'm going to drive out to the shore alone, instead of it being the start of us living together. *That's* what the big deal is."

Peter shrugged, "Do you want us to drive out with you? We could drop you off, and you could ride back to the city with Alex."

In her heart, Kat knew she should be adult enough to drive out alone, but having the company sounded so good. "You wouldn't mind? I know it sounds stupid, but I think I'll lose my mind if I drive out there by myself."

"No problem. Give us five minutes, and we can leave."

***

The drive out to the shore was the longest drive there Kat could remember. Other than a little bit of chitchat on the way, much of the trip had been in silence, with soft music playing on the car stereo.

As they pulled into the driveway of the house, Kat felt nauseous with nerves. Had she overstepped in buying the house? Would Alex see it as a romantic gesture, or one of her trying to make decisions without him? She suddenly realized that a rental car was already parked in the driveway and that Alex wasn't in the car. Was he walking around the building? She couldn't see him anywhere.

Peter cleared his throat. "Okay, kiddo, this is where we leave. You need to do this part alone."

"You sure you don't want to come in for a minute?"

"No." Peter gestured toward the house, "Go!"

Walking up the slate walkway as the jeep drove away, Kat tried to keep her breathing regular. "Alex?"

There was no response from outside the house, so Kat assumed maybe he'd walked down the beach a bit. She'd go inside and put her bag down, then go look for him. Kat put the key in the lock. Opening the door, she realized that the house was warm—clearly, the heat was on, and music was playing inside. Kat's voice shook as she called out, "Alex?"

Alex came around the corner into the hallway and smiled, his delight was clear, "Welcome home."

Stepping into the kitchen, Kat suddenly realized that the kitchen looked ready to use, a bottle of champagne in an ice bucket on the counter next to *their* glasses, a bouquet of roses sitting on the counter next to a small wrapped package. Kat looked at Alex. "How? What?"

He pulled her into his arms. "When I left you last night, Pete, Luke, Josh, and Beth helped me plan to get the house ready for us to visit today. We have groceries here for a couple days. Luke snuck clothes out so you have some here, and they helped me put this together."

Tears started to fill her eyes. "You did this for me?"

"For us."

She smiled. "Our glasses."

Alex brushed back a tear from her cheek, "Champagne?

"Please."

He kissed her, feeling her breath catch with desire. "How about we sit on our couch?"

"*Our* couch. I like that."

"Me too." He led her to the couch, "I know we may change furniture, but it's still our couch right now. I *did* have them deliver a new bed this morning." His eyes darkened with desire. "This is our house, and our bed, just ours. That's why I had you meet me here. I was still putting this together."

She was still so stunned all she could do was nod. "Thank you. Wow."

He poured them each a glass of champagne. "To a new beginning and to the woman I love more than anything."

"To a new beginning, and to the man who makes me complete."

Alex handed her a small wrapped package. Opening it, Kat's breath caught as she saw the playbill and two ticket stubs from the opera so many years ago. "How?"

"I kept them. Then, I got them out last fall and had them framed." He stroked her face. "It was supposed to be one of your Christmas gifts, but instead it's a housewarming gift."

"That's amazing."

He kissed her hand. "Kat, I absolutely love this house. It's perfect for us. I can't imagine a better space even if we'd designed it from the ground up."

"I know. And once we add on the addition it'll be even better."

Alex leaned forward and kissed Kat slowly and gently. "Our house." He then pulled a small box from behind a cushion and handed the box to Kat. "I've carried this around for months, hoping to get up the nerve to give it to you."

Kat opened the small velvet box, and gasped. Nestled on a cushion was a gold band studded by a large round white diamond. It was surrounded by white and black opals.

"I had it made to match your bracelets." As he slid the ring on her finger, he asked, "Kat, will you marry me? Will you marry me, have children with me, and grow old with me?"

"I'd love to. Yes!"

Alex gathered Kat close and kissed her deeply. "I love you."

"I love you."

"No matter what, this is forever."

"At least that long."

Epilogue

Fourteen months later, Alex came up behind Kat as she stood on the balcony of their bedroom, looking out at the ocean as she did almost every night. Wrapping his arms around her, his hands settled gently on their growing child. "I love you. You know that, right?"

She leaned back. "I know. And I love you."

"Happy?"

"So happy." Her voice caught. "Still scared, but so excited."

Alex rubbed her belly, holding her safely in his arms, knowing her constant caution of their unborn child. "I know, baby. But, everything is going to be fine." He kissed her neck, his hands sliding up to stroke her breasts. "And who knows, I may convince you to have five or six more babies with me."

Her breathing quickened with desire. "Really?"

Slowly, he dropped gentle kisses down her neck to her shoulder, "Uh-huh."

She turned in his arms, "So then maybe we should practice making love?"

Alex immediately felt himself respond, still entranced by his bride. "Practice makes perfect."

"Then let's practice."

Alex picked her up in his arms, feeling her arms go around his neck as she kissed him. Minutes later, he placed her gently on the bed, and all conversation stopped as they made slow, sweet love.

About Anna Belle Rose

Anna Belle is an educator, a graduate of Middlebury College, Castleton University and Union Institute. She lives on their small family farm in Central Vermont with her husband and youngest son. When not writing, she enjoys time with her husband, children and grandchildren, traveling, gardening, cheering for the Red Sox, and taking care of her alpacas, bees and chickens. Anna Belle is also an avid knitter and spinner, and often her best ideas for novels come when at the spinning wheel or in the garden.

Social Media Links

Website: www.authorkfrancoeur.com

Facebook page: www.facebook.com/authorkfrancoeur

Twitter: https://twitter.com/KFAnnaBelleRose @KFAnnaBelleRose

Acknowledgements

To Amie, thanks for teaching me the benefits of deleting. To Sora, thanks for showing what true tenacity is every single day. To Ryan, Ben and Linnea, thank you for cheerleading. To my parents, thanks for not laughing when I told you I wanted to write a romance novel. To Amy, thanks for always being happy to edit it one more time. To Courtney, thanks for your fine eye. Finally, to Paul, thank you for your love, patience, humor, and belief in me -- it means more than I can express.

www.ingramcontent.com/pod-product-compliance
Lightning Source LLC
Chambersburg PA
CBHW070406260626
47161CB00001B/296